CINNAMON ROLL

A BOLD BREW NOVEL

ANNA ZABO

Editor: Mackenzie Walton, www.mackenziewalton.com

Copy Editing: Lynda Ryba, fwsmedia.net

Cover Design: Cate Ashwood, www.cateashwooddesigns.com

Print ISBN: 978-1-947550-04-9

For Annabeth, because this project gave me my words back.

CONTENT NOTES

This novel contains frequent descriptive on-page sex and kink with enthusiastic consent, including bondage, pain play, D/s, orgasm denial, anal play, and use of toys.

There are mentions of past sexual and relationship trauma, and a very brief non-graphic description of a past attempted sexual assault of Tom.

Characters consume alcohol socially. There's mentions of being buzzed.

CHAPTER ONE

MAXIME DEMERS EYED the ad pinned to the community bulletin board on the wall of the Bold Brew coffee shop. Well, well, well.

Gay sub seeking Dom for pain play, bondage, & sex. Assholes & jerks need not apply. Ask for Tom.

Max ran a finger across the phone number listed under the ad and tapped the paper once. The author was Tom Cedric. *Had* to be. Max didn't know Tom's number, and he didn't know Tom personally, but he and Tom shared friends and they'd seen enough of each other from a distance over the years. Max understood all too well the quip about assholes and jerks.

Tom had *terrible* taste in men. Every guy he'd seen Tom date fit that description to a T.

It wasn't any of Max's business, but that ad wasn't going to bring Tom the Dominant he wanted. Max suspected the result would be quite the opposite: even more jerks.

Then again, stranger things had happened in this coffee shop, so maybe he'd be wrong.

Ech, leave it, Maxime.

He had no time for subs or significant others. The fall semester was in full swing, he was teaching four courses instead of his usual three, and he had his own research to attend to, if he could squeeze that in.

Tom was a lawyer. He could take care of himself.

Rather than linger at the bulletin board, Max headed to the counter to order. Lupé was on this afternoon, and their smile, as always, was warm and friendly.

"Find anything?" They nodded at the bulletin board.

Max shrugged a shoulder. "Just looking. You never know what you might see."

"That's true. I found an awesome four-poster bed there." They grinned, then gestured dramatically at the drink menu. "New fall specials! What'll it be, Professor? Feeling adventuresome?"

Max laughed. "Lupé, my dear, this is *me*." Of course he'd try something new. He'd try most things at least once. "Why don't you pick for me?" He gave them a smile and a wink.

They pretended to swoon, then rang Max up. Years ago, when Lupé had started working at Bold Brew, they'd looked Max up and down and decided he was a little too pretty for them. "Sexy French pirate isn't my thing," they'd said. But Lupé still bantered and flirted, even now that they had a partner.

"You going to tell me what you're making?"

"Nope." They waved him away. "Go set up your grading nook, and I'll bring it out to you."

Max chuckled and headed over to the fireplace near the front of the shop. He tossed his jacket, a tweedy green-and-brown a former girlfriend had said practically screamed college professor, over the lounge chair, then pulled the side table over so he could unpack his satchel.

He settled in. Laptop. Stack of essays. Three pens—orange,

blue, and black. He didn't use red. That had always felt too critical, and he'd vowed early in his career not to become like one of the professors who'd set his teeth on edge.

He still expected the best out of his students, but he tried for kind *and* fair. Students were *human* and often stressed in ways he hadn't been at their age.

He wasn't far into reading the first of the essays when Lupé arrive with his drink. "One very special drink for a very special professor to enjoy while he grades his very special papers!" Lupé said in Spanish.

Max answered in kind. "More like one tired professor who is utterly grateful for the caffeine." He took the drink from Lupé and savored the scent. The coffee smelled of autumn and came with a nice leaf design on the frothed milk.

Cinnamon, nutmeg, a hint of cloves. Something else. Chocolate?

He took a sip and closed his eyes, letting the taste melt over his tongue and flow down his throat.

Yes, all the above, plus a sharp sting of heat. He flicked his eyes open and met Lupe's amused smile. "Mexican chocolate?"

Lupé shook their head. "Belgian chocolate, but that's chili you taste." Lupé rested their butt against the armrest of another chair. "What do you think?"

Max took another sip before answering. "It's divine. Like a warm fall day that has the promise of a crisp evening."

That got a laugh from Lupé. "You should've been a poet, Professor. You have a way with words."

Max scoffed. He liked words, but he loved languages. "Is there a name for this?"

"Campfire Mocha, and you just gave us a great description for it!" Lupé stood. "Enjoy, Professor. Holler if you want another." With a wink and a smile, Lupé headed back to the counter.

"Gracias," Max called out, and received an air kiss in response.

Best coffee shop in town.

Max indulged in another sip, then got back to reading his students' essays. He was about halfway through the stack and three quarters through his second Campfire Mocha when the shop door's bell rang. Max glanced up to see Tom Cedric eyeing him, his mouth pulled down in annoyance before he looked away.

Max got that from quite a few people when he occupied this seat in the coziest corner of the shop. Right by the fire, patrons could pull up two chairs close and have a private, intimate conversation. Prime real estate. But there *were* other seats around, including a couch, so he never felt bad about planting his ass and staying for several hours, especially since he always bought a pastry or two, and enough coffee to vibrate himself home.

Maybe Max was on Tom's asshole list. The man tended to avoid Max whenever they were in the same space, despite whispers he had a crush on Max. He surreptitiously watched as Tom headed to the counter, then to a table near the bulletin board, a cup of water in hand. He took a seat facing the front of the shop.

Interesting. Waiting for someone? Not that it was any of Max's business.

Max forced himself back to grading. After a few minutes, the bell on the door rang again, and a man in a hoodie entered, crossed the shop, and took a seat across from Tom. They conversed for several minutes before Tom shook his head once at what seemed to be a pointed suggestion. The man rose, planted his hands on the table and spoke again, words too low for Max to catch, but the tone was biting and sharp.

Max glanced over to the counter, seeking out Lupé, who

was also watching the exchange, arms crossed. Good. Lupé was closer, if there was trouble.

Just then, Tom laughed, and that, too, was caustic. Then he pointed. To the door, Max realized.

The man huffed, spun around and stomped away. As he passed, Max heard him say, "Fucking bitch." Then he was gone.

He could stay gone, as far as Max was concerned. He turned his attention back to Tom, who was staring up at the ceiling, annoyance plastered on his lovely face. When Tom's gaze dropped, Max buried himself in his grading.

He was *not* getting involved and he certainly didn't want to let Tom know he'd been watching. Besides, he needed to get this stack of papers done.

Max tried very hard not to watch as similar situations played themselves out three more times that evening. Swaggering men approached Tom. Calm conversation, then the men did or said something rude, and Tom pointed to the door.

At least the assholes had the decency not to make *too* much of a scene.

After the latest one, Tom folded his arms on the table and laid his head down. The groan that escaped was loud enough for Max to hear.

Poor guy. Max had been correct, though—that ad wasn't working for Tom. How many other meetings had Tom had before today?

Too many, from the looks of it.

Something akin to need itched in Max, poking his legs and turning his mind. *Fuck*. He never could say no to a sub in need. And this was *Tom*.

Max set aside his grading, stood, and headed to the counter.

Lupé raised an eyebrow. "Another?"

"No." Max chanced a glance at Tom, but his head was still

down. "What's his regular?" He chose Spanish, but kept his voice low so it wouldn't travel far.

Lupé made a silent "o" with their mouth, then said, "Tall cap with skim milk."

A simple brew. "Make him one. Dust it with some cinnamon sugar. Poor man looks like he needs something sweet in his life."

They got a curious look, then smiled. "Ah, Professor. A sweet from the sweet, eh?"

Max shrugged. His personality wasn't sweet, per se. He cared about people and was too much of a Dominant not to take charge of a situation. "More like a treat for a fellow human traveling through the world."

"There you go again. Poetry. In several languages"

Max handed over his card. "Hardly."

When Lupé handed the card back, they asked, "Do I tell him who it's from?"

"If he asks, that's fine." Autonomy was important. If Tom was interested, Max would know. If Max had been slotted in as an asshole, Tom was free to ignore the drink entirely.

Lupé gave him another long look, then nodded once.

Max returned to his grading, and watched Tom as Lupé took the drink to him.

There was a conversation, and Tom locked eyes with Max, before thanking Lupé. He took a sip and his shoulders relaxed. A moment later, he stood, drink in hand, and made his way toward Max.

A thread of exhilaration traced up Max. He set his pen down and leaned back as Tom drew close.

Rather than say anything, Tom pulled the other lounge chair close and sat. Finally, those dark honey eyes homed in on Max. "If this were a bar, I'd think you were trying to pick me up."

Max chuckled. "But it's a coffee shop." He wasn't trying to pick Tom up, even if the man was certainly worth the attention. Pale skin. Light brown hair. Caramel eyes. Long nose. His type, in more ways than one from everything he knew about Tom.

He *really* didn't need a sub right now. Even one with a pretty mouth.

Tom's smile was enjoyable and his limbs loose and calm. "You're Max, right? I've seen you at munches and around, but I don't think we've ever talked."

They hadn't. When Max had been unattached, Tom had someone else, and that someone else was often overly possessive. There were games Max didn't play, and fighting against an overcompensating Dom was one of them. The few times when Tom had been single, he'd very much avoided Max.

"Maxime Demers, but yes, Max is fine." He extended his hand.

Tom's hand was electrifyingly warm and strong. "Tom Cedric. Only my mother and certain judges call me Thomas."

They both let go. "Noted." Some of the men Max had seen Tom with had called him Tommy, which had grated on Max's ears.

"You're a professor, right? Languages?" Tom grabbed his coffee and sipped, watching Max over the rim.

Oh, dear. Perhaps Tom was trying to pick *Max* up. "Linguistics."

"What's the difference?" There was honest curiosity there.

"Linguistics is the study of languages, how they evolve, the foundations and structure. The semantics." Max gave a light shrug. "Languages are...individual languages. How to speak them. Vocabulary. Grammar. Idioms."

"So similar to the difference between practicing law and studying...say, the legal system?" Another sip. Another look with those eyes.

"Maybe? Law's not my forte." Max's cup was woefully empty for this kind of discussion. "But you're a lawyer, if I'm not mistaken?"

Tom's smile turned almost conspiratorial. Very nice. "You know something about me!"

Max chuckled, and picked up a pen so he'd have something to toy with in the face of those disarming dimples. "I do go to the same munches, you know."

"But you never talk to me." Amusement in his voice, and yes, interest.

Max should put a stop to this. There wasn't enough time in his life for dating. Or flirting. Or whatever it was they were doing. "You're usually occupied." Or running in the other direction.

Tom's smile vanished. "Yeah. I guess I am. Or was." He twisted his lips into an ugly frown. "You watch the performance?" He poked his thumb in the direction of the bulletin board.

Max nodded. "Those men were answering your ad?"

"Yeah, except they were all assholes." Tom sighed, then gave Max an appraising look. "You read my ad?"

Max tapped the pen against his right hand. "I always read the board. You never know what you might see."

Tom's gaze flicked from Max's pen to his face. "You didn't call me."

He spread his hands, pen gripped lightly in his left. "Maybe I'm an asshole?"

That earned him a laugh. "No. I don't think so." Tom lifted his coffee. "You wouldn't have bought me a cappuccino in my hour of need."

"Ah, you have me." When Max tapped the pen on his hand again, he realized he wielded his crops in a similar manner. That shouldn't have been so exciting. Hell, he shouldn't have been turned on. He certainly shouldn't have been having vague thoughts of helping Tom.

Maxime, what are you doing?

"Why didn't you call?" The question was soft, and there was a heartbreakingly vulnerable tone in Tom's voice.

Max dropped his hands to his lap. "I only saw the ad today, but I didn't think it would bring you what you wanted."

"What do you think I want?" Tom wasn't soft now. Everything about him was tight and agitated.

Max held Tom's gaze and his own tongue, waiting for the heat in Tom to abate.

Eventually, Tom cooled, and he sighed. "I mean, the ad's self-explanatory. I want a man to tie me up, make me hurt, and then fuck me." He cocked his head. "I know you like men, and I know you're a Dom."

Max nodded. "Yes. And a Dom *is* what you asked for in the ad, but I think you want something more."

"What's that?" Two brittle words through a smile that wasn't friendly.

"A Dom who will treat you with the respect you deserve." He spoke softly, but made sure every word was as clear as the finest crystal.

Tom inhaled sharply, his eyes fluttering and lips parting. Then the hope, oh such hope, lit in Tom. Fear, mixed with desire. He set down his empty cup.

Max hadn't intended to pick Tom up, and this wasn't that. This? *This* was the beginning of negotiation. He wondered if Tom understood. "Would you like another cappuccino?"

Tom didn't move. "Yes, please."

A deep pulse of satisfaction thrummed through Max. Grading be damned, he'd finish later. Someone needed to treat Tom correctly, show him what a Dom *should* be. Might as well be Max, then Tom could find the right man, the non-asshole Dom.

Max collected their cups and rose. "I'll be back."

———

TOM STARED at the chair Max had occupied, his heart pounding in his throat and every nerve tingling.

Of course he knew who Maxime Demers was. He knew all about Max, from where he worked to how well he could wield a flogger. His gaze drifted to the stack of papers. He didn't know linguistics from literature, but he remembered the first time he'd seen Max, six years ago, here in Bold Brew about a week after Tom had moved to Laurelsburg. A white man with longish dark hair, eyes the color of summer storms, and a long, solid body Tom wanted to climb. He'd been wearing jeans and a forest-green button-down, sleeves rolled up to reveal well-toned arms.

Max had been grading papers then, as well.

A week after that, Tom had seen him at the kink munch in Bold Brew's back room and had nearly lost his senses. Max's pants had been black leather, the shirt burgundy, and his vest cinched tight to show off his trim waist and torso. He'd been holding a crop like he knew how to wield it. Later demos and parties had proven that, yes, Max knew *exactly* how to use a crop.

Tom shivered.

Max had been with a woman at the time, but that hadn't stopped Tom from watching him or asking about him. Seeing someone with a partner didn't define their sexuality or even their availability. Turns out, Max was about as pansexual as a person could get. Also monogamous, like Tom. But, as Max had said, Tom was usually with someone when Max wasn't. And when they were both single?

God, *no*. Max Demers was too good for the type of sub Tom was. Hell, Tom should go over, thank him for the coffee, and get the hell out of here. Two things kept him in the chair. One: for years, his law partner Aaron Taylor had wanted to give Max's number to Tom, and Aaron saw things Tom didn't. The other? Max, in his captivating accent, had voiced *exactly* what Tom wanted.

Respect.

No assholes, indeed.

Tom sat back in his chair and took a deep inhale to slow his heart. As far as he knew, Max was single.

Max returned, carrying two cups. He handed one to Tom, then reclaimed his seat, much like a monarch would.

Watching Max move was a *treat*, from the way he claimed his space to the way he held a flogger, crop, pen, or that damn mug. "What are you drinking?"

Max peered into his cup. "Lupé calls it a Campfire Mocha. It's got a kick to it."

"And what am I drinking?" Tom took a sip. Same hint of cinnamon and sweetness to this cup as in the last.

"It's your regular, with a dusting of cinnamon sugar." Max cocked his head. "Do you like it?"

Now *this* was like being picked up at a bar, other than it being Bold Brew and Max being surrounded by papers. "Yeah. I like cinnamon."

"I thought you could use something sweet to chase away the bitter."

He could listen to Max's voice all day. "Yeah. Those four guys were all dicks."

"So I gathered." Max tilted his mug this way and that. "One of them had unkind things to say about you as he left."

Tom snorted. "Those were the ones I weeded out from the messages, too." He wrinkled his nose. "I swear, how hard is it to find a decent guy?" He'd had this exact same conversation with Aaron many times. Of course, Aaron *had* a decent guy, and had gone and found another to boot.

Tom couldn't even be mad about that.

Max watched him, that bemused smile on his face again.

"What?"

"Nothing." He sipped his drink, but his eyes danced.

"No, seriously," Tom said.

"It'll make you angry with me." There was the glint Tom associated with Doms, right on schedule.

"Well, now I really want to hear what's on your mind, Mr. Linguistics."

"Doctor," Max corrected. "Or Professor." His grin was feral. "You have a difficult time with all this because you have the absolute *worst* taste in men."

Heat spiked through Tom, and he twisted in his seat. The emotion that rose wasn't anger, but annoyance. Deep down, he knew Max was right. Still. "Fuck you," he muttered.

"Not tonight." Silky smooth, and soft as sin.

Tom's breath caught, and a different heat flooded his senses. "What?"

Max leaned forward, and Tom couldn't look away. "You heard me."

Tom nodded. That was all he could think to do.

The approval in Max's smile made Tom both focused and lightheaded.

"Now," Max said, resuming his original position, and crossing one leg over the other. "Tell me what you want."

"What I really, really want?" Tom deadpanned.

Max gave him a look that was part amusement, part annoyance. "Yes, Tom." That held the clip of a Dom. "What you really, really want."

"I don't know," he said automatically, then added, "Maybe that's the problem."

"Perhaps." Max's smile was soft.

Tom should've been angry, but there was no malice in Max. Amusement, yes, but not in a way that belittled him. Tom sipped his coffee and considered the question—really thought about it. He'd wanted to talk to Max for ages, it was the least he could do for both of them. "It's so much easier to say what I don't want. What I want seems too expansive. Too much to even voice."

Max pursed his lips, then took a sip of his own drink. "What do you like?"

That was less terrifying to contemplate. "Sex," he said. "Not all the time, but I'm very allosexual, so it's up there."

Max nodded. "Noted. What about romance?"

Tom couldn't help scrunching his face. "I specialize in divorce. Romance and I have a strange relationship. There's something to it, since I know happily partnered people. My law partner. The owners here. But me?" He shrugged.

Max seemed to mentally note this. Watching him this closely was a thrill. His expressiveness. His gaze. Handsome as fuck. "Have you ever been in love?"

Tom shook his head. "I thought I was once in high school, but that was more infatuation with an older boy, you know? Honestly, when I go looking for men now, it's not for hearts and flowers." He lowered his voice, despite which coffee shop they were in, despite his ad on the corkboard. "I like pain. I like the edge of it. The sharpness. I can't even say why." He met Max's gaze.

"There's nothing wrong with that." Max sipped his coffee, and seemed like he wanted to say something, but he huffed.

"What?" Tom wanted to know what was going on in that mind.

That led to a touch of embarrassment on those cheeks. In a Dom? "Oh, I was going to launch into a whole lecture about theories around sadomasochism, but figured this wasn't the time for that, and I don't think you're a novice."

"Can take the professor away from teaching, but can't take the teaching away from the professor?" There was something charming about that. So much about Max was charming.

"A bit of that, I suppose. It's why I do the munches and demos." He set his cup down. "But you're not here to listen to me ramble about why people like us"—he gestured between them—"do what we do."

No. Tom wasn't sure why he was here, except Max had bought him coffee. "The thing is, I hate being humiliated. Or belittled. Which makes me a horrible sub."

Max's expression flashed through a host of emotions, including fury. "No." His accent wrapped the words with weight. "It doesn't make you a horrible sub." Anger flickered in Max's face, and he looked away. "Ech. Whoever taught you that —" He shook his head.

In that moment, the world shifted or the floor dropped. Tom's mind lurched. "I—but —" He stopped.

Max studied him. "Do you think all Doms are assholes?" There was a seriousness to that question.

"No." Max didn't seem to be. From what Aaron had said over the years and from what Tom'd seen, Will wasn't. "But all the ones I end up with are."

Max grunted. "You keep finding the wrong Doms."

Tom twisted in his seat, fear rising out of his soul, cracking his chest open. "It's me. The problem is me. I don't know what I want and..." He gestured in frustration.

"Tom, you're not the problem. I think—" Whatever Max had been going to say was lost when his phone chimed loudly.

They both started at the sound. Max glanced at the screen, then frowned, picked the phone up, and scrolled.

Tom didn't know French, but he understood cursing when he heard it. "Bad news?"

"Ech, it's... I have a demo tomorrow."

"Impact play, yeah, I—" When Max glanced up, Tom felt heat rise to his cheeks. "I was planning on attending unless you don't—"

Max frowned at his phone, then at Tom. He set the phone aside. "Of course you're welcome to my demos." He gestured at the phone. "Unfortunately, the sub who was going to work with me just texted. She's come down with a stomach bug of some kind and doesn't want to get anyone sick." He rubbed his forehead. "But it's far too late to find someone else, so I'm going to have to cancel."

"Oh." Disappointment fluttered through Tom. He enjoyed watching Max work, dreamed of that kind of Dom. A thought floated across his mind, landed, and pecked at his brain. "Um..."

Max closed his eyes, sipped his coffee. He flicked them open. "Yes?"

Tom hated when men prompted him like that, but that single word from Max wasn't spoken with exasperation or coated in scorn, so it didn't feel horrible. "What would a sub need to do during the demo—I mean, aside from letting you lightly beat them?"

Max quirked his lips. "This is teaching, so they'd have to be willing to work with me and share some of what they're experiencing when it comes to impact play. Also, I had intended to cuff my friend to a cross, since she doesn't mind. It's a good visual for pointing out places to strike and not to strike."

Tom held Max's gaze. "I could do that for you, if you'd like."

There was a shift in Max's body and his lips blossomed into a pleased smile. Tom was left breathless.

Pleasing Max. Obeying him. Maybe Tom was too into the idea, and he couldn't envision Max taking him on as a sub. Not after this conversation. But the offer to fill in at the demo was out there now, hanging in the space between them.

"I believe you'd do a fine job," Max said. "If you trust me."

Tom didn't know Max, not really, but every demo and munch Max had ever been a part of had been calm and professional. When Tom had seen Max at parties, he'd been kind to his subs. Aaron's husband Will knew Max from Laurelsburg University, and had never uttered one bad word about him.

"Jess, Ralph, and Aries trust you," Tom said. "They have for years." The triad who owned the coffee shop didn't put up with shit.

Max gave a little nod of concession. "They do, at least when it comes to kink. I'm sure they wouldn't trust me behind the coffee bar."

"I trust you," Tom said. "At least with the kink."

Max laughed. "Let me text Ralph to verify the switch in personnel is okay, but I'm sure he'll be fine with it."

More than fine, it turned out. Max got a reply text almost immediately, and turned the phone around so Tom could read it.

Lawyer Tom? He's perfect. He'll do well for you.

"I don't know about perfect." Mostly, Tom'd been told how difficult he was as a sub. "But now what?"

Max glanced at the text, then placed his phone face down on the papers he'd been grading. "Ralph has an uncanny awareness of people." He shook his head, as if clearing a thought. "For the demo, please show up a half hour early, and we'll go over the details, but the general flow is me discussing the demo ground rules, consent, then explaining each toy or implement. They usually have a cross set up for impact play demos, so that'll be waiting for us."

Tom's entire body sparked and fizzled at the thought of Max cuffing him and stretching him out, even fully clothed. "What should I wear?"

"Up to you. You've been to other demos. Generally, subs wear clothing that shows off the body somewhat, but not obscenely so." Max's gaze flicked over Tom, and that sly smile set Tom alight.

"So not a jockstrap?"

Oh, *that* was a look. Max tented his fingers. "Not for the demo, no matter how lovely that ass of yours looks naked." He paused. "Also far too tempting."

A shiver ran up Tom's spine. "Are we flirting?"

Max let out a bark of laughter, then picked up his coffee. "Is this how you flirt?"

No. Never. Never like this. "I—" Time to change subjects. "What was it you were going to say before you got the text, about what you think of me?"

He grunted. "Before I answer, would you be willing to tell me when and how you got into kink?"

Was Max as calculating as a professor as he seemed to be in this conversation? Woe be to any student that tried to pull a fast one. Tom's lawyer instinct clicked on, but he answered anyway. "I've always been interested in kink, I think. I was fascinated when they tied characters up in cartoons when I was a kid. When I got older, I started fantasizing about being the one tied up. Then I found adult media when I was old enough, and that was like having a door opened to all the possibilities beyond sex."

An understanding smile formed on Max's lips.

"As to how—I had a college boyfriend who was into kink.

He was a jerk, but sex with him was out of this world. He was the first person to flog me until I cried, then fuck me senseless. I'd never been so turned on or satisfied before."

Max seemed to chew on *that* while sipping his coffee. Finally, he said, "I don't think you're the problem. You seem like a decent person, and I believe you know what you want."

The praise made Tom's skin itch. "I don't know about decent. You've never seen me in court."

Max's lips twitched. "You're a lawyer with your own firm. I suspect you wouldn't get very far in your profession if you weren't a hard-ass in court."

That was true. "I co-own the firm," Tom murmured, "with Aaron."

Max waved those words away. "You have a perception issue, either with what a Dom can be for you, or what you can be for a Dom, or both. That's why you end up in the hands of men who mistreat you."

"They don't mistreat me!" The words flew from Tom's mouth.

Max raised an eyebrow.

Shit. Maybe they did. They were all assholes. Or jerks. Or both. He'd stick around for a bit, to see if this time he could endure the humiliation, the degradation, but the outcome was always the same. "All right. But I don't stay when they do."

Max nodded. "You have a great deal of pride, I think." Tom made to rebuke, but Max held up a hand. "It's not a flaw, Tom."

That stopped him cold. "For a lawyer, no, it isn't."

"It's not for a sub, either."

He opened his mouth to argue, but the only data point he had was himself, so he flattened his lips together. The more he thought about it, the more Max might be right. All the subs he knew in healthy relationships had a great deal of pride. And also the respect of their Doms.

Aaron and Will, for example. There wasn't a lawyer in a fifty-mile radius with more pride than Aaron Taylor.

Max cocked his head, and there was a questioning look in his eyes.

"How do you say, 'I'm a fool' in French?"

Max said a phrase so fast, Tom could barely catch the syllables. "You're not a fool. You've had a series of bad experiences that have shaped your understanding of you in relation to kink. But not about kink itself. You need different data. Different experiences."

"You sound like a scientist."

Max chuckled. "I *am* a scientist."

Tom kept his yapper shut. Was linguistics a science? He made a mental note to look that up later. "I'm not much of a scientist."

"Ah, but you are a lawyer. I can make a case to you that not all Doms are assholes, and show you what a decent Dom/sub relationship is like."

Lightning straight to Tom's head. "Are you—are you answering my ad?"

Max pondered for a moment. "I am, though I hadn't intended to."

That dropped a stone into Tom's stomach. "Why not?"

"Time." Max waved his hand at the papers in front of him. "I'm somewhat overcommitted at work this semester."

"That hasn't changed in however long we've been talking." A horrible thought occurred to Tom. "I'm not a *project* to you, am I?"

A mix of embarrassment and mortification crossed Max's face. "No," he said, as if testing the word for the truth. "Not as such. You're—" He huffed a laugh. "Honestly, you're someone I've been attracted to for a while. At the very least, I can give you a taste for what a Dom/sub relationship can be like, if you found the correct person."

Elation twisted in Tom's stomach, mixed with a hint of disappointment. Max wanted him, but... "Short term?"

"I'm a romantic at heart," he said. "Or alloromantic, whichever you prefer. I don't know if you'd be comfortable with that, long term."

While Tom hadn't said it, he'd implied he was aromantic. "I mean, I might be demi? I might actually be allo? I have no idea. I've never been with any guy long enough to figure any of *that* out."

This time, the expression that flew over Max's face was, well, akin to deer in the headlights.

"So what happens next?" Tom asked.

Max cast his gaze around at his papers before landing back on Tom. That strange sense Tom had caught him off guard lingered. "Well, I need to finish grading my students' papers."

"And I'm a distraction?" Tom grinned. Max liked him. He wanted Tom. This was... overwhelming.

Max's chuckle was self-deprecating. "A welcome one to be sure, but yes."

"Well, I guess I should thank you for the coffee, head home, and see about an outfit for tomorrow?"

Max nodded. "You should also give me your number."

That sent all kinds of fire through Tom. "Okay." He rattled off his number for Max to enter into his phone, then pulled his out when Max texted him.

"My class schedule and office hours vary, but you can text me any time. I use the 'do not disturb' feature when I'm busy. Or asleep."

"Same. My schedule isn't regular either. Clients. Court cases. All that." He rose. "Thanks for the coffee. I'll see you tomorrow."

There was that sly smile again. "You will, yes."

He headed for the door, but before he got far, Max's voice struck, much like the soft fall of a deerskin flogger. "Tom."

A command lurked there. Tom turned. "Yeah?"

"Take down your ad." The smile was still there, but a dark smolder lay in those words and in that look. "Unless I don't meet with your approval?"

Oh. Fuck, did Max meet with his approval. Tom's sudden spike of desire was dizzying.

"Yeah, you do." His voice was gravel. "I should remove that, huh?"

Max nodded, and that also left Tom dazed.

How would it feel to be touched with those hands? Held down by that body? He stilled his thoughts and changed directions for the bulletin board. He didn't bother unpinning the tack, just yanked the posting off the board, the paper tearing easily. The space and the pin were available for someone else.

Tom balled the ad up.

Max was going to dominate him. First, they'd run a demo together, then...then he'd find out how Max put those demos into practice. God, that thought had him hot all over. He turned, caught Lupé saluting him, a quirky smile on their lips.

When Tom passed, Max was intently reading, a pen in his hand, but Tom's movement must have caught his eye, because he looked up.

The smile, the crinkle of skin around his eyes—that was like sunlight on a crisp day. Tom grinned, but kept going.

Tomorrow. That word echoed in his head. He'd submit to Max tomorrow.

CHAPTER TWO

TOM ARRIVED forty minutes before the start of the demo, ten minutes before Max had asked him to be there, and headed to the counter to ask for a water from Blake, the coffee shop manager.

"You're doing the demo with Max, right?" His pink hair was extra bright tonight, somehow.

Tom nodded. "Yeah. I'd have a coffee, but I don't want to be too hyped up."

"First time demoing?"

He chuckled. Yeah, he was a nervous wreck. "That obvious?"

"Nah. I've just never seen you be part of the demo before." Blake handed over a cup of water. "Max is good. You'll do fine."

A little heat rushed to Tom's face. "Thanks." He saluted Blake with the water, then headed to the back room. Tom wanted to find out how fucking good Max was.

This was only a demo. He was just helping Max out. Except...it wasn't. It was almost like an audition. Tom shoved *that* thought out of his mind.

The private room had been rearranged to allow for a stage

of sorts. Most of the tables had been pushed against the walls, and in the center of an area, close to the back of the room, a St. Andrew's cross had been set up.

Tom's breath caught and his skin tingled. A slow sip of water helped steady himself. He set the cup and his bag down on a table closest to the cross, then stripped off his leather jacket.

This was hardly the first time he'd seen a cross—hell, he'd been strapped to countless numbers of them. Wasn't even the first time he'd seen this cross in this room.

But this was Max. And him.

Tom strode up to the cross and touched the leather. Equal parts excitement, arousal, and fear stripped through him. Max was what? A new friend? Tom's new Dom? A wingman to finding a Dom? He wanted Max, wanted Max to want him, but the man was entirely too good to be true and Tom...

He was the fuckup who picked the wrong guys. Like Max had said.

As if Tom had summoned him, the door swung open and Max walked in, coffee in hand and a duffel over one shoulder. He was dressed for the cold fall day, wearing a long dark blue wool coat paired with a rust-and-blue knit scarf. He had black leather gloves on.

Fucking beautiful. Looked like a fashion model or movie star.

"Ah, you're early." Max paused by the door. "Do you mind if I lock this, so we won't be disturbed while we go over things?" His gaze captured Tom.

Not a fashion model. Max was a Dom. Someone Tom wanted to obey. His tongue cleaved to the roof of his mouth, so he nodded his agreement.

"Thank you." Max locked the door. "There."

The room felt warmer. Smaller. Intimate. Tom shivered, even though he was still in his sweater and jeans.

Max looked him over again, a frown marring his face. Tom had no idea what Max saw in his inspection, but it must have prompted his next question. "Are you still up for this tonight?"

God no. Yes. Tom swallowed, his throat dry as a crumpled autumn leaf. He claimed his water, and a sip allowed him to croak out, "Yes. Just nervous, I guess."

Max's smile returned, small but warm. "Understandable. It can be quite a lot to be the center of attention." He joined Tom, setting his coffee and duffel on the table.

Then Max took off his coat, and Tom lost the ability to speak again.

Leather pants. Black. Not skin-tight, but snug enough to show off Max's long legs and thick thighs, and hint at other assets.

And his shirt? The same fucking one Max had been wearing the first time Tom had laid eyes on him. Forest green and crisply pressed. Sleeves cuffed at the wrists. It wasn't buttoned up completely, and a black shirt peeked beneath. A belt with a simple silver buckle tied the outfit together.

"My eyes are up here," Max murmured, amusement licking each word.

Tom snapped his gaze up. "Sorry—I—God, you're gorgeous." That last bit came out before Tom could snatch it back.

Max's amusement softened. "Thank you." He gestured at the table. "Shall we sit?"

Tom pulled out a chair and sank down onto it. "Yeah, sorry."

"You don't have to apologize for being honest." Max sat and stripped his gloves off his hands. "Nor for being nervous."

"I've scened before. Entirely naked for a room full of people. I don't know why this has me so..." Tom waved his hand, then picked up his cup.

"Tied up in knots?" It was almost a deadpan.

Tom choked on the water. "Did you just pun?"

That *grin*. "My dear Mr. Cedric, I can pun in four different languages."

"Only four?"

"Ah." Max nudged his leg, and *that* expression Tom knew from other Doms, that little hint of excitement they got from the thought of punishment. "Don't get ahead of yourself."

He enjoyed pushing the edge, but they weren't Dom and sub tonight, not in that way. "This is just a demo. In clothing." No reason he should be worried. Or excited.

Max reclaimed his coffee and sipped. "Yes, a demo, in clothes. But we're teaching. The focus will be there, but different from a public scene. Also, you're submitting to me for the first time, albeit in a light way. There's quite a bit at play here."

Tom hadn't thought about the teaching aspect. Submission? He'd thought about that too much, even if he kept telling himself it didn't count. "So how is this going to work?"

"Well, here's what I had in mind." Max outlined the general form of the demo, then pulled the duffel over. "I brought a number of impact toys, and some cuffs, if you prefer to be restrained on the cross."

Tom wanted that. He shifted, getting a little hard as Max pulled out three sets of leather cuffs. An irrational desire to get on his knees and beg zipped through him. That made Tom sit upright. He hated kneeling. "I—cuffs are fine." Normal. "I like being restrained."

That smile did nothing to quell Tom's dick. Max pushed the cuffs over. "Your choice. Some people like the softer interiors and some like a harder bite."

Max could have pulled out rope and Tom would have said yes to being bound tight enough to leave marks. Still, he fingered the cuffs, then chose the ones with some lining, but not the very soft, fuzzy set. "I shouldn't get marked on my wrists. I have a case coming up." Wasn't anything big, arguments in front of a judge, but there were things you didn't show off. Tattoos. Cuff burn. Bite marks.

He was getting *way* ahead of himself.

"Understandable." Max took the other cuffs and put them back in the duffel. "Now talk to me about toys." He gestured at the spread he'd brought.

A crop, a paddle, three different floggers, and two canes, one of natural material, and the other fiber.

Yeah, wow, Tom wanted all of those. He poked at the fiber cane. "This thing hurts."

"I know." There was glee in Max's voice, and Tom looked up to a grin that melted him, then lit him on fire.

"I didn't take you for that much of a sadist."

Max laughed. Outright. "I'm very much a sadist, but only when my partner loves the pain I give them. Nothing gives me that kind of pleasure—nothing in the world."

Oh god, how was this man real? "I really like canes, but they make me scream, and I'm not sure that's what you want in a demo."

Max shifted in his seat. "Not for a demo, no." Husk in his voice.

So, Max could be cracked. The warmth in Tom was getting to be too much, but he wasn't ready to strip off his sweater.

Max cleared his throat, then took a long swallow of his coffee. "I don't intend to hit very hard. Enough to sting, maybe make you gasp, but we do want to keep this educational and not voyeur-bait."

"Yeah, I figured you should know what gets me off, so you can go lighter on that." And Max would know, and think about it.

"Mmmhmm." A snap in that sound. "I'm *sure*."

Tom shrugged and picked up the paddle. "Believe it or not, I've never been paddled. That'll be interesting."

"Never?" Max raised an eyebrow.

"Spanked, yeah, but—" Tom smacked his palm. Stung across the length of his flesh. "Always with a hand. Never with something like this."

"And your verdict on spanking?" Max's gaze was captivating.

There was the dry throat again, and the desire to slide off his chair to the floor. "I hate it so much that I love it." Spanking had that edge of humiliation he loathed, coupled with the pain he loved and the intimacy he craved so badly. "Hard to explain."

"We don't have to discuss it now." Max didn't break eye contact, even when he took another sip of his coffee. "I'll be gentle with both the hand and the paddle."

Now implied a later. Tom shifted in his chair again. "Clothing will help."

A nod from Max. "Creates a distance, which we're both going to need."

Tom's turn to stare. "You actually want me."

Those lips curled into a smile that had the edge of disbelief. "Are you only now realizing that, Mr. Cedric? After our conversation yesterday? I told you to *take down your ad*."

God, the way he said it. That accent. "I—uh—yeah. I mean —" Tom waved at himself.

Both of Max's eyebrows went into his hair. "That's something else we're going to have to talk about." He glanced at his watch, then tapped the handle of one of the floggers. "These?"

Oh shit. Fuck. Max wanted him. They were negotiating. They'd been negotiating. Yesterday hadn't been a mistake. "They're fine," he stammered. "I don't like the ones designed to make you bleed. I'm not keen on blood." Sometimes broken skin happened. He hated the mess of cuts too much. Reminded him of different cuts from fights he'd had.

Max nodded. "Noted. It's not my kink either, and far outside of what we'll be demoing here."

Another sip of water cooled Tom slightly. "We're not entirely talking about the demo, are we?"

Max drank his coffee, then smiled but said nothing.

Fucking hell, Tom liked this. This banter, this *interplay*. Being on the same ground as Max. "What else?"

"For tonight? That's it. I'll also talk a little about restraints for impact play, and if you're willing, we can demonstrate some positions with normal furniture." He gestured to the tables and chairs. "And the wall and such. Not everyone will have a cross ready to go."

"That's fine—but no kneeling."

Max nodded once. "I'll remember." He took another peek at his watch. "I should unlock the door soon. People always arrive early."

Tom did, when he wasn't encumbered by an asshole Dom. "I should change."

"Do you plan to use one of the bathrooms, or is here fine?" A simple question, but there was interest there, despite the nonchalant way Max finished his coffee.

"Here's fine. I'm not getting naked."

Max's smile hitched, but he didn't comment any further, so Tom stood and pulled off his sweater. Underneath, he had on a black tank undershirt, one that fit tight across his chest and back.

Max's smile widened, and he shifted in his seat again.

Tom never thought he was attractive enough to catch the eye of fucking hot Maxime Demers. Apparently, he'd been wrong. He dug into his bag and pulled out a pair of black yoga pants. These weren't as tight as the tank, but this pair was clingy enough in the ass and thighs, where it counted. He stepped back to undo his belt and jeans, then let them drop to the floor.

His boxer briefs, however, left little to the imagination. Especially given his current semi-hard state.

Max checked him out, shamelessly, too. "My eyes are up here," Tom said.

That got him a chuckle. "Your eyes are a lovely shade of brown I enjoy immensely. But this is a view I haven't seen before." His gaze lingered low, then drifted up Tom's body. "Do you mind me looking?"

Not a question he'd been expecting. "No. Not at all." Warmth grew on his face. "I didn't think you were that interested in my body."

"So you've said." Max stood. "Put on your pants, Tom. There's something else we should do before I unlock the door."

It wasn't a command. Still, Tom drew on the yoga pants. "What else is there?"

"Me touching you." Max closed the distance between them. "The demo will require it, and I don't think cuffing you to the cross should be the first time I lay hands on you, do you?"

"N-no." God, Tom felt like a college kid again, face to face with his first Dom, not two decades beyond. "Wouldn't be the first time you've touched me. We shook hands."

"I'm talking about *touching* you, Tom. Running my hands over your chest and back. Cupping your ass." Max stopped just inside arms-length. "Consent is important," Max said, seriousness deepening his voice. "May I touch you, Tom?"

No Dom had ever talked to him like this. Not one had ever asked him that question. It was the sexiest thing he'd ever heard. "Yes. Yes, you can." He paused. "Do I call you Max, or Sir, or...Professor?"

Max grunted. "Never professor. Not as a submissive. I know

people get off on that, but ethical student/teacher relationships are sacrosanct to me. I don't mix them with kink, ever."

That hadn't occurred to Tom. "Is that why the demos you do are always twenty-one and up?"

"That's exactly why. A few seniors from the university might attend, but I teach freshmen and sophomores, so it keeps problems down to a minimum."

Smart. "So what should I call you?"

Max placed a hand on Tom's chest, warm through the cotton of the tank, and stepped closer. "I enjoy being called Sir, if that's agreeable to you?"

This close, Tom felt the warmth of Max's body, and inhaled the scent of leather and coffee. "Yes, Sir," he whispered.

The sound Max made was more of a purr. He smoothed his hand over Tom's chest, brushing over one nipple. "I don't think I will demo much on your front. It's a delicate place for beginners."

Tom nodded. "I know."

Max's expression shifted, but smoothed out a moment later. "Turn around, please?"

Tom turned. "Sir."

"Oh, I do like that." Max's breath tickled the nape of Tom's neck. "And this." Warm hands traced over Tom's shoulders and upper back. "Nice and broad. Strong."

The touch continued, stroking down either side of his spine, eliciting a shiver. He was fully hard now, noticeable through his pants. So much for this not being a voyeuristic event. When Max cupped his ass, he couldn't hold back the soft moan.

"Very spankable." The touch lingered for a bit, then Max's hands were gone. "I wish I could continue to drive you wild like that, but we should move our things to the side, and let the early birds in."

Fucking hell. Max *was* a sadist. Teasing Tom without any release was *torture.* "Maybe later, Sir?" He turned to face Max.

Tom could get used to Max's sly smile. "That's something else we can talk about after."

Heat blazed through his body. "I should have asked for ice in my water," Tom murmured.

Max grinned. "I'll give you a minute to—ah—calm down." He stepped away and pushed the table they'd placed their bags on closer to the cross. "I'm going to lay the toys out here, and the cuffs. We can toss our coats and things on a chair or two over there." He waved to the side of the room.

Together, they finished setting up. Tom took a long drink of water, and yes, he was calmer now. Also buzzed with that heady hint of subspace.

Felt good, and he didn't have the bitter taste of resentment in his mouth from a jerk of a Dom. "How are we going to do the cuffs?"

Max pursed his lips. "I think, for the demo, you should put on the cuffs. It's less intimate."

They'd already flirted close to intimate when Max had laid his hands all over Tom. "Makes sense."

There was a gentle rapping on the door. "That'll be Ralph. Can you think of anything else we need to discuss before I let the masses in?"

Tom ran the demo through his mind. "I don't think so."

Max grinned. "Then here we go." He headed to the door, unlocked it, and poked his head out.

Tom took a deep breath. This was either going to be one of the best times of his life, or a complete disaster.

———

MAX UNLOCKED the door to the private room and pushed it open. "My apologies," he said to Ralph, and to the people waiting for the demo. "I had a few things to go over with Tom."

"Good of him to step in on such short notice." Ralph grabbed the door and pushed it open wide.

They let the small group of folks enter before Max replied, "It was. He's going to do just fine."

Ralph gave Max a *look*.

"What?" He feigned innocence.

"I know you, and I know him. Be kind to him, and yourself."

"I will." Yes, there were hints of mental scars in Tom, and that alone was enough to warrant caution. How badly had his search for a Dom gone all these years? "I'll be careful."

"Be gentle," Ralph said.

Max surveyed the room. A few people were talking to Tom, and he was smiling, relaxed. "He doesn't want gentle. He deserves kind, though."

"There's the Max I know."

He blew Ralph a kiss, then headed back into the room. Tom glanced up, and his smile came with that hitch of breath Max found alluring.

Tom was expressive and delightful. Also sexy as fuck. This demo would be fun.

Afterward, they'd sit and have another chat, because this was going to go farther damn fast, given both their temperaments.

But right now? There was a demo to run.

He said hello to the folks he knew, was introduced to others, and made polite chat until it was close to the hour. About the time they needed to meander to the front, Tom caught his attention and raised a questioning eyebrow.

Max nodded and met him at the front. "Are you ready?"

"Yes, Sir," he said, his tone a little cocky.

It was a tease, that, and Max enjoyed the *Sir* thoroughly. If all went well, perhaps he'd hear it from Tom's lips more often. If hubris wasn't setting him up for a fall, he could be the right Dom to show Tom how pleasurable both discipline and respect could be.

Max plucked a crop off the table of toys, faced their audience, and tapped the end against his palm while scanning the crowd. That had the desire effect—as he caught the attention of the audience, they stopped chatting and took their seats. Next to him, Tom muttered, "Well, shit."

Joy flared in Max's heart, and he smiled at his audience, then nodded to Ralph, who closed the door to the room.

He began. "Welcome, everyone. I'm Master Maxime Demers, and this is a BDSM demonstration of impact toys and a discussion of elements of pain play. I'm joined by Tom Cedric, who has graciously agreed to be my partner for the evening."

Tom stood with his hands clasped behind his back, his nervousness evident in his eyes and tight shoulders, but he nodded to the crowd.

Max placed a steadying hand on Tom's shoulder, gave him a reassuring squeeze, then let go. That seemed to help.

"Let's start with some ground rules." Despite his desire to keep his work and play lives separate, Max fell into a similar mode to his first day of lectures, firm but fair. "Please put your phones away. If you must text or take a call, you can step outside to do so." He pointed to the door with the crop. "It's a matter of privacy, both yours and ours."

Small amounts of nervous sounds drifted over the audience, and Max let that ebb before continuing. "Remember, this is a demonstration, not a scene. Any impact I deliver to Mr. Cedric will be light." He gave Tom a look. "Though it may sting."

For his part, Tom shrugged. His smile was on the lopsided,

embarrassed side. "I may get a little aroused. Just a warning," he said.

"And that's perfectly normal. There are many things that turn us on, but impact play, with or without much pain can calm and sooth, rather than sexually arouse. Or it'll feel good."

Max pointed to himself. "While I enjoy causing pain in a scenario such at this—" He waved to the cross. "If it's not what's wanted—say, if I accidentally stepped on Tom's foot and injured him—I'd feel awful."

There were some murmurs around the room. "It's a complicated subject, and if you're newer to BDSM, I strongly advise doing your research—and not only via the internet, though that's a good starting point. Remember, not everyone out there who says they're a Dom is a *decent* one.

"Before this demo, Tom and I discussed everything, including which toys I'd use, because consent is important. If he'd said, 'no crops,' I'd discuss crops, but not demonstrate on him." He slapped his hand hard with said crop. A few people jumped at the sound, as did Tom. Max grinned at him.

"But I said yes."

"Not that exact word, but you did consent."

Tom nodded. "And if I change my mind?"

Good question. "Tell me. Or use a safeword, if we negotiated that."

Tom crossed his arms and considered this. His acting was decent. "We didn't talk safewords."

"I was thinking traffic lights."

"Ah, red, yellow, green." Tom nodded. "Those are easy to remember. We can use those."

The ease at which they fell into the teaching together was remarkable. Together, they moved through negotiating consent and safewords, what to do when using a gag, and touched briefly on types of situations where partners might not use safewords, but rely on other ways of communicating.

"There's a lot of trust involved," Max finished. "So be sure you have a partner who respects you."

"Sir?"

Tom addressing him as such flared deep pleasure in Max. "Yes, Tom?"

There were spots of color on Tom's cheeks. "Do you have a safeword?"

"Yes, yes I do. It's *flower*." He focused solely on Tom for a moment. "Thank you for asking."

The hesitant smile Tom gave Max was *everything*. He savored it like a small sip of fine wine, then turned to their audience. "That's something I should mention: both Dom and sub absolutely have the ability—and should—end a scene if they don't feel comfortable."

"Consent," Tom said, "works both ways." He voiced that as if this was the first time he'd considered the concept.

Max shoved down the anger in his chest. "Yes, it does." Gentle words. "And since we've negotiated this demo and we have our safewords, let's get started."

"Yes, Sir." Tom grinned widely.

"Before I discuss these—" Max waved the crop, then placed it on the table of other implements. "—for impact play you don't need anything other than a consenting partner." He gestured to Tom. "You don't need restraints." He launched into different positions, including someone lying over another's lap, then demonstrated a few with Tom bent over a table, braced against a chair, and then the wall. "Very few people have BDSM furniture lying around their homes."

Tom still had his hands against the wall. "Do you?"

Max swatted his ass, reflexively, and the gasp Tom made was like honey. "Wouldn't you like to know," Max said.

A little titter of laughter behind them. "Behave," Max murmured low.

"I am," Tom replied, equally as soft.

Oh, he was one of *those* subs. Honestly, Max should have expected it. "That," he said, turning to the audience, "is a good segue into where you can hit someone."

Max pointed out safe places to hit. "When in doubt, the ass is ideal." He swatted Tom's backside, softer this time.

Tom rose up on his toes. "Ow."

"That was barely a love tap!"

Another flash of that gorgeous smile over his shoulder, and another round of laughter from behind them.

"Now, he complained, but didn't safeword," Max said. "So we'll keep going. Let's move to the cross, so I can talk about shoulders and back a little more."

He handed Tom the cuffs he'd chosen. "In many cases, a Dominant places the restraints on the submissive, but not always. There are no set rules as to how a relationship can play out." He paused, then added, "I personally think it's important to remember we all grow and develop over time, and our relationships, whether kinky, romantic, or friendly, evolve with us. Always leave space to negotiate and change."

"You're a philosopher." Tom's voice was low, but the audience heard.

Max shrugged. "Connections are important. They take work."

Tom nodded, and so did many in the crowd.

"Now comes the fun part." Max pointed at the cross. "If you'd please, Tom."

"Yes, Sir." Tom strode to the cross and stretched his arms up for Max to clip the cuffs into the restraints that hung down from each arm. These were nylon webbing. Adjustable and less noisy than chains, though Max enjoyed the latter on his own equipment.

He fastened Tom onto the cross, adjusting the straps so there was a hint of tension in his arms. "You can play on either side of the body, but the back is more forgiving, and similar across genders when it comes to striking areas. Also, bruising is more easily covered."

"Good thing for folks with unforgiving day jobs," Tom said.

The audience chuckled, and Max used that to move into talking about aftercare for both Doms and subs, and types of products used to sooth angry, welted, or broken skin. Then he went over areas to strike again, and emphasized where one shouldn't land a blow. Kidneys. Spine. Tailbone. Joints, including the shoulder joint. Max pointed with his reclaimed crop. "The upper back, to either side of the spine is good, as are the ass and thighs." He gave Tom's right thigh a little whack. Enough to sting.

Tom hissed and danced a little. "Thighs are diabolical. But I like that. It's sharper than on the ass."

"Try different areas. Talk to each other." Max flicked the crop in the air. "Let's talk toys."

He set down the crop and held up his hand. "First implement, and one most have." He launched into how to spank, with cautions about avoiding injury both to the submissive and the dominant. "Spanking will make your hand sting, even if you're wearing leather. It's a very personal way to give pain."

"It can be humiliating," Tom said. "Which may not be your thing. But can also be very sexy."

"For both people," Max said. "May I use my hand on you, Tom? It occurs to me we didn't discuss that in detail."

"Yes, Sir, you can."

Music to his ears, and to his dick. Rather than give in to the urge to cup Tom's ass, Max focused on explaining hand positions and the difference between clothed and unclothed. Finally, he hit Tom's ass, hard enough to get Tom's attention.

Tom's fingers curled around the nylon webbing attached to the cross.

"How was that?" Max kept his demo voice.

"Light," Tom said. "But nice." There was a headiness to his words.

Yes, Tom like being spanked. Max talked a little more about hands, then gave Tom's other cheek a blow, to balance things out. This time, Tom gasped.

Nice indeed. "Shall we talk paddles?"

"Oh god," Tom murmured, not quite soft enough, and the room chuckled. He hung his head for a moment, but there was a smile there, one the audience couldn't see.

"I've never been paddled," he said, loudly enough.

"Paddles *are* a different experience." Max launched into the basics, then picked up one. "This was designed by our very own Vann Gelens, who's hiding in the back of the room there." He pointed Vann out. "Fine craftsmanship, and he's not paying me to say that."

"My work has its own impact," Vann said.

Max rolled his eyes to the chuckles, blew Vann a kiss, then discussed how to use the paddle. When he was finished, he paused. "Shall we?" The audience was eager, but Tom fidgeted on the cross. Max stepped into Tom's line of sight.

"I'm fine," Tom murmured. Then added, louder, "I'd say give it your best shot, but I think that'd be asking for it."

"Indeed." The blow Max gave was slight, a graze more than a blow.

"Hmm." Tom considered the impact. "Could you hit me a bit harder? I'm not getting a sense of that."

Max's own desire was to hear Tom gasp and moan, but this

was still a demo. So he swung with enough force for Tom to feel, but not much beyond that. A warm-up blow.

Tom arched his back and went up on his toes in response. "Oh! Wow." He took a deep breath and settled back down on his feet. "That *is* different."

"Could you describe it?"

Tom shifted his weight from side to side. "It's...a lot sharper, I suppose. More expansive. Less forgiving?" He turned his head. "Maybe because it doesn't flex like a hand would."

"And like a cane or a crop, I can put my wrist into it." Max demonstrated for both Tom and the crowd.

From there, he moved onto floggers, showing off the different types and cataloging the kind of impact they would make, before demonstrating on Tom.

Tom seemed to melt into the cross. "This part, when it's light, is soothing," he said. "Rhythmic. There's a hint of pain, but it's far down."

"That's something a Dom can use to build on—bring the pain up slowly." They both spent a little time talking about different styles and mood.

"Sometimes I want a good hard flogging, or caning, or whatever. Lots of pain, quickly. Other times, I want rhythm and buildup." Tom shrugged, which was a feat in the bonds.

There'd also a wistfulness about the latter part, which set Max's teeth on edge. This was neither the time nor place to discuss Tom's past Doms. "Ready to move onto canes?"

"I'm always ready for canes." Tom's eyes were closed, but his lips turned up into a smile so sexy, Max was glad only he could see it.

Joy bloomed in Max, and he let that grow as he explained caning and different cane materials, as well as the dangers of improper wielding. When he finally demoed on Tom, he pulled a few hisses and some dancing from him, and that was a delight.

"Sorry," Max said. "That's probably a little too hard."

"You're not sorry," Tom quipped. "That was fine. Felt good." He paused. "It stung, but I like that. Makes everything more real. Or less real. Something like that."

Max nodded, more for the audience than Tom. "I'm not a masochist, but I've been told by those who are that there's a paradox there. Yes, pain. Yes, it hurts. Yes, sometimes you want it to stop. But under the right conditions, it feels so good that you want it to go on forever."

There were some nods and murmurs around the room. Max set down the cane. "I'm out of toys, so now let's talk about the front of the body." He touched Tom's back lightly. "Are you okay to be turned around?"

Those warm brown eyes flicked open. "Gonna keep me bound up?"

Max couldn't judge whether that was a request to be bound or to be freed. "I'd like to, but this part can be done off the cross, if you'd prefer."

Tom shook his head. "I like being tied up for you."

Desire ripped through Max, and he quashed it right down. If they hadn't had an audience, he'd have taken that serenely smiling mouth and claimed it as his own. Instead, he brushed his hand over Tom's back. "Then tied up, it is." His own voice was husky and dark.

Tom's grin deepened into something devilish. "Yes, Sir."

Oh, Tom knew how to play.

Max quickly unclipped Tom, had him face forward, then stretched his arms back up. He stepped back and admired Tom for a moment. Beautiful, especially with that edge of snark and subspace. Tom's hair was disheveled and the hardness of his dick was evident through his pants. He met Max's inspection and grinned.

They were both enjoying this demo.

"Right," Max said, then picked up his crop. "The front." He pointed out safe areas of play on the front of the body. "Breasts can take play, but be more careful about breast tissue. Also, be aware of a submissive's preferences and abide by them. Not everyone who has breasts wants them touched or emphasized. Same with genitals. Careful play, yes, but abide by preferences."

"Thighs are good," Tom said. "Though it sucks when the crop or whip or whatever wraps around your limb."

Max swatted Tom's right thigh with the crop, and Tom jumped, then settled back on the cross. "Yeah," Tom said. "Like that. No wrap."

Max chuckled, then turned serious. "Wrapping does suck. Remember, the person delivering the blows must be careful and controlled. The idea is to cause pain that pleases both of you." He scanned the audience. "I'm sure there are questions?"

As expected, hands went up.

"Let me free Tom, then we'll get to those questions."

As he unclipped Tom, hot breath blew past Max's ear. "You could have left me up here."

"I know," Max answered, his breath not more than a whisper. "But demo, not a scene."

A chuckle. "Pity."

Yes, and no. "Behave."

There was a twinkle in Tom's eye. "Do you want me to?"

No, and yes. "For now. Until our audience is gone."

After that? Well, they'd see.

Both he and Tom pulled chairs out and sat before fielding the questions. The topics were interesting and ranged from practical to philosophical. Several were for Tom, specifically, and he answered those with grace. When there were no more hands, Max stood. "That's the end of our demo. I hope you've all enjoyed it and learned something."

Ralph cleared his throat, thanked both Max and Tom, and

gave a little rundown on upcoming events, then the room was in motion again.

Moments later, Max found himself surrounded by several people and answering more questions. A quick glance found Tom in a similar state.

A little spike of possessiveness slid through Max, but he let it go. Tom was fully able to handle himself. He'd done fine with those jerks yesterday. Max didn't need to protect his subs.

His sub. Tom. Max also shoved that thought aside and answered a question about wrist strain and flogging.

After a few more minutes, the room cleared out, with Ralph ushering out the last of the stragglers. "Max and Tom need to pack and head home. Let's give them a chance?"

Ralph nodded to Max. "Nice demo. Whenever you want to do another, let us know."

Max gave him a bow. "Always a pleasure."

Ralph rolled his eyes and laughed, then headed out of the room. The door swung closed, leaving Max and Tom alone.

Tom's gaze was on the cuff that still encircled his left wrist, his fingers gliding over the surface.

If Max had to guess, Tom was floating a little in subspace.

"That went well, I think," Max said.

Tom jerked his head up. "Yeah, I think so too." He rubbed at the cuffs. "I guess I should give you these back." Longing echoed in Tom's voice.

Need in another was like honey to Max, and he never could resist. "If you'd like."

Tom focused on him. "They're yours."

"Yes, they are." He stepped closer to Tom, not enough to enter into his personal space, but Tom straightened his back and his eyes widened. "Those are *my* cuffs on your wrists, Tom."

Tom gave a little croak. "Are you—what are you saying?" Red touched the tips of his earlobes.

Max wanted Tom's snark. Wanted to bend him over the nearest table, pull down those yoga pants, and mark his ass. Watch him squirm and cry under his hands.

"I have a choice for you. Regardless of what you decide tonight, I'd like to continue our conversation, our—relationship."

Tom stilled. "Okay."

"The first option is you take off my cuffs, hand them back to me, and we say goodnight. At some point in the near future, we meet again and talk more about us."

He nodded once.

"The other option is you keep those on your wrists, come home with me, and find out exactly what my hand feels like on your bare ass, how hard I can hit, and exactly how much you want to scream for me."

Tom's mouth opened a fraction, and he swayed on his feet. Eyes wide, pulse visible on his throat. Fear laced through Max that he came on too strong.

Then Tom exhaled and licked his lips. "I'd like to leave the cuffs on, Sir."

Max gripped Tom's hips and pulled him forward. "Good."

The small moan Tom made when their bodies touched was a lovely sound, and the press of Tom's erection was perfect. Max wanted to take those parted lips against his own and devour that shocked expression.

Instead, he kissed Tom's cheek. "The quicker we clean up, the quicker we can get to my house and you can get under my body."

Tom shivered against Max. "Yes, Sir." His breath was a whisper of lust and gravel.

Max let go. "Toys in the bag, then coats on."

"Should I..." Tom took a breath and steadied himself. "Should I change into my other clothes?"

Max considered the question. This outfit left Tom more

vulnerable, but that was a precarious position for so new a relationship. "Up to you. It is a bit cold out."

A nod, but Tom made no movement to don his other clothes. Instead, he picked up Max's duffel, and started putting the toys away. Max slipped his crop inside the bag, then stroked a hand down Tom's back. "Think about which toy you enjoyed the most tonight. I'll ask later."

Tom turned to Max. "Do you always give your subs so much...room?"

"No. But I enjoy knowing my subs enjoy the torment I'm giving them." He paused. "Do you mind having a say in how I'm going to make you scream and come?"

There was something delightful about making Tom tremble using only words.

Tom swallowed. "No. It's just...different."

"Yes." Max gave him another kiss on the cheek. "Perhaps that's a good thing?" He hovered his lips close to Tom's.

"I...can't believe this is real."

Neither could Max. "Coats. Bags. Let's get out of here. My house isn't far, but I'm not willing to wait much longer to have you alone, Tom."

There was another swallow, then a dazed smile. "Sir."

They were outside the coffee shop a mere two minutes later.

CHAPTER THREE

AS MAX HAD TOLD TOM, he didn't live far from the coffee shop. Maybe a ten-minute walk, though maybe it was closer. Tom's concept of time was fuzzy.

Max had dropped Tom into subspace, and hard. Words. Touches. Those chaste kisses on the cheek that Tom wanted to be wicked and on his lips. Or his chest. Wherever Max wanted.

Knowing Max desired *him* was enough to keep him semi-hard during the walk, which was impressive, given the cold.

The chill of the evening did clear his mind from some of the fog of subspace, though. Maxime Demers was taking him home, at least to spank, maybe to fuck. There had to be some kind of mistake. Tom gave a little exasperated huff at himself.

Max glanced his way. "Too cold?"

Tom had to laugh at that. "No. Well, maybe. But I don't mind." He paused. "Did you want me to put my jeans and sweater back on?"

Max had a scarf causally wrapped around his neck. "No. Jeans are more work to take off."

Tom lost the rhythm of his steps for a moment. "You're so—" He stopped, unable to describe what Max was doing to him.

"Different?" There was a teasing there.

"You have no idea." Max was unlike any Dom he'd ever been with. He was *kind*. Thoughtful. Sexy. Tom kept waiting for the other shoe to drop, but that hadn't happened.

Didn't feel like it would, either, and that was so *weird*.

"My law partner's been trying to get me to let him give you my number for ages. I probably should've, huh?"

This time, it was Max who slowed his steps. "Perhaps. Though, how we ended up here might be for the best." He came to stop in front of a huge old Victorian house, complete with a metal fence around the property and a little gate. "And here we are."

The place looked *exactly* like the kind of house a professor might have. Or a Dom. Or a Gothic villain. "You're leaning into the whole sexy European intellectual thing, aren't you? Do you have little wire reading glasses? Brandy by the fire?"

Max opened the gate and gestured for Tom to precede him. "No reading glasses yet."

When Tom stopped on the stoop of the house, Max wrapped his arms around him and pulled him back, his grip almost painful. "That's sexy *French-Canadian* intellectual, Mr. Cedric."

Tom couldn't tell if Max was hard, given all the layers of clothing between them, but he groaned anyway. Felt so good to be restrained by this man.

"Behave," Max murmured into his ear.

"Do you want me to?"

A huff of a laugh. "You're going to find out, aren't you?" Max moved him to one side and let go. A moment later, he had the door unlocked and once more gestured that Tom should go first.

The foyer was tiny, a closet of space between the front door and the rest of the house. Tom caught glimpses of that space.

Arches. Hardwood. Stairs and a banister, but most of his attention was fixed on Max, since as soon as the door clicked closed, he had Tom again and spun him so they were face to face.

Not much difference in height, but Tom was looking up when his back hit the wall. Max hadn't shoved him there, but it felt *right* to be against that hard surface, inches from Max.

Slowly Max pressed a hand to Tom's chest, over his heart. "Before we go any further, I need you to understand something, Tom."

"Yeah?" His heart was beating so fast.

"You can always say no or tell me to stop. Anytime, for any reason. I won't get angry. I won't be upset. I may worry, but that's because I don't want to harm you. Do you understand?"

Wonder opened up in Tom. Also something sharp, like the pull of an old wound. "I—yeah. I'll tell you."

"Good." Max traced his hand up, skimming Tom's jaw before cupping the back of his neck. "May I kiss you?"

"Oh fuck, yes." It burst out of Tom, and before he could say anything else, Max had his mouth and Tom was moaning and opening against lips and tongue. No space separated them now. Max's weight, his hard body, crushed Tom into the unyielding wall.

The kiss was masterful, dominating, and everything Tom had hoped for. He gripped Max's coat, needing to be stripped and flogged and fucked with the same commanding presence.

When Max finally relented and opened up space, he was smiling, and breathless. "Well, you're going to be fun." Super-sexy voice, all dark and passion.

"Just don't ask me to kneel."

Max cupped his face. "I don't need you to kneel." Those words were dark, as well. "I won't ask you for that."

Tom didn't know how to reply.

Max claimed his mouth again, and Tom twisted against him, moaning into that heat. They still had their coats on, still had bags on their shoulders. He never wanted the moment to end. This was paradise.

Then Max pulled away. He stroked Tom's throat. "Always tell me what you don't want. What you crave. I'll make submitting to me worthwhile."

God, he hoped so. Hoped this wasn't some weird-ass dream he'd wake up from, then have to trod to work and help people split up. He placed his hand on Max's heart. "I want the respect you offered. But sometimes I need to be pushed. Test my limits?"

The curve of Max's smile was soft and devilish. "Oh, that I can do."

Max's chest was warm under Tom's hand, even through his coat. "I promise I'll tell you if it's too much."

"I'll hold you to that." Max plucked Tom's hand off his chest, then kissed the knuckles. "Why don't we pause and take our coats off?"

Tom chuckled. When Max gave him space, he dropped his bag and stripped off his outerwear. Max took his coat and hung it on a hook to the left of Tom, then removed his own and hung it next to that. He grabbed his duffel of toys. "These go downstairs. Care to join me and them?"

"This a casual way of inviting me into your dungeon?"

Max's laugh was full throated. "Something like that. Though I don't think of it as a dungeon." He beckoned Tom forward. "Later, I'll give you a tour, but I don't have the patience for that right now."

Tom didn't, either. He followed Max through what looked to be a living room, and into a gorgeous kitchen. Gas stove. Old touches with modern appliances. "You cook, don't you? Shit."

"I do," Max said. He smiled over his shoulder. "And I'm good at it."

Of course he was. That fit Max. How many times had Tom bitched to Aaron that Max, from what he'd seen at munches, demos, and parties, seemed too good to be real?

Here he was in Max's house and so far, everything seemed way too good to be real. And yet...

Max opened a door and flicked a light switch. "Basement. I had it finished before I moved in. I'll admit there is something sexy about luring submissives down these stairs, but *dungeon* isn't the right word." With that, he headed down.

As if that wasn't the bait Tom needed. Not that he required encouragement, but he *was* curious.

When he reached the bottom, he stopped and looked around, his heart thudding. "Okay, not a dungeon." Despite the cross and rack. Even with the strategically placed anchors in the large oak beams that ran the length of the ceiling.

The place looked like a speakeasy. Except where there should have been liquor, behind a bar complete with a polished wooden bar top and stools, there were cuffs and floggers and collars and dildos and...chastity devices.

Oh *shit*. Tom headed to the bar, and he placed his hands on the cool, smooth wood. "Are those... Those are cock cages."

Max drew close. "They are."

"I've never..." Tom turned and found Max watching him, gaze flicking over him before meeting Tom's.

"Never been caged?" Max spoke the words lightly, as if they had no weight.

"No."

"Do you want to be?"

"I don't know." Only answer Tom could give. He'd thought about being caged in the past, been curious, but whether from fear or desire, or both, he didn't know.

Max cocked his head. "Something we can revisit. Too early for that, anyway." He smiled. "You said to test your limits, but let me earn some trust, eh?"

Tom stared at Max in wonder. "I...can't believe you're—earn *my* trust?"

Max's expression faltered and he took both of Tom's hands in his own. "Tom..." He seemed to search for words. Finally, he squeezed Tom's hands. "Yes," he said, with gravity, "Earn *your* trust."

A strange feeling floated into Tom's chest and tumbled against his ribs. Not fear, but with that weight. A hint of pain, too, but like the kiss of a flogger, this felt cleansing, and anchored him in the moment. "All right," he whispered.

Max drew him into a kiss, and this wasn't the consuming one they'd shared twice upstairs. This kiss was gentle, unusually so. Tom whimpered. So much was gentle about Max, and so much hinted at hardness and pain.

Max slid his hands into the back of Tom's yoga pants. "I'm going to strip these pants and your underwear off, and you're going to bend over one of these bar stools, yes?"

Oh god. "Yes, Sir."

"Very good," Max purred into his ear, then pushed off his yoga pants. The boxer briefs took more effort, given how hard Tom was, but in no time, he was bent over one of the bar stools, ass up, his bare skin exposed to the cool air of the basement.

"Do you *like* my bar?" Max's voice was conversational.

"Yeah," Tom croaked. The floor was wood, or something made to look like wood. The bar stools were covered in leather. His hard cock pressed into the padding. "What I've seen of it."

"We can spend our time touring this space tonight." Max skimmed a hand over Tom's ass. "Not a single mark from the demo. Ech. I suppose that's good."

"You're very controlled," Tom murmured.

"Safeword, Tom? Or shall we stick with traffic lights?"

Oh. He didn't want to use the word he'd used with all those other Doms. "Traffic lights, Sir. Red. Yellow. Green."

"Very good. Do you remember what I asked you to think about before we left Bold Brew?"

What toy Tom had liked the best. "I do, Sir." That had been in his mind during the walk to Max's.

Fingers danced along his ass cheeks. "Do you have an answer?"

"I...do. I have two, if you don't mind." Other Doms would be mad at Tom for not answering as ordered, but Max seemed to want true answers, not precise ones.

"I doubt I will. Tell me."

The command burned through Tom, shivering delight over him. "I enjoyed the crop the most, especially when you used it on my thighs at the end." Tom licked his lips. "But the paddle—I want more of the paddle."

"Now that's interesting." Max skimmed his hand up Tom's back, under the tank he still wore. "Did you enjoy the paddle?"

"I don't have enough experience to decide. It hurt like spanking, a little," Tom said. "I just know I want more."

"All right." Max stroked Tom's ass again, his other hand landing on the small of Tom's back. "So, the paddle. We'll see, once I'm done with you, whether you love or hate it."

"Or both," Tom muttered.

Max chuckled darkly. "Or both. But first, I'm going to indulge in my delight." Then he spanked Tom, on one cheek, then the other. The sound of the blows registered first, then the shock, then the pain. By the time Tom flinched, Max had laid another two down, and started into a slow rhythm.

The pain was exquisite and sharp, as was the realization that it was *Max* spanking him. Tom squirmed on the barstool. "Please, no."

"That's why I asked for safewords again," Max said. "You're going to take these blows, Tom. I'm going to redden your ass with my hand, warm you up, *then* we'll get started."

The pain was so damn good, as was the way Max held him still when he tried to avoid the blows. Every so often, Max broke the rhythm, either pausing for longer so Tom could catch a breath, or following up rapidly so he couldn't even think before shouting. By the end, there were tears in his eyes, a buzzing in his head, and he was rock hard against the barstool.

He registered the spanking was over when Max fluttered fingers over his ass. "So nice," he said. "All those cries for me."

Okay. Max *was* a sadist.

"Thank you, Sir." Tom's voice was rough.

"I didn't even have to tie you down." Amusement there.

Tom had wrapped his hands around the legs of bar stool. Still had a tight grip on them. Pride flared. "I like being tied down, but I can control myself."

"I'm not poking fun at you." A soft pat on his back followed those words. "You did exceptionally well under my hand, especially for someone with a love/hate relationship with spanking." Max paused. "While I wasn't as cruel as I could've been, I wasn't *kind*."

"I...liked that. Could have taken more."

"I know." That came out as a purr. "Do you think you can hold on like that for a paddling? No shame if not."

From the few blows he'd taken? No.

"Please tie me down, Sir?" Strange to ask for such a thing.

Stranger still, when Max answered, "Of course."

Max helped Tom right himself, then brushed the tears from his cheeks before giving him another soft kiss that took all the air from Tom's lungs. He kissed Max back, wanting more of his taste, of his sweetness.

He'd always enjoyed being devoured by lips and tongue,

being taken by another, but he never understood the pleasure of just *kissing* until now. Max smiled against his lips, then he pulled away. "Let's take this tank top off."

Yeah, good. Tom lifted his arms, and Max pulled the tank off. It fell to the ground somewhere behind him.

In the soft light of the sexy speakeasy, Tom found himself floating as Max, still fully clothed, stepped back and appraised him. "I'd thought you'd be quite enjoyable to see naked. You very much are." He cocked a finger. "Let me show you another part of my bar."

Tom followed. There was a cross, and a frame, both with chains, something that looked suspiciously like a sex swing, a spanking stock, a padded massage table, and—

"Is that a pool table?"

Max cocked his head. "Yes?"

"Do you actually play pool on it?"

"I have, yes. Most of the time, I practice shots. Sometimes I bend a submissive over the edge and fuck them until they come around my cock."

Tom swayed on his feet and Max took his elbow, steadying him.

"I really should tie you down." Max's amusement colored every word.

"You have this way of dropping the filthiest words into the simplest of conversations."

Max pulled Tom close, his shirt brushing Tom's chest and those warm leather pants pressing against Tom's hard cock. "I like shocking you." Max kissed his neck. "You look amazing when you're so turned on you can hardly stand."

They'd known each other for *years*. They'd finally talked yesterday. "Really should have let Aaron give you my number."

Max bit his shoulder, and all Tom could do was cling to him

and moan until he relented. "Enough." There was heat and annoyance there. "Past is past, Tom. Don't dwell there."

Yeah, that's not where he wanted to be right now. "Fuck me on your pool table?"

"Not tonight," Max said. "We'll see about some other time."

"Guess I need to earn it."

Max had a smile Tom couldn't read with his head was spinning from lust and need. "For tonight, we'll use this table." He drew Tom over to the massage table. "Let me place you."

A part of Tom registered that Max hadn't chosen the spanking stocks, which would have required kneeling. Gratitude nipped at the edge of Tom's lust. Max hadn't just listened, he'd heard what Tom had said.

Tom ended up folded over the massage table, supported by enough of his core that he could collapse safely. His dick had no purchase, but could be stroked by Max, if he chose.

Max hadn't touched Tom's cock yet. There were many places he hadn't touched, and Tom wanted those fingers and his mouth on every bit of him. He squirmed as Max looped rope through the rings on his cuffs, and tied his arms down to the middle legs of the table. A kiss to the back of his neck. "Spread your legs for me, Tom. Nice and wide."

Heat raced through Tom. He was tied to Max's table. Vulnerable.

Fear nipped into him, then exhilaration. Open and exposed for *Max*. He widened his stance.

"A little more."

The few extra inches drove home how helpless his position was. He'd need to stay this way while Max paddled him.

"This is nice." Max's hands cupped Tom's ass, and his fingers skimmed near to his hole.

Tom gasped and rose on his toes.

"Very nice, too." Max's voice was wicked. "Have you ever been plugged, Tom?"

"N—no." He cleared his throat. "But I've been fucked with toys."

"Mmm. You did say you like being fucked."

Tom could get used to that low murmur. Sexy. Hot. "Hard. Yeah."

Those fingers stroked up and down his crack again, mind-numbingly close to his ring. "Tempting."

Max's touch was gone, and his steps clicked a short distance away. Tom couldn't see what Max was doing, but when those footfalls returned, something cold, hard, and flat was pressed against his ass.

"Same paddle as before. I'll start softly, and we'll see how it goes."

"Green, yellow, red," Tom murmured, more to himself, but Max patted his ass.

"Good," he said, then hit him.

Tom rose on to his toes in shock. It *stung*, more than before. Probably because he was naked and well-spanked. The heat of the blow spread out, as did the pain, and he settled back down. Then the next blow came. That stung, too. The third *hurt* and had him on his toes, gasping.

By the time the fifth came, tears pooled in Tom's eyes, and the room had receded into the thudding of his pulse, the sound of the paddle against his ass, and his own cries and curses. Every blow was bite and fire, and he knew he couldn't stand the next. When that came, he screamed for Max to stop.

But he *wanted* one more. Then another. And another. Until he was outright sobbing.

The blows stopped. "Shh." Max murmured. "You're good. You're fine. You did so well, Tom."

His brain was on fire. His ass. He needed to be fucked so badly, but he couldn't stop the tears or the trembling of his legs.

Max kissed his neck. "Brave, brave man, to let me do that to you."

"You're too good," Tom slurred out. "Too much."

There was a pause, then "Am I?"

"Yeah."

Another kiss to his spine. "I enjoy making my subs feel good." Max slid his hands around Tom, and finally circled fingers around Tom's cock. "You're still rock hard."

Tom could barely breathe. "Please," he whispered. "Please, Sir."

"Pain does turn you on." Max's lips brushed Tom's skin.

"You turn me on." The truth slipped out. "Pain's good, though."

Max chuckled, and started stroking. "I'm glad. It's a delight seeing you writhing and hearing you cry for me."

Warm leather pressed against his very sore ass—the hard ridge of Max's cock. "You turn me on, too."

Tom could only moan and whimper as Max rocked his leather-covered erection against him.

"Yeah," Max said. "Like that." He backed off, and there was the distinct sound of a bottle top snapping open. "I hadn't planned to fuck you tonight, but you deserve the reward, and I very much need to feel you come around me."

Tom couldn't get words out before the cool slick of lubed fingers were pressing into his crack and over his hole.

Max wrapped a slick hand around his cock again. "I've wanted you for a while, Tom."

The only sound that came out of Tom—the only sound he could make—was a low groan when Max pressed a finger inside him.

Max cursed in French, then spoke in English. "Fuck, you're tight."

Oh, did Max take care to open him, leaving him breathless and close to coming between the fingers pumping his ass and the grip pistoning his cock. "Sir, I can't..."

"Not yet." The words were sharper than a lash, and the order settled into Tom's bones. He gasped and twitched under Max's ministrations, his orgasm hovering so close he could taste oblivion, but never reach there. Max was etching a different kind of pain and pleasure into Tom's soul.

"Sir," he croaked.

"No." Max pressed fingers against Tom's prostate. "You can do this for me. Wait for me. Obey me."

Obey Max. He wanted that. Wanted to please the man trying to make him come, then telling him not to. Absolute torture. Tom's blood sang.

Finally, Max withdrew his fingers, and relented on Tom's cock. Tom couldn't help moaning at the loss of fullness.

A playful slap sent pinpricks of pain through Tom. "Greedy, aren't you? Give me a moment." Then there was the delightful sound of a zipper being undone, of a condom being unwrapped, and that lube bottle again. Max placed a steadying hand on Tom's thigh, and—oh god, the pressure, the stretch of Max entering him. Tom gasped and moaned. "Oh fuck."

Max felt huge. The stretch went on and on, until Max stopped and sighed. Another murmur in French, then one in English. "Fucking gorgeous. Next time, I'm going to make you watch me take you."

Next time. Assuming Tom survived this. He wasn't sure if he would. He tried to say something, but only a breathless croak came out. His whole body shook.

The chuckle from Max was dark. "Oh, my dear, I'm only halfway in." He pulled out, then pressed in more.

Fuck. Tom was gonna die. What a way to go.

When Max fully seated himself, Tom let out a cry. Max's thighs met Tom's ass, and the sharp pain from the spanking and paddling ignited up Tom's spine and into his brain.

Then Max started moving inside him, and Tom lost all ability to think. There was only the stretch and burn of that cock pounding him, and the sharp slap of pain when Max pressed against Tom's sore ass. Tom's own groans and curses rang in his ears. Eventually, Max sped up until he was ramming into Tom. Pleasure turned red and gold, filling Tom and pouring fire into his bones. Pain, perfect and heady, chased Max's every thrust, and Tom's cries turned to sobs.

Helpless. Bound. Being fucked hard and relentlessly against his beaten ass by Max Demers.

Couldn't have been more perfect if Tom had dreamed of it.

"There you go," Max murmured. "Beautiful." He took Tom's cock again and pumped it, pushing Tom over the pain into bliss. There wasn't time to warn Max he couldn't stave off the orgasm any longer—Tom rocketed past the threshold and spilled over Max's hand, his mind a whirl of ecstasy and pain. His cries echoed in his ears.

Max groaned deeply and plowed into Tom hard, as if trying to merge their bodies together, and Tom soared into a white-hot cloud of bliss.

He didn't know how long he was lost in the haze, but words filtered through. Max's voice. Tom's name.

"Tom. Hey, come back down please." Concern there.

He groaned against the table. "Here. Maybe." Or maybe this was a dream. Everything burned. Everything glowed. Max was still inside him. "Oh god."

A kiss to his back. "Give me a moment, and I'll untie you."

"Sure." He was fine. Floating. Impaled. That didn't last long. Max pulled out, and Tom groaned in disappointment.

"Oh." Max's voice was raw and thick, "You'd very much enjoy being plugged."

"Like being fucked." Tom closed his eyes. "Was perfect."

A huff of a laugh. "Oh my dear, you're something." Max patted Tom's ass, and that sent a delightful shower of pain up his nerves.

"Ow."

Another laugh. "Now you say *ow*." He coasted a hand up Tom's spine, then kissed his cheek. "Thank you for that, Tom."

Confusion flickered through Tom's mind. "For what?" He tried to focus on Max.

A frown marred his expression. He shook his head and said something in French. Then he smoothed a thumb over Tom's cheek. "For gifting yourself to me."

Something cracked and tumbled inside Tom, and he found himself blinking away tears.

Gifting.

He was still processing that word when Max untied him from the table and eased him up to something approaching standing.

"How do your hands feel?" Max asked. "I had you tied up for a while."

"They're fine." He leaned heavily against Max. "I'm sorry I'm such a wreck."

"Oh, Tom." Max kissed him—one of those gentle kisses that took away Tom's breath and scrambled his mind. He didn't know what to do with those kisses, or the emotions that bubbled in his chest.

Max maneuvered Tom over to the bar stool he'd been spanked on, and helped him sit. The pressure on his ass stung and cleared his mind.

"Seriously. I'm not usually this much of a wreck." He scrubbed a hand over his face. Doms hated when he got like this, and he had to get his head together or he'd never make it back to his place tonight.

Max ducked down behind the bar, only to appear a moment later with two bottles of water. "Here." He handed one to Tom.

Tom took it, peered at it, then cracked it open. By the time he'd taken a sip, Max had pulled over another stool and taken a seat next to him.

Max opened his own water and sipped, then spoke. "Tom, I take it as quite a compliment that I was able to fuck you senseless." There was a hint of annoyance there.

Tom couldn't grasp the emotions that zipped through him. "But—" He paused. "Are you mad at me?"

"No!" Max looked like he'd been slapped. "God, no." That came out softer. "Holy shit, Tom. Absolutely not."

Tom took another sip. He felt—he didn't know. Shaky. Alive. A mess. He ached all over. That had been the best sex of his life, and he'd just asked Max if he was mad at him.

Max set down his bottle of water and stood. He took Tom's face in his hands and stroked his cheeks with his thumbs. "Would you mind looking at me?"

That was harder than Tom had anticipated. He hadn't realized he'd been avoiding Max's gaze until he peered up into those eyes. God, Max was beautiful. His long hair was askew, his shirt unbuttoned, exposing his chest and the curls there, but what was hardest to behold was amount of concern in his frown.

"I'm fine," Tom stammered.

"Are you?" Those thumbs stroked over Tom's cheeks again.

Yes. No. He couldn't say.

Max's expression softened. "I have a feeling no one has ever told you what an absolute delight of a human being you are."

Tom croaked.

"See? Or that you're a tremendously responsive submissive. Your willingness is a *gift*."

"No." Tom could barely breathe. "No one has ever told me that."

"It's not a lie."

"That was the best I've ever—" And his fucking voice shattered.

Max kissed him, and Tom's tears welled. He jammed them back down. "I'm not used to someone kissing me like this," he murmured against Max's lips.

Max pulled back. "Like what?"

"I don't know—like you care, I guess?" The words were out before they registered.

They obviously had an impact on Max, because he wrapped his arms around Tom, and kissed him again. Hard and tender and—everything.

Tom threaded his hands into Max's hair and kissed back, trying to explain with his mouth how much Max had undone him with one damn scene.

Max softened his hold and hummed appreciatively. Eventually, he broke the kiss. "You're not used to this, are you?"

Tom pressed his forehead against Max's shoulder. "Used to what?"

"Being cared for."

He was glad his face was hidden, because he wanted to cry again. "No." His voice was raw. "I'm not."

"All right. I can work with that." Max rubbed his back. "Let's get you cleaned up and tucked in bed."

That sent a bolt of shock through him. "What?"

Max opened up space and peered at him. "Pretty sure that was in English." He had an imp's smile.

"It—yeah. But—you want me to *stay*?"

That same set of emotions Tom had seen before flashed across Max's face. Anger. Sorrow. Care. "Of course I do." Those words were carefully spoken.

"Oh." Tom tried to come up with some reason he shouldn't —but bed and sleep sounded amazing. Maybe if he rested, he could wrap his head around this night. "Okay."

"Let's go upstairs," Max said. "I'll take care of you, Tom. Everything's going to be okay."

Maybe. Maybe not. Right now, all Tom knew was that he trusted Max, so he followed him up and up and up.

———

MAX HAD to coax Tom up to the second floor to get cleaned up. Took even more coaxing to convince him to slip under the covers into Max's bed.

"But it's your bed," Tom protested.

"Yes?"

"Where—are you going to sleep with me?" There was that same profound look of confusion Max kept glimpsing every time he did some motion of ordinary aftercare.

They hadn't discussed Tom staying over, and that was Max's fault. Too late to rewind the clock, though. "I'd like to, but I can sleep in the guest room, if you're uncomfortable with that."

"I—" Tom looked so damn lost.

Yes, Tom was crashing from the scene, but this was more than that, and it made Max want to hunt down every last one of Tom's exes.

Tom looked up and focused on Max. "You want to sleep in the same bed with me?"

Max nodded. "If that's okay with you."

Tom furrowed his brow. "Yeah, it's fine. I just—don't understand *why*."

Oh my god, Tom. Max bit his tongue to keep that

exclamation in, then he spoke. "Can I explain tomorrow? I don't think either of us is up for the conversation tonight."

Tom seemed to accept this. "Yeah. Yeah, you're right."

So finally—finally—he got Tom into bed. Once there, Tom melted into the mattress, enough so that he barely grumbled when Max tended to his well-abused ass. "Don't need anything."

"Humor me," Max said. "I like giving aftercare." He wondered if Tom even understood the concept.

"Oh," was all Tom managed, before mumbling something unintelligible and dropping into sleep.

Max closed his eyes for a moment, then headed into the bathroom to perform his own ablutions. When he finished, he paused, hands curled around the edge of his large white basin sink, and stared at himself in the mirror. *What have you gotten yourself into, Maxime?*

Tom Cedric. Gloriously masochistic, wonderfully expressive, lovingly submissive. Tom, who didn't know how to respond to a Dom who wasn't utter trash.

This was going to be complicated. Especially since Max liked Tom. More than liked, perhaps. He wasn't possessive about his submissives, and while he'd enjoyed and connected, and even loved most of them, what he felt ramming around in his chest for Tom was different. Harder and deep.

He wasn't sure he should trust *that*—but also knew himself.

This wasn't some flash-in-the-pan infatuation. Nor was he being a knight in shining armor attempting to *save* Tom. He wanted Tom to understand what a *decent* Dom/sub arrangement was like. He also didn't want to overstep any boundaries Tom might have about relationships.

Sex and kink were easy. Fucking Tom had been as exquisite as beating him, and there was so much more Max wanted to do with Tom, if he were willing.

There was also a budding friendship. Maybe something else, though the *else* might be a deeper platonic relationship, given Tom's disinterest in romance. Max didn't know.

They needed to talk—about what Tom had experienced, what he felt, what he wanted. However, the other edge to that sword was that Max had to figure those things out as well. He knew, as instinctually as breathing, he wanted more time with Tom, in whatever form that could take.

He gave his mirror image a shrug, and headed back into the bedroom.

Tom was deeply asleep now, all tousled hair, with his face mashed into the pillow. He barely stirred when Max slipped into bed.

Whatever the outcome tomorrow, Max was grateful for the demo and for the incredible scene that had played out in his basement. If nothing else, he'd had one moment of bliss with Tom. Max switched off the light, and with the lulling warmth of Tom's body next to his, he quickly drifted off into sleep.

CHAPTER FOUR

WHEN MAX WOKE and blinked blearily at his clock, he wasn't surprised to find that he slept about an hour later than normal. It hadn't been that late when he'd poured Tom and himself into bed, but it had been an eventful evening. Sleep had come hard, fast, and long.

His stomach whined, though. In his haste to have Tom, he'd completely neglected dinner. No idea if Tom had eaten before the demo, either.

Max flinched. Not his finest hour as a Dom, there. He shifted to see if Tom was awake.

That answer was no. Tom was plastered to the bed, his head half under the pillow, mouth open slightly, and was sound asleep.

Beautiful man. Max wanted to trace the smooth, worry-free contours of Tom's face, so different from the fraught looks he'd seen previously. At this moment, Tom was at *peace*, and that was lovely.

Max slipped out of bed and headed into the bathroom. Apparently neither flushing the toilet nor running the sink had disturbed Tom, because he hadn't moved an inch from where he lay.

Max grabbed a pair of flannel pants, set out another for Tom, paused to admire his slumber, then headed downstairs to put on some coffee and figure out how to talk to Tom about everything they needed to discuss.

Max was staring out the back door into his yard, listening to the coffeepot gurgle when he heard the stairs creak, announcing Tom descending to the first floor.

He glanced over his shoulder and watched Tom, in the pants Max had left for him, inch his way into the kitchen. "Hi."

There was the fear and the apprehension Max kept seeing. "Good morning. Coffee's nearly done."

"Yeah?" There was eagerness there. "Beans from Bold Brew?"

Max turned around and leaned against the door. The glass was cold against his bare back. "Yeah. The breakfast blend. I usually stop in the shop before going up to LU, but some mornings, it's easier to make some here. Especially if there's hockey practice in the morning." That didn't happen often, but you only got so much rink time.

Tom stopped in the center of the kitchen. "Wait. You play hockey?"

"I am, in fact, somewhat of a Canadian stereotype, yes." Max deadpanned that, but added a smile.

Tom shook his head. "You're on a *team*?"

Max pushed off the door and waved a hand. "It's a beer-league team some of the faculty and staff have for fun."

"Huh." Tom looked around the kitchen. "There's so much about you I don't know, even though we've been going to the same munches and parties for—" He shrugged a shoulder almost helplessly.

"Years?" Max filled in.

Tom nodded. "And you know my best friend's husband."

"Will Taylor. Yes." Art department. Dominant. Good man. "Not as well as I believe you know your law partner."

Tom scrubbed a hand through his hair. "Yeah. I guess we should talk, huh? About last night, and everything else."

So much for worrying about bringing that topic up. "Coffee first." As if to punctuate that, the coffeepot spitted and hissed, announcing the end of the brew cycle. Max laughed and gestured to a little table he had set up against a window—a kind of breakfast nook. It overlooked the fence he shared with his neighbor, and a trumpet vine that was dormant this time of year. "Do you take anything in your coffee? Cream?"

"Yeah, some milk or cream. I can't drink it black." Tom headed for the table and sat gingerly. "Shit, that's good."

Max couldn't help the smile. "Enjoying the aftereffects of my handiwork?" He poured two cups, and headed to the refrigerator for creamer. After pouring some in both, he took the mugs to the table.

Tom had a rueful smile. "I do, yeah. I like the reminder. It helps me focus." He paused. "Is that strange?"

"Not at all." Max slipped onto his seat and sipped the coffee, letting the warmth and the earthy flavors center him. "I wanted to ask if everything I did last night was to your liking? That was a lot to take in, and perhaps I should have—" He waved a hand. "Gone slower? Been more gentle?"

Tom wrapped his hands around his mug, cocked his head and watched Max. "I keep thinking I'm dreaming. You're so thoughtful and careful. You took me home, beat my ass, brutally fucked me until I couldn't think, then tucked me in your bed. Now you're asking me if you screwed up?"

Max's cheeks heated. "Yes?"

"I don't—" Tom stopped. "Last night was perfect, Max."

Relief wound through Max. "The paddling?"

Tom dropped his gaze to his coffee, then sipped. "Good. Really good. I like being caned better, but that was intense and sharp, and you know how to make someone *feel* it."

Max couldn't help the grin. "That's the whole point, isn't it?"

Tom coughed a laugh. "I guess so. Did *you* like it? I've never asked any Dom that before, but the demo got me thinking. I assume you do, since—" He shrugged.

"Since I'm the one beating your ass?"

"Something like that."

Max considered how to answer. "Yes, I enjoyed paddling you. Spanking you. It's power and control. But it's also you giving that to me."

"A gift," Tom said. "You said that last night."

When Max had thanked Tom, who'd looked at him as if he'd grown antennae. "I did. Yes."

Tom sipped his coffee again. "Sometimes I think we're speaking different languages." His voice was almost a whisper.

Maybe they were. "I care about you, Tom."

Tom raised an eyebrow. "Is this where you're going to tell me that you're falling in love?"

Max shook his head. "No. Too soon for that. I care about your experiences with me, whether you enjoy how I give you pain, how I fuck you. I want that to be good for *both* of us."

Tom blinked a few times, frowned, and drank more coffee.

The anger Max had pushed away for two days came boiling up. "I don't get my jollies from smacking you around, fucking you until I come, then leaving you with the scraps of whatever pleasure you can get from that."

Across the table, Tom sat bolt upright.

Fuck. But he'd started, so he needed to finish. "You're a beautiful, intelligent, expressive man. A gift. I *care*, Tom, and

I'm mad because I shouldn't be the first person to tell you this, or who wants kink and sex to be good for you, as well."

Tom's cheeks were ruddy. "I—" He seemed to search for words. "Thank you." He blew out a breath. "You're right, I'm not used to someone caring about me when it comes to sex and kink." He turned to stare out the window. "Too many jerks."

Max leaned back in his chair, and bumped Tom's foot with his own. "Hey."

Tom met his gaze.

"I'm not perfect. I *can* be an ass, Tom. Selfish, and all those things. I derive a tremendous amount of pleasure from being sadistic." Max gave a self-deprecating laugh. "I enjoy that infinitely more when my ministrations are appreciated by a partner."

Tom's lips hitched up. "Back to being the philosopher?"

"It's not called a PhD for nothing."

Tom's smile was a sunrise, all light and promise. "Okay, so if I tell you when I don't like something, or when you *are* being an ass, you'll actually listen?"

"Exactly."

"Hence you basically telling me to test you at some point."

Max nodded.

Tom grunted and looked back out the window. "Last night, you were so fucking dirty. Those cock cages. Asking me if I'd ever been plugged. Telling me what you wanted to do to me. It was so fucking hot. I wanted to let you do whatever you wanted."

Max's brain tumbled, but he stayed silent.

"That was thrilling and terrifying. You *did* do what you wanted, and, fuck, I can't even describe it. You also did what *I* wanted." Tom's brown eyes were peering at Max again. "That's what I want. More of that. Push me."

"It'll come with the price of me taking care of you," Max said. "Like last night. Aftercare. Consent. All of that."

Tom's voice got husky. "Yeah, I know. I want that, too. Maybe you're right. I deserve someone who respects me."

Max rose—he couldn't stop himself—and had Tom's face in his hands. "You do. And I'll do my best."

Tom hiccupped a laugh. "Is this where you kiss me?"

Rather than answer, Max took Tom's mouth with his own, and gently tangled their tongues until Tom gave a sweet little longing moan. He tasted of coffee and need. A moment later, Tom's hands were in Max's hair, fingers scraping against his scalp.

Felt good. Real. As if Tom needed to be part of the kiss and not just consumed by it. Max lowered himself onto Tom's lap, and wrapped his arms around him.

Tom spoke against his lips. "Well, that's a first. A Dom in my lap."

"Get used to firsts, Mr. Cedric." Max brushed his lips, then nibbled his neck. "I'm going to give you as many as I can."

Another groan. "How is it you can get me hard with just *words*?"

Max bit Tom's shoulder, strong enough to make him hiss. "Not just words."

"No...fuck." Tom rolled his hips under Max, and yes, rock hard. "Can I—can I ask you a question?"

Max pulled back to see Tom's face. "Of course."

"How big *is* your dick? Because it felt like you were going to split me in two when you were fucking me."

Ah, yes. While Max had seen all of Tom last night, the opposite was not true. "Why don't you feel me up?"

There were those wide eyes again. "Really?

Max leaned in to nibble at Tom's earlobe. "Put your hand in my pants and wrap it around my cock, Tom."

A groan, then Tom did as told, brushing his fingers against Max's length before wrapping his hand around the girth. He stroked Max slowly.

Warmth to Max's balls and up his back. He sucked on Tom's neck, then whispered, "What do you think?"

"No wonder you took your time opening me." Tom kept up the lazy strokes.

Lengthwise, he was average, but his girth was considerable. He hadn't realized that until he'd gotten into kink and seen a whole variety of dicks and toys.

"Fuck." Tom squirmed underneath Max.

Very likely, very soon. Max cupped Tom's cock through his pants, then swallowed Tom's moan. It was a pleasant way to spend the morning, feeling up a willing partner. Being felt up in turn. Kissing and nipping at Tom's mouth, neck, and shoulders.

Tom was breathless. "Can I see you naked?"

"I think we can arrange that, though you'll have to let go."

There was a murmur of dislike, but Tom pulled his hand back from Max's pants and let him stand. His focus was on the bulge tenting Max's flannel pants. Without any teasing, Max hooked his fingers in the waistband and pushed down. When the pants hit the floor, he deftly stepped out and kicked them to one side.

Tom had his hand in his own pants, stroking his cock. He met Max's grin with one of his own. "You know, you're beautiful too."

"Thank you." He leaned down and took a taste of Tom's mouth.

When he drew back, Tom's cheeks were ruddy. "Can I— will you—?" Such a pleading look.

Oh, sweet man. "Tell me what you want, Tom." He had a decent idea, from Tom's body language and that hunger when he focused on Max's dick.

Tom swallowed. "Make me suck your dick. Use my mouth. Fuck my face."

So Tom liked that kind of play. "Rough?"

A nod.

Max gripped Tom's chin. "Then get your hand off your cock. If you're good, I may let you come later."

Tom did as told, trembling in Max's hand.

He stared into Tom's eyes. "If you need me to stop, slap me twice on the thigh. Otherwise, I'm going to fuck you without any mercy at all."

Tom's groan was honey. "Okay."

Consent given, Max loomed over Tom, and tightened his grip. "Better fucking open that mouth for me."

That made Tom's eyes widen, but he didn't obey, so Max gripped his hair tight and forced his head back, mindful of his neck. Tom yelped and danced in his chair, then finally opened his mouth wide.

Max straddled Tom's legs and Tom bent forward, giving Max a workable angle.

"That's better." He let go of Tom's chin, and slapped his cock against the side of Tom's mouth. "You have the prettiest lips. I've been wanting to see them stretched around my dick. Better be worth it, or I'm going to upend you and make you pay." He shoved his dick into Tom's waiting mouth.

There was a touch of fear in Tom's groan, but he didn't tap out. He gripped Max's legs, and he worked to both breathe and obey.

That sight, Tom's lips stretched wide, was as gloriously decadent as Max had thought. Wasn't hard to let go, grip Tom's hair in his fist, and start thrusting, pressing in as deep as he could before Tom started to panic.

"You need to do better, Tom," Max growled, and fucked his face harder.

Tears welled in Tom's eyes, but also a fierceness Max hadn't seen before. Tom shuddered and fought back. He didn't struggle, didn't push Max away. Instead, Tom sucked and licked and opened himself to Max.

"Fuck." Max was going to lose his mind. He caught himself on the back of the chair, and gave Tom everything he'd asked for —a rough, brutal face fucking.

Tom relished meeting Max's thrusts, sucking and mouthing Max's cock like it was the only thing that existed in Tom's world, as if he'd been born to pleasure Max.

Max wasn't going to last. Blow jobs usually didn't get him off that hard, but seeing Tom's mouth full of his cock, hearing and feeling the whimpers, watching the tears slide down Tom's cheeks, even as his eyes were pits of fire...it was too much.

He yanked Tom's hair. "You like that, don't you? My fat cock in your throat?"

Tom moaned, and the vibrations nearly undid Max. "Bet you want to suck my come out, eh? Drink it down? Greedy, horny thing that you are." He quickened his thrusts.

Tom's grip on his thighs tightened, and his groans and gasps were deeper and more frantic—almost panicked.

A lance of fear slid through Max, and he peered down, trying to judge if Tom was okay or if he was the one that needed to tap out of this. But when Tom's gaze met his, the fire was there. Tom's nails bit into Max's thighs, urging him deeper.

Tom wanted this. Wanted more.

Max threw caution to the wind and chased his orgasm with dark joy. He grasped Tom's head and fucked him hard, until Tom was gasping with each thrust. In the end, Max spilled himself into Tom's mouth, cursing in a mix of French and English.

Tom's moan was triumphant and defiant, and he swallowed most of Max's seed, though when he pulled out, some dribbled from his lips. There were tears in Tom's eyes and on his cheeks, but those plump lips curled up into a smile. "Made you come."

Goddamn this man. Max yanked Tom up and kissed him, chasing the taste of himself and Tom's strength. Then he spun him around, yanked his pants down and delivered four sharp, hard blows to his ass.

Tom yelled and squirmed.

"That," Max said, "was for your lip." Then he righted Tom and kissed him again—this time gently. He spoke against those lips. "And that was for everything else."

Tom trembled against him. "Oh, god. I think I like you, Max."

The words cracked Max's heart open, and the only thing he could do at that point was wrap his arms around Tom and hold on.

———

TOM'S ASS HURT. His throat hurt. His *mind* hurt.

Max Demers was the absolute perfect man. He could have used Tom a little harder, in retrospect, but in the end, Max had let go and fucked Tom like a demon. And Tom had made Max lose control and come hard and fast.

He wanted to do that again, complete with giving Max lip and getting punished for it.

Now Max was holding him as if he wanted to protect Tom from the world. Or maybe Tom had broken Max.

"Hey, you okay?" Tom's voice was cracked and rough, the sign of a well-fucked mouth and throat, and he tasted Max with each swallow.

Max stirred. "That's usually my line."

"Yeah, well." Tom shrugged.

Max kissed him on the forehead. "I'm fine. You?"

"Perfect." Because he was. "Was I good enough for you to let me come?"

"Yes, though I'm going to make you wait, unless you're feeling very—" He whispered in Tom's ear. "—very desperate."

That didn't help. At all. "If I say I am, you'll make me wait longer."

Max's dark chuckle was answer enough. He broke the embrace, collected his pants, donned them, then stole another kiss. "I wish we'd talked more about your likes and tastes. I have a personal kink for orgasm denial. So yes, the more you want, the longer I'm tempted to make you wait."

Tom squirmed at the thought of Max driving him high, then not letting him come. "You didn't make me wait last night."

"True." Max gestured to the table again. "Let me get more coffee."

Tom sat, gingerly. The brief spanking had reignited all the bruises and welts from the previous night. God, he loved that. Tomorrow in the office would be *interesting*.

Max deposited a refilled mug in front of Tom, then took his seat, looking so relaxed. Glowing, even.

Tom sipped the brew, and he didn't sound so horrible the next time he spoke. "You really like fucking, don't you?"

He didn't expect the bark of laughter, or the trace of color on Max's cheeks. "Quite a bit, yes. Especially when my partner wants to be fucked." He leveled a look at Tom.

Tom shrugged. Yeah, he liked being fucked. A lot.

"That's also why I think you'd enjoy being plugged. You love being stretched full with cock, don't you?"

God, Max and his casual dirty talk, especially with that accent. "I—" His own cock hurt from the thought of having a toy in his ass for however long Max wanted it there. "Yeah, but I think this might be about you wanting your dick in me all the time."

That got him a chuckle. "I have my fantasies."

That made Tom shiver. "You keep asking me what I want, but you haven't said what you want." He took another gulp of coffee.

Max sat back and got that contemplative look. "There's a lot of layers to that." He scrubbed a hand over the stubble on his chin. "On the whole, I want you to know that Doms aren't assholes hell-bent on using you—that *I'm* not like that."

"I don't think you are!"

"But other Doms?"

Tom flicked at the handle of his coffee mug.

Max gave a satisfied grunt. "I also want to see you in the throes of pleasure, Tom. I've watched you at parties. I've seen your scenes."

He cringed. Most of those scenes hadn't been great. They'd scratched his itch for pain and he'd been fucked, but it hadn't been pretty or even enjoyable. "Okay."

"More personally," Max said, his voice sounding like velvet-coated sin, "I want you under my hand in the throes of pleasure and pain, for *me*." He paused. "I'm a tad selfish. Now that I've had a taste, I want your screams and cries, and your orgasms. I want *my* bruises on your skin and my toys on and inside you. And yes, my cock inside you."

Tom squeezed his eyes shut, because he was gonna come just listening to Max. He gripped his mug to keep from shoving his hand into his pants and jerking off to Max's voice and those words.

"Am I turning you on?" Max purred.

"Yeah," Tom said. "Every time you talk like that." When he opened his eyes, Max was sipping coffee, his eyes dancing. "You're not going to let me come anytime soon, I bet."

Max's smile softened. "We never ate dinner last night, and I'd like to talk about past partners and personal pitfalls before the day is over. Breakfast first, then you decide if you want to have the more serious discussion sooner or later."

He didn't want to have it at all. "I don't suppose we can push it off until another day?"

The smile slipped away entirely. "No. That's non-negotiable, Tom."

Figured he couldn't get away with that, and he probably needed to explain a few things. "Okay. Sooner. Get it over with."

Max made a face. "It's not like dentistry."

Except it was. "Breakfast?"

That word made Max sit up. "What would you like?"

Not *where do you want to go.* "You're going to cook for me?"

He gestured around the kitchen. "Fully functional space."

"Uh..." No one had ever cooked for him, discounting his parents and holiday meals with friends, but those didn't count.

Max cocked his head. "Eggs? Pancakes? Waffles? Bacon? Some combination of those? I wasn't expecting company, so I don't have any pastries, but I have bagels in the freezer, and there's always French toast. I suppose I could whip up a tart or pie..."

The list made Tom's head swim. "Um. Why don't you decide this one? Anything's fine for me."

"Are you sure?" There was that damn look of concern again.

Tom laughed. "I made a lot of decisions lately."

That got him a chuckle. "Fine. Waffles and bacon, then." Max headed to the cabinets, opened them, and started pulling things out. "And while I'm cooking, you can tell me about your last relationship."

Oh god. "Do I have to?"

Max paused. "If you absolutely don't want to, then no. But I'd like to know what made you tack that ad up."

Which meant the same thing, because Frank was pretty

much why Tom had gotten desperate enough to try that scheme. "Okay. Let me see how I can explain that."

He was quiet for a while, as Max moved around the kitchen, pulling out a waffle iron, several mixing bowls, and ingredients.

"Sometimes, I think there's a sign on me that attracts the wrong kind of guy. You're not the first person to tell me that I date the wrong men." Aaron had, often enough. Will, as well. Lupé. Ralph. Basically everyone at Bold Brew. Candace up at Mansion House.

"It's a small community," Max said.

Yeah, it was. Tom scrubbed a hand over his face. "So, when I got to Laurelsburg, I heard about the parties up at Mansion House, and tried to figure out how to get an invite. I hadn't actually realized that I could just ask my barista."

Max laughed at that.

Tom launched into the rest of the story. He'd searched for locals on Kinkbook. Found some guys into pain play and rough sex, and one who thought he could get them into the parties at Mansion House. They'd hooked up. The pain play had been okay. A little rough around the edges, but nothing Tom couldn't handle. The sex had been hard and fast, and that had been okay, too.

"Scratched the itch." Tom shrugged.

"But?"

"Well, he got...possessive and domineering. Wanted me on my hands and knees all the time. Naked. Available for him at all hours. I was okay with trying a weekend slave scene, but then he tried coming to my office and bossing me around. No warning. Nothing. Barged right in while I was with a client."

Max stilled. "You threw him out."

"Of course I did. Dragged him out of there and literally tossed him on his ass. Told him we were done, and that he needed to get his head screwed on straight." Tom drummed his fingers on the table. "A week later, he called and dangled an invite to Mansion House, and asked to get back together. Fool that I was, I said yes."

Max grunted.

The party had been fine. "You were there, with Susan, I think." Tom recounted some of the events, and Max nodded.

"I remember. It was the first time I'd seen you at Candace's. I asked after you." He paused, then added darkly. "Oh, *that* guy."

Yeah, *that* guy. Despite having gone to the party with Tom, the dude tied up and flogged a different man. Told Tom no one wanted a bitchy fuck like him.

Tom had left, walking the entire way back to his apartment, because of course the fucker had insisted on driving. Had taken hours to get home.

"Candace banned him after that."

Tom nodded. "I'm surprised you asked about me, given—" He waved his hand.

Max grunted and cracked an egg into a mixing bowl.

"Anyway, it was Ralph who pulled me aside at Bold Brew to let me know that Candace had extended me my own invite."

"Why did you never come by yourself? Play with one of the unattached Doms?"

Tom should have. Especially since once or twice Max had been unattached and willing to dominate. "I didn't think anyone would want me."

Silence expanded between them for a time, as Max whipped up what Tom guessed was waffle batter. There was a faint scent of cinnamon in the air, and maple syrup, too.

"After that first dude, I wanted someone outside of Laurelsburg." Except the internet wasn't the best place to shop for Doms. He didn't need to fill Max in about the men he'd taken to Mansion House. Max had seen that play out. "The next guys were better than the first one, at least."

Max gave him a dubious look, "I suppose."

Tom grunted. "Yes, I know. They were jerks, too."

More silence. Then, Tom sighed. "So, Frank was the last one, and I thought maybe he'd work since I'd seen him at Bold Brew, and the munches, and at Mansion House."

Max nodded. "I know who Frank is."

Of course. "We were out at that club on Jefferson Highway, and I had one too many, and—lost my head a bit. He felt me up while dancing, and that was okay, but I wasn't up for exhibitionism, and I needed a piss, so I went to go do that and—" Tom blinked and stopped.

Silence. Absolute dead silence. Max had stopped moving.

"In the bathroom, he tried to get me on my knees to suck him off," Tom said, trying to keep his tone light. He knew what it sounded like, what it was. He'd spent time talking with a therapist afterward. "When he tried a little too hard, after I'd said no, I punched him in the balls."

"Good." Max ground out the word. "Is that why you don't kneel?"

Tom nodded. "That, and other Doms being complete assholes when I was on my knees. I...have some issues. I just want someone to beat me, fuck me, and wreck me who isn't an asshole with no understanding of boundaries." He focused on Max. "I should have told you that on Friday."

Max set the bowl he'd been working with aside, and dusted his hands together. "You did, more or less."

"You were right. I want respect." Tom paused. "I deserve it."

"Yes," Max said gravely, "you do."

Tom huffed a laugh. "Bet the tale of your last partner isn't as fraught."

Max shrugged. "It's pretty short. I met Rosalind at Mansion House. She lives a couple towns over, but knows Candace through a connection with the art scene. Rosalind is an interior designer. She enjoyed bondage and some light pain play. I do enjoy tying people up. But, as it turns out, she has a professor kink."

"Oh shit! Did she tell you?"

Max scowled and shook his head. "No, she did *not*." He gave a little exasperated croak. "Then she showed up at my office, dressed like a Catholic schoolgirl."

Tom blew out a breath. "What happened?"

"Well, luckily, it was nearly Halloween, so no one blinked. None of the students dress like that anyway, but oh, it became obvious what she wanted from me. So I took her to dinner over at Olympia, we had a nice long chat about our kinks, and then we broke up because we were not compatible in the long run, even without the schoolgirl/professor dynamic that I absolutely cannot do."

Tom rewound the conversation a little. "You're not into light pain play."

"No," Max said. "I'm quite the sadist."

Good. "You weren't *that* rough with me this morning."

Max grunted. "I wasn't. Not until near the end. I was worried you wouldn't tell me if it was too much, but I had to trust that you would."

Tom sat back against the chair with a thump. "Trust—me? Oh." He'd had so many Doms walk over his needs that it never occurred to him that trust flew both ways. "I'll safeword, or tell you no. I promise."

Max nodded. "After hearing your tale, I believe you." He headed to the fridge. "Do you have a preference for how you like your bacon cooked?"

Tom cringed. "Yeah. But you're going to hate it."

Max closed the door to the fridge, bacon in hand, and raised an eyebrow.

"I like it well done."

"You mean burnt," Max said, a little curl to his lip.

"Yeah. Exactly."

Max rolled his eyes, but he burnt several pieces of bacon for Tom, and served those with two Belgian waffles topped with fresh whipped cream and a blueberry compote he just *happened* to have lying around. There was also maple syrup and butter and more coffee.

The bacon was perfect. Tom crunched down on a piece. "Thank you for this." He waved the bacon at Max.

Max looked bemused, and nudged Tom with his foot. "I abhor burnt bacon, but I'm glad it's to your liking."

A sense of calm mixed with a heady giddiness washed over Tom. He was comfortable. Safe. Max was kind. He *liked* Max and was enjoying his company. Plus, Max wanted to fuck him as much as he wanted to be fucked, and with the same kind of intensity.

He dug into his waffles and tasted the same hint of cinnamon as in the coffee on Friday, sharp and earthy under the sweetness of the blueberries and syrup. "Tell me about hockey."

Max's fork hovered for a moment. "Not much to tell. Like I said, it's a faculty/staff pickup team playing in a beer league. We have games against a couple local teams, and a couple teams from nearby towns. It's just for fun."

"But what position do you play?" Tom had to know, since he'd been wavering between guessing forward or defense.

Max took his time eating before replying. "Do you play?"

"I did as a kid. Wasn't great, but I *loved* watching games. Still love skating, and it's more pleasant without people crashing into you."

"Checking is the best part," Max murmured. "Though we don't get *that* physical during game. All of us are too damn old."

"So, defense?"

Max's lips quirked up. "Yup, though like every Quebecois kid of my generation, I wanted to be Mario Lemieux, play forward, and win a Stanley Cup."

"Alas, here you are, a linguistics professor," Tom couldn't help teasing. "In a little Pennsylvanian town."

Max sighed dramatically. "My young playing career was cut short at the age of thirteen when realized I was spending more time reading on the bench during practices than actually playing hockey." He had a rueful smile. "Coach said I was too reckless. Kept turning over the puck or taking penalties. Or both."

Tom shrugged. "Sounds like a defenseman."

Max mock-kicked him again. "Behave."

Tom chuckled and ate more waffle. "Habs fan?"

"Much to the chagrin of my parents, I was a die-hard Penguins fan. I was that kid who wore black and gold in a sea of red when the Pens were in town."

"Mario Lemieux."

"Exactly, and then I was hooked." Max paused and looked thoughtful. "A few times my folks took me and my sister down to Pittsburgh for a game. Those were special."

There was something odd about connecting this man to a family. Max had always seemed so solitary. Even when he had a partner. "Does your sister play?"

"Used to." Max sipped his coffee. "Goalie. She coaches youth hockey back in suburban Montreal, and works with my folks." He expression turned contemplative. "I should call her soon." He poked at his plate, then the smile was back. "What about you? Siblings?"

Tom rotated his cup in his hand. "Just one. An older

brother. He's living in Europe, so I rarely see him. My parents are in North Carolina, and they never quite got used to me being gay."

Max pushed back a little from the table. "Mine are fine with my sexuality. They were unhappy with my move to the States, though."

Tom's parents had never liked his brother living in Europe. "I guess that's the tour of relationships, sports, and family." He finished his waffle. "And breakfast." Tom laid down his fork. "Thank you for this."

"I enjoy cooking." Max rose and grabbed their plates. "Speaking of tours, let me show you the rest of the house."

Three stories, plus a basement. Tom followed Max all the way to the top, which contained a whole guest suite.

"It's woefully out of date," Max said. "The last project I have for the house."

It was pretty seventies. Odd green carpet. Orange wallpaper. "Good bones, though. What are you thinking of having done?"

Max leaned against the wall, his blue-and-green plaid flannel pants clashing horribly. "This will sound—sappy? I think that's the best word. I'm leaving it until I have a partner to share all this with." He waved a hand to encompass the house. "Everything else that I've done has been to my taste. I want to leave something for them, so this place can be theirs, too." He paused. "Assuming anyone wants to live with me."

Tom took in the third floor. "Leaving this space for a partner is thoughtful. I don't know anyone else who'd do that." He focused on Max. "Your house, what I've seen, is beautiful. I can't imagine anyone who wants to live with you saying no to this."

Max smiled, but there was a sadness to it. "That's kind of you to say."

Tom wanted to probe that sadness, but they had combed through so much, and the thought of Max not having a permanent partner was a question mark.

Tom followed Max to the second floor. He'd already seen the main bedroom and the attached bathroom, but there were other rooms—another bedroom and an office—and a second bathroom. The first floor contained a formal dining room, a living room, the kitchen, and a tiny office in a sunroom. "It's not heated," Max said. "So I only sit out here in the summer, when I can open the windows and listen to the birds."

There was a porch off the kitchen and a backyard beyond that. Max waved toward the fence. "I have a small garden, though I am not very much of a green thumb."

"There's something you're not good at?" Tom feigned surprise, and peered out the kitchen door.

Max chuckled, then pulled Tom close. "Yes, there are things I'm not good at." He caught Tom's hands and brought them to the small of Tom's back. "And many things that I excel at."

There was no space between their bodies now, and Max pressed him up against the door, his lips hovering close to Tom's. "Should I treat you to more of my talents, or let you wonder what I might have done to you?"

Lust ripped through Tom. "Can I help you chose?"

Max's amusement was a whisper of breath before his lips met Tom's.

This kiss was deep, consuming, and commanding. Tom couldn't have broken free had he wanted to. Max had him trapped against cold glass and wood, their erections rutting against each other. Max slid his lips down to Tom's shoulder and bit. Hard.

Pain flashed through Tom, stealing his breath. He thrust against Max, as the ache swept into his skull and turned to bright spots of pleasure.

There'd be a bruise. More than one, because Max bit him a second time. Tom voiced both pain and desire, and tried to free his hands. Max slipped his thigh between Tom's and leaned in. "I still haven't decided if I'm going to let you come, but I'm going to fuck you again, and you're going to pick your torment."

Tom caught his breath, and followed the shift to this being a scene. "Yes, Sir."

"Very good. Down the stairs, Tom."

Max let him go, and Tom headed into the basement, trying not to seem eager to be punished.

CHAPTER FIVE

MAX ADORED EAGER SUBS, the ones who wanted the pain he could give, who wanted torment, lack of control, and release. Such joy to give someone what they wanted and watch them fall into bliss and contentment.

Tom ran down the stairs to the basement before Max. Pure pleasure to see.

What Tom knew of kink seemed to revolve around brutal fucking and impact play, plus humiliation and attempts at control by men who had no idea how to properly treat submissives. Max shoved his annoyance aside when he reached the bottom of the stairs.

There were aspects of kink Tom hadn't experienced, and Max wanted to share those and see Tom dissolve into pleasure again and again.

Over at the bar, Tom stood with his hands on the smooth wood bar top, and stared at the toys on the shelves behind it. Max joined Tom, placed his hands on those hips, and pulled him close. "See anything you like?"

Tom's breath hitched. "Yes, but it's not for me to say, is it?"

It could be, but he'd given Tom many choices the previous

night. "Not this time. I'm going to give you an old experience and a new one."

Max had seen Tom flogged at Mansion House, watched how he fell into the rhythm and pain, how he stretched himself out for the blows, and gave himself over afterward. He kissed the back of Tom's neck, then swung around to the other side of the bar. On the counter, he placed a new set of cuffs, similar to the ones Tom had worn before, another set for his ankles, then drew out two floggers—one to warm the skin up, and another to sting and burn.

Tom inhaled sharply.

"That's the old. For the new—" Max tapped his lips and surveyed the shelves.

He hadn't enjoyed watching Tom being fucked. The Dom had been reasonable with a flogger but cruel with his words, and hadn't had any thought about Tom.

Some partners liked that kind of relationship, especially in public. Scenes were *scenes*, after all. But Tom never seemed to enjoy the sex. Sure, he came, but it was, as Tom put it, scratching an itch. Max didn't want that.

He wanted desire and need, on both their parts. Gags were a thought, but those required more trust than Max felt he'd earned. So, he plucked one of his thinner plugs off the shelf. Simple. Metal.

"This, I think." He took it to the bar sink and gave it a wash. It was clean, but he always washed his toys before and after use.

Tom made a croaking sound.

Max didn't even look up. "Are you hard, Tom?"

There was a breathless laugh. "I haven't stopped being hard since you fucked my face."

"Good." Max finished washing the toy, dried it and placed it and the towel he'd used on the bar, along with a bottle of lube. He grabbed a condom and stuffed that in the pocket of his pants, then rejoined Tom on the other side. "Now, stand right here."

Max positioned Tom, then pulled over a bar stool and took a seat in front of him. Both Tom and the toys were within easy reach.

Indeed, Tom was hard, his flannel pants tenting obscenely. Max hooked his fingers around the waistband, and pulled them down, rendering Tom naked again. "Kick those off to the side, please."

Tom did, and they joined the yoga pants from the night before.

Once more, Tom vibrated before Max, all need and want, sprinkled with that heady hint of fear. His gaze was focused on Max, but it occasionally flicked to the toys on the bar top.

Max clicked his tongue, and Tom yanked his gaze back to him. "You'll experience all those in due time."

"Yes, Sir," he whispered.

Max cupped Tom's balls and rolled them, eliciting a lovely groan from Tom. "You're so responsive. It's a treat." When Max wrapped his hand around Tom's shaft and stroked him several times, Tom rose up onto his toes, keening in the back of his throat.

"So *very* responsive. Look at your cock, Tom."

Tom obeyed, his eyes wide. Max caught a dab of precome on his thumb, and as expected, Tom focused on that. Max lifted his thumb and licked the wetness off.

Salt and musk—some of Max's favorite tastes.

Another moan escaped Tom. "God."

Max stroked Tom's jaw. "Has no one tasted you before?"

"I—no Dom, no."

"Pity." Tom had a cock built for sucking. Max would add that to the list of experiences. "My turn to strap leather on you. Your wrist."

Tom obliged, and Max finally had the pleasure of buckling his cuffs over Tom's flesh. Tom's breath was slow but strong, though he trembled slightly as he stood.

Max repeated the order and the motions with the other wrist, then slid off the stood to admire Tom. So strung out, hard, and unsure of himself. Absolutely delightful. Max pushed the stool away. "Put both hands on the bar, and spread your legs wide."

Another hitch of breath, then Tom obeyed. Max circled behind, admiring the colors rising on his ass. He tapped the inside of Tom's thigh with his hand. "Wider."

A little groan, and then he did.

"Now that's a view." Tom wanton, his cock thrusting forward, balls hanging low, and that absolutely stunning ass marred and marked with Max's ministrations. He cupped the flesh there, feeling the raised skin under his fingers.

Tom groaned and hung his head. "Fuck."

"Mmm. Eventually." Max picked up the ankle cuffs, then knelt to encircle Tom's ankles.

Tom's whole body vibrated. Whether from fear, excitement, or desire, Max couldn't tell. Time for some torture, then. He slid into the space between Tom's legs, caressing the outsides of each. He leaned his back against the bar. When he looked up, Tom was staring down, his mouth slack, as if he had an inkling of what might be to come.

"How still can you hold yourself, Tom?"

"I—" He exhaled. "How still do you want me to be, Sir?"

This time, Max ran his hands over the muscles on the insides of Tom's thighs. "As still as you are right now. Stay that way while I suck your cock and finger your hole."

Tom's "Yes, Sir" was all breath.

Max did reposition Tom to get the ideal angle, and in that time, Tom's breathing hitched.

"I don't know if I can do this, Sir." That was the first time trepidation had colored Tom's voice.

Max smoothed a hand down Tom's calf, meant to soothe. "You can. You have a great deal of control over yourself." He found Tom's gaze. "You did ask me to push you."

Tom closed his eyes. "Yeah, I did."

Max patted his leg, then took the tip of Tom's cock into his mouth, lapping at the precome there. Savoring the taste.

The moan from Tom was half keening, and his whole body shook. "Oh my god."

Max chuckled, and Tom shuddered, and then Max got to work, sucking and licking, and sliding his mouth on Tom's shaft.

"Fuck, Sir! I can't! I can't!" For all that shouting, Tom didn't move much.

Max gave Tom's calf a squeeze. A whimper and some gasps for air later, Tom settled, even as Max worked that dick over with mouth, tongue and lips.

He fucking loved giving blowjobs, especially when combined with submission, bondage, and orgasm denial. There was something so luxurious about bringing another to the edge, then making them stay there until they were strung out from pleasure with no release.

He wanted Tom there, so Max backed off. "You taste divine."

"Fuck, Max." Tom caught his breath. "You're too good."

Not Sir this time. Interesting. "That's never been a complaint before." Max slicked a finger with his spit, and went back to work on Tom's dick. Then he slid his wet finger over Tom's hole.

Tom cried out, his legs buckled, and he caught himself on the edge of the bar. Max yelped and grabbed Tom's thighs to keep them from taking his head out.

"Oh fuck, oh shit," Tom panted. "You okay?"

"I'm fine," Max said, breathless between his legs. "You?"

"Yeah, I—I'm not sure I can stand yet, though. Uh."

Well, this was a predicament. "That didn't work out as I had planned."

Tom's wheeze had laughter in it. "You think?"

They managed to untangle themselves, and ended up sitting side by side on stools at the bar. Tom leaned his elbows on the wood and scrubbed his hands through his hair. "Fuck, I'm sorry for killing the mood."

"That's on me, not you." Max coughed a laugh. "So much for being a sly and clever Dom."

The smile that broke out on Tom's face was breathtaking. "You're a great Dom. That was one of the *hottest* things anyone has ever done to me. I *wanted* you to finger fuck me, I just couldn't control the reaction."

Max grinned back. "We can try that again sometime, perhaps with more support for you. Though, I do enjoy that kind of bondage, so maybe not."

Tom blinked. "That's *bondage*?"

"All the ropes are in your head." Max tapped the side of his.

Tom got a faraway look. "Huh." His gaze wandered to the bar top, and the plug that sat there. "I was curious about how that was going to feel."

"I still intend to plug and flog you, never you fear." Max cupped the side of Tom's face and kissed him.

Tom met him with lips and tongue. Rather than the dominating kiss Max had intended, this was one of exploration, as if they hadn't kissed before. There was wonderment in Tom's lips, surprise in how his fingers traced over Max's neck and shoulders.

Tom was the one who broke the kiss. "You're not mad at me?"

Despite being utterly fluent in English, the question took

Max time to parse. So much lay behind it that he didn't understand. Then he did, and rage and sorrow flowed in equal measure.

"Tom," he said gravely. "Of course I'm not mad at you. You did nothing wrong. As I said, if anyone is to blame, it's me."

Tom seemed as if he'd argue that point, so Max touched his lips with a finger. "I'm not one bit mad."

"Oh," Tom said, then sucked Max's finger into his mouth.

Hot. Wet. Velvet. Max moaned as Tom sucked it like a cock.

"God, your mouth." Max reclaimed his finger and rose. "So many things I want to do to it."

Tom gazed up at him. "Please, Sir."

Max tapped him on the thigh. "Up, Tom. Let's try that again, shall we? Hands on the bar as before."

Ordering Tom to spread his legs wide, caressing his ass and thighs, and planting kisses on his back had Tom trembling and cursing in no time, and Max's own desire kindled again. He adored Tom's curses and shudders. Those moans.

Max grabbed the bottle of lube, clicked it open, then dribbled some down Tom's crack. When he followed the lube with probing fingers, Tom gasped, loud and sweet. This time, Max wasn't slow—he thrust into Tom, driving him up onto his toes.

Tom's lustful cry was decadent, and Max wanted to drink that down. He drove his fingers in, then fucked Tom hard, keeping him on his toes and rocking him against the bar.

"Please," Tom moaned. "Oh, god, please."

"You're not coming any time soon, Tom." Max added more lube, and another finger, then resumed his punishing thrusts.

Tom groaned and pushed back on Max's hand. He leaned over Tom and kept fucking him. "Like this, Tom? My fingers in your ass?"

"Yes," he gasped out. "Please!"

Max withdrew his fingers. "You're to come only when I say."

"Y-yes, Sir." Tom shook, and had a death grip on the bar.

If Max hadn't spilled himself down Tom's throat, he would've been tempted to skip straight to fucking Tom into the oblivion like they both wanted. But different desires roiled through Max now, to tease and torment. To make Tom scream.

Max fetched the plug, slicked it and Tom's hole, then gently pressed the tip against Tom's ring.

Tom yelped and rocked forward. "C-cold!"

Yes, it was. That was part of the delight. "You can warm it up, Tom."

Max pressed forward. The plug opened Tom and slid in, the wide head stretching his ring, then disappearing into Tom's ass, until only the flanged base remained outside.

Tom's spine was as straight as a rod. "Oh my god," he said. "Oh fuck." His legs shook.

Max gripped Tom's hips, pulled him off the bar and back against his body. "Do you like that?"

Tom moaned, then hissed. "I—god, I can feel it."

Wicked delight flared in Max. "That's the point."

"It's—fuck." Tom shifted, then groaned.

Perfect. "Now imagine being tied up and flogged," Max purred into his ear.

Tom squirmed against Max. "Old and new."

"Exactly so. Come with me."

"I'm not sure I can walk." Tom was breathless.

Max stifled a laugh. Being plugged was a strange sensation indeed. "That's not a very large one. I'm sure you can."

In the end, Tom managed to make it to the cross, though his gait and his expressions were a delight to behold, full of grimaces and sighs of pleasure. Tom stretched his hands up high for Max to clip him on. "Do you—have any idea what this feels like?"

Max gave his ass a slap, and that had Tom rocking against the cross. "Yes." He pressed the flange of the plug, tilting and angling it until Tom was groaning and humping the cross. "And I know how to move it so it presses into you right—there."

Tom squeezed his eyes shut. "Max! Sir!"

"Behave, Tom. I intend to come inside you again. It's your choice whether you get to join me."

That quieted Tom.

"You wanted me to push you."

A swallow and a nod, but not a safeword. So Max bent and clipped Tom's ankle cuffs into the restraints at the base of the cross.

Tom hung there against the padded wood, arms and legs spread wide, Max's leather around his limbs and a glint of silver on his ass.

"Good." Max retrieved the floggers, set the harder one aside, and shook out the softer. "Just your back. Your ass has more than enough to handle at the moment."

That got Max a chuckle, which turned into a gasp when he laid down the first blow. The second wasn't any harder—they both needed to be warmed up, and Max wanted Tom deeper in subspace.

The motion and sounds, those were heady for Max. The rhythm and swinging soothed, but that moment when Tom flinched, then hissed—that ignited Max's blood, and so did Tom's groans and the way he danced and jerked to the tempo of Max's blows.

"Oh my god," Tom said. "It's—fucking me."

"Enjoying that?" Max kept up the rhythm of the flogging.

Tom groaned, a sound that was half pleasure and half torment, and that was answer enough.

After a few more strokes, Max paused and picked up the other flogger, the one that would leave welts and give Tom the pain he wanted.

Heat coursed through Max. Tom was on his cross, in his leather, impaled by his plug, his for the taking. He shook out this flogger, then slowly started again.

Tom jolted on the cross, his gasp filled with the edge of pain. After a few more blows, Tom's reddened skin turned darker, and the moans took on a hard edge.

"There you are, Tom. I see you," Max murmured, then struck harder, keeping the rhythm slow. Tom's whole body relaxed and glowed. As Max worked, Tom's moans turned to sharp gasps that twisted into cries.

Max's own breath was heavy and his cock hard, but his focus was on Tom, his rising welts, the timber of those cries and sobs, and the tremble in his arms and legs. So beautiful, especially with the glint of silver between his cheeks and the way his hips twitched.

This glorious man was stunning in his pain and pleasure, his whole being flush, his yells sheer music. Max wanted to devour those cries, dig his fingers into those welts, then kiss away Tom's tears.

They were both close. There was a dizzying dark height Max wanted to reach, Tom too, and he'd bring them both there. Max paused for a beat, then laid down the next blows hard, heavy, and fast.

Tom shook on the cross, his whole body twitching against the flogger, his cries long and harsh and edged with sweet agony. Tears slid down his cheeks. "Sir, please, please!"

Yes, there. Perfection. Max's body thrummed and his soul burned. The last blow made Max grunt with exertion and Tom scream and flail against the wood, his face wet from crying.

Max dropped the flogger and was to Tom in an instant. "Shh. Shh. It's over, Tom."

He sobbed. "No, please, I need..."

Max drank that in, dug his fingers into Tom's ass cheek, and lifted.

Tom gasped and twisted, his hips jutting forward.

"More?" Max growled. "Shall I keep flogging you?"

"No—want you." Tom tried to swivel his head, tried to meet Max's gaze. "Take me. Use me. Fuck me up. Make me scream."

Good god. Lust and need twined in Max, wrapping him in a heady, dark desire. He mouthed then bit Tom's shoulder, right on one of the marks he'd left before. "I can do that for you." His voice was rough. "Stretch you wide with my cock. Make you feel every inch, and all these marks... Hurt you so good."

"Please!" Tom's consent was music.

Max unclipped Tom, and hauled him from the cross and to the floor. He scrambled up onto his hands and knees, crawling away, but Max caught him around the waist and yanked him back against his body.

They were both on their knees now, both panting.

Max grazed his teeth along the side of Tom's neck. "You want to be fucked? Want something thicker than this plug in your ass?"

Tom struggled and gasped but didn't answer, so Max pushed him forward, held him down, and grasped the flange of the plug. He was gentle with the removal, and so aware of the long, strangled moan Tom made, that glorious sound. There'd be a ton of cleanup later. Right now, he didn't care.

Under Max, Tom squirmed again, so he held him down firmly, and slapped his ass until Tom was gasping and crying again. "That's what you get for not waiting. Now, behave."

This time, Tom obeyed. There were tears in his eyes, but a smile curved his lips. "I'm behaving."

Max gave him another hard smack, and Tom moaned.

Fuck, did he need to be inside Tom. Buried to the hilt. Thank goodness he'd had enough sense to bring the lube over. He dug the condom out, pushed his pants down and prepped himself, then he was grasping Tom's hips again, and thrusting deep into his tight heat.

Tom's cry was sweetness and light. Max curled his fingers into Tom's hips, and rammed into Tom's ass, driving his cock in as deep as possible, over and over, until Tom was shouting and scrambling for purchase on the floor. Max grabbed Tom's shoulder and pulled him back, wrapped both arms around his torso and held him tight. Then he thrust into him hard.

"This what you want, Tom?"

He response was a strangled cry.

"A fat cock in your tight ass?" He held Tom still and pounded him hard and as fast as he could. "Fucking you until you scream?"

"Yeah." The words poured out of Tom. "Need to scream. So fucking good."

It was. Max's arms ached, the floor was hard, and they'd both feel this later, but right now? He found Tom's nipples, twisted them cruelly, and set about fucking him as brutally as he could manage.

Tom's cries became incoherent and loud, and his body taut with pain and pleasure.

Max was close, so close to heat and darkness and light crashing over him. He bit Tom and tugged at his nipples. "Jack off. I want you to come on my cock. Hear you scream for me."

It was a wonder that Tom could obey, given the stream of cries and moans pouring out of him, but he grasped his shaft and beat himself off.

What a sight to behold, Tom frantically pumping his cock

while Max pounded into him. "Yeah, that's it. Make it good for me. Want to see it."

Tom's whole body tightened. "Max," he moaned. "Max!" Then he was coming, coating his hand with ribbons of semen. His body clenched around Max's cock.

Max pounded into Tom, chasing his own orgasm, then he was there too, crying out until all that was left was light and bliss.

They were both slumped over on the floor and panting when Max could focus again.

"Tom," he croaked. *Fuck.* He needed to be more together. "Tom?"

There was a laugh. "Oh my *god.*"

Max pressed his head against Tom's back and breathed out relief. "Ouais." He didn't want to move, but lying on the floor would become painful soon, and he couldn't imagine it was comfortable for Tom. "Give me a second."

Tom groaned. "Please don't move yet. It's gonna hurt."

"I know. For me too."

There was another laugh. "You're fucking fantastic, you know that?"

Max cracked open an eye. "You liked all that?"

"God, yeah. Brutal. But I never felt unsafe. Out of my mind, sure, with the flogging and that—thing up me."

Max chuckled "Anal plug. Next time, it'll be thicker."

"Fuck." Tom slumped farther against the floor.

"Speaking of your ass, I should pull out."

"Yeah, I know." Tom sighed. "Wish you could stay in me longer."

Max kissed Tom's back. "So do I." Then he slid out of Tom and untangled himself.

They were both a mess of groans and aches. When they were upright, Max tossed the condom and surveyed the scene.

That was a mess, too. Lube. Semen. The plug. He'd have to spend time cleaning.

Not now. He had other plans now.

Tom leaned against the cross. "I'm going to feel every second of that tomorrow."

Max huffed a laugh. "Me too." He met Tom's gaze. "Thank you for giving that to me."

That mix of confusion and joy was heartbreaking to see. "I —" Tom took a breath. "You're welcome." That was a whisper. "Thank you for—" He gestured to the cross and the floor.

"Messy sex?"

Tom laughed, then sobered. "Honestly, that was best flogging and fuck of my life."

Max hoped he kept his shock and dismay from his expression. "I'm glad I could give that to you then." He scrubbed a hand through his hair. "Care to join me for a shower upstairs?"

Tom got another befuddled look, then brightened. "In that slate monstrosity of yours?"

Max nodded and held out his hand. Tom sucked in a breath, then let Max draw him out of the basement and up the stairs.

"I'm not used to this," Tom said on the flight to the second floor.

"I know," Max replied. "Humor me?"

Tom coughed a laugh "I'm not complaining. Normally, I'd be putting my clothes back on and heading home while the other guy was in the shower."

This time Max couldn't keep quiet. "Those fucking assholes."

Tom was quiet until the stepped into Max's en suite bathroom. "But you're not them." Tom's eyes were so dark in this light.

"No. I'm not." Max gestured at the shower. "After you."

Built for two, with several different showerheads, the shower was an obnoxious luxury, but also a huge relief, both after a long day at the university or a brutal hockey game.

Or intense sex with a man Max could come to adore. Or cherish. Or both.

Slow down, Maxime.

While they cleaned up, Max kissed Tom and ran his hands over the bruises and welts, and enjoyed Tom's hisses and moans. Then they stepped out.

"Fuck, you're good with a flogger." Tom dried his front, and let Max pat his back dry and apply salve.

There were so many things Max wanted to tell Tom. That he was delightful. That Max wanted to hunt down every Dom who mistreated him.

Instead, he kissed one of the bite marks he'd left on Tom's shoulder. "Let me get you something to wear."

Tom ended up in another set of flannel pants, this time with a T-shirt. While Max was putting on clothes, Tom muttered something about needing his underwear, and headed downstairs. When Max followed, he found Tom standing in the foyer, a bundle of his clothes in his arms.

Tom looked up at Max on the stairs. "Should I put these on? I mean—we're done, right?"

Max took the rest of the stairs quickly, and closed the distance between them. Slowly, carefully, he took hold of Tom's arms, cradling his elbows, and waited until Tom met his gaze.

"I was hoping you'd stay longer. I can make lunch or dinner —I don't know what time it is. Or we can watch a show or talk or—"

Tom's lips parted.

"If you want to go home, of course you can, but you don't have to because the scene is over."

Max let go and stepped back, giving Tom space.

Those brows furrowed, and he peered at the bundle of clothes in his hands. "I wouldn't mind staying. I don't want you to go out of your way, though."

"Tom." Max's voice twisted. "You're my *guest*. Nothing is out of the way."

"God." Tom shoved the bundle of clothing into his duffel and straightened. "I'm a fucking mess, aren't I? Can't even do this right."

Max's endorphins were crashing, so Tom's must have been too, especially given the emotions dancing over his face. That, coupled with Tom's past, must have been a heavy combination.

"Tom, it's fine." Max opened his arms in an invitation.

Tom hesitated, then wrapped himself around Max. "I *am* a mess, though."

"Subdrop," Max said. "Come. Couch and TV time."

Tom hiccupped a laugh, and let Max draw him into the living room. "Read about that. Aaron lent me books way back," he said. "Finally opened one. Is this the whole aftercare thing you're doing?"

"Partly." Max pulled Tom down onto the couch, then wrapped himself around Tom. "It's also because I'm selfish and want more time with you." He kissed Tom, who made a surprised sound, then melted against Max.

They stayed like that for a time, Max exploring Tom's mouth until Tom was kissing him back, his fingers wandering over Max's neck and jaw, then sliding into his hair.

"I like this," he murmured when they both finally came up for air.

"Me too." Max held Tom tighter.

They lay in each other's arms, TV forgotten, food forgotten, existing in the same space and time, curled into each other. Content and snug, Max realized Tom was snoring, so there wasn't anything more to do, but relax and slip into sleep.

———

TOM DIDN'T WANT to move. He was warm, safe, and comfortable, but he had no idea where he was. This wasn't his apartment; he knew that without opening his eyes. There was a faint scent of bacon in the air, spices, and something like pine or juniper, and his place never smelled like that.

Then he remembered, and the knowledge was a bolt of electricity through his body.

Max Demers's house. On his couch. In his arms.

He'd fallen asleep *cuddling* with Max, after what had been best damn flogging and dicking of his life. His back was achy and tight, and he'd been well fucked in both mouth and ass, and his orgasm had blinded him with the intensity and pleasure.

Max hadn't thrown Tom out when it was over. He was the opposite of an asshole, and yet a Dom who was both inventive and deliciously cruel.

Aaron often teased that Tom acted as if Max was a cinnamon roll of a man, too good, too pure for Tom's world. He *was*, though. Max was entirely too good. Plus, he left Tom sticky.

That bubbled up a snicker, one he was too old to let out, but it shook him enough that Max woke.

"Oh." His voice dripped with sleep. "Hi."

"Hey there," Tom replied. "We fell asleep."

Max's smile was soft. "Yeah. Was good. Needed it."

Tom had never read anything about what Doms needed after a scene. Heck, he'd barely read about subs. He knew about being wiped out after scenes, but he'd always made it home before faceplanting into his bed, or would catch a nap somewhere if he crashed up at Mansion House.

"If I move, am I gonna hurt you?"

"Mmm." Max shifted a leg. "Don't think so. Should sit up anyway."

They untangled and sat up. Tom winced. "Oh man. I'm gonna feel this for days."

Max scrubbed a hand through his hair, which was a hopeless mess. "Good or bad thing?"

Tom laughed. "Good thing."

"I'm glad." A smile warmed Max's face.

Tom believed him. "Thanks for letting me stay."

"I would never throw you out after a scene like that." Max's voice was deep and thick. "Ever. It's unconscionable." A grin blossomed. "Plus, I did want you to stay. Selfish."

Tom kissed Max. He didn't really know why. The kiss was sweet, a sip of Max's lips, and a delighted rumble flowed from Max. "Maybe," Tom said. "Maybe not."

Max chuckled. "Let me see what time it is. I don't know about you, but breakfast is wearing off." He pushed himself off the couch and headed to the kitchen, a picture of messy relaxation, all flannel pants and wrinkled T-shirt. This time, the chuckle made it out Tom's lips.

Max peeked around the corner, hair every which way. "What?"

"You look more student than professor right now."

"Ech." He waved that away and vanished back into the kitchen. "You hungry?" he called.

Tom's stomach gave a whine. "I could eat."

The sound of pots and pans and cabinets being opened filtered into the living room, and a strange sense of euphoria hit Tom, welling up from deep inside. This was—nice. Good. Was this *normal*? He had no idea.

"Max, are we in a relationship?"

The sounds of activity stopped in the kitchen, and Max reappeared. "A kinky one, yes."

"This is very different from the kink relationships I've had before."

Max rubbed the back of his neck. "I've gathered." He gestured toward the kitchen. "Could we talk in here? It's nearly four, so I'm going to make us dinner."

Nearly *four*? "Shit, we really slept."

"The scene took a while, I think. I lose time when I'm in the zone."

Tom stared at Max, then rose. "Sure. Dinner. Talk. Sounds good." There was a hell of a lot he didn't know about BDSM, it seemed, despite the munches, demos, parties, and Doms. Maybe he knew things intellectually, but everything with Max was nothing he'd ever experienced before.

Max "threw together" a dinner of steak, fresh green beans, potatoes, a salad, and some sort of artisan bread he had lying around, then followed with a batch of brownies he "whipped up" from scratch.

"Do you do this for all your subs?" Tom nibbled at a brownie. Fantastic.

Max waggled his head. "Not exactly," he said. "I've cooked for a few, though."

Tom filed that away. "So, we're in a relationship?"

"Well, you wanted a Dom for sex and pain play. I said I'd show you what a Dom/sub relationship could be like. So yes?" Max broke his brownie in half and took a bite.

Right. Tom rolled his shoulders out. "Makes sense."

Their conversation drifted to Max's job, his course load, and how tough it was balancing that, hockey, and personal time, especially teaching an additional course this semester. Tom discussed his work as a lawyer, including some amusing stories.

"You know what's the worst? Tree law. Never seen people get more upset than about trees and property lines and overhanging branches. Divorce is less vicious."

Max laughed at that.

At the end of the evening, when Tom had changed back into his jeans and sweater, Max took him into his arms. "Thank you for your help at the demo." His grin was fiendish. "No idea how I'll ever repay you." Then those lips were on Tom's and it was all he could do to hold on while Max kissed deep into Tom's soul.

He was breathless and dizzy when they came up for air. "Well, we could do this again sometime."

Max's smile was all teeth and happiness. "That sounds lovely."

Tom didn't want to leave, didn't want Max to let go. This weekend had been a kinky, sexy fairy tale, but the sooner he stepped into reality, the quicker he could process what had happened between him and Max.

Max opened the door. "Are you sure I can't drive you back?"

"No, I need the walk, and it's not far. I'm in the Crimson Building on Main, not too far from the courthouse."

"Above the old pharmacy. I know those apartments." Max pulled him in for a kiss that seared its way to Tom's toes. "Be safe, and have a good night, Tom."

"Bye, Max." Tom took the steps down to the walk. At the gate, he glanced over his shoulder. Max leaned against the doorframe, a smile on his face.

He—Tom Cedric—had made Maxime Demers happy.

Tom waved, then headed to his own apartment. Soon enough, the weekend would roll through his mind for him to pick apart. He wanted to cling to Max's smile for as long as he could.

CHAPTER SIX

TOM'S NIGHT in his own place on Sunday had been strange, but walking into his firm on Monday was odder still. This wasn't the first time he'd come into work with his ass bruised and aching from a weekend spent being fucked, so nothing should have been that different. But everything, from the air in the Laurelsburg streets, to the coffee he'd picked up at Bold Brew, to the damn cream paint on the walls of the office hallway seemed sharper. Vibrant. Like he was lingering in subspace.

Aaron was in his office and working already, on the phone with someone, judging from the shut door and the low murmur of his voice. Neither their admin, Brook, nor their paralegal, Kip, was in yet.

Just as well, since the quiet firm gave Tom time to settle into his office and wrap his brain around work. Except every movement reminded him that he'd spent the weekend with Max.

This wasn't going to be easy.

He took several gulps of his coffee, turned on his computer, and double-checked his calendar before sorting through his emails. Thank goodness his client appointments were in the afternoon. He made a point never to schedule anything, client-wise, before noon on Monday. Sometimes he had to appear before a judge, but lately the fates had been kind, as if judges also hated early Monday court dates.

Despite the aching in his ass and back, his mind settled into the business of lawyering quickly, and he was almost in a groove when Aaron rapped on the open door.

Tom looked up and found Aaron leaning on the doorframe, arms crossed. "Hey, so how'd all your appointments go?" There was an eager smile on his face.

Tom stared back. "Appointments?" He had no idea what Aaron was talking about.

Aaron looked as confounded as Tom felt. "Hello, your *ad*? For Mr. Not-a-Jerk-Dom?"

Oh god, *that*. Tom made a face. "Shit. I forgot all about those."

Aaron pushed himself off the doorframe and made a choking sound. "You stood those guys up? You were salivating in hope on Friday!"

Had he been? He'd remembered being excited, but also apprehensive. Then again, Aaron took everything with more intensity than Tom intended. "No, no. I went. I just forgot that I had met all of them."

"You...forgot." Aaron shook himself. "Okay, there's more going on here, isn't there?" He kicked Tom's door closed, then settled into one of his guest chairs. "Out with it."

Tom giggled, the giddiness boiling up fast. He pushed a hand through his hair.

Aaron's eyes widened. "Thomas Cedric, what have you been up to? And do I need to get *you* a lawyer?"

"No lawyer. But I owe you a dinner, or maybe several, because you were right."

Aaron crossed his legs and waved a hand dismissively. "You

know I'm always right. But you'll need to be more specific about what. Yes to dinner, though. I'll decide how many when you tell me what the hell's going on."

Fair enough. "So the ad was a total bust. Every guy was a complete ass, as you predicted. The whole thing, from start to finish, was horrible. Weeding through the texts and calls to get to *four* guys who were so full of themselves, it's a wonder their egos didn't explode all over the shop."

"Well, shit," Aaron said.

Tom's laugh was bitter. "Yeah. Afterward, Lupé comes over and hands me a cappuccino. On the house."

"That was nice of them."

"Wasn't from them. It was from Maxime Demers—he'd watched the whole shit parade."

"Sexy Cinnamon Roll Professor bought you coffee?" Aaron sat up bolt straight. "What did you do?"

"Well, I'd had such a hellish time, I figured why not talk to him? Couldn't be any worse than what I had gone through. So I got up and introduced myself."

"And?"

Tom leaned back and smiled.

"Out with it, Cedric." Aaron mimicked Tom's posture. "And make it good."

"All right." So he went through that conversation with Max on Friday night. "Then he gets a text from the sub he was doing that impact demo with."

Aaron nodded. He'd known about the demo, but he and his partners had opted to skip. They already knew all about impact toys.

"You were going to that, right?"

"Yeah," Tom said. "Had planned to, so I volunteered to be his sub for that night."

Aaron got a *look*. "Just for that night, huh?"

Heat crept into Tom's face. "He offered to show me what a non-asshole Dom could be like."

Aaron sat up again. "Oh, *please* tell me you took him up on that, and didn't beg off for some fucking *foolish* reason."

More heat coursed through Tom.

Aaron got his smug, pleased look. Same one he had when he caught the opposition doing something imprudent. "Sooooo, was he all that and a bag of chocolates?"

"Oh my god, you have no idea." Tom leaned farther back and stared up at the ceiling. "I spent that night and most of Sunday at his house. He cooked for me."

"Well, good." The normal teasing clip was gone. "You fucking deserve someone who respects you."

Tom sat up and met Aaron's hard gaze. "That's what Max said."

Aaron nodded slowly. "Uh huh. So why do you owe me dinner?" A smile blossomed on his face. "And are we talking pizza dinner or steak dinner?"

"I should have let you get his number ages ago."

"Mmmhmm. That's a given. Answer the *other* question, counsel."

Tom rolled his eyes. "Steak. As if you'd settle for pizza."

"Not when you owe me." Aaron rose and his serious lawyer face appeared. "I'm ecstatic for you, Tom. Max is a decent guy." Then the cocky smile came back. "And he's hot and sexy, and I'd bet *anything* he's fantastic in bed."

Tom lobbed a stress ball at Aaron, who caught it deftly. "Just how sore is your ass, honey?"

He wasn't about to tell Aaron that. "You instituted the 'no oversharing at the office' rule, *darling*."

Arron tossed the stress ball back. "Pizza for lunch?"

"Get out of here, Taylor, and let me work."

Aaron rolled his eyes. "Work." He air-quoted the word, but opened the door and headed out. "Serious about pizza, though."

"Whatever," Tom said. They had several hours before lunch, and Aaron's culinary moods could change on a dime.

Strangely, the conversation settled Tom into the day more than emails or trying not to think about Max. Maybe he needed to tell a friend what had happened, or he needed Aaron snarking at him. Or perhaps, he needed Aaron being happy for him and telling him Max was a good thing.

Because the amount of joy in Tom's heart was *terrifying*, and he had no idea what to make of that.

———

AROUND LUNCHTIME, Tom and Kip were in Tom's office and halfway through drafting a divorce agreement for one of Tom's clients when his phone honked—his tone for an incoming text—then honked a second time.

Kip looked up. "You going to check that?"

"It's probably spam." Or some dude texting him about the ad. He'd gotten several of those while at Max's. Thank god his phone had been happily buried in his duffel. When he'd finally dug the thing out, he'd rolled his eyes.

"I wonder how many of these things I'm going to get." He'd looked at Max and grinned. "Should I tell them the position's filled?"

The smile that had spread over Max's face had been warm and cocky and—everything. "Yes, I believe you should."

So he'd giddily answered each one with, *Sorry, the position's been filled.*

His phone honked a third time, and Kip gave him a look. "If you're not going to check that, at least put it on do not disturb. You have the most *annoying* notification sound."

Yeah, Aaron had said that too. Tom grabbed the phone, glanced at the messages, then stared.

All three were from Max.

The first one read:

Hey there, been thinking about you. Wanted to see how you're doing.

The second and third followed that up with an invitation.

If you're not busy this week, I'd love to take you to dinner.

Or have you over to eat. Whichever you prefer.

"Oh," Tom said. "Shit." Max was asking him to dinner. That felt rather like a date.

Except he didn't date. Especially didn't date Doms.

"Something wrong?" Kip asked.

Tom shook his head. "No, Just something unexpected."

"Finally got asked out on a hot date?" Kip waggled his eyebrows.

Heat rose to Tom's cheeks, and he stammered out nonsense syllables.

Kip slapped a hand over his mouth, horror in his eyes. "Oh shit! Did you? I was just teasing!"

They all did that here. Snarked, teased, and joked. Made the lawyering easier when things got heavy. Plus they all knew Tom had shit luck with men.

Tom peered at Kip, then at his phone. "Yeah. Seems like."

Kip's eyes were wide. "Is he cute?"

Aaron must have overheard from the hall because he leaned into Tom's office. "He's the gorgeous Mr. Professor Sexypants!"

"Doctor." Tom grabbed his stress ball again and flung it at Aaron, who ducked.

Kip started laughing.

"Fuck you, Taylor."

"Happily married," he said in a singsong. "See also, Dr. Sexypants."

Tom ran out of curse words, so he picked up the other stress ball—the one he saved for when he was *really* annoyed, and tried to bean Aaron with it.

Of course he ducked. "Hey Kip," he said. "Want to have pizza for lunch? Tom's buying."

There was no answer because Kip was laughing so hard he couldn't breathe.

Soon enough, Tom laughed too. "Fine, I'll pay. Let me—uh —reply to these texts?"

"Oooh, I'll give you some privacy." Kip rose, grinning from ear to ear.

"God," Tom murmured, and turned away.

Hi! I'm fine. Aaron's giving me no end of shit because I told him we were seeing each other.

And yes to dinner. Wednesday? I have client meetings Tuesday and Thursday. Those wipe me out.

Tom grabbed his coat and scarf off the back of the office door, shrugged them on, then stepped into the hall.

Before he could put his phone in his pocket, it honked again. Kip was right. That was an annoying sound, and he had no desire to be irritated with Max.

Have a hockey game Wednesday. Would you like to

come watch? We can get dinner afterward. We're
playing our local rival, so it should be a decent game.

That sounded astounding. So different from the texts from past Doms ordering him to come over to be flogged and fucked.

Shit, he really *did* have bad taste in men.

He looked up from his phone. Aaron was watching him from the other end of the hall. "You okay?" He had a concerned, furrowed look.

"Yeah, I—hang on."

I would love to watch you play. That sounds great.

Excellent! I'll text you the info once the rink time is set.

They each sent bye texts with emojis that *weren't* hearts. Tom shoved his phone into his pocket and joined Aaron and Kip. "Yeah, okay, my treat."

Aaron grasped his shoulder. "You sure you're fine?" Even Kip looked concerned.

Had he not paid attention to how many people cared about him? Or wanted him happy? "God, yeah. Just realizing how much I wasn't."

Brook had errands to run at lunch, so it ended up just the three of them.

They were silent as they walked down the stairs to the street. Finally Kip spoke. "Sometimes, all it takes is one person being kind." There was a contemplativeness to his voice, but also deep empathy, as if he'd walked those streets himself.

Tom stuck his hands into his pockets. "Lots of people are kind to me. You two, for instance. I guess—" He cut himself off, unsure of how much to unburden himself to his co-workers in the middle of the business district of Laurelsburg.

Aaron clapped him on the back, and the silence stretched all the way to Mario's Pizza.

He and his co-workers always looked slightly out of place in their suits and ties, though they all were considered regulars by now. Mario nodded as they entered, and they grabbed a table in the back.

They piled their coats on the fourth chair and settled into their seats. "Maybe I've been working divorce cases too long," Tom said. "I think it's made me cynical."

"Nah," Aaron said. "You've always been a cynic."

Yes, but no. He'd never thought about having a sex and kink partner who was also a friend. Friendships were important and hard work, and he'd no desire to lose one when the sex and kink fizzled, or got overbearing.

He barely lasted for more than a month or two with Doms before he'd had enough of them and how they treated him.

He met Aaron's gaze. "I like Max and he likes me."

Aaron nodded. "That's good, Tom. That's how it's supposed to work."

It was Kip who asked, "Wait, you don't normally like your boyfriends?"

Thankfully, the server came to take their order, so he dodged that question. They split two pitchers of Coke and a large pepperoni pizza, since Mario meant *enormous* when he said *large*. There might be leftovers, but Tom was reasonably hungry, so he doubted it.

Kip rubbed his hands together. "So—boyfriends? Don't you like them?"

Fuck, Tom hadn't dodged after all. "I mean..."

"No," Aaron said. "He doesn't like them."

Kip got this incredulous look. "Then why date them?"

Tom shrugged and muttered, "Sex?"

Kip opened his mouth, then shut it and frowned. Finally he

said. "I can't imagine being intimate with someone you don't *like*." He paused. "Then again, I'm demisexual, so that's kind of par for the course for me, I suppose."

Their drinks came, and Aaron poured them each a glass. "I've had meaningless hookups—not for a very long time—but they *can* be fun, if you're into that."

Tom shrugged again and drank his Coke, letting the sweet fizz soothe away some of the tightness in his chest. "I suppose I never thought about friendship and sex together. I never wanted to ruin friendships by—" He waved a hand. "So I never bothered getting to know the guys."

"No," Aaron said. "You don't pick up anyone you want to get to know."

Tom cringed. "Maybe," he muttered.

The pizza came, and with it, the realization that Aaron was correct. It was much easier to be banged by a guy you weren't going to develop anything with, because then dumping his ass wasn't a loss.

Tom chewed on a slice. "Shit." Kip glanced his way and he met the younger man's gaze. "I'm a little fucked up when it comes to relationships."

"Perfect for a divorce lawyer," Kip deadpanned.

Tom chucked darkly.

"No," Aaron said. "You're a good divorce lawyer, but you're not fucked up when it comes to relationships." He grabbed another slice of pizza. "You're stellar with clients and most of the judges think well of you. Hell, even your opponents in court respect you. And you're a great firm partner."

There was truth to that.

"It sounds like you need to merge the 'good relationship' part with the sex part, and you'll be fine." Kip took a long drink of Coke. "You know, no one at school prepares you for *these* types of conversations with your bosses.

"We shouldn't be having this conversation," Tom said. "Technically."

Aaron shrugged. "We've never been conventional."

Kip laughed. "Yeah, well."

Thankfully, the conversation moved back to more normal things, like scheduling snafus and opposing counsel woes. All the while, both Aaron and Kip's comments bounced around in his brain.

As he'd told Max, he'd never been a romantic, and he'd never been in love. Those hadn't been important when it came to fucking, but neither had friendship. Tom grabbed another slice. He'd think about it later. After lunch, he needed to finish that agreement draft, then meet with a client. He couldn't afford to have his head full of fog.

Come Wednesday, he'd see what he could do to merge the relationship part with the sex part. Deep inside Tom, the thought of having both sparked a kind of hope he'd never felt in his life.

———

MAX COULDN'T KEEP thoughts of Tom out of his mind as he worked through his Monday routine. That wasn't uncommon when it came to his partners, but he found himself wanting to *tell* someone about Tom, which was unheard of. Co-workers asked him how his weekend went, expecting, "Oh, it was fine, how was yours?" and what he wanted to say was, "I met the most amazing man. I've known him for years, and I finally got to speak to him."

That seemed too much for conversation around the department coffeepot.

He'd settled for texting Tom between lectures, and ended up with a Wednesday dinner date after his hockey game. Other partners had watched him play, but the thought of Tom being there was spread warmth in his soul.

Oh good god, Maxime. You're crushing on him. He felt like a teenager, rather than a man on the cusp of forty. It was ridiculous.

His loopiness must also have been noticeable, because when Dr. Madeleine Charrington, head of the Physics Department, sat next to him in the faculty dining room, she gave him a once-over and said, "Did you know you're glowing?"

Max choked on his water. "What?"

Madeleine was a tall white woman with long blonde hair braided back into a ponytail, and her smile was cool but sly. "You look like you're incredibly happy. Glowing. Did you get your course load lightened?"

"Oh god, no," Max said. "Still teaching one too many classes." Honestly, it wasn't that bad if he kept up with the grading and prep. "I'm considering shifting some of the material around to have either fewer papers or fewer exams. I doubt the kids would mind fewer assignments, but that's also less they can work on to increase their grade if something goes south."

She sipped her coffee. "You hate leaving students behind."

He did. When he'd started at LU, the administration worried that his classes weren't hard enough because he didn't fail many students, but then someone sat in on his lectures for a week, and that went away. "The point is to learn." They argued pedagogy as a matter of course. Hard science versus soft science. The never-ending battle.

"Mmm," she said. "You haven't told me why you're so happy, though."

He shrugged. "It's nothing."

She set down her coffee. "Dr. Demers, stop bullshitting me. You've never developed the knack for lying, and you've the poker face of an excited toddler on Halloween."

He didn't know whether to laugh or give in to his embarrassment, so he did both.

"The unflappable Maxime Demers," she purred.

"You are an evil person, Madeleine." He poked at the ravioli they had on offer in the dining room. "And I have *never* said I'm unflappable."

"You're dodging the question."

"Yes, I am." He sipped his water and decided eating might be the better option.

Her shoulders dropped. "Oh, come on, Max. Throw me a bone, here, or I'll be forced to head to administration and ask your fan club."

Or maybe not.

That he was considered one of the more attractive people on campus wasn't a secret. He tried to stay on the correct side of that by not dating anyone working at the university, and by being careful with students. But some of the folks in admin had formed an unofficial fan club for their faculty/staff hockey team, and that had morphed into a gossip group about team members, including him.

"You wouldn't," he said.

Madeleine gave him a look he well knew from that same hockey team.

"Oh captain, my captain," he muttered, and she laughed. "All right," he said. "I met someone over the weekend, that's all."

She raised an eyebrow. "This one is different, then. I've seen you when you've started relationships before."

Max finished his ravioli. What *was* different about Tom? Maybe the fact that they'd been in each other's orbit for years and Max had watched Tom with shit boyfriends for all that time. Perhaps it was his beautiful brown eyes, or his inherent sexiness. Or his submission. Or—

"Glowing, Maxime. You should see yourself." Madeleine

peered over her coffee mug. "At least give me a name and pronoun."

He had to laugh. "Tom and him. We've been on the edge of each other's circles for years, but never talked before. I've always been curious about him."

She made a little agreeable noise in her throat. "He's into the stuff you're into."

His interest in kink was also not a secret at the university, given the munches, demos, and the parties over at Mansion House. He'd hardly ever mentioned it. Still, a creep of worry worked its way up his spine.

That, too, must have registered, because Madeleine waved her hand. "I've been living in this town longer than you. Not my thing, but I have no issues."

He gave a light shrug. "Yes, he is."

Her brow furrowed for a moment. "Tom—" She sat up. "Not the cutie lawyer Tom? The one who works with Will Taylor's husband?"

Oh shit. He'd forgotten about that connection. "That's the Tom, yes."

She got a look. "Oh, no *wonder* you're glowing."

Embarrassment finally won. "Madeleine, *please.*"

She laughed, and a few other faculty members looked their way. "Oh, no, Dr. Demers. I'm going to enjoy this! You're embarrassingly happy about your *boyfriend.*"

Another colleague and member of their hockey team—Dr. Jeremy Braden—chose that moment to sit down at their table. He was a Black man with short silver hair at his temples. "Max has a new boyfriend?"

"That he's happy about." Madeleine wagged her fork at Max. "It's adorable."

"You should invite him to the game." Jeremy started in on his burger.

Max scrubbed his face, even as his emotions tumbled. Embarrassment for being teased by his colleagues, but joy. Joy that he was with Tom. He shouldn't be this happy.

Because you like him, Maxime. Quite a bit.

"I already invited him," he said.

Madeleine clapped. "Excellent. I can't wait to meet him."

Jeremy scoffed. "Max never introduces us to his dates."

He didn't because he kept pleasure and business away from each other. Wasn't sure why he bothered, since Laurelsburg was small. Everyone knew everyone else, practically.

"We're going to dinner after the game. I'll have him come around to the locker room."

Jeremy put down his fork. "Whoa. You're serious about this dude."

Was he? Yes, yes he was. "We've only been dating a few days."

"How long have you been pining for him?" Madeleine asked.

He rolled his eyes. "I didn't pine for him. We...orbited each other."

"Mmmhmm," she said.

Max's phone chimed a reminder for his next lecture. "Ech," he said. "And now you'll gossip about me." He stood and collected his plate, utensils, and glass.

Madeleine blew him a kiss. "Yes, but we're friends and you love it. Besides, it's only fair."

Perhaps. Two months previously, he'd conspired with Madeleine's wife, Annabell, to throw her a huge birthday shindig. Madeleine *hated* fusses made over her, but Annabell loved surprising her, and well, he never passed up the chance to kindly needle his friends.

"Fine," he said, "But no sharing with admin."

Jeremy put his hand on his heart. "We solemnly swear."

Max rolled his eyes, then bussed his dishes before heading to his office.

Glowing? Maybe. He was happy, and perhaps giddy. There was such a thing as topspace, but he didn't think this was that.

He liked Tom Cedric. And now, at least for a time, he had him.

CHAPTER SEVEN

AFTER A FRUSTRATING DAY of work on Wednesday, Tom headed to his apartment to strip off the suit that helped define his lawyer persona, along with the annoyance at clients and their exes on the divorce side, and the thoughts of mortality that came with working on a will for another client.

A shower eased the tension from his muscles, and let another kind of anxiety sneak in.

He was going to watch Max play hockey, which shouldn't have been a big deal, but his skin buzzed and his mind whirled.

He'd never interacted with his Doms other than while fucking. Tom hadn't wanted to deal with those jackasses outside of being beaten or fucked. There were some who'd had blown up his phone with messages; one recently had been so insistent Aaron had taken it upon himself to scare the guy off by pretending to be from the Drug Enforcement Agency. That had been embarrassing, harrowing, and hysterical.

The only reason Tom "dated" them was that he liked the continuity and routine of a single sexual partner.

Max could be—was becoming—a friend. He was an amazing lover and far sexier than any human had the right to be.

Was it a romance? Tom didn't know. Romance had always been for other people—like Aaron and Will, and their Kelly. Like the trio from Bold Brew or the couples he knew from the scene.

Nice concept, but impractical for Tom's life.

He might be aromantic, but Tom wasn't sure if he had enough data to decide if he was, or if he was demi. He hadn't *liked* the men he'd dated, so how would he know?

But Max? He liked Max. He also liked hockey. Max and hockey? That sounded like a great combination.

When it got close to game time, he threw on a Penguins sweatshirt he'd bought while a law student at the University of Pittsburgh, and headed over to Laurelsburg's city park.

He'd been impressed with the ice rink in the park when he'd first moved into town. The setup was pretty swank. Indoor sheets for the summer, plus an outdoor one for the winter that they converted to dek hockey in the summer. Apparently, Laurelsburg had won a contest to have the rink spruced up, and they'd maintained the rink well afterward. There were tons of youth programs, a good number of adult ones, and quite a lot of free skate times all year round.

As he walked up to the complex along the park path up a hill, the sound of music filtered through what was left of the leaves on the trees. A bunch of folks were skating on the outdoor rink, with more waiting to rent skates. At the main entrance to the indoor facility, a trickle of people was entering, either for classes or, like Tom, to watch the amateur hockey matchup for the night.

What he'd learned from Max was that the LU faculty/staff team was called the Shrubs, and they'd be taking on the Cavemouth Lions from a town over. Tom made his way to the designated rink and settled in by the glass, on the side of bleachers where the LU team, in their red-and-gold jerseys, were warming up.

The moment Tom spotted Max on the ice, every limb tingled and his mouth went dry. His heart had already been thumping hard in anticipation and nervousness. Strange feelings to have while watching his Dom play a game.

Max was hard to miss, though. For some foolish reason, he wasn't wearing a helmet, so his shoulder-length hair flowed as gracefully as his skating, and his last name was emblazoned on his back, across his shoulders. He wasn't holding anything as he skated backward in a large loop, laughing with another member of his team, who followed him. That player had a full face cage like college hockey used, but even through that Tom saw the smile.

Max crossed over to skating forward, headed to the bench, and grabbed his helmet. The white woman sitting next to Tom sighed. Her companion, a stout person with light brown skin sitting on the other side of her, chuckled. "So hot. That hair. That face."

"Hottest potato at LU," the woman said. "Except he never mixes business with pleasure."

Tom turned a little, because this had to be about Max.

They noticed, but didn't seem upset by it. The woman who'd made the potato comment waved. "Hey, you new to watching the Shrubs?"

"Yeah," he said. "Friend suggested I come and watch him play."

"Oh, cool! They're fun to watch. She gestured at her companion. "We're their unofficial cheerleaders. I'm Cara, and this is Zane. I work in admissions, and they work in finance." Zane also waved.

"I'm Tom," he said. "I'm not part of the university." He paused. "I don't know that much about the team. Want to fill me in?"

Both Cara and Zane looked eager. "Hey," Zane said. "Why

don't you switch places with Cara? We can tell you who's who and all that."

Seemed like a good idea, so they did.

Zane started first. "So—do you know hockey?" They eyed Tom's sweatshirt peeking out from under his coat.

Tom laughed. "Yeah. Played as a kid. Was in Pittsburgh for grad school and did the whole student ticket thing to watch games. Now I watch 'em on TV."

"Oh, that's good! We can skip the boring bits," Zane said.

Between the two of them, they rattled off all the players, from the goalies to the forwards and the defense. "Do you see number 65 there, the tall white woman with the blonde ponytail?" Cara pointed out a player on the ice.

Tom nodded.

"That's Dr. Madeleine Charrington, the captain. She's the head of the physics department, and can score a goal from anywhere on the ice."

"She's fast, too," Zane said.

Apparently, Dr. Charrington had grown up in Minnesota, and had played at an elite level at her university, missing the call-up for the national team due to grad school pressures.

"We have a couple almost-pros, and everyone else is pretty darn good," Cara added. "Other teams love and hate playing us, because we're really competitive."

"But," Zane said, "they've all been working harder, so they can try to whoop our asses. The Lions beat us twice last year, and they've been gunning for us ever since."

"Bunch of lucky bounces," Cara said.

Tom laughed. "Isn't that the way, though? Just need one to turn the momentum." He was pleased he ended up sitting with to these two.

Max had been holding out on him! He'd said that the team was a fun thing the faculty and staff did, not a team that regularly won the area-wide league cup. "Five years running!" Zane said.

"So, watch Charrs," Cara said. "And Bones there—the Black man wearing number 7. Great shot. And Maximilian the Great, our sexy French-Canadian defenseman, he's over there —number 85."

Tom wondered if all those nicknames had been earned or whether it was particular to these two. "The Great?"

Zane laughed, and Cara blushed.

"Don't mind her," they said. "She, like *so* many, has had a crush on Dr. Maxime Demers for ages."

Cara reached around Tom and gave Zane a shove. "Like you haven't."

"Anyway, he's one of those offensive defensemen. He has more goals than some of our forwards, much to their chagrin, even when we win the game."

That fit in with Max's personality, especially given that he'd wanted to be Lemieux as a kid. Tom nodded, solemnly.

"His *actual* nickname on the team is Demmy," Zane said. "Aside from the swoon-worthy hair and that lovely face, he's fun to watch on the ice. Excellent skater."

They chatted longer, and Cara finally pried Tom's profession out of him.

"Oh! The First Name Firm!" she said. "I walk past your office every day on my way up to LU!"

"First name—" Then it hit him. "Cedric and Taylor. Holy shit!"

Zane gave him a look. "You've never heard people call you that before?"

Cara burst out laughing, and a moment later, Tom joined in. "I honestly hadn't, but I don't talk to people about the firm that much, socially. Who brings up law firm names up in casual conversation?"

Hell, most of the men he'd been with didn't even know his last name, and barely remembered his first. He'd been called Tim too many times to count. Tom stared out at the ice, his brain skidding to a stop as a buzzing took up shop.

Max knew Tom's name.

"Hey, you okay?" That from Zane. "I don't think I've ever heard anything bad about your firm."

He smiled at his companions. "I'm fine. That thought triggered another and my brain went off on a tangent."

After that, Zane and Cara told him about the other team, and he listened as best he could, his mind drifting back to Max in that same, smooth way Max moved around on the ice.

Max *knew* Tom.

Last name. First name. Snippets of his past. Max had cooked for him. Talked to him. He'd also explored Tom's body and had fucked him without mercy. Tom still had a few bruises on his back from that flogging.

Tom ached for Max, both sexually and for this friendship they were building. He didn't understand the emotions he had for Max, only that it was a great deal more than lust.

"Incoming hottie alert!" Zane said

Tom looked up to see Max skating toward them. His helmet had a full face cage, but nothing could keep *that* grin hidden.

Something in Tom's chest leapt and twisted in joy, and he found himself laughing. Of course Max would find him in a crowd, would look for him in the bleachers.

Max slammed his body against the boards, in front of Tom, the glass and baseboards flexing and swaying against the impact. When Max turned, he pointed at Tom.

Tom waved, the giddiness a different kind of high than the one he felt during sex or kink—but as welcome and as needed. Max gave him a little salute, then skated back to the bench, while the referees check the nets.

Next to him, Zane coughed, and Tom turned, his cheeks hot.

"Mr. Hot Potato Professor is your friend?" Zane raised an eyebrow.

"Yeah," Tom breathed out. "We're dating." Holy shit, Maxime Demers was his boyfriend. His Dom.

"You're *dating* Dr. Demers?" Cara looked as excited about that as she had about Tom watching the game. "Wow!"

"Yeah, that's kind of how I feel, too."

She gave an exaggerated sigh. "Which means you're *both* off the table."

Wait, *what?* His confusion must have been all over his face, because Zane laughed. "Honey, you're also quite the hot potato. *And* a fancy-pants lawyer."

"Oh! Uh…" Tom shrugged. "Thank you? Honestly, I'm not fancy. I do family law, sometime property stuff."

"So no *Law and Order* stuff." Cara mimicked the *dun dun* of a gavel.

He shook his head. "More like meetings with clients, arguing behind the scenes with other lawyers, and really boring court dates."

"Still," Zane said. "Hot potato."

"Oh my god." Tom was saved from any more embarrassing conversation by the game starting, thank the hockey gods.

This game took less time than a pro game because the breaks between periods were only long enough to run a Zamboni over the sheet, then they were back at it. There wasn't anybody checking, but there was damn good hockey to watch. Speed, excellent passing, and some great playmaking.

As Cara and Zane had said, Charrs and Bones were the ones on the LU team to watch. They set each other up well, and got good shots off.

The opposing goalie played well, though, including

absolutely stoning Max on a breakaway. Even from across the ice, Tom felt Max's frustration. Two more times, the Lions goalie robbed the Shrubs of a goal, and kept the score at nothing apiece.

Max stole the puck a bunch of times, but also turned over a few, including one that gave the Lions a chance to score.

"Ugh, Max," Tom muttered under his breath when Max headed off at the end of his shift "Get it together."

"Demmy's getting frustrated," Zane said. "Not that I blame him."

Neither did Tom, really.

Luckily, the LU goalie also held her own, snatching pucks out of the air. She was damn good, and wicked with the poke checks, which made up for her smaller stature when compared to the Lions goalie.

The game turned around in the second period when the Lions were sloppy with a pass, and Charrs stole the puck with Bones right with her in a two-on-one breakaway. Tom yelled and cheered as much as the other LU supporters when Bones managed to flick the puck over the Lions goalie's glove, off the crossbar and in.

That opened things up. Max fired a slapper from the blue line that was tipped in by an LU player Cara called Sunshine.

This friendly beer-league game had a very serious tone to it. "Are all the games like this?" Tom asked Zane.

Zane shook their head. "Not always. The rivalry between the Lions and the Shrubs goes back a couple of years. I think it's because they started bringing a lot of family and friends to games here since the rinks are so close, and LU answered in kind, getting more people here and traveling to their home ice and well—" They gestured around them. "Here we are!"

The third period was a nail-biter. The Lions scored on a breakaway, then Max's defense partner tripped a Lions player and went to the box, and the Lions scored on the power play, tying the game up.

"Well, shit." Tom leaned on his knees.

Cara and Zane agreed with that assessment. The next ten minutes of play were a furious back-and-forth contest. Both goalies played lights out. Tom caught a glimpse of Max's expression during a break in play. Mouth pulled into a thin line. Gaze focused on the blade of his hockey stick as he cleaned the snow off the edge.

"God, he's even hot when he's pissed off," Cara murmured.

He was. He looked different in this environment, but also utterly the same. There were so many aspects to Max, from the professor to the dominant to the cook to the athlete. Tom was glad to see this one—even if LU lost the game.

He didn't want them to lose, though. "Come on, Max."

Puck drop was near the Lions' net, and the players set up on the other side of the glass from Tom. Before the ref dropped the puck, Charrs said something to all the LU players on the ice—calling out a play, probably.

The faceoff was a fury of action and competing sticks, but Charrs got the puck back to the blue line. Max passed it to Bones, who then faked a shot to Charrs and sent it back to Max, who had pinched up the wall to an open space. The puck sailed off Max's stick hard and fast, and shot past the Lions goalie and into the net.

Everyone, including Tom, was on their feet, screaming. Max pumped through a triumphant celly, then headed to his teammates for hugs.

There was still two minutes on the clock, but the Lions couldn't get another one in behind the LU goalie, and the game ended, three to two in favor of the LU Shrubs.

After the celebrations in the stands and a salute from the teams, the crowd trickled out.

"Hey," Cara said. "See you next game? You might be Dr. Demers's lucky charm!"

Tom laughed. "I don't think he's superstitious, but I'll probably be at the next game."

He shook hands with both of them, then headed out to wait for Max, but Max's voice echoed across the rink.

"Tom!"

————

"TOM!"

Max hoped to hell his voice projected up and over the glass. Sound was weird in rinks.

Guess it had, because Tom stopped short and whipped around. Max skated toward him, knowing he had only a few moments before the Zamboni would be out. Thankfully, the staff and refs liked him, but he didn't want to press his luck.

He gestured for Tom to go to the far side, close to where the visitor bench lay, then headed off the ice by the benches as the staff cracked open the Zamboni doors.

Good. Close, but good.

He headed up to where Jean, one of the rink's security guards, sat behind a rope. Several years ago, with a different set of teams, things had gotten ugly, so now very few folks were allowed back into the locker area during the games.

"Hey Jean," Max said.

Jean, an older Black man with silvering hair, raised an eyebrow at him. "Well, here comes trouble."

Max met that with a laugh. "I'm here to plead with you to let me bring my boyfriend back."

"I don't know, Demers. How serious is this?"

Oh *lord*, not Jean, too. Everyone was acting like he'd never dated anyone before. "When have I ever asked you to let me bring someone back?"

Jean cracked a smile. "Not once. Just talked about 'em."

Tom came into view around the curve in the boards. "That's him," Max said, pointing.

"Uh huh. I'm only doing this because I like you, Demers." Jean wagged a finger at Max.

Max grinned. "And I bring you those maple sugar candies you like."

"Oh man." Tom stopped shy of the rope, his hands in his pockets. "Those things are good."

Jean turned that gaze onto Tom and crossed his arms. "Don't try to butter me up, Mr.—"

"Cedric. Tom Cedric."

"The lawyer?"

"Yeah." He scrubbed his hand over the back of his head. "That one."

Jean turned his attention back to Max. "You know the rules, Demers."

Tom took a step back. "Hey, I can wait—"

Max cut Tom off. "Ech. Fine. Two dozen chocolate macarons and maple candies."

Jean cracked a smile. "Chocolate and mint macarons."

"Chocolate and mint," Max agreed, then switched to French. "Please? I think you're terrifying him."

"Done." Jean turned to Tom. "You watch this one." He nodded to Max. "He's slippery as the devil. But maybe you can make him an honest man."

If the comments before hadn't frightened Tom, that one did the trick. Tom's eyes got wide, and he stammered.

"Oh my god, Jean." Heat flew up Max's neck. "We've haven't been dating a week. Don't marry me off yet!" He pulled the rope stanchion out of the way. "Come on, Tom. I want you to meet some friends."

Jean smiled to Tom. "He's never brought anyone back here, you know."

Tom slipped past the rope, looking like he expected to be arrested for loitering. "Never?"

Jean laughed, and Max swallowed all his embarrassment, took Tom's hand, and pulled him away from Jean. "No one's been as interested in the hockey."

"They came to your games, though?"

"Yeah, a couple did, but they sat toward the back, and..." He stopped by the door to the locker rooms. Time for some truth. "I wasn't comfortable with them meeting my co-workers."

"Oh." Tom breathed the word out. Slowly, a beaming smile emerged. "Max," he said. "Thank you."

Trepidation and joy tripped over inside Max "Let me introduce you to some folks." He pushed open the door.

Most of Max's teammates were entirely out of their gear, and the sound of rushing water could be heard from the shower area. "I should warn you," Max said, "we all change out in the open."

"That's fine. I know where to keep my eyes," Tom said.

Despite the chaos of the locker room, Max introduced Tom to Madeleine, Jeremy, and Michelle Summers, the admin of the chemistry department.

After those three, Max regretted suggesting Tom meet everyone, because they all told Tom about Max. Madeleine was the worst. "Max is a good guy, and you're the first person he's dated who he talks about at work. He's been adorable."

"Madeleine, really?" Max said. "I need to shower. But now I'm afraid to leave you with these people."

Jeremy slapped him on the back. "You stink, Max. Go. We'll keep Tom entertained."

"That's what I'm worried about." He picked up his shower kit, underwear, and jeans.

Tom laughed. "I'm sure it'll be fine."

"You don't know them like I do."

Madeleine, all six foot four of her, swung Max around and pushed him toward the showers. "Go, Demmy. No one's going to bite him while you're gone."

"Yes, Captain," he quipped, and headed out.

Max wanted to bite Tom. Would have, had the locker room been empty. Instead, he took a quick but thorough shower, and pulled on his clothes, anticipation and dread gnawing at him. Anticipation for dinner out with Tom, and apprehension as to what his colleagues were saying to him.

He rounded the corner and heard Tom sputtering. "I—uh. *Bubbly?*"

Madeleine laughed loudly.

Oh fucking *hell.* Max tossed his shower kit in his duffel and set about toweling off his hair. "Good god, what has Madeleine been telling you?"

Tom's gaze swept over Max, lingered on his bare chest. Then he broke into a sly smile. "She's says you've been bubbly."

There was that ball of embarrassment, rising to the surface again. Thank goodness he was ruddy from the shower. "Well..."

"He's been talking about this night since Monday," she said.

Jeremy chimed in. "It's been fun to see unflappable Maxime with a crush."

Max buried his face in his towel and groaned. He did have a crush, but he didn't need Jeremy and Madeleine telling Tom that.

Tom plunked himself down on the bench next to Max. "Okay, tell me more. I've got to hear this."

Max popped out from under the towel. "Please, no." He

glared at his colleagues. "You two will be the death of me." Then he turned that gaze to Tom. "You, as well."

Madeleine snickered. "You love it, Demers."

"Ech, this is why I don't bring my dates back to the locker room."

"And," Madeleine said, "exactly why you brought Tom."

Max froze at that, because it struck a nerve, hard. There was truth there. "Maybe."

Tom got that deer in the headlights look again, but didn't say anything. He met Max's gaze, and he couldn't tell if Tom was horrified or pleased.

That could be bad or wonderful. Max balled up his towel and threw it into the hamper across the room. Michelle, who'd been watching, listening, and packing, gave a mock clap, then waved. "See you guys."

Jeremy plunked down next to Tom. "Hey, I throw a Thanksgiving potluck every year for staff. Make sure he brings you. You'll fit right in, and Max never brings anyone."

Tom gave a little croak. "Uh, sure. I mean, if we're still..." He let that trail off.

If they were still dating by then. Max pulled on his long-sleeved Laurelsburg University T-shirt. He hoped they'd still be dating by then, but the party was still several weeks away. "I promise I'll bring Tom, if he wants to go."

Tom's horrified look waned. "I'll make sure he does."

Some tension in Max's stomach eased, and he smiled at Tom. "Shall we get out of here?"

Tom rose. Together they said goodbye to everyone, Tom congratulated them on the game, then they headed out of the locker room and toward the parking lot.

Well, that had been a success. Hopefully dinner would be as enjoyable.

CHAPTER EIGHT

THE COLD AIR outside the ice complex hit Max's warm, damp skin, and goose bumps rose over his arms. Felt good for the moment, so he didn't bother shrugging into his coat. He was giddy from the game and from how everyone had taken to Tom.

Next to him, Tom gestured at the hockey sticks Max carried. "Do you want me to take those? Free your arms up?"

Not a bad idea. He handed them over. "Thank you."

Tom's breath steamed in the lights illuminating the lot. "Aren't you cold?"

It was below freezing out and the temperature was pecking away at Max's scalp through his damp hair. "Not yet, but I will be. I hate being overheated, though." He glanced over at Tom. "Did you walk or come in your car?"

"Walked." Tom rubbed his hands together, then shoved them in his pockets. "No sense in us both having cars here. I figured we'd either end up at a restaurant or your house."

"That makes sense." Max fumbled with his coat to fish out his keys, then clicked the unlock button for his truck.

Tom stopped short, shock written in his face. "You drive a *truck?*"

Max chuckled. No one expected a liberal arts professor to be driving around in a big red GMC pickup. "Yes?"

"It's huge!" Tom hadn't stepped any closer, as if he couldn't believe his eyes.

"Yes." Max's grin was wicked, then he sobered. "I walk more often than not in town. So I suppose it's a shock, but I wanted something that could haul building supplies, and that had four-wheel drive because of the ice and snow here. This lovely vehicle came in handy when I worked on the house." He threw his duffel in the bed of the truck, strapped the duffel down, then gave the truck a pat. "The sticks go in the cab."

"I hadn't thought about needing a truck for house renovations." Tom handed the sticks to Max. "I have a tiny Honda Fit. Aaron teases me about it, because I should be driving a BMW or something."

Max stared at Tom. "Are you talking about the same Aaron Taylor who drives a Prius?"

Tom grinned. "Yup!" He made a popping sound on the end of the P. "To be fair, Will has an SUV."

Max laughed, opened the truck up, and slid the sticks behind the front seats. "As for this, I didn't do all the renovation work myself, but I did most of the insulation and a good bit of the painting. Plus the garden, and I constructed most of the kink furniture." He gestured to the passenger side. "Door's unlocked. Hop in."

"Hop is right." Tom scrambled up while Max slid into the driver's seat.

If Tom had a Honda, he was practically driving on the ground. "After being three inches off the ground, it must be quite a climb."

Tom laughed. "I forget how low Hondas are until someone else gets in, and they fall into the seat." He belted in. "I suppose you can't go to First-Rate Finishes and order a St Andrew's cross or a spanking bench."

Yes and no. Max turned the car over, then backed out. "I might be able to order from them. I know I could order pieces off the internet, but I'm particular when it comes to my furniture."

"You don't say." That was said with a complete deadpan.

Max gave him a look before putting the car into drive. "Behave."

"Oh, I am." There was the cocky, bratty submissive Max already adored. But Tom sobered quickly "Thank you for sharing this with me."

Max shifted in the seat, that flare of embarrassment returning. But this time, it was coupled with joy. He concentrated on the road and eased out the tightness in his throat. "Thank you for being someone I want to share with the important people in my life."

Tom was silent for too long after that. The joy in Max morphed into a cold stab of panic. Fuck. He pressed his lips together. Maybe that had been too strong, but everything else in this evening had pointed to Tom being excited to be dating Max. Guess he'd been wrong.

Finally, Tom cleared his throat. "You know, this sounds like a lot more than you showing me how a good Dom treats a submissive."

Max kept his voice soft. "Does that bother you?"

"I don't know," Tom said.

Quiet settled between them again. Eventually Max broke that. "I can adjust my expectations." He tried to keep his tone light, even as his heart dug its way into his stomach. "Do you have a place you'd like to go to eat?"

"Somewhere quiet? The rink was loud." Tom sounded apologetic.

Max turned off Main, and down one of the streets that would take them past a set of strip malls and big box stores. "There's a little French bistro off Jefferson Highway that's quiet."

"Le Petit Chateau?"

"That's the one." It was an indulgence, a long shot, but he didn't want Tom to go home, and that was the first place that came to mind when Tom said quiet.

Le Petit Chateau was for beginnings and endings, Veronique had once said. Max eased out a breath, then another. Tom was running scared. Physical intimacy was easy, but emotional? Max suspected Tom had little experience with that.

You came on too strong, Maxime. Except he had to be true to himself.

Tom exhaled. "I've heard good things, but have never been there."

That was surprising, though the type of law Tom practiced probably didn't require expensive client dinners. Certainly none of the fucking rat bastard men Tom had dated would ever have taken him to Le Petit Chateau.

Max bit back on his sudden anger. Now was not the time, nor was it his place to be furious about Tom's former Doms.

"Max." Tom's voice cracked on the vowel. "I don't know what's going on in my head. Everything with you is so different, and I don't want to fuck things up. Please don't be mad at me."

It was dark on this portion of the road, so Max couldn't take his eyes away from the windshield. He rolled his shoulders, releasing the building tension. "I'm not mad. I don't want to fuck things up either," he said. "But I don't know what you want from me beyond sex and kink. If the answer is nothing, that's fine, but then we *can't* do this dating sort of thing." This time, his voice caught, scraping over the hurt in his heart.

Tom made a pained groan. "I want to be your friend, Max. I don't know how to *do* that with the sex and the kink."

Max turned off the highway, which had turned into a two-lane state road, onto an even smaller, winding one. "Oh my god, Tom," Max murmured. He'd had an inkling Tom's relationships hadn't been good. But to never be friends with your lovers? "Shit."

"I told you I was the issue." Bitter words there.

Max couldn't think of anything to say that made sense, so silence slipped between them for the rest of the ride. Then the familiar huge stone house appeared, all lit up, along with a sign that read *Le Petit Chateau* in a beautiful script.

Tom huffed a laugh. "*Petit*, huh?"

Everyone knew at least that much French. Max chuckled. "It's smaller than Mansion House." He pulled into a spot under a soft amber light. It illuminated Tom's hair through the windscreen.

Tom remained quiet when Max put the truck into park, and more silence descended when he turned the motor off.

This wasn't good. Max turned to face Tom. "Are you afraid of me?"

Tom met his gaze, his frown creating shadowed furrows in his brow. "No," he said. "I know you won't hurt me, not in the ways I don't want."

Max couldn't help the smile, even if his heart was sinking down and down.

Tom continued. "But now that I know you better, I don't know which I want more, your friendship or everything else."

"You've never had both before?"

He shook his head.

Fuck. Max ran a hand through his damp hair. "Let's go eat some good food in a quiet corner, and maybe we can figure this out, yes?"

Something unlocked in Tom. He took a breath, his shoulders loosened, and he nodded. "Okay. Let's try that."

When they got out of the truck, Max donned his coat and scarf. The truck had been warm, but now his *insides* were chilled.

They got some *looks* from diners exiting the restaurant as he and Tom strode toward the door, but Max paid them no mind. Tom, however, did a double-take, likely at what the diners had been wearing. Suits or better. Long dresses under expensive coats. "Uh, are we properly dressed?"

Max gave a sharp laugh. They both had jeans on. He was in an LU shirt, and a Penguins logo was peeking out from under Tom's coat. "No, not at all. But they know me here, so it'll be fine."

They were *exceedingly* underdressed. Normally, coming here in an ill-fitted suit made Max's teeth ache, but tonight, he was so far beyond caring about his state of dress. There were more important matters, like Tom and keeping this new relationship from falling apart before it had even had a chance to blossom.

When they stepped into Le Petit Chateau, Tom made a soft, worried croak, and muttered, "Max..."

He understood. The dining room beyond the host stand was full of dark wood, crystal, rich red accents, and people dressed to the nines. Max hadn't buttoned his coat, the red-and-gold lettering of his Laurelsburg University shirt quite visible underneath. His hair was likely a wet mop of long tangled locks. Any other place such as this, they'd be tossed on their asses.

But rather than the maître d' scowling in contempt, Gabriel's eyes widened. "Monsieur Demers!" He took in Max's state and that of Tom, and continued in French. "We had no idea you'd be joining us tonight. Please tell us what you and your companion need."

French came so naturally here. "Ah, Gabriel, it's a story and a half. I'm sorry to intrude on you like this. Tom and I are having some serious discussions and we wanted a quiet, private location with excellent food. I could think of no other place than this. Would the drawing room be open?"

Gabriel nodded, taking everything in stride. "The drawing room is yours for the evening. Veronique isn't here tonight, but I'll let Bernard know you've arrived. If you'd come with me?" He gestured for Max and Tom to follow and headed into the restaurant.

Max slid into English. "He's going to show us to our table."

Tom stared at him, a dazed look in his eyes.

Max nodded into the room and followed Gabriel, Tom close on his heels.

Le Petit Chateau wasn't a casual dining establishment, not with its elegant and well-dressed clientele. Had Max not been who he was, he'd only be able to come here on rare occasions. He didn't have the wealth necessary to be a frequent visitor, otherwise.

Laurelsburg wasn't home to billionaires, but Max had learned over the years that there was money in these hills. Mansion House wasn't the only mansion out there in the surrounding countryside. Oil, coal, and steel had built much of this area, and that wealth hadn't left.

Max felt the stares of the diners and smiled, taking enjoyment in their curiosity and discomfort.

Let them wonder.

Gabriel led them to a small, intimate room in the back of the restaurant. The decor was modeled after an old-fashioned study or smoking room, a place where secrets could be shared, where no one would disturb. Books lurked behind glass panels along with old liquor bottles. A single table for two sat in the room, though there was space for more.

This was a room for business deals, clandestine meetings between lovers—or a place Max could attempt to woo Tom and see what lay underneath his sudden fear. Or perhaps this would be a place to let Tom go.

Gabriel gestured to the table, and spoke in French. "I'll take your coats and bring tonight's menu, and we'll give you some time to settle in."

"Thank you very much, Gabriel. Your accommodations are perfect, as always." Max turned to Tom. "Please." He waved at one of the chairs. "Have a seat. Gabriel will take our coats."

Tom did as told, and Gabriel took both the coats, then brought menus, including an extensive wine list.

When Gabriel left, Max turned his attention to Tom. "Please order something to drink, if you'd like." He kept his tone careful and soft. "I won't, since I'm driving."

Tom opened the wine list and skimmed, looking dazed around the edges. "I'm guessing every single wine on this list is good."

Max couldn't help chuckling. "Yes."

"Have you ever tried any of them?"

He nodded. Quite a few. Some he would never have afforded anywhere else. Veronique had made it clear early on that she'd be offended if he didn't order anything he'd like. "Sometimes I grab a rideshare over and back, so I don't have to worry."

Tom studied the list again, biting his lip. "I do want wine, but everything here is—" He looked up and whatever he'd planned to say died in his throat.

God. Perhaps this hadn't been the best plan after all. How horrible did he look? "Tom," Max said. "Order whatever you'd like. It's fine."

Tom held Max's gaze. "Are you secretly filthy rich, or a French prince, or something?"

Max gave a small bark of laughter, and grinned at Tom. "No to both. I'm well enough off, and Québécois. The owners are Parisian, and—let's say amused by my French. I'm one of the few fluent speakers for miles, so they tolerate me." He paused and added, "I can inflect a Parisian accent and vocabulary, but I'm far too Québécois for that, so I don't."

There was much more to the story, but that would do for now.

Tom was a picture of confusion. "So, not a prince."

"No. I'm the son of a baker, which is probably disappointing." He'd have to tell Veronique about the prince comment later. She'd be amused by that, especially given how she upheld Max's parents.

"I don't know about disappointed," Tom said. "I like bread."

So did Max. Bread was a part of his life he'd wanted to share with Tom. He didn't know how to start the conversation they needed to have, or where to begin, so the silence stretched between them, itching like a new wool sweater.

Thankfully, that was interrupted when one of the servers, Fleur, entered the room. "Monsieur Demers, it's good to see you again. Have you decided on wine?"

"Alas, I'll only be sipping water tonight." He turned to Tom and switched languages. "Did you figure out a wine?"

Tom glanced down at the menu, then back up. "No."

"May I order one for you?" he asked gently. Consent. Always consent.

Tom nodded.

"A glass of the Château Pichon Baron for my friend, and water for both."

"Excellent choice." Fleur took the wine list from Tom, then slipped from the room.

"I also asked for water." When silence fell between them

again, he studied Tom, but still didn't know what to say, how to unlock the puzzle of what lay between them.

Tom flipped open the dinner menu and scanned. Then he raised his gaze and pinned Max to his chair. "Are you breaking up with me?"

That was one way to broach the subject. Max shook his head. "No. I'm trying to figure out how to convince you not to break up with me. How I can remain your friend and be your lover and your Dom, too."

"Oh," Tom said. "Shit."

Shit indeed. Max chuckled, though it tasted bitter. He picked up his menu and looked over the night's selections. As usual, there were no prices. "Everything is good here," he said. "Order whatever you'd like."

"This place is—" Tom shook his head, and went back to studying the menu.

When Fleur came with Tom's wine, their water, and a basket of warm bread, Max gave his order in French. Tom gave his in English.

"Very good, sir," Fleur said to Tom. She took the menus, then vanished out the door, leaving them alone in the quiet space.

"How did you manage this?" Tom waved his hand to encompass the room.

A smile tugged at Max's lips. That was a story he didn't share, but maybe it was time to give Tom a piece of his life that no one else had.

He took one of the rolls, cracked it in half, then spread butter over one side. "The first time I came here, I'd been in Laurelsburg a month. The head of my department brought me here for lunch. The prices are better during daylight and within the department budget." He'd been almost ten years younger then. "We spoke English the entire time, as we do in the department. Not everyone in linguistics is a polyglot, though the head knew Middle and Old English, Gaelic, Welsh, and a smattering of Old Norse."

Max held up the bread, which was golden and flakey. A *good* roll. "This was not what they served then. The bread they had was some awful commercially made roll. Tasted like yeast-flavored paper."

Tom wrinkled his nose.

"Yes, that's much the face I made." Max had been incensed. If nothing else, a French restaurant should take its baking seriously. Everyone had been saying how good Le Petit Chateau was, yet his first impression had been that damn roll. "I suppose it's a fault, but I'm not good at hiding my emotions."

Tom said nothing, but amusement was written all over his face.

Yes, Max deserved that look. "Anyway, the server made a snide comment to another about the plebeian and the bread." He paused. "He doesn't work here anymore."

Tom sat up straight. "You said something. In French."

Good guess. "Not right away. The chef came out later—he'll come out tonight—to ask us what we thought of the meal. We were merely faculty, but the university has big donor dinners here." Max nibbled the bread, and there it was, that specific taste he loved. They hadn't changed the recipe. "You should try the bread, before it cools."

He hadn't meant to, but he said that like an order. Tom started and reached for the bread. Max waited while Tom buttered it and took a taste.

"Oh shit, this is good." Tom sipped his wine and his eyes fluttered shut. "Really good."

Warmth suffused Max. "When the chef asked our opinion, we were complementary of the meal, but I, much to my department head's chagrin, told him that he'd cheapened everything on the table by serving cardboard rolls."

"In French?"

Max chuckled. "Oh no, in English." Honestly, they should've picked out his accent and known. "That server? He muttered another insult that I will *not* repeat." He still fumed when he thought about it. "That's when I stood up and ripped him a new asshole, albeit in my very *Canadian* French. But he understood, *despite* my accent." Max leaned back and let the memory come. The shock on everyone's faces. The utter dismay in the department head's eyes. *So* worth it. "The chef was horrified at the server, but also at my dressing his meal down over *rolls*. We went back and forth several times, until I told him I could make better bread in my torn-apart kitchen than what he'd put on my plate."

"How is it that you didn't get thrown out?" Tom took another bite of the bread. "Sounds like something straight out of a reality show."

"Turned out the owner had been watching the whole episode play out, and she was extraordinarily amused by two grown men arguing over dinner rolls." Max savored another bite of bread, then continued. "She sauntered over and challenged me to do what I'd said—make better rolls."

Tom leaned forward. "Oh *shit*. You can bake!"

"I have, in my skull, a whole set of recipes memorized, because I got up in the middle of the night, every night, for *years* to help my family make bread. I'm passionate about baked goods, even if I did disappoint my parents by neither becoming a hockey star nor a world-renowned baker."

The myriad of looks that passed over Tom's face intrigued Max to no end. He saw questions there, and curiosity. The things Tom could learn about Max, if he asked, if they had more time together. "You took her up on the offer," Tom said.

Max nodded. "I called my parents first, because I knew I'd be handing over a family recipe at the end of this exploit, and they had some suggestions about how to modify it. But yes, I showed up, pre-dawn, about a week later with ingredients in the back of my pickup, and made them an entire day's worth of complimentary rolls."

That had been both exhausting and exhilarating. He hadn't wanted to take over the family business, but he'd missed baking on that scale.

Tom took another nibble, then spoke. "These rolls?" He held his piece up.

"These exact rolls." Max wished he hadn't been driving, because indulging in wine would've been perfect at this moment. "By the end of that night, both the owner and the chef were calling my cell for the recipe. Everyone who dined that day and that evening had said wonderful things about the *bread*, and how they were so glad they'd changed the recipe, because those old rolls had been *awful*. Like cardboard." He popped the last piece of his roll into his mouth.

From across the table, Tom stared at Max. "And *that's* how you can walk into this place and get a private table?"

He smiled, but kept his mouth firmly closed.

———

TOM'S MIND swam with questions, so many that he didn't know where to start. Obviously, there was a ton about Max he didn't know. He wanted to dive into Max, his warmth, his interests. Uncover all he could.

But Max was Tom's Dom and that meant sex and pain, not friendship. Except—they could be friends, too.

Fuck.

The food came after the story, and that gave them

something safe to discuss. The meal was astounding, as was Tom's wine. Everything smelled and tasted divine, but the ache and tension he'd held before crept back as the silence stretched between them.

Finally, he set down his fork. "How are we going to make this work?"

Max put down his own utensils and sat back in his chair. "I've had one-night stands. I've also had scene and sex partners for one scene or party." His voice dipped. "You've watched me fuck some of them."

Heat poured into Tom's bones, and he looked at his plate, because that was safer. "I liked watching you. Maybe I shouldn't have, and we wouldn't be in this—" He waved a hand, then met Max's gaze. "Maybe I should have just drunk your damn coffee and let it be."

"There's no shame in watching, or wanting," Max said. "I've also watched you be fucked at parties, Tom."

That didn't help. "You're infuriating," Tom snapped. "Did you know that?"

Max shrugged. "Am I? Because I don't think you're mad at me."

Tom wasn't, but he couldn't sit anymore, so he pushed his chair back, rose, and paced in the small room.

Max was irritatingly silent, but he watched, concern marring his brow.

"I want—" Tom stopped, his mind a wash with thoughts. His head hadn't been this tangled in ages. Everything was usually very orderly, and during even the most complex court cases, he could tease out what he needed. Everything came down to compromises or scorching the earth for just reasons.

There were no reasons here, only emotions. His own damn mess and the man sitting at the table, the one who delighted and terrified him.

"Yellow." His legs wanted to buckle. "Yellow."

"All right." Max's voice was soft and soothing. "We'll stop, and when you're ready, you can tell me what you need."

Tom shook his head. "I don't want you to stop. I want my *brain* to stop doing what it's doing."

Max rose and closed the distance to Tom. It was then Tom noticed that Max, for all his calm demeanor, had moist eyes. He cupped one side of Tom's face, then the other. "Do you want me to push your limits, Tom?"

Terror lanced through him, then hope. "Please."

A nod, and Max kissed him.

Tom clutched Max for support. This was the tender kiss, the one where Max explored and nibbled, and sipped on Tom, feasted on their closeness, and sent light into every part of Tom's soul.

A deep longing unfurled in Tom, for more of *this*. A moment with Max. Fine food, a room that smelled of wine, lamb, steak, and steaming vegetables. The gentle murmur of music in the background.

Max's lips on his. This was the opposite of a flogger landing or a cane striking his skin, and yet somehow everything was the same, as well.

Max broke the kiss, licked his lips, then stared at Tom. "Good wine."

Tom nodded. The best red he'd ever had.

A sweet smile alighted on Max. "I like you, Tom. Quite a bit. You're a wonderful, interesting man."

"Thanks," Tom said. Max's next kiss started sweet, then turned dark and passionate. The sips became bites and the tastes turned to demands. Tom moaned and stepped into Max's warmth and his hard body.

Max slid his hands down until one was on Tom's shoulder and the other cupped his ass, grinding their bodies together.

Every bit of Tom's body hummed and the chatter in his head quieted. He wanted *this*, as well, hanging between the promise of sex and the temptation of pain and submission.

He gasped when Max broke that kiss.

"There are so many things I want to do to you." Max's voice was a purr of words. "So many ways I want to pleasure you."

Oh *fuck*. He couldn't look away from Max.

"But here's a secret about me, Tom. I enjoy sex and kink so much more with a friend. Partnering with someone you like is sublime if they—if we—want that. Most people who date the same person regularly do so because they enjoy that person, you know."

Tom was deliriously hard, but the teasing gave him something to push against. "I know how relationships work. I'm a divorce lawyer."

Max kissed his forehead. "You know how relationships end."

That stopped Tom's brain. He stared back at Max.

A chuckle escaped Max. He loosened his hold and drew Tom back to the table. "Your lamb is growing cold. Why don't you finish it, and the wine, and then I'll offer you a suggestion?"

Tom lowered himself into his chair. "You must think I'm fool."

Max took his seat and shook his head. "I don't."

Knowing Max, that was true. The man was too good, too much. Sexy. Understanding. Thoughtful. "And you bake, too."

"Hmm?" Max's lips hovered at the edge of his water glass.

"It's just—you speak a bunch of languages. You're stunningly handsome. You can skate backwards, you cook *and* bake. And you're nice."

"Oh." Max sipped his water and then dipped his head. "I suppose that's true."

"But also, you're a Dom and a sadist."

Max straightened and nodded. "People can be many things."

"I know." Tom took another taste of the wine. "Might be easier if you *were* some secret prince."

Max grinned. "Then we wouldn't be eating here, so you're stuck with the son of a baker."

The wine made Tom warm and loopy, but also loosened his tongue. "Aaron says I'm good with relationships. Like with clients and stuff, and with him and Kip—our paralegal—and Will, and people at the coffee shop."

"You strike me as someone who cares about others."

"I do. I mean, I don't just do divorce, but that's the main focus. Some people drift apart. Others—man, they're getting screwed over, or screwing others over." He blinked a few times.

"But you've never liked anyone you've dated?"

"Maybe dating isn't the right word for what I was doing."

Anger and sorrow flickered over Max again. "Perhaps not."

Tom took several bites of his dinner and tried to puzzle out how to explain himself to Max. Finally, after another gulp of wine, he started.

"When I first moved here, when I first saw you, I wanted you," he said. "Gorgeous. Sexy. Great smile. You were in Bold Brew, grading papers, like you always are, but you were talking to someone, and I nearly ran into a table because I was..."

Smitten. He didn't say that. He didn't finish the sentence, because Max wore a tiny smile and ruddy cheeks, and was staring down.

"Then I saw you at a munch. Then a demo. Then at Mansion House," Tom said. "And I knew with absolute certainty that you were out of my league."

Max's gaze snapped up. "I am certainly *not* out of your league."

The food was gone—only the wine was left, so Tom picked

that up, swirled it, and drank. "I date assholes, Max. I don't think I know how not to date them. I don't know what to do with this." He gestured to his head. "All that's in my brain."

"Maybe dating isn't the right word for what you were doing." Max parroted Tom's own words.

"I was getting fucked and beaten. Scratching my itch."

"Until you couldn't stand the way they treated you."

Yup. He'd leave and lose a piece of self-respect every time.

Max sighed. "Would you like to hear my suggestion?"

"Sure." Tom shrugged. Couldn't be any worse than now.

"Let me *date* you. Let me be your *friend*." Max paused. "And when you need that itch scratched, let me fuck you. Let me tie you up, whip your ass, and make you scream."

That sounded ideal. "What if—"

Max cut him off. "What if it doesn't work out? If we develop a friendship and the sex and kink thing falls apart? Or vice versa?"

"Yeah." Tom didn't know why that scared him so much. "Mostly the friend part. I don't want to lose you."

"I'm not keen on losing you as a friend either." Max ran a hand through his hair. "I want this, Tom. You think me infuriating? You should sit in my skin for a little bit." He said that softly.

Oh. "I—shit."

Max waved the concern away. "You said you weren't romantic?"

"Not really, no."

"And you've never had sex with a friend?"

"No. Granted, most of my friends are taken, or not into kink. I'm gay. So that also limits the pool..." Tom trailed off.

"Of the men you've submitted to, that you've let fuck and beat you, you've never become friends with any of them." There was an edge to Max's voice.

Max had uttered a sad, true statement about Tom's sex life. "I don't think I liked any of them."

"I was wrong," Max said. "That Friday night when we finally talked, I was wrong."

An awful sharp pain cracked open in Tom's chest. "About me?"

A nod. "I thought you needed a Dom who would treat you with respect to show you that we weren't all assholes, because you deserve better."

"And now?"

"You need a man who can be your friend, who you enjoy being with, and who you want to Dominate you."

That didn't sound bad at all. "Maybe I need both."

"Maybe you do." Max paused. "Do you want me to push your limits, Tom?"

That question again. It pierced his chest and slid down his spine to his balls. "Please."

"I can do that. I want you to trust me outside of the kink as you would inside. Trust that when I ask you to dinner or when I want to spend time with you, that it's because of the friendship. I think what's between us can last more than a couple of fucks. I'm also not going to break up with you at the first hint of trouble. We're adults. We can talk."

Tom shivered. "You made me waffles." Not the most *adult* reply, but that's what sprang into his mind and soul. Max feeding him had made him feel warm and safe, almost like Max holding him down and fucking him had.

"I did. I'd like to make you more breakfasts and dinners." He smiled. "Maybe bake bread for you, too."

That sounded fine. Tom brushed a hand down his chest, where a strange warmth had grown. It was comforting, not terrifying. "We can try that."

"Good." Max finished his meal while Tom finished his wine,

letting the alcohol seep into his bones and joints. Calm finally descended on his skull—the panic of earlier gone. That might have been because of the wine, but he didn't think so.

Max was as grounding as he was terrifying. "I do like you," Tom said. "I don't know what to do with that."

"Enjoy it?"

Tom leaned against his chair. "Maybe that's the answer." He closed his eyes.

Max huffed a laugh.

Soft footfalls made Tom blink his eyes open. A man dressed in the whites of a chef entered the room. "Maxime," he said.

There was Max's sly smile. "Bernard." He rose and shook the man's hand. They exchanged what sounded to be pleasantries in French, then Max turned to Tom. "This is my friend, Tom Cedric."

Tom rose and offered his hand.

"Ah," Bernard said. "Any friend of Maxime is welcome here."

"Thank you. The meal was delicious."

"So glad you enjoyed it." Bernard smiled. "And the bread?"

Max laughed. "I told him."

"So he's going to say it was the best part of the meal." Bernard poked a finger at Max and switched to French.

Max held up his hands in mock submission and replied back.

This felt *right*, being here. Tom didn't understand a lick of French, especially not at the rate Max and Bernard spoke. But this was Max opening up a window into his world and letting him in. Tom dropped a hand to the chair to steady himself.

Max hadn't brought him here to break up with him. He'd chosen this place to share. To save. Maybe Tom spent too much time at the end of relationships. Maybe he took the friendships he had for granted.

"The best part of the meal was the company." He spoke quietly, underneath Max and Bernard's happy chattering.

Max heard, though, because he stopped talking and turned, his whole body swinging as if pulled by those words. In that moment, Tom realized how much power he held between them.

"Tom," Max said.

Bernard clapped Max on the shoulder. "I was going to ask you whether you wanted dessert, but I think I know that answer." He gave Tom a little bow of the head. "Pleasure to meet you, Monsieur Cedric. I hope we'll see you more often." He gave Max's shoulder a squeeze. "Maxime."

Max gripped Bernard's arm. "Thank you. Please pass on my regards to Veronique for the time and space."

Bernard nodded solemnly, and they exchanged farewells in French. Tom almost understood those.

When Bernard left the room, Max came to Tom. "Thank you," he said.

"For making your evening hellish?"

Max cupped Tom's neck and pulled him in for a kiss. Wasn't long enough to discern what type of kiss this was, because it was interrupted by a discreet cough.

Max pulled back slowly, all smile and sparkling eyes, then turned.

The maître d', Gabriel, stood at the doorway of the room, wearing a smile of his own, and holding their coats and scarves in his hands. They took them, and thank-yous were exchanged, both in English and French.

When the maître d' had left, Max smoothed out Tom's scarf. "I'll admit this evening was rocky. But I won a hockey game, had a very nice meal, and you're still here with me, so I'm counting this one as good." He used the scarf to pull Tom in and brushed their lips together. "Thank you for your trust."

"It's all I have to give," Tom said.

Max kissed his forehead again. "Come on."

Tom didn't feel as strange walking through the dining room now. Could've been the wine. Or maybe Max's story. When they got outside, and the cool air cleared his head, he stopped dead in his tracks, halfway to the truck. "Max."

Max stopped and turned. "Yes?"

"Did we just walk out without paying?"

Max's grin in the lamplight was both wolfish and downright sexy. "Yes."

Oh. "Can I ask about that?"

"Let's say they still owe me, and leave it at that for now. It's nothing untoward, but I want to keep a little mystery about me."

Laughter bubbled up in Tom. "I'm afraid to ask." He followed Max to the truck, and climbed in.

Max turned the engine over and rubbed his hands. "Ech, now I'm cold."

Tom wasn't. He was warm, sleepy, and relaxed. "You're too good for me."

"I'm not," Max said. "And I bet your friends would agree."

"God, I think everyone agrees." Tom put on his belt and leaned back in the seat. "Did you know you have a fan club?"

Max groaned. "Oh god. You sat with Cara and Zane." He pulled out of the parking spot and headed back to Laurelsburg. "Please don't tell me their nicknames for me."

Tom had to laugh. "Okay, but they seem like nice people."

Max waved a hand. "They are. It's fine. Just sometimes it's a bit much."

"To be the hot professor?"

"Believe me, the moment a hotter professor shows up on campus, I'll be the first to celebrate. Hell, I'll bake them a cake."

"I'm sure there's more than one of you on campus. Maybe you should start a club?"

Max laughed, then sobered. "Would probably be more like a therapy group."

"Ooof."

"It's really not all it's cracked up to be."

"What about being a sexy hot Dom?"

"Ah," Max said. "Now that *is* everything it's cracked up to be."

The banter continued and segued into discussing their favorite podcasts. Max, it turned out, listened to many in different languages, and tended to listen to ones about history or science.

Tom added his favorites. "I love the true crime ones, especially when they get into the nitty-gritty of historical cases."

Turned out they listened to the same historical murder podcast.

"I do have to keep my hand in English, too." Amusement laced Max's voice, and Tom couldn't help laughing.

"I'm glad I can be part of your practice," Tom quipped. As they entered Laurelsburg, Tom fell silent when he realized they weren't heading to Max's house.

Of course Max noticed the shift in mood. He sighed. "You're tipsy, Tom. And we've had an emotional night. Part of *friendship* in this kind of relationship is knowing when we both need time alone."

Tom wasn't sure that's what he wanted. Needed? Probably. "You know I'm going to go over everything that happened tonight, multiple times, right?"

Max pulled over to the curb near Tom's apartment building, and put the truck into park. He shifted in his seat. "Maybe you need to do that, though in my experience, it doesn't help."

Tom wrapped his coat tighter around him. "I know."

"Besides," Max said. "It's a school night. I have an eight-thirty lecture tomorrow that I'm only half prepared for."

"So even if you wanted to..." Tom let that trail off. Max *didn't* want to, Tom was sure of that.

Max reached over and gripped Tom's shoulder. "Tom, I haven't stopped wanting you. I enjoy spending time with you. I love kink with you, and I love fucking you into oblivion." His hand slid up to Tom's neck. "I'm trying very hard to pace myself."

"Why?" All that sounded fantastic.

"Because I'm thirty-nine, and I don't think you're much younger, and both you and I have jobs that require our attention."

That was a pretty good reason. He still groaned in frustration.

"Tom, Tom," Max murmured. He tugged. "Come here."

Tom went, unbelting himself and sliding over to meet Max's embrace, his kiss.

God, he wanted those kisses, whether they were soft or hard. Enjoyed kissing back and hearing Max moan. His hands were tangled in Max's coat, and Max's were in Tom's hair.

Those fingers tightened in Tom's locks, pulling at the roots. It wasn't painful, but he became sharply aware of everything, and yelped into Max's mouth.

That earned him a chuckle, then words against his lips. "If this weren't a busy street, I'd blow you right here and now."

"Oh my god." Tom couldn't remember the last time anyone had gone down on him in a *car*. That was high school stuff.

Max pulled Tom's head back and kissed his throat. "I'll save that fantasy for later, I think."

"Please," Tom whispered.

Max nipped at Tom's neck, then eased back. "Are you free this weekend?"

Tom ran through his mental calendar. "I—think? Sometimes I meet with clients on Saturday. But—yes?"

"Let's pencil in some time Saturday evening, shall we?"

Something in Tom's soul smoothed out. Bubbled, even. "Yes, Sir."

Max smoothed a thumb over his cheek, then gave him a quick kiss. "Better go. We're fogging up the windows, and I don't want to explain to the cops why I was feeling you up."

Tom laughed. "Because you want to suck my dick." He reached for the door, then paused before opening it. "Max, I—thank you for riding that out with me."

He nodded. "Our friendship is important to me, Tom, regardless of anything else. I think we can have it all, though." He got his devil's smile. "Also, someday I want to ride you."

The two statements collided in Tom's brain, and nothing came out of his mouth but a wheeze.

"Goodnight, Tom." Max's smile was evil.

"Goodnight, Sir," he murmured, because it seemed the right thing to say. He climbed out of Max's truck, and headed into his apartment building.

His unit was on the fifth floor, and by the time he got to his door, he was sorting through the night, like he'd predicted.

Even after he'd crawled into bed and turned off the lights, his mind circled through the evening before it landed on those last minutes in the truck, what Max had said, and what that meant.

Max valued Tom, and his friendship. He loved fucking and flogging him. Then Max had casually slipped in that he'd like to ride Tom's cock.

He rolled *that* thought around. He was too tired to get that hard, but lust wound its way through him, anyway. Topping as a sub. How would that work? Then his brain supplied the memory of a couple different BDSM scenes he'd seen, and he shivered. Would Max tie him down first? Did Tom want that?

Hell yes.

Were they *really* dating?

Yes, they were, and that was okay. Good, even. He liked the budding friendship with Max. Maybe he *could* have it all.

Exhaustion crept up on Tom, cleared his head, and pulled him down into sleep.

CHAPTER NINE

ON THURSDAY MORNING, Tom checked his schedule. He had a noon appointment with a client on Saturday, so he fired off a text to Max, letting him know he wasn't available until the late afternoon. There wasn't a reply right away, but then Max had said he had a lecture at eight thirty, so he was likely deep into teaching.

So Tom stuck his nose down into paperwork, and got started on the day.

There was something mind numbing about legal procedures, and those soothed much of Tom's worries away, until Aaron rapped on his door. "Hey, how'd the hockey game with Dr. Hotty go?"

Tom started. "Uh—fine? Fine. Yeah."

"Uh oh." Aaron stepped into the room.

Oh god, he didn't need to be cross-examined by Aaron —*fucking*—Taylor. Tom raised his hands. "No, it's fine. The game was great. Lots of fun. He invited me back to the locker room, and I met a bunch of his co-workers."

"Uh huh." Aaron crossed his arms.

"Then I panicked because he's way the fuck too good for me

and nearly broke up with him, but he took me to that really expensive French place outside of town and kept me from falling apart, so I guess we're *dating* dating."

The expression Aaron got would have been amusing if it hadn't been aimed at Tom. "Oh my god, you're impossible. He's not too good for you." He marched over to Tom's desk, reached past him, and grabbed his stress ball. Then he beaned it off Tom's head. "He's *perfect* for you, you nincompoop!"

Tom sat there stunned. "Really?"

Aaron threw up his hands. "Oh my god, *yes!*" Then he marched out of the office, leaving Tom to stare at the empty door.

A minute later, his phone chirped several times, his new text alert. He rotated around.

That's fine. I had a thought about Saturday. Do you have ice skates?

He stared at that text, then typed in a reply.

I do, yeah. I try to get to the rink a couple of times in winter.

Would you like to go ice skating with me, Tom?

A weird, bubbly sensation filled Tom's chest.

Are you asking me out on a date?

Yes. Come skating with me? We can go to dinner first. Though I do desperately need to do some grading Saturday, or they're going to yank my tenure.

They can yank your tenure for that?

*No. But I don't like leaving my students in a lurch.
Skating?*

A skating date. Dinner. God, that sounded great.

*Yes, skating. Why don't I meet you at Bold Brew after I
finish w/ my client? I can do paperwork, too. Then we
can either eat there, or somewhere else.*

Perfect. See you then!

He contemplated whether to send an emoji, and ended up
replying with one word.

Awesome.

That was how he felt. Along with giddy and excited and—
he didn't know. How had he felt about meeting new friends?
Not like this.

He'd been excited to meet Aaron, even flirty, then horribly
embarrassed when Aaron confessed he had a husband. But a
fellow lawyer who was queer? That had been a breath of
fresh air.

The day after they'd seen each other at the same kink party,
they'd met at the courthouse, hedged around the subject of kink
for a moment, then they'd gone out for drinks and decided to
open a law firm together. All that had been heady, life-turning
stuff. He'd been pumped and joyful to start a new venture.

What he felt for Max was nothing like that. There were
similarities, but this was—god, he didn't know. Tom levered

himself out of his chair and made his way to their break room to get some coffee.

He wasn't surprised to see Aaron there, sipping a mug and staring out the window. "Hey, everything all right with you?"

Aaron turned and raised an eyebrow. "With me?"

Yeah, Tom was the one with all the issues lately, but it had been Aaron not that long ago. "I realized I haven't asked you how your cases are going, or any of that."

Aaron cracked a smile. "Too absorbed with your cinnamon roll."

"Ugh. I left my stress ball in the office." Tom padded by him, grabbed the coffee carafe, and refilled his mug.

Aaron chuckled, then sobered. "Cases are fine. Tough, but fine. Pulled Judge Townsend again, though."

"At least he's fair, just a hardnose." You had to have your ducks in line, a tidy appearance, and know your shit when you faced that judge.

"That's the only good thing about that. I'll be fine. So will my client." Aaron took a sip of his coffee, then gave Tom a look that he knew all too well. "You want to talk about Max?"

Tom shrugged. "You'll tell me I'm overthinking everything."

"You're overthinking everything."

Tom rolled his eyes. "Fuck you, Taylor."

Aaron chuckled. "Against the rules."

It was, but also they were incompatible anyway. "He asked me to go ice skating with him on Saturday."

That got a rise out of both of Aaron's eyebrows. "A date?"

"A date." Tom huffed out a laugh that was a little too high pitched. "An actual fucking date."

"Dude. Told you." Aaron topped off his coffee. "He's good."

"Yeah." Tom pushed a hand through his hair. "I'm not used to that." Or the giddy feeling when he thought about Max.

"Happiness looks good on you." Aaron walked through the

doorway, and paused outside. "Or maybe it's indigestion. Who knows!" Then he was heading down the hall.

"Taylor!"

There was an evil chuckle from the hall, then the click of Aaron's office door shutting closed.

Tom sighed, then laughed at himself.

Happiness, huh? A date? He might as well enjoy it.

––––––

SATURDAY'S CLIENT meeting ran longer than Tom expected, so he was glad he'd suggested meeting Max at Bold Brew to finish up the paperwork. This one was going to have *paperwork*. A messy divorce. Tons of assets. Kids. Pets. Cheating. The whole nine yards. He had notes to type in and contingencies to plan for his client, and a list of items for Kip to research.

Even with his head full of business, the moment he walked into Bold Brew and saw Max sitting in his usual spot, that bubbling feeling rose in his chest. When Max looked up and smiled—there went years of law school and practice, right out of his head.

He managed to walk to the chair next to Max and set his satchel down. Max stood and, with a cocky smile, held out his arms for an embrace. Of course Tom went and of course Max kissed him. In public, in Bold Brew, a week after they'd done that demo together.

It wasn't a chaste kiss, but it wasn't one of Max's dominating kisses that had Tom hard and moaning in need. This one was long enough to heat Tom's blood, deep enough to remind him of all that had happened between them, and short enough that he didn't lose his balance or his decency.

"It's good to see you," Max murmured when he was done.

Tom was breathless. "Same."

Over at the counter, someone gave a little round of applause. Tom looked, then rolled his eyes. "Kelly. Goddamn it." Of course Aaron and Will's partner would have a shift tonight.

"Ah, yes. The joys of living in a small town." Max gave Tom's arm a squeeze. "Go get a coffee. Tell Kelly it better be on the house."

Tom snorted, then shucked his coat while Max settled back into his seat. Then he headed over to Kelly, who was looking very smug. "You know, I get enough of that from Aaron."

"And the way I hear it, you give as good as you get." Kelly took his smile down a notch. "You should see how happy Aaron is for you, though. Good on you for hooking up with the professor. He's a great dude."

"Uh huh. He told me to tell you that my drink is on the house."

Kelly burst out laughing, then held up his hands. "Fine, fine. Your usual?"

"Could you dust it with cinnamon sugar?"

Kelly nodded, then set about making the drink. "Heard good things about the demo, too. People liked you working with him. Good banter, they said."

Yeah, that described that night. "I can't believe it's only been a week."

The screech of frothing milk covered Kelly's obvious laugh. When he brought the drink over, he said, "Enjoy it." He nodded over to Max. "Enjoy him, too. It's about time."

"Thanks." Tom picked up the drink, then headed to Max's grading nook. Maybe happiness could go along with sex and kink. That was what other people had.

Max watched him move his bag and settle into his seat. Tom

took a sip, then met his gaze. "Apparently, you're a great dude, and it's about time we hooked up."

"Ah, yes. Strangely enough, I keep hearing that, too, but in reverse."

Tom stared at him. "People think *I'm* a good guy?"

Max's smile shifted. "You are, Tom." He opened his mouth to say more, then shook his head. "How was your client meeting?"

Tom sighed. "Wasn't bad, just long, and this is going to be one hell of a divorce." He gestured to his satchel. "I have a ton of notes to organize."

"Well, I have a pile of grading. So, we're even."

They settled into their respective work. It was surprisingly pleasant being in Max's company, and after about a half hour, he understood why Max graded here. The music in the background was light enough not to be disturbing, the chatter of people and the sounds of coffee being made and bites being served created a kind of white noise. The fireplace was lit. Everything was toasty, and when Tom looked up, Max was *right there*. Within arm's reach. His boyfriend.

He must have laughed, or snorted, or something, because Max glanced up, a questioning look on his face.

"Sorry, I was—this is really nice."

Oh, that smile. It lit up so many places inside Tom. "I'm glad." Max glanced at his watch. "Are you hungry?"

He wasn't yet, so they settled on working until the daylight faded and twilight took over. This time, when Max posed the question, Tom's stomach rumbled. "Eat here? Or should we take this show on the road?"

"I'm just as happy to stay here. I'm going to have to run home to drop all this off and get my skates." Max eyed Tom. "It seems you might need to do similar."

He nodded. No way he was leaving client paperwork out at a skating rink. "I do like their turkey bacon cheese panini."

Max set aside his papers and rose. "That sounds like an order. Something to drink?"

"Just water."

Max headed to the counter, and Tom watched while he bantered with Kelly. This was so nice. There'd be skating, too. Then afterward?

His brain twisted at that. Sex. Kink. That didn't fit in with pleasant afternoons and evenings in Bold Brew and ice skating. Then it struck him that it was *Max* who'd gotten up to order for them. Was that a Dom thing to do? Didn't seem like it. That *was* a friend thing, though. He'd gotten beers for Aaron and Will countless times when they'd gone out together. Or one of them had. Didn't matter.

Did this? *Was* he overthinking things?

He must have had quite the expression when Max returned with their order number, because he tossed it on his chair, then tilted Tom's chin up with two fingers so their eyes met. "What's going on in there?"

Tom's breath caught. This was Max as the Dominant. "This is strange for me."

"Is it?"

Tom really couldn't nod. "Yeah."

Max cocked his head. "Do you like it?"

"Yeah." Quite a bit. "I—like I said. My brain."

"Mmm." Max withdrew his hand, but Tom kept staring up at him. "See how it goes? Then you can overanalyze it later." Max's grin was more teasing than taunting.

Tom huffed a laugh. "Ah, fuck you."

"Later, very probably," Max murmured.

That sent a bolt of lust through Tom. "Okay."

Smiling, Max reclaimed his seat, set the order number on his stack of graded papers, then got back to grading.

Tom returned to his paperwork, but the warmth in his soul and the tumbling in his chest made it hard to be the cynical divorce lawyer he needed to be. All that his client had undergone tugged at him, as did the general asshole nature of his client's ex. He started making a list of information he needed Kip to dig into. He wanted everything he could legally get on the ex.

Didn't take too long for the food to come, and Kelly brought it over rather than shouting out the number, since there was a lull in customers.

"Thank you," murmured Max.

"You guys are some of my favorite people's favorite people." Kelly looked as if he might say more, but the front door opened. "Whoops. Work calls."

Tom breathed out a sigh and finished packing his satchel. "I'm so getting it from Aaron on Monday."

Max poked at the layer of cheese on his French onion soup. "Thankfully, Will isn't up on campus much. Though I'm certain I'll bump into him in here sometime next week."

The panini was as good as always, and they lapsed into a comfortable silence as they ate. Finally, Tom spoke. "I know I keep saying it, but this is *nice*."

Max met his gaze. "Spending time with someone you like?"

Put that way, Tom sounded like a colossal mess, not a thirty-six-year-old man who co-owned a law firm and was successful with his life. "Yes. With someone I like, who enjoys me and isn't a giant dickwad."

A smile tugged at Max's lips. "It's what you wanted from your ad. At least the 'not a dickwad' part."

While he ate, Tom mused about the ad he'd pinned to the

corkboard on the other side of Bold Brew, and about what he'd thought he'd might get from it.

A Dom, yes. A boyfriend? No. Max Demers? Never in a million years.

Yet, he was in the middle of a date with Max, who'd thoroughly fucked and beaten him the previous weekend.

Max said something and Tom looked up. "What?"

Max set down his spoon. "What's on your mind, Tom?"

"You," he blurted out. "Me. Dating. I like this." He was repeating himself, but he couldn't put into words how he felt.

Max's smile was charming. "Let's finish up so we can hit the ice, eh?"

Tom insisted on bussing their dishes when they were done, then they donned their coats and headed outside. On the sidewalk in front of Bold Brew, Max kissed Tom. Despite the onions, this one was lovely, too. "Meet you in—say—a half hour at the rink?"

"Absolutely." Impulsively, he grabbed Max by the lapels and pulled him in for another quick kiss. "See you soon."

Very soon. Yes. Tom liked everything about this, even if his brain didn't know what *this* was.

CHAPTER TEN

MAX BREATHED in the cold evening air and blew out a cloud into the darkening night.

After all the years of going to the ice rink for hockey—throwing his gear into the truck and driving over—it was odd to be walking with only a pair of skates. He had to dig out his old skate bag, since they normally lived in the duffel with the rest of his equipment.

But here he was, on a crisp fall night, walking toward the rink to meet with Tom and skate together after having spent a lovely afternoon working together in Bold Brew.

Max couldn't wait to see Tom on the ice. He was so damn happy to see Tom out in the world with him. Max loved kink and sex, but not everything had to be about that.

He crossed over the main road by the park and headed up the path toward the rink, leaves crunching beneath his shoes, and contemplated Wednesday night. The hockey game and the aftermath had terrified Tom, and he'd caught inklings of that fear in Bold Brew, but that seemed to have settled down. Now Tom seemed bewildered but happy. Max could work with that.

The only issue Max saw was that Tom was the kind of

person he could fall hard for. Love was a dangerous thing; past experiences had taught him as much. And while Tom hadn't come out and said the word *aromantic*, that's what the other words Tom had said led Max to believe.

Though Tom could be passionately romantic in his own way, from the kisses, to the looks, to those damn gorgeous smiles. Then again, that might be Max projecting.

He had to let Tom lead in this, find his footing in their relationship. What they had was a growing friendship that Max adored, and they were exceedingly compatible when it came to sex.

His colleagues had liked Tom. Will and Kelly liked Tom. He didn't know Aaron as well as Will or Kelly, but the friendship he had with Tom was obvious.

Most of all, Max liked Tom, more than a little.

Tom, it turned out, was waiting for Max at the rink. He had on his wool coat, the dark blue that looked fetching with his lawyerly suit. The suit was gone, replaced by jeans and a rust-colored turtleneck. He had on a black tuque with a Penguins logo straight out of the '90s, and wore a blinding smile that made Max's heart flip.

Oh hell, he was falling in love with Tom.

Maxime, go slowly.

He ignored his own advice and jogged the rest of the way to Tom, then gave him another very public, but not long, kiss.

Tom always looked startled when he did that. Or dazzled.

"You don't mind kissing in public? I should have asked before now," Max said.

"After the amount of kissing we've done in private?" Tom caught Max's hand, and twined their fingers together. "I have no issues whatsoever."

"Public's different than private," Max said.

Tom was holding his hand, also in public, and leading him

toward the ice. That didn't help the ratcheting up of affection for this beautiful, complicated man.

Tom was beaming. "I haven't skated since spring. I kept meaning to go to the public skates in the summer, but I can't bring myself to step out on ice in July, even when it's blazingly hot out."

"This is the perfect weather for skating." Crisp air, but not so cold as to be uncomfortable. The night smelled of woodsmoke, the promise of winter, and the memory of summer.

When they reached the benches outside the rink, Tom finally let go of his hand.

"The perfect night," Tom said. "I can't wait to get out there." He plopped down on the nearest bench, and toed off his shoes, then patted the seat next to him. "I know you skate all the time."

Max settled down next to Tom. "Yes, but outdoors is different." For one, he was here with Tom. For another, this was relaxing. "Hockey's fun, but it's also a lot of work and thinking. Here I can just skate and be with you."

Tom's grin was toothy. "I'm the added bonus, huh?" He opened his skate bag, drew out his skates, and stuffed his shoes inside.

"You're the main attraction."

Tom huffed out a laugh. "You're unreal."

"Am I?" Max worked his shoes off, set them aside, and opened his own bag.

"Yeah." Tom was quiet. Sober. "An honest-to-goodness cinnamon roll."

Max knew that meme. "Too good, too pure for this world?" Couldn't keep the incredulousness out of his tone. He lowered his voice. "You know for a *fact* that I am not at all pure."

There was the shiver Max liked seeing. Tom finished lacing one skate on, then met his gaze. "I think 'pure' when it comes to you is different than when applied to other people."

"Mmmhmm." Max finished tying his skate laces. "And good?"

Tom took off his blade covers. "You're *amazingly* good." His cheeks were ruddy. When he stood, he held out his hand to Max. "Skate with me?"

Max slipped the covers off his own skates, rose, and took Tom's hand. "You lead, Tom." Not everything was dominance and submission. He didn't have to be the one propelling them forward.

Besides, he wanted to watch Tom skate.

The ice wasn't the best, given the number of people on the rink, but it was still perfect. And Tom? He could skate very well. When he hit the ice, he shot out into the crowd, a grin on his face and Max on his heels.

There was an easy fluidity to Tom's skating, the kind born from hours on the ice as a child, when falling down didn't hurt, especially encased in padded equipment, but there was also more elegance than Max usually saw from hockey players.

He caught up and slipped his hand into Tom's. "Did you also have figure skating lessons?"

Tom laughed. "I did both as a kid for a while. Loved being on the ice. You can tell?" He paused. "Of course you can. Canadian."

Max gave Tom's hand a squeeze, since smacking him on the ass wasn't appropriate. There were tons of kids on the ice, despite the clock ticking into the evening. "Something like that," Max said.

Truth was that he'd taken lessons, back when there'd been a glimmer of hope that he could've made hockey into a career. The idea had been to gain an advantage, and it had helped somewhat, but not enough.

Tom bumped him. "Tell me?"

So he did, recounting some of his lessons, pausing in the

middle of the rink to spin and jump. Then he explained how young Maxime was far more interested in languages. "I had such passion for all the different languages. I wanted to know how they'd come to be. I was fascinated with how they were alike and different, how we talked and shared ideas. That overtook hockey as the love of my life."

He crossed over to skate backward, trusting that Tom would let him know if he were about to run into anyone. "After a couple years, it became obvious that my hockey talent and IQ, while decent, wouldn't be enough to crack into the majors. There was a tiniest of chances I could've played in the minors, if I'd applied myself."

Tom gabbed Max's other hand and swung him out into the middle, then around so they were both skating forward again. "I'm guessing you decided to apply yourself academically, instead."

"Exactly. I was digging into French syntax and comparing it to English, even before high school. Then I started learning about other dialects, and other languages, and their histories."

"How do you stay fluent?" Tom asked. "I took German in high school and college, and can still read a little, but I probably know more Latin now."

"Because you use or see the Latin more frequently. If you had someone to speak German with, I'm sure much of it would come back." Max pulled Tom over to the boards, past where a group of girls were hanging out, so they could catch their breath. "And to how I do, there are colleagues at the university who are native speakers of many of the languages I speak, so I seek them out and we have some lunch dates to chat." He pushed his hair off his forehead. "Or, in some cases, I converse with people I run into in stores or Bold Brew or wherever."

"I don't suppose German is one of those languages you speak."

Max had an idea where this was going. "It is," he said, slowly, and in German, "but I'd rather hook you up with a conversational partner, than be that person myself."

Tom's brows knit and his mouth formed half words. "I got the gist of that, I think," he replied. "So, yes, but you'd rather not talk in German with me, and I should find someone else?" He looked a little dejected.

Max took his hand and clasped it to his heart. "Close. I can help you find someone to converse with other than me."

"Oh," Tom moved closer. "Why not you?"

Max brushed at the strands of sandy hair sticking out from under the tuque. Light shone in Tom's eyes. "Because," he said as he leaned in, "there are other things I'd rather do with you."

The kiss he stole wasn't pure by any means. He stopped before it turned obscene, though.

Tom gave a little grunt of frustration. "You kiss too damn good."

"Sorry. Shall I make my kisses worse, then? Be like a fish, or an aunt?" He puckered his lips up and went in for another.

Tom rolled his eyes and pushed him away.

Max glided backward down the boards a few inches, and laughed. Over Tom's shoulder, he spotted some younger folks—students—who looked familiar. They were smiling and watching him. "Oh no," he muttered, but it wasn't enough to dampen his humor.

"What?" Tom closed in and took his hand again, and they skated in the direction of traffic.

"Ech, a couple of my students spotted us." Max lifted Tom's hand and kissed it.

Tom glanced over his shoulder, his mood also light. "What, professors aren't supposed to be cute with their boyfriends?"

Tom claimed him as a boyfriend. Joy leapt in Max's heart,

and he sputtered, "I startle them buying coffee in Bold Brew! We're not supposed to be out and about being human."

"You practically live in Bold Brew!"

If he had his way, he'd spend less time there in the future. He'd have to cram grading in between lectures. He wanted to see more of Tom. "It's the shock of seeing someone outside of the venue you know them in."

Tom's expression turned thoughtful. "Like only seeing someone up at Mansion House, and then seeing them in the grocery store."

Max gave a bark of a laugh. That had happened to him a couple of times. Once it had been a guy he'd had an impromptu scene with, one that had been delightfully dirty and full of cock and ball torment. He'd thought the gentleman was from out of town, but there he'd been, in the supermarket. They'd stared at each other for a moment, then walked in opposite directions. He hadn't disliked the man, but the scene had specifically been a one-time thing, for both of them. "Life can get complicated."

"Tell me about it. I've run into my clients' exes—or soon-to-be exes—around town."

"Oh good lord," Max said.

Tom chuckled, but it was without humor. He launched into a story of having to leave a shopping cart full of food in an aisle and leave a store to keep one person from harassing him. "Most folks are reasonable in person. They realize taking their frustrations out on the opposing lawyer isn't a wise decision."

Max had to laugh.

After that, they headed off the ice to grab waters from the concessions stand set up next to the rink, but were back out once they'd chugged those. During a slower song, Tom pulled him into a tight circle in the center of the rink. "Ever learn to ice dance?"

"Alas." Max took Tom into his arms. "No. And we'd need toe-picks for that."

Laughter bubbled out of Tom, and then *he* was kissing Max. Deeply. Passionately. They rotated to a stop in the middle of the rink, and everything in Max's mind stood still as well.

Tom had never kissed him before, not like this. Every other time, Max had initiated. Tom had kissed back, with lust, with sweetness. He'd stolen kisses after Max had kissed him, or he'd crawled up Max like he needed to merge their bodies together. But Max had made the first move every time.

He welcomed Tom kissing him, relished it. He didn't always want to dominate, didn't want to turn every situation into a scene. Tom's hands were in Max's hair and their bodies pressed together. He explored Max's mouth with his tongue, then pulled back to meet his gaze.

"I don't know what you do to me." Tom's voice was barely audible over the music. "Half the time, it terrifies me, the stuff I feel. I don't get it."

Max gripped Tom's waist. "I'm sorry." It seemed the only thing to say.

"Don't be." A smile blossomed on Tom. "The other half of the time, I'm so happy I could scream."

That was how Max felt about Tom, as well. "Should we take this conversation somewhere more private?"

Tom blinked, as if only realizing they were standing in the middle of the ice rink, then he laughed. "Yeah. Two more times around, then we go?"

In the end, it was more like eight times—Max lost count— but eventually Tom led him off the ice, and they changed back into their shoes.

"Your place or mine?" Tom said.

The obvious choice was Max's. Big house. No neighbors.

But he'd not been to Tom's. "Would it be an issue if I said yours?"

That same shocked look Tom had sported on the ice returned. "You want to see my place?"

Max nodded. "If you wouldn't mind."

"I don't have any toys," Tom said, then blushed. "Well, I do, but not..."

"Like the ones I have at my house?"

He coughed a laugh. "Exactly."

Oh, *Tom*. Max leaned in. "The only things I need are your body, your mind, and your consent."

Tom's lips parted. "Okay, my place, then."

Max's heart flipped. Yes, he was falling in love with Tom. And like Tom, a little terrified at what he was feeling.

———

TOM GRASPED Max's hand like a lifeline, because he was drowning in the waves of uncertainty and elation crashing in his head.

Max wanted to see his place. No one ever wanted to see his place. Even Aaron rarely stopped by. The apartment wasn't bad, not at all. The apartments in the Crimson building had been renovated when he'd moved to Laurelsburg. Since the landlord lived in the building, everything was well maintained. But his space was kind of bland. He hadn't done much to personalize it, figuring he'd eventually buy a house. Then six years passed.

Now Max would see it, lack of art and all. Tom almost pulled Max to a stop to ask if they could go to his place instead, knowing full well that Max would agree in an instant.

Consent. Permission. If Tom changed his mind, Max would

always be fine with that and do whatever was necessary to make sure Tom was safe and secure. Respected.

The least Tom could do was open up his home to Max, including the bare walls and his small collection of dildos, vibrators, and masturbators.

They crunched through the park path, Max's hand in his, then padded down their town's sidewalks, their breaths clouds in the moonless, star-speckled sky, until they reached the Crimson building. He let go of Max to unlock the main door, then led him to the elevator up to the fifth floor.

His was the unit in the back, away from the noise of the street, and with a view of the hill on which Laurelsburg University sat. From his living room and bedroom, the tops of the older academic buildings peeked through the autumnal colors of the trees.

He turned on the lights and tossed his keys in a bowl on a table by the door. "It's a little..." He trailed off. Plain. Boring. Messy. All those were true.

Max looked around. "This is fine. Bachelor pad." He unbuttoned his coat.

Tom shrugged his off and hung it on a coat hook next to the door. "You have an entire house."

Max handed his coat cover. "It's close to the university and became available at a good price just after I got tenure. It seemed like the right moment."

What to say now? "I'm used to this place. It's close to the firm and the courthouse. I keep thinking I should buy something more permanent, especially given the rent, but I haven't."

"Nothing wrong with that. A house is a lot." Max glanced around the room again. "Especially for one person."

"Do you want to see the rest?" There wasn't much other than the room they stood in now—the combined living, dining, and kitchen space, and his bedroom and bathroom.

Max's lips quirked up. "Sure." Though for the life of Tom, it felt like he'd intended to say something else.

He led Max into the bedroom. "This is it. Room two." White walls. Dark furniture. A bit of a mess, with business clothes thrown over a chair in the corner by the walk-in closet.

Max stepped into the room and peered around. "Spacious."

"Boring," Tom said. "It's not—I don't bring people here."

That got Max's attention. "Never?"

"Well, Aaron's been over to watch a movie or three, or to listen to me complain about guys, but that's pretty much it."

Something sharp and wicked flashed across Max's face, and that look stole Tom's breath. Max strode farther into the room, walking into the space as if claiming a piece of it. He peered into the bathroom, then the open closet, then pinned his gaze on Tom. "Toys?"

Lightning over his nerves. "Dresser. Bottom drawer." He pointed, and Max crossed the room and crouched down.

"May I?"

With those eyes on him, all Tom could do was nod. He wanted Max to see, to open all his drawers, tease out all his secrets, and turn Tom inside out.

Granted, Tom was already inside out, had been since their initial conversation in Bold Brew. All his emotions were tangled up and leaking out and his whole world was off kilter.

Max slid open the drawer.

That, at least, was one place Tom kept well-organized. Masturbators. Dildos. Vibrators. Lube. Condoms.

"Oh, these are nice." Max lifted one of his dildos out, a long, thick, and dark blue cock. He held it almost reverently. "I am still amazed you hadn't been plugged before me."

Tom hadn't been. Had wondered, yes, but not enough to explore on his own. "Guys want to fuck me. They don't want to keep me." The words spilled out of his mouth. "What's the use of plugging a hole you're only gonna fuck?"

The sound Max made was something between a hiss and a growl. "Fuck *them*." He put the dildo back and closed the drawer, then stood and closed the distance to Tom. "They know nothing about being a good Dom. Or a good lover, for that matter." He opened his arms.

Tom stepped into that warm embrace and pressed his face against Max's shoulder. "Maybe. Maybe not." The words were muffled by Max's sweater.

Max held him and pressed a kiss to his temple. After a couple of moments, he spoke. "You are so much more than a hole for a dick, Tom. You know that, right?"

Intellectually, yes. He was a lawyer. He had friends and clients. People genuinely liked him. Baristas teased him at Bold Brew.

But his sex life—the kink—dating—whatever you wanted to call it, had always revolved around him being the end game for some guy's cock.

When he didn't reply, Max opened up space between them. "Tom."

"I hate that you're so nice." His voice cracked and broke. There were no tears. Never were when he was angry.

He was furious. Not at Max, but at himself.

Max's touch was soft. Those thumbs against his cheek. "You don't." He nudged Tom. "Here, come sit on your bed."

Tom sat and peered up at Max. "I've broken the mood, haven't I?"

Max shook his head. "The mood changes. It's like a tide, rolling in and out. Sometimes it calls for sex or a flogging, other times, just a kiss. Or maybe nothing at all. It is what it is."

Tom sighed. "I wanted you to fuck me tonight."

Max caught his chin before he could look down. "I very

much want to fuck you, Tom. I want to pound you down into your mattress and claim what no one else has yet—you in your own bed."

God. Sometimes the mood was a fucking storm. He was hard and wanting in no time flat from hearing those words on Max's lips. "Oh."

Max knelt down, pressed Tom's knees apart, and slid in between them. He tugged at Tom's belt. "As I recall, you said no Dom has sucked you off."

Tom's head might crack open. "No—I—no. None of them. Well, you—but—"

"Ah yes, when I killed a scene with an ill-timed fingering." He worked Tom's jeans open, shoved down his underwear, and freed his dick. "But I didn't swallow any of your come, which was a shame," Max said. "Because you have a lovely cock, and what little I had tasted was exquisite."

"I—" Tom lost the ability to speak when Max wrapped a hand around his shaft and stroked. He lost his entire mind when Max slid his mouth down over his head.

The heat was astounding. The slick velvet of Max's mouth. His tongue sliding over his head, around the shaft. Everything.

"Oh god." He braced himself with one hand, and gripped Max's hair with the other. "Oh fuck!"

Max chuckled, and Tom couldn't keep the moan back. He'd blown so many men, understood exactly what Max was doing, but experiencing it like this was a whole different story. Nothing like a frantic high school blowjob. He couldn't help thrusting in time to Max's sucking and bobbing.

That got him an appreciative purr.

This wasn't Max being a Dom—this was him being a lover.

Tom's brain tripped over that. They were *lovers*. Max was in Tom's apartment, kneeling on the floor of Tom's bedroom, with his lips spread wide around Tom's cock.

Fire and heat rained inside Tom, his nerves a jangle of pleasure and bliss, and his balls tightening each time he pushed into Max's mouth. He was thrusting, actually fucking Max's mouth. Not hard—but Max made no move to stop him. He licked and sucked and then opened his throat and took Tom right down to the root.

Tom wasn't the one with a cock in his throat, but he couldn't breathe, couldn't speak for the pleasure of that heat and tightness. He groaned and squeezed his eyes shut. Wasn't going to last. Not like this, not with Max on his knees, feeling his lips against his shaft, hearing him moan and groan. The wet, obscene noises of oral sex.

"Max," he managed to gasp out. "Going to—"

Max slid his mouth off his dick, and pumped it with his hand. "Good. I want to choke on your come, Tom." Then he was sucking Tom again, and there was nothing to stop Tom from gasping, moaning, and thrusting into that amazing mouth.

Bliss chased up Tom's spine to his head and down into his balls, then he was shouting and coming while Max inhaled his dick and Tom couldn't think or see.

Max didn't choke, but there was jizz at the corner of his mouth when he finally pulled off Tom's dick, and he was breathless, his mouth well-fucked.

He also looked pleased as hell and so damn sexy, Tom whimpered.

Max grinned, licked the remaining semen off his lips, then climbed over Tom, laying him flat against the bed. "Good?" His voice was wicked.

"Yes." Despite getting blown, Tom's throat was raw. "Oh my god. I thought I was going to die from that."

Max laughed softly, then kissed him. Hard. Relentlessly.

This was Max, the Dom, but he could taste himself, even as Max stretched him out and pressed him down into the bed.

Max's dick was rock hard against Tom's thigh, and he pushed Tom's arms up above his head. When he broke the kiss, he whispered against Tom's lips, "You feel how much I want you?"

"Yeah."

"That's because I loved sucking your cock and drinking your come. Tasting you." The next kiss was gentle. "Sometimes, all I want to do is make you scream in pleasure."

He shivered against Max. "I—don't have anything against that."

Max groaned. "We're both wearing too many clothes."

Between the two of them, they managed to strip everything off each other in record time, tossing clothing off the bed every which way. By the time they were naked, they were both laughing.

Max pulled Tom down onto the bed again, this time with his back against Max's chest. "You're so fucking gorgeous." He kissed the base of Tom's neck.

"Have you ever looked in the mirror?" Tom said. "It's no wonder you have a fan club."

"Don't remind me." Max nipped at Tom's shoulder. "The only fan I need is you."

That was what made Tom melt, made his insides flip, and his mind try to figure out what the heck was going on. "Always wanted you," he murmured.

Max smoothed hands over Tom's chest. "Always?"

"Yeah. Can't believe you're here." He laughed. "A cinnamon roll."

"You know—" Max kissed across Tom's shoulder. "Cinnamon has *bite*." He punctuated that by pressing his teeth into Tom's shoulder. Max found Tom's nipples and pulled and twisted them.

The pain was sharp and sudden, and Tom would have

elevated out of Max's lap, had he not been encircled by those strong arms. He struggled, the pain a fiery pleasure in his veins. "Please!" he gasped.

Max let up, but only a little. He kissed the skin he'd bitten, but still pulled and teased Tom's nipples. "Do you want more?"

"Always want more with you." He wanted to be consumed by Max. Overcome by him. Out of his mind in lust and pleasure.

Max twisted Tom's nipples again. "Too bad you don't have clamps in that drawer of yours."

Except, he did. "Do. They're—" He waved at the drawer, but couldn't articulate anything more when Max tightened his grip.

"Get them." He spoke so softly. "And the lube and condoms, too."

That had the same effect as a growled order. When Max let go, Tom was over to the drawer in an instant, opening it and digging out the old clamps. They had a chain that hung between them, and cruel little teeth, not sharp enough to break skin, but enough to make Tom twist and moan in pain that was on the edge of too much.

He'd hated the clamps when the guy who'd originally bought them had put them on him, but that might not be the case with Max. He grabbed the lube and the box of condoms, then crossed back over to the bed and handed everything to Max.

Max set aside the lube and the box, then examined the clamps closely, even closing one on his finger. He didn't wince, per se, but his eyes flickered at the pressure. "Did you buy these?"

"No." Tom sat on the bed next to Max. "A previous Dom did. He was—he liked seeing me in pain." He shrugged lightly.

Max turned the clamps over in his hand, his brows knitting together.

Tom put a hand on Max's knee. "I *like* pain. You know I do. I want you to use these on me."

Max met his gaze. "Are you sure?" That was Max the friend and the lover.

Tom swallowed. "I didn't like when he used them because he enjoyed seeing me humiliated while in pain. You're nothing like that. I want you to use them, Sir."

Max cupped his neck like he always did, and pulled him into a kiss Tom couldn't label. It was breathtaking and dominating, and then tender and soft. He moaned into it, and chased after Max, wrapping himself around that warmth and the man he trusted.

"Thank you," Max said.

He opened space between them again, and pinched one of Tom's nipples. The touch, that stab of pain and pleasure, zipped through Tom, then it was followed by the sudden sharpness of the teeth of the clamp pressing into his tender flesh.

"Oh fuck," he moaned, then bit his lip.

"Ah, yes," Max said. "Look at you." He teased then clamped the other nipple.

The pain was hell and heaven, then settled into an ache that went on and on, almost too much. The clamps hurt as much as they had before, but the pleasure that rippled through Tom, especially when Max smiled—was new.

He sucked in a breath, and another, and his cock stirred.

Max slipped a finger under the chain that lay against Tom's chest. "You're stunning," he said. He pulled the chain up slowly, until it tugged at the clamps.

Little jolts of awareness flashed through Tom. He rose with the chain, but a simple click of Max's tongue stopped him. The teeth dug in and his nipples stretched. Was torture. He wanted more. Less. He bit his lip, then finally moaned, "Max!"

"I'm here," he said. "You're so beautiful like this. At my literal fingertips." He gave the chain a harder tug.

Tom gasped and yelped, then moaned as the sensation turned to gold over his nerves.

"Ah, there you go," Max murmured. "Good." He let the chain drop slowly, then pumped his cock before patting his lap. "I've been wanting to spank you over my knees."

It was one thing to be bent over a stool or other surface, quite another to be over Max's naked legs. Tom hesitated for a moment.

Max lifted an eyebrow.

This wasn't edgy, but it was extraordinarily intimate. Warmth that had nothing to do with pain or pleasure spread in Tom's chest. He crawled forward, allowing Max to position him. His cock ended up trapped against Max's thigh.

Max collected Tom's hands and placed them at the base of his spine, pinning him down. His chest, with the cruel clamps painfully digging into his nipples, lay against the bedspread. Sparks of awareness rose every time he—or Max—shifted on the bed.

He never expected to be upended on his own bed. This was his safe place, a space away from kink. Except Max had become a safe space, and the kink they did together was a different kind of haven.

Max rubbed his free hand over Tom's backside. "Your ass is delightful, did you know that?"

"Other people have said it's nice." Tom laid his head carefully. His view was of the dresser and floor. The skin where his and Max's bodies met was burning hot.

"That's one of the very few things your past Doms got correct." Max stroked Tom's ass cheek. "I should've had you pull out your favorite toy from that drawer of yours and fucked you with it." He skimmed a finger down Tom's crack, and lingered over his hole.

Tom groaned and squirmed at the touch, making the clamps bite in. His dick thickened against Max's thigh.

"Now, isn't that a pretty sight," Max murmured. "Next time we're at my house, I'm going to do such things to you, Tom. Make you moan like that for me all night."

"Don't have to do much," Tom said. "Just be you."

"No toys necessary." Max landed a sharp blow on Tom's ass.

He hadn't been expecting it. The sting and shock had him arching back, which moved the clamps and sent all kinds of pain into his skull. Before Tom could reorient himself, Max spanked him again, this time harder.

"Oh fuck." Tom twisted in Max's grip, so aware of both their nakedness, of his cock pressed against Max's thigh, and Max's length brushing his hip.

Max chuckled, then struck again, then again, falling into a rhythm that had Tom panting and groaning, and the ecstasy of pain turned to bliss. The clamps flared burning heat over his chest, while Max's hand struck, sometimes in rhythm, sometimes not, over his ass and thighs.

"Fuck, baby," Max muttered between blows. "You're so goddamn gorgeous."

No one had ever called Tom *baby* before. He cried out when Max landed a particularly hard blow, then moaned and whimpered when they stopped falling. Tom's head rang with heat and light and echoed with the slaps of flesh on flesh. He was hard, and so was Max.

He didn't realize he was sobbing until Max stroked his back. "Shh. Done for now, Tom."

"Was good," he managed to get out. "So good. Hate it, but so so—"

Max gave him a smack, and Tom gasped again. "Good?" Max purred the word.

Exactly. Tom sighed into the bedspread. "Even the clamps." His nipples ached and throbbed—but that had flooded his brain with the bliss that came on the heels. He was light now, safe.

"I'm glad." Max's hand still clasped Tom's wrists. He stroked Tom's ass. "Because I like those clamps on you."

Tom shivered, and Max chuckled.

Beneath Tom, Max shifted, then the sound of the lube bottle clicking open filled the room.

Tom gasped even before the cold liquid hit his flesh, then moaned when Max's fingers spread lube over and around his hole, teasing the ring but not quite pushing in.

"Oh fuck," he groaned.

"Greedy thing," Max said. "Always wanting something inside you, eh?"

"Yes, Sir."

"Mmm. Good thing I enjoy filling you." He slid a finger inside, and Tom moaned into the bedspread.

Max fucked him like that, Tom twisting against his grip, but his struggles only seemed to make Max tease him more. Eventually, Max slipped in another finger.

Every time Max slid over Tom's sweet spot, he couldn't help shuddering and moaning.

"See," Max said. "I could watch you do that all day. Hell, I jerk off to the memory."

Tom squeezed his eyes shut and rocked against Max; the image of Max jerking off to *him* flickered through Tom's head. "Sir," he gasped. "Oh fuck." He was so close already.

He rarely came twice so close together in one night, but Max had a way of turning him on, even when he thought his body couldn't draw out another orgasm.

He could live in the bliss Max plied from his mind. The pain, the pleasure, the security of it all

"Not yet," Max said, and withdrew. "I want to fuck you into your mattress, Tom." He released Tom's wrists and smacked his ass. "On your back."

Tom scrambled to obey, hissing when the chain of the clamps caught on the bedspread, then pulled free. Max gave his ass several more stinging blows before Tom lay down in the center.

Max loomed, naked at the foot of the bed, casually stroking himself. His grin was *everything* as he grabbed a condom, then pushed the box off the bed.

Tom had never found a Dom putting on a condom all that sexy. The act was a necessity, a prelude to being fucked.

But Tom was transfixed by Max opening the wrapper, and rolling the condom over his dick, his thickness spreading the latex. Those fingers, those hooded eyes, and that turn of his lips were pure sex, and Max lubing his dick was sublime.

Max made the ordinary into something erotic and overwhelming. He turned Tom's brain inside out with a laugh or a simple touch, then turned his body inside out with a whip or a flogger or his hand.

No other Dom—no other *person*—could ever do to Tom what Max did. He was certain of that. He'd been fucked so many times in so many ways, and none of those compared. As Max crawled up the bed, Tom realized he didn't want anyone else.

"Please," he said. "Sir."

There was laughter in Max's smile. "Always happy to oblige that begging." He lifted Tom's ass, his hands hot against the stinging flesh he'd marked.

Tom hissed, then moaned when Max breached him and slid in deep.

"Ah, fuck," Max murmured. "You're so good."

Tom wrapped his legs around Max, then reached up and pulled him down into a kiss. There was a little shocked "Oomph" from Max, but then he was kissing and fucking Tom, moaning into him.

Maybe that wasn't a submissive thing to do, but he wanted Max feral and passionate and plowing into him. Tom raked fingers down Max's back, and devoured that mouth when he could, when they both weren't panting and groaning and trying to meet every thrust and roll with one of their own.

Max dug into Tom's ass, lifting so the angle was perfect, and Tom cried out. "Fuck. That!" He couldn't breathe for the light and heat in his body when Max rammed in harder.

Tom couldn't make out what Max was saying, except that it sounded filthy and appreciative. He wasn't going to last, not with Max pounding into him like that, not with the clamps pulling and dragging on his nipples, and certainly not when Max smiled his evil grin against Tom's lips, and wrapped a hand around Tom's cock.

Light and heat flared, stealing his breath and flooding his head with pleasure and bliss. "Max!"

Max was there, holding Tom. Moving inside him. "Want you to come for me." His accent was thick and sharp, making every word musical and perfect. "Now, Tom."

Everything broke apart as Tom crashed into bliss, emptying himself over Max's hand and moaning out his release into the air. Max groaned and thrust harder, grinding into Tom until he too was coming and gasping.

When it was all over, they lay entwined in each other's arms. Tom kissed Max's cheek, and Max murmured something in French that sounded sweet and tender.

"Hmm?" Tom nudged him.

Max buried his head into the crook of Tom's neck and—held him tighter.

Apprehension trickled through Tom. "Max, are you okay?"

A weak laugh was the answer. "I'm the one who's supposed to ask that."

Yes, but also no. Tom tipped Max's head up to meet his gaze. "I—kind of took over a little there."

"Less scene and more—" Max seemed at a loss of words. Finally, he licked his lip and said, "Lovemaking."

Oh. Tom had an inkling of what was bothering Max. He brushed those locks out of Max's eyes. "Was a lot more like that, wasn't it?"

Something shifted in Max's eyes. He nodded, carefully, then shifted his body. "I need to—"

When he pulled out, they both moaned. Max untwined himself to deal with the condom, and Tom was suddenly very aware of the clamps on his nipples. "Shit, this is going to hurt." He touched one and winced.

Max slid back onto the bed. "Do you want to pull them off, or should I?"

God, Tom didn't know. "Don't yank the chain to try to whip them off. Fucking Julian tried that, and I nearly punched him."

"I remember that asshole. Cut through the scene like a rusty knife." Max paused. "They didn't come off, eh?"

Tom shook his head, and Max winced.

"All right," Max said. "I'm going to—" He unclamped one, even before he hit the last word, and Tom shouted and pulled back.

"Fuck!"

Max actually looked apologetic. "I can do the other, if you'd like."

He nodded. Probably the easiest solution. "They really hurt."

"And it's not the kind of pain you like." Max said.

"No, it's—fuck!"

Max held the other clamp in his hand. "Sorry. It's easier when you're distracted."

Tom stared at him. "You really don't like hurting me when I don't like it."

Max stared back. "I—" He clamped his mouth shut, as if biting back a set of words. His shoulders dropped. "I want you happy, Tom. Creating the pain that you like, seeing you writhing in *that*, brings me joy." He licked his lips again. "My pleasure is deep and dark. I absolutely love seeing you in pain. Tasting your tears. All that." He held up the clamps. "But taking these off? That's not a pleasure for me."

Julian had loved hurting him, especially in ways Tom didn't want. That had been true of so many other of the men he'd fucked, but Julian had been an *expert* at that.

He shivered, both from the memory and from the air cooling his damp skin. "I should grab a shower."

Max edged away. "I should probably head home."

"Stay." The word burst out of Tom's soul. "Please?" he added.

There was a profound look of shock on Max, and he didn't move, as if he wasn't sure what he'd heard.

"I want to sleep with you tonight. You don't have to go, unless you want to."

"I thought—" Max sank into the mattress as tension eased out of him. "I'd like to stay."

That same warm, bubbly feeling flickered up in Tom and climbed into his chest. He slid across the bed, wrapped his arms around Max, and kissed him, trying for one of those soul devouring kisses Max liked to give.

Max kissed him back, stroking his hands down Tom's spine. After a bit, Tom broke the kiss. "Better?"

Max huffed a laugh. "Yes."

"I'd suggest you'd join me in the shower, but it's tiny. I clobber my elbows sometimes."

Max pressed his lips to Tom's shoulder. "I'll clean up after you. Next time you want to spend the night at my place, we can shower together."

Tom brushed his fingers though Max's hair. "What you're saying is that you'd love to fuck me in your shower."

Another chuckle. "Well, that too."

He pecked Max on the temple. "I'll be right back."

It didn't take that long for either of them to shower, and while there were red marks on Tom's ass and thighs, those wouldn't become bruises. His nipples, however, had borne the brunt of the abuse. Back in bed and sitting against the headboard, Tom touched one gently. "I wonder if they'll bruise."

"Maybe." Max ran a hand over Tom's shoulder. "I've seen that happen."

"I usually like bruises, but this could be inconvenient."

"So, perhaps not the clamps in the future," Max said.

"I really enjoyed them. Maybe not quite as long, though."

That lit a smile on Max's face. "Your choice, of course."

His choice. Because this thing they had, this relationship, was about finding their way together. "Hey, Max?"

"Yes?"

"Are you falling in love with me?"

Max froze, and terror flashed over his face.

Oh, shit. "It's okay if you are—or aren't—I thought maybe—"

Max exhaled. "I'm—it's too early to say. I really enjoy being with you." Fear was laced into his expression and voice. "I don't know if love would change things for you." He pulled his knees up, and wrapped his hands around them. "I understand you might not ever feel the same way."

Tom didn't know how he felt. No—that was a lie. He wanted this badly. But was it real or something so different that he was jumping after it without thought. "This is new to me, which is fucking *odd*, I know. I'm thirty-six. I've been hooking up since high school. Been into kink since college. I've never had a romantic relationship with anyone. Never wanted one."

Max turned his head and studied Tom. "You were tired of being fucked by awful people. Hence the ad."

"Yeah. No jerks. No assholes." Tom chuckled. "Instead, I found a friend, who's also a lover and a Dom. I need to sort that out. I don't want to stop doing what we're doing, but I can't stick a label on what I feel right now." Even if he wanted it to go on forever. He closed his eyes. "I'm not sure I trust myself, either."

That was met with a silence punctuated only by Max's breathing. After a few moments, Tom opened his eyes and peered at Max. He had no idea how to read that expression. Sad? Concerned? Loving?

Max stretched out his legs. "We've only been seeing each other for a week, which isn't much time, but we've been in the same circles for years."

"Yeah. I know." Tom slid down under the covers.

"What I'm trying to convey is that we've taken a long time to come together. Years. We've also become very close over a short span of time." Max picked at fluff on the bed sheet. "I can wait. I've waited. I shouldn't have, in retrospect, but that's not the point. The point is, when you find a label, or if you decide you want something more, or less, or *different* from what we have right now, I'll be here. You can take your time."

The emotions that cascaded through Tom weren't easy to label either, but relief was there. Gratitude. That warm, strange bubbling that made his eyes sting. "Thank you."

Max lay down, and they each turned to face the other.

Before Max could say anything, Tom wrapped his arms around him and buried his face against Max's shoulder.

He didn't want more words. He wanted touch. Heat. Comfort.

Max might have sensed that, because he held Tom. Kissed his brow and cheek. Drew soothing circles on Tom's back until Tom was on the verge of falling asleep. "Should get the light," Tom murmured.

"I think I can manage that." Max climbed out of bed and must have found the switch for the overhead, because the room plunged into darkness. Then he slid into bed and wrapped Tom up in that warm embrace.

He wanted Max here, in his arms. He didn't *need* to know what to call it—this was enough.

CHAPTER ELEVEN

MAX DIDN'T KNOW if it had been the skating or the night he'd spent with Tom afterwards that had shifted something, but there'd been a subtle change, a movement away from a strict Dom/sub relationship to something more intricate and wonderful.

He'd hesitated to put a name on what was between him and Tom. Tom hadn't.

Labels were important, as were names. He didn't remember where he'd read "to name it is to know it," but he understood the idea, even if he argued against the concept.

Language was complex, a set of ideas imbedded into sounds, pictures, or motions. Some people needed labels and names to map out their inner workings, but others didn't. Sometimes the language a person knew didn't house concepts for what they felt, and left them without a way to describe their emotions or state of being.

Max could name what he felt for Tom, but he wouldn't take the choice away from Tom to find his own path, his own words.

The Sunday after skating, they'd woken up late and spent time in Tom's bed exploring each other in ways that scenes and kink didn't always allow, and then in ways kink did. Max had fucked Tom with the largest of his dildos, pounding him into an incoherent screaming orgasm, then used his own cock later to make Tom scream again.

He adored that Tom was so vocal, that he couldn't hold his passion in. Drove Max wild to hear those cries and shouts, and his own yell had been nearly as loud.

Tom, however, had buried his face into the pillow. "Fuck, my landlord lives upstairs. His photography studio is next door. I'm not going to be able to look him in the eyes next time I see him."

"Rhys Campbell?" Max had patted Tom on the ass. "I doubt he'll mind that much, considering you don't normally bring dates up here."

Tom had sat up. "You know Rhys?" Then he'd shaken his head. "Of course you know Rhys. You know everyone. We both do."

Max had laughed at that. Yes, they both knew most of the same people, especially those related in some way to Bold Brew or the kink scene or both.

When they'd finally left Tom's apartment, they'd taken their skates with them, picked up coffee and pastries at Bold Brew, then gone skating again. The evening had been full of laughter over dinner at the Italian place across from Tom's building, plus a bit of embarrassment when Rhys Campbell had walked in for takeout and seen them together.

Rhys had given them a look of recognition, then a longer one of comprehension, then had gifted them quite a cocky smile before strolling out.

"Never living that down." Tom took a long sip of wine. "Ever."

"What? He never has lovers over?"

Tom shrugged. "Not that I've heard."

After that, they'd spent too much time saying goodbye on the sidewalk in front of Tom's building, then Max had strolled back through town to his own house, put his skates in his hockey bag, and flopped happily onto his couch.

He woke up there the next morning, not nearly as happy and in a panic before he realized he had enough time to shower and change his clothes before his first lecture. The rest of Monday was a mess of lectures, grading, office hours, a faculty meeting, and ribbing from his colleagues at lunch as to why he was so discombobulated.

"Given your state, I suppose things must be going well with your lawyer boyfriend?" Madeleine gave him a knowing smile.

Heat had crept into Max, and he hoped it didn't show on his face. He tried to find a quip to throw back, but he was too tired, so he shrugged. "Yes. Very well, indeed."

Jeremy laughed. "Woo, Max finally found his match!"

Max rolled his eyes. "Ech, please." He took a gulp of coffee. "Would anyone have any objection to me inviting him to practice Tuesday night?"

That got him another round of comments, but also agreement that Tom would be welcome, and could bring his skates.

Alas, a series of texts killed that idea.

Can't. I have court first thing Wednesday. Pretty complicated divorce, and I need to be sharp, which... It's us.

Max chuckled.

We'd end up fucking like mad, and both of us would be late Wednesday. Totally understand. Offer stands for any practice. The next game is Friday, if you'd like to watch.

Yes to the game! And I'd love to come and watch
practices. Don't know about skating. I have no gear.

Max reassured Tom that his skates would be enough. They could lend him a stick to play around with, and had enough extra gear they could dress him, too, if he wanted to see how rusty he was.

The urge to text Tom throughout Monday and Tuesday was unusual. He'd never been so taken with anyone he'd dated, but he tamped down the desire. He had copious amounts of work and didn't want to be a pest. Tuesday night after practice, though, he stepped off the ice to find a message from Tom.

Hope practice went well. Wish I could have been there.

He must have been grinning like a damned fool, because a balled-up towel hit him in the side of the head. "Demmy! Share with the class!" That from Michelle.

"Not on your life." He stuffed his phone into his locker, grabbed his shower things, and headed to clean up. Afterwards, when he was safely sitting in the cab of his truck, he replied back.

Was good. Missed you, though. Good luck tomorrow.

Thanks!

There was a smiley with a halo after the text.
The only acceptable response was the devil smiley.

Goodnight, Tom.

At least by Wednesday, Max was caught up on sleep. He

even got himself into Bold Brew early enough to snag his usual grading location, and worked through a good portion of his grading backlog, class prep, and student emails before noon. He was standing in line with the lunch rush for a coffee refill when Will Taylor walked in.

His grin told Max that Will knew all about him and Tom. He'd expected that given his marriage to Aaron and relationship with Kelly.

"Hey Max, how are you?" Will's smile didn't diminish.

Max chuckled. "I'm fine. What brings you into Bold Brew? Lunch with Aaron?"

That grin turned personal. "Ah, no. He *just* got free from court and still has a busy day ahead. I'm here to pick up coffee and donuts to feed the victorious lawyers."

Tom's case must have gone well, too. "Would you mind a companion in that mission?"

Will laughed. "I was going to ask if you wanted to come along. Both Aaron and Kelly have been feeding me little tidbits about you and Tom. I want to see this wondrous miracle of Tom dating someone decent for a change with my own eyes.

"Oh my god." Max shuffled forward in line. "Honestly, if I ever see one of his exes, I may need Aaron's help."

"You'll need my help to bail both of you out."

That got a laugh out of Max. When they got to the front of the line, he insisted on paying for Tom's half of Will's order, which included a cappuccino with cinnamon sugar, along with his own coffee. Will was kind enough to wait while Max packed his messenger bag and donned his coat, then they headed out of Bold Brew and toward Tom and Aaron's office.

"Have you been to the office yet?" Will eyed him.

"No. We haven't been dating that long. I didn't want to intrude."

"Good thing I'm giving you an excuse, then." He paused. "Want me to tell them you're coming?"

"Nope." Max grinned into the autumn sunlight. Seeing Tom was going to be a *delight*.

Will cackled. "Ah, yes. There's the Max I know.

He really couldn't gainsay that. "It's the little pleasures in life. I'm only going to get to surprise him like this *once*."

"You'll come up with other ways to surprise him, I'm *sure*."

Yes, yes, he would. If he had his way—if Tom wanted it—this would the first of many surprises.

They neared the law office, and Will chuckled. "I can't *wait* to see this."

———

TOM LEANED back in his office chair and tossed his stress ball to Aaron, who caught it deftly and tossed it right back.

"Don't need it. No stress here." Aaron launched back into the story of his morning. "So then Judge Vasquez calls us both up, and the opposing counsel is sweating bullets. He had to have amazing wet patches under his suit jacket. Vasquez rips into him for wasting the court's time."

"You've got to be kidding me. Not even in chambers?"

"Nope, right there in court, with the jury and everything. Needless to say, it was like someone flicked a switch over to our side. Everything after went smoothly, and it took the jury no time to come to a verdict. Boom, done."

What a morning *that* sounded like. "Bet your client is pleased!"

"Oh my god." Aaron rolled out his shoulders. "Ecstatic. So relieved. I have a bunch of follow-up paperwork and calls and shit today, but that verdict was worth every fucking minute I put into this. To see counsel's face and his client go down like that?

Those fuckers." Aaron stretched his arms behind his head. "So what happened with yours? This was the divorce with the big house and the second house he bought for his mistress, yes?"

Tom nodded and set his stress ball down. He didn't need it either. "My client pretty much got everything she wanted. Some concessions—they're selling the mistress's house and splitting the assets, rather than her getting the whole thing—but she's keeping the house, he has his fancy-ass cars, but most importantly, she gets primary custody of the kids, and Mr. Big Spender has to pay child support out the wazoo."

"Good job all around." Aaron stretched his legs out.

Just then, Will's distinctive voice echoed down the hall. "Hey, did someone order coffee?"

"We're in Tom's office!" Aaron shouted.

Tom laughed. After cases like that, Aaron was loud and happy and probably didn't need coffee. Or sugar. Yet, inevitably, Will arrived with both.

But when Will stepped into Tom's office holding a coffee cup in one hand and a bag in another, there was another person behind him, one so familiar that Tom's heart leapt for joy, even as his brain sputtered to a halt.

Max. Right there. Holding a cup of coffee in each hand, and smiling that devil's smile of his.

"Oh, hey!" Aaron said, "It's Professor Cinnamon Roll!"

Oh, for fuck's sake. "Taylor!" Tom whipped the stress ball at Aaron, who, once more, caught it.

"Cedric," he replied. "Play nice in front of the guests."

Will laughed. Hard enough that he had to pass the coffee he was holding to Aaron.

"Better give me the donuts, too. I hate when they get crushed." Aaron took the bag.

"Oh god, that's worth the look Tom's giving me, for sure," Will said.

Tom continued to glare at Will, until Max huffed a laugh. "Hello, Tom. I brought you coffee."

God. Max. He had on the brown wool coat with his rust-colored scarf. No hat, so his long hair was windswept, and he hadn't shaved in a few days, so his scruff was perfect. Gorgeous Max. In his office.

"Hi." Tom's voice practically squeaked. He cleared his throat. "What are you doing here?"

Max held up one of the coffees. "Seems you could use this." He strode right across the office to Tom's desk and handed over the cup.

"Thanks."

Max still had that sly grin. "I was in Bold Brew when Will came in, and I asked if I could tag along. Provide another set of hands."

"And what a lovely set of hands they are," Aaron said.

Max rotated and gave Aaron a look.

He raised both of his in supplication. "I'm just saying. I've seen you use them very effectively."

"Is he always like this?" Max asked

"Yes," both Tom and Will said, almost at the same time.

Aaron huffed and crossed his arms.

"Come on." Will patted Aaron on the shoulder. "Let's leave Tom to his guest."

"Let's leave Tom his donut, too." Tom patted his desk.

Will rolled his eyes, took the bag from Aaron and handed it to Max, who passed it to Tom. Inside were two chocolate-cherry glazed donuts and a handful of napkins. He snagged one and some napkins, then handed the bag back. The donut he set on top of a napkin on his desk.

Aaron stood and shook hands with Max. "It's good to see you, seriously." He glanced over at Tom, then back to Max. "Be good to him."

"I endeavor to do only that."

Will tapped Aaron's shoulder again. "Come on, babe." He gave both Tom and Max a nod, then pulled his husband from the room.

Max closed the door. The click of the latch sent a shiver down Tom's spine.

Max returned to the front of Tom's desk, set his coffee down on the desk and his messenger bag on the floor. "Hello, Tom," he repeated.

None of his lovers, save from the first one in Laurelsburg, had ever come here. After that fiasco, he hadn't wanted any of them to. But Max? He wanted Max around all the damn time.

"You're here," Tom blurted out. "In my office."

"Yes." Max cocked his head. "Should I go?"

Tom was out of his chair in an instant. "God, no." He practically reached across the desk. "Please don't go. I was just —" He shoved a hand through his hair. "Surprised."

A grin alighted on Max's lips, then a long appreciative look up and down Tom's body. "Oh, I like the suit."

He had to glance down to remember which one he'd worn. It was his gray tweed three-piece, one that he'd had made for him, so it fit exceptionally well. "Thanks. I have a few custom ones. Judges can be prickly about appearances."

"Hmm." Max came around to Tom's side of the desk. "So woo them with fine fashion?" He slid his hands under Tom's jacket, catching him at the waist.

Warmth flooded Tom and his throat dried when he met Max's gaze from inches away. "More like look the part of a top-notch put-together lawyer who knows what they're doing."

Max moved his hands up Tom's sides. "Do you know what you're doing?" His voice was low, and his lips so very close.

"Right now? Not exactly. But I suspect it's going to involve kissing. Maybe moaning."

A huff of laughter brushed Tom's lips before Max's mouth met his.

He'd been right about the moan. When Max pressed their bodies together and deepened the kiss, one caught deep in Tom's throat.

Max hovered his lips over Tom's. "You look stunning. So much so I want to take every stitch of that fetching suit off you and bend you over your desk."

Fuck. Oh *damn*. Lust swept up Tom and he was rock hard against Max. "There's no rule against it. Just—can't be too loud."

Oh, that grin. Max let go of Tom and stepped back enough to strip off his coat and scarf. He tossed those onto the guest chair. "Ever been fucked in your office?"

Tom placed a hand on his desk to keep himself upright. "No. And—I have nothing here. No condoms. No lube. Never needed them." Nor was he about to go ask Aaron, who probably had both in his desk.

Max tilted his head again, seemingly taking in all of Tom. "Then perhaps not a fuck." He strode over and moved both coffees and the donut on its napkin to the side, away from Tom's laptop. "Take off your jacket and place both hands on the edge of the desk, please."

Desire flooded Tom, setting his bones on fire. God, he *needed* this. Max was—a gift. His dominance. His subtle ways of asking for consent and his not-so-subtle ability to take over. Tom flipped his laptop closed, hung the jacket on the back of his chair, and did as told.

"Nothing on camera, eh?" Max caught Tom's hips again, and pulled them back until Tom was stretched out.

"I prefer not. Even private stuff has a way of becoming public." His breath hitched between sentences. This stance. Max's heat behind him. Tom had no idea what was about to happen, but he was sure it would blow his mind. "Besides, I'd make a horrible cam boy."

Max reached around and undid the buckle on Tom's belt. "I don't know about that. You're stunning when you're turned on. I bet you could rake in quite a bit of cash." He unbuttoned Tom's pants and pulled the zipper down.

The thought of performing on camera was a turn on and a non-starter. "Lawyer," he said. "But—" Words failed Tom when Max slipped his hand into his pants and cupped his balls and rock-hard cock.

"But?" Max purred in his ear, his own bulge evident against Tom's ass.

"Could—roleplay for you—sometime?"

Max rocked against Tom and stroked him through his underwear. "Now, that's interesting to know. We'll have to explore that, perhaps in your apartment with those lovely toys of yours."

Tom had to bite his tongue to keep the moan in. The office was so quiet, and he didn't need Aaron or Will to hear him. Thank goodness Kip was off for the day.

But a whimper spilled out when Max pushed Tom's suit pants down to the floor, and the cool office air hit Tom's bare legs.

"You're so hard for me." Max palmed Tom's dick. "You'd let me fuck you right here, wouldn't you? Hold those screams in while I rammed my cock inside you." His breath was hot against Tom's ear.

Tom exhaled and hung his head. If he had lube and condoms? "Absolutely," he whispered.

"Something for both of us to look forward to, then."

He did groan at that, deep and quiet in his chest.

Max kissed Tom's neck, then peeled his underwear off. Those joined his pants at his ankles. Max slid his hands up

Tom's sides, under his shirttails. "Next time maybe I'll bring a surprise of my own." He drew his hands away, and must have stepped back, because cool air rushed in against Tom's ass and legs.

Max stroked one ass cheek, then the other. The blows that landed after were sharp, hard, and fast, the sound cracking into the room and the pain dancing up Tom into his brain. He arched his back, a gasp in his throat.

Max caught him around the chest and pressed his jeans-covered bulge against Tom's stinging ass. "I couldn't resist," he murmured.

Tom didn't have the breath to answer. His mind swam with want and desire, the pain, taking him back to Max spanking him, paddling him. He needed more. Pain. Pleasure. He rolled his ass against Max. "Sir."

"Fuck, you're so utterly perfect," Max said. Then he pulled away and pried Tom's cheeks apart.

What came next was something almost out of porn. Spit, then Max's finger circling his hole, teasing and probing. More spit, and Max plunged a finger in. Tom hung onto his desk, trying not to collapse from the pleasure and absolute eroticism of Max finger fucking him in his own damn office. That, more than the stokes over his prostate, had him mewling and gasping into the silence of the room. His orgasm built so damn fast.

He'd submitted to Max. Obeyed him. Let Max fuck him over his desk. Though he wore his tie, his shirt, and his vest, he might as well have been naked and tied up at a play party for the intensity of the pride and abashment lacing through him.

Max wrapped a hand around Tom's dick and stroked.

It was all Tom could do to hold in the cry. Bits came out. A gasp, and soft keen of pleasure. Tears in the corner of his eyes.

"Look at you." Max's voice was rich with delight and praise. "Magnificent." He said something in French, but that slid right past. He nuzzled Tom's neck. "Do you want me to make you come, Tom?"

Yes. And no. He wanted— "Whatever you want, Sir." That came out as gasps.

"Oh, Tom." Max drove his finger in deep, stroking and teasing Tom's prostate until Tom could barely hold his arms up. Then Max slowed both the fucking and the stroking. "I'm going to take this pleasure for me, then. Drink your want and need. Make you spend the rest of the day thinking about my cock inside you. Have you fantasize about it tonight." He withdrew both his hands and snatched some tissues from the box on the desk. "I don't want you to come again until I'm buried inside you. Do you think you can do that?"

Only the last bit—not coming—would be hard. Tom swallowed, his whole body shaking. He ached with unfulfilled need. His ass hurt. His dick. Balls. His mind—that soared. "Yeah. I can do that."

"Good." Max patted his ass, cleaned off the spit, and slowly drew Tom's underwear back up.

Tom let go of the stance to put himself back together—tucking, zipping, buttoning, and buckling with trembling fingers, his mind and body still buzzing with submission and lust. Then he met Max's gaze and nearly crumpled from the pride he saw there.

Max leaned in and stole a kiss. "Bathroom? Unless you have some handy wipes in here?"

Tom laughed. "Down the hall. First door on the left." He sank down on his desk chair. "I should wash up, too. But—I need to sit for a moment." He was still damn hard, and the thought of going out of the office like that, with Aaron and Will there—well.

Max chuckled and left, leaving Tom's door a slightly ajar.

Tom stared at his closed laptop. The donut. The coffee.

Holy shit. That had been an experience. The smacks against his ass and the finger fucking still blazed through him. But it had been obeying Max that had brought him joy.

By the time Max returned, Tom had his dick under control. His brain buzzed with the aftereffects of submission, but that felt *good*. He rose when Max entered.

Max wore a playful smile. "Beware. Aaron and Will are being inquisitive."

Of course they were. "Lurking in the hall?"

"More lurking inside what I'm assuming is Aaron's office."

That was kitty-corner to the bathroom. Tom rolled his eyes and headed for the door, but Max stopped him with a touch to the arm, then cupped his neck to reel him in for a scorching kiss.

That didn't help Tom's dick at all. He moaned in frustration, and that was answered by a laugh he knew well. "You're evil," he murmured.

"I'm a sadist." Max stole a kiss, then drew back. "Should I stop?"

"God no." Tom let out a breath. "Just—you turn me on like no one else."

"And now I'm not going to let you do a damn thing about that." Max's grin was wicked.

No jerking off. No nothing. "What happens if I disobey?"

"I don't think you will." Max stroked his fingers along Tom's cheek. "No punishment, though. I'll just be disappointed."

That thought, of *disappointing* Max, twisted Tom into knots. "Oh."

"The best ropes, the best cuffs, those are the ones in your mind." Max opened a little space between them. "If you're willing to play this scene out."

Hell yes he was. "For you, I am."

The smile on Max was not his sly or devilish one. This looked of joy, as if Tom were giving him a grand gift.

Maybe he was.

Shit, Tom *really* liked Max, not only as a Dom. He loved that joy, that happiness. "I should—" He held up his hands. "Especially if I'm going to eat that donut. Which I am."

Max nodded. "Go. I'll be here when you get back."

He went. And yes, Aaron and Will were lurking in Aaron's office. He headed into the bathroom to clean up, then stopped by Aaron's on the way back. "Don't think I didn't notice you stealing my stress ball, Taylor."

Aaron's eyebrows went up. "Are you accusing me of theft, counselor?"

Tom crossed his arms. "I am."

"Well. Possession and all. You threw it at me, Cedric."

"Uh huh. I'm just telling you that it hasn't escaped my notice."

"Despite Max Demers distracting you," Will said.

Tom couldn't keep heat from dancing up his spine. "I'm capable of remembering what happens when Max is around."

"Good thing, since I suspect we'll be seeing more of him, somehow." Will turned to Aaron. "Which reminds me —pay up."

Aaron shook his head. "You can't prove anything happened."

"You bet on *what* exactly?" Tom glared at Aaron.

"That you and Max would get up to no good," Will said.

Oh god. Tom shoved a hand through his hair. "How'd I ever end up friends with you two?"

Will snorted. "Because Aaron's queer and kinky and where are you going to find a law partner like that? Also, you adore us."

He did. That was the problem.

"Hey," Aaron said, "I said you wouldn't. I defended your honor."

"I said you absolutely would, because Max is a snack and a half." Will stuck out his hand to Aaron. "You know I won."

Tom's cheeks had to be red. "Fuck you both." He shook his head. "Aaron, pay your husband." Then he marched back to his office.

Max was lounging in Tom's guest chair, sipping his coffee. He looked at Tom and raised an eyebrow. "Did they give you grief?"

"None that I didn't ask for." Tom plopped down into his chair and claimed his coffee and donut. "They had a bet as to whether you and I would fool around."

Max laughed. "Who won?"

Tom sipped his coffee, which was still warm, surprisingly. "Will."

"Of course." Max eyed Tom's donut. "I don't suppose I could beg a piece of that?"

Tom broke the donut in half and passed one part to Max. "I don't need all the sugar, especially after—" He waved his hand.

"Me finger-fucking your ass?"

God. His cheeks were burning. "Yes."

Now there was Max's devil smile. "I've heard all kinds of filthy things from that lovely mouth of yours. You can't possibly be embarrassed."

"I'm not." Tom's reaction was more visceral than that. "When you say it like that, I remember in detail, exactly what happened."

"I see." Max took another sip of his coffee and a tentative nibble of the donut. "That's interesting."

Ah fuck. He'd given his Dom some fodder.

Tom stilled his movements. Max was still his Dom. A friend, a lover, a Dominant. He wondered if he'd ever get used to that, or the floating feeling that came with it. "I can't believe you're here."

"But I am, and so are you." Max held up the donut piece. "This is very good. I don't make donuts—lack of equipment. But this..." He stared at appreciatively for a moment before taking another bite.

Tom laughed. Max was perfect. Too good. Too pure. He grabbed his half of the donut and took a bite. It was very tasty.

They chatted a little longer, mostly about schedules. The next time they'd see each other would be Friday, after Max's game. Hopefully that night would end with Tom in Max's bed, or Max in his, especially if he had to wait to relieve the desire that would build up between now and then.

"I'd like to take you to dinner again at Le Petit Chateau. This time, more appropriately dressed. Would you be amenable to dinner there on Saturday?"

"That depends on how badly you intend to wreck me on Friday."

Max laughed, then was all teeth and light. "Not so badly that you won't enjoy dinner on Saturday, but quite enough that I will *greatly* enjoy taking you there."

"That sounds like an evening I should either fear or look forward to." He paused. "Or both."

"Both." Max grinned.

As they were laughing, Tom's phone chimed. "Ah, damn. That's the warning that I have a client meeting in a half hour."

Max glanced at his watch. "I should head out. I have office hours coming up, and plenty of grading to do." He rose.

Tom met him on the other side of the desk and Max pulled him into a long, slow kiss. When they broke it, Tom whispered, "I'm glad you visited. And that Will won the bet."

"I'm glad I visited, too." Max cupped Tom's ass. "And I am greatly looking forward to Friday."

"Me too." The headiness of what lay ahead, the weight of Max's command, and the buzz of his body ignited his soul. The hard press of Max's cock against his didn't help at all. Or rather it did, and that was a problem. "You should go before my client arrives."

A huff of laughter.

They untangled, and Tom saw him out. Turned out, Will was heading home, as well. Once their respective lovers were gone, Aaron gave Tom a rueful look. "It's like we have jobs, or something."

"Right?" Tom tugged at his clothes. "I should make sure everything's in place."

Aaron gave him a once-over and shrugged. "You look fine."

He wasn't one to bullshit. "I'll take your word for it."

Aaron shook his head. "You two are adorable, you know that?"

"Ugh. Can it, Taylor." But Tom couldn't help the smile pasted on his face.

Thankfully, his next client was one of his non-divorce cases, this one a name change, so joyfulness wasn't out of place.

If Max were going to visit more often, Tom really needed to check his schedule against Max's—and get a few supplies.

CHAPTER TWELVE

ON FRIDAY AT THE RINK, Tom found Zane and Cara down by the glass on the LU side. Zane patted the bench next to them. "Have a seat, lucky charm!"

"I'm not sure how lucky I am." Tom sat and set down the backpack he'd brought with him.

Once more, the view was superb while the team warmed up. Max noticed him and gave him a smile as he skated past the boards. God. Shivers down Tom's spine.

He'd been thinking about Max since his Wednesday visit, which had been hellishly frustrating, especially since he'd managed to obey Max's order.

Only this hockey game to get through. *That* had Tom's blood stirring.

Max made another round past the glass, same smile on his face. Of *course* he knew what he was doing.

"Mmm. You bring the hottie potato around," Cara murmured.

Yeah. He did. Emotions flipped inside Tom. Not jealousy. Lust, but also more. Hope? He didn't know—never knew with Max. Hot potato, indeed.

Max was becoming his best friend. The best Dom he'd ever had. The most expressive and tantalizing lover. Tom bit his lip to keep from groaning.

This was going to be a long hockey game.

The seconds ticked down, the buzzer blared, and the teams set up. A puck drop later, and the game was on.

This opponent was another team from Laurelsburg, Two Mugs After Hours. Cara said they were a bunch of business folks who got together to play hockey, then have a few beers. "They put the beer in beer league, but they're also good. And sneaky."

They were, too, catching the Shrubs flatfooted down ice, and getting a goal past the goalie into the net.

Max looked pissed. He hadn't been on the ice during the goal, but he had this grim look of determination.

"Demmy's gonna get a goal tonight," Zane said. "He has that look."

"Either that, or he's going to drop gloves." Cara bounced her knees.

"Max fights?" That shocked Tom to the bones.

"Not really," Zane said. "He chirps enough that others want to fight him, but he rarely ends up in a tangle. Mostly, he makes them pay in other ways. Steals pucks. Gets goals."

Now that sounded like Max.

The game got chippy before the first intermission, but everyone settled down in the second period, and the Shrubs got on the board with a beautiful goal from Charrs. True to Zane's prediction, Max scored, not once, but twice. The first one, he waltzed around the other team's D like a fucking forward and put it in. For the second, he one-timed it from the circle.

Tom ripped up his voice yelling after those.

The Mugs fell apart in the third, and the Shrubs beat them handedly, five to one. Tom cheered each of the LU goals with the other supporters, clapping and shouting in the stands. Shared high-fives with Zane, Cara, and those around them.

"See? You are Max's lucky charm!" Cara said.

Zane rolled their eyes. "Don't embarrass the poor guy!"

Tom laughed, heat in his cheeks from happiness. He said his goodbyes as they all filed out of the stands.

This time, Tom didn't head back to the locker room, but waited for Max by the front. Didn't take long for Max to appear. He gave Tom a quick kiss. "I'm unshowered and disgusting, but I didn't want to waste any time getting home." He gestured to the parking lot, and they headed for Max's big red truck. Tom held out his hands for Max's hockey sticks, and Max handed them over. This felt eerily familiar, except the thrum in his stomach was from anticipation and need, not fear.

That vanished once they were free of anyone that could overhear. "You'll be joining me in the shower, Tom. But don't expect me to have any mercy on you."

Tom clutched the sticks tighter. That could be a good thing —or an extremely frustrating thing. "Here I thought you'd be in a good mood after two goals, one of which won the game."

Max's smile flashed in the light of the parking lot lamps. "I'm in an *exceptionally* good mood because of that." He tossed his bag into the bed and clipped it in. "I fully intend to enjoy your company, with all that entails. You'll enjoy the experience, as well. Eventually."

Tom handed over the sticks. "But not right away?"

Max stowed his sticks in the cab. "Depends on whether you're more frustrated or masochistic at the moment."

Oh. Tom shivered.

"Get in the truck, Tom." Max rounded to the other side while Tom scrambled to obey.

Once they were in the cab, belted in, and the engine turned over, Max locked gazes with Tom. "Did you obey me?"

Tom nodded. "I'm not sure how, but yeah."

Max smiled. "You're strong and determined."

"I wanted to please you." He spoke the truth into the dim light of the truck's cab.

Max brushed his fingers high on Tom's thigh—both a comfort and a tease. "You have. You do." Then he put the truck into drive. "And you will, undoubtedly, please me a great deal tonight before you get the orgasm you so richly deserve."

Tom's heart hammered in his chest as they headed out of the rink and on the streets that would take them to Max's house. So many emotions tripped over themselves. Elation. Pride, trepidation. A burning desire to be the best damn submissive Max could want.

The drive took no time at all. They stowed the gear in the garage, Max quickly laying out his equipment to dry. When they entered the house proper, they shed their coats, then Max nudged him. "You and your backpack—upstairs, please."

Tom went, his dick already thickening. The backpack contained his toiletry bag and a change of clothes to lounge in—they'd stop by Tom's apartment tomorrow for an appropriate suit before heading to Le Petit Chateau. In the bag, under the clothing, was the one item Max had ordered Tom to bring: those wicked little nipple clamps.

He didn't want to wear them again. He couldn't wait for Max to place them on him.

Tom entered the bedroom, and Max wrapped a strong hand around the back of his neck, sending heat to Tom's balls. "Put the bag on the bed, then strip. Fold your clothes neatly, and place those next to your bag."

"Yes, Sir."

Max let go of Tom's neck and stepped back. He made no move to undress, just stood there. Waiting.

Tom swallowed and did as told. When he finished, he faced Max.

Max hummed appreciatively and flicked his gaze over Tom. "I'm never going to get tired seeing you like this."

Those words only made Tom's cock ache more.

Max pulled off his T-shirt and deposited it in a hamper by his closet. "Tell me about Wednesday night, when you were lying in bed and trying not to think about my cock in your ass."

Tom gave a grunt of frustration. "That was the worst. Thursday night, too. I was so damn hard trying not to think about you fucking me. I could ignore it when I had something to do, but in bed, all I could think about was you inside me. Flogging me. Plugging me. Or—even like now."

"Now?" Max pushed off his jeans and underwear, and both ended up in the hamper, too. Along with his socks.

"You talking to me. Ordering me."

A smile spread across Max's face, and his cock filled. He stroked himself a few times. "Tormenting you?"

That, too. Tom nodded.

Max crooked a finger. "Come here."

Tom went, and found himself wrapped in Max's arms, his sly mouth on Tom's. Everything was heat and light and he was so damn keyed up. Max's shaft slid along his, then Max gripped both their dicks and stroked. Tom lost his mind at the pleasure and keened in the back of his throat.

Max chuckled darkly. "Oh, that *is* nice."

"Fuck, I can't—" Tom clung to Max's arms and fought against the onslaught.

"Yes you can." But Max stopped, stepped away, and smacked Tom on the ass. "Into the shower with you."

The blow hadn't hurt, but it did tumble Tom even further into subspace. He obeyed, stepping into the bathroom and that lovely slate shower.

Max joined him, turning on the showerheads and setting the water to a good temperature. "I do need to actually clean myself after that game," he said. "You might as well do the same."

The first part of the shower was actual showering, and that relaxed Tom, soothed away some of his frustrations, even with a naked and gorgeous Max next to him.

The ache for release returned when Max turned him toward the shower wall and murmured an order into his ear. "Hands on the wall, Tom. Spread your legs for me."

Tom had barely gotten into position when Max slid a hand over his ass and between his legs, stroking his taint and fondling his balls. Tom gasped and hung his head, water dripping from his hair down to the wet shower floor. The spray splashed around him, but Max blocked most of it.

He was going to lose his mind. This teasing, this torment. Felt so...good.

"Sir." It came out as a whisper.

Max kissed the back of his neck and teased his hole with a finger. "What is it that you want, Tom?"

Everything. Nothing. To be lost in pain or bliss or both. To be with Max. To see that smile and hear his voice. Feel those kisses. Figure out what this *thing* was between them. "Whatever pleases you the most."

"Oh." That breath flowed reverently across Tom's ear. "Tom, Tom. What a treasure." Max bit his shoulder, hard.

Tom arched against the pain, reveling in it, letting it slide over him like water, like Max's hands over his skin. His groan bounced off the slate tile.

"Fuck," Max ground out. "I had plans for you in the basement, but I can't wait that long." He shut off the water and pulled Tom from the shower. There were kisses and bites. Tom's fingers found Max's wet hair. Max's hands landed hard on Tom's ass until they were practically climbing each other.

This wasn't a scene.

This was new and amazing and he never wanted it to end.

They stumbled into Max's bedroom, and against the bed. Tom's flailing knocked his backpack and the carefully folded pile of clothes to the floor, but Max didn't say a word. He hauled Tom onto the bed, and they tangled and kissed, cocks jutting against each other, mouths tasting and nipping and kissing.

Max scraped his teeth over Tom's skin, and his fingers found Tom's nipples, twisting and pulling at them until Tom was writing and moaning under him.

"Fuck, baby, I need to be inside you. Want you coming around me."

That wasn't an order, but a plea. The words stabbed into Tom and rearranged his world. Dom. Friend.

"Max," he said, because it was the only thing that made sense.

Max pulled back, and the concern in his eyes was breathtaking. "Is this okay?" Honest worry. "It's not—" He seemed at a loss for words. "I want—"

Not a scene. Not pain. Not dominance. They were on equal footing. Tom closed his mouth over Max's and attempted to kiss him back with the same soul-rending passion Max used. Must have worked, because the whimper that sounded between them came from Max.

He broke the kiss and stared into Max's frantic expression. "Whatever you want, Max. Anything."

Max closed his eyes for a moment and seemed to catch his breath. His smile was caught between joy and something that was too close to sadness. That vanished when he kissed Tom.

"I wish I could show you yourself." He spoke against Tom's lips. "You have no idea."

Max levered himself up enough to wrench open the nightstand drawer and root around. He drew out a bottle of lube, then searched around in the drawer again. "Fuck. I don't usually—ah!" He drew out a condom. "Not expired. Thank god."

Max didn't regularly keep condoms in his bedroom. That flashed through Tom like lightning. He'd never considered that this—that he—wasn't normal for Max.

"You don't fuck in your bed?"

Max stilled, though his breath came hard. His hair was a tangled wet mess and his eyes smokey dark. "No. I make love to people here. And not that often at all."

Oh shit. Oh fuck.

This was all-out heavy lovemaking, the kind Tom never, ever had before. He'd caught glimpses at parties, and read about passion in books.

Tom didn't know what expression had appeared on his face, but Max's turned utterly hopeless, and he pulled away. Tom grabbed his arm in desperation. "No, Max, I want you."

Max froze, and this time his eyes were wide.

"I meant what I said. What pleases you the most, Max. Fuck me, beat me, or"—unexpected tears sprang to Tom's eyes— "make love to me. Whatever you need the most." His voice cracked into a whisper.

Max said something soft in French, then kissed Tom. They wrapped themselves in each other's arms, and in that instant, everything *fit* for once in Tom's life.

The way Max touched and teased Tom with mouth and teeth and hands brought such joy. There was pain, because this was Max and it was him. Biting, pinching, and slapping. Enough to make Tom gasp and moan and beg for more. Then Max was kneeling between Tom's legs, rolling on the condom, and slicking up.

He eased his way into Tom, his gaze focused on where their

bodies met. "Always amazing." He was breathless. "You taking me inside you."

Then he met Tom's gaze, and Tom's entire world vibrated. Tom didn't know what Max was doing to him. Everything had changed, every damn thing. He closed his eyes and arched against Max's thrusts, and the absolute pleasure of being filled by his cock. He never wanted this to end.

Max made love, and Tom was utterly lost.

He understood the physical nature, the thrusts and the moans. The way he clung to Max. The bites and fingernails against skin. Max's weight pressing him down. The ripples of absolute bliss when Max plowed him right. That hand around his cock, drawing pleasure out of him. Tom knew that.

But it was *Maxime Demers* inside him, on top of him, kissing him and whispering how beautiful and perfect he was. Saying how much he wanted to see Tom come after obeying him for so long. How proud he was.

Whispering that he needed Tom in his bed and in his life.

Those sweet, aching whispers into his ears were what pushed Tom over the edge after more than two days of frustration and lust.

Max *needed* Tom.

His chest felt like it might crack open, he sobbed out Max's name, and he came so blindingly hard that there were tears in his eyes.

Max added his cry, and his thrusts turned frantic and perfect, driving even more ecstasy from Tom. Then they were holding each other and breathing against each other's skin. Max trembled in Tom's arms.

"Hey." He stroked Max's back. "You okay?"

The answer was a laugh that was more of a croak. "You keep stealing my lines."

They were both a mess, honestly. "Even Doms need aftercare."

Max peered at him. "Been reading those books of Aaron's?" A teasing lilt there.

"Yeah, a little." A question wormed through Tom's mind. "Hey, how long have you known Will?"

"Can we—pause for a moment?" Max shifted and eased out of Tom.

Tom closed his eyes. "Ah, fuck."

"Pain?"

"No. Always feels like a loss when you do that." Tom cracked his eyes back open.

Max kissed him on the brow. "I'll be right back. Promise I'll answer your question." He slipped out of the bed to deal with the condom. When he returned, he had a damp washcloth and a towel for Tom to clean himself up.

"Almost feel like I need another shower," Tom said.

Max tossed the towel and cloth into the hamper. "I don't. Post-shower sex smells better than post hockey-game anything."

"I don't know, I've read some jock porn."

Max laughed. "Oh my god." He sat down on the edge of the bed. "To answer your earlier question, I've known Will about as long as you've known Aaron, more or less since they came to Laurelsburg. Will was in Bold Brew and mentioned he was a new professor at LU. Blake was the barista on duty, and pointed me out."

Tom digested that information, his emotions churning up another question. "How long have you known I wanted you?"

"Ah." Max seemed to consider the question. "That's harder to answer. Will told me early on that his husband's new law partner had a crush on me. I knew who you were, but I didn't pay what Will said much mind right away." He rubbed his arms. "Are you hungry?"

The change in questions derailed Tom's thoughts, but his stomach answered for him. His brain caught up. "God, you must be starving." An entire hockey game, then a round of sex? Shit.

Max shrugged. "Food was secondary to you tonight." He rose and dug out a pair of sweatpants from a dresser, along with a bright yellow T-shirt Tom recognized.

"Someone's been to a Penguins playoff game."

Embarrassment laced Max's laugh. "Well, they're not *that* far away."

Tom scooted to the edge of the bed and rescued his clothing and backpack. He chose the sweats he'd thrown in his bag over his jeans, and pulled out an old Pitt Law School T-shirt. Seeing that focused his brain. "Want to finish answering my question?"

Max rocked his head from side to said. "I'm figuring out how to explain the rest."

"You're usually pretty good with words."

"The thing is, before Will mentioned the crush, I'd made note that you'd always avoid me."

Oh. Shit. Tom met Max's gaze. "Uh."

Max's smile was rueful. "Let's take this to the kitchen? I can cook and talk."

They headed downstairs, and Tom took a seat at the table by the window while Max started pulling out a pot and a skillet.

"Don't need to do anything fancy." Max had already done enough for him.

"Ech. It's tomato soup and grilled cheese. Not fancy at all."

An understatement, because the soup was homemade, and Max pulled out several varieties of cheese, butter, and a fresh loaf of bread he'd likely baked himself.

Tom raked his fingers through his damp hair. "I did avoid you. I was so afraid you'd try to talk to me."

"Mmm. I gathered you didn't want me around." The

kitchen quickly started to smell amazing as Max cooked. "You were aggressive with other men, so I figured Will had to be wrong."

Tom gripped his hair. "Ugh. No. I—you were out of my league."

Max turned around. "No. I'm not. At all." He dusted his hands together. "I realized Will might be telling the truth when I paid more attention to how you were being treated by the men you submitted to."

Tom met Max's gaze. "How so?"

Max shook his head and didn't answer. He didn't have to.

"They were shit to me."

"Yes." Max's voice was sharp. He turned back to the pan on the stove. "Then there was your ad."

"Which you weren't going to answer." That came out more annoyed than Tom had intended.

Max voiced something between a laugh and exasperation. "This part we've discussed before." He glanced over his shoulder. "I suppose the coffee was my way of testing Will's theory."

"I was so out of fucks to give that day, I decided it didn't matter if you thought I was a fool or too—" Tom waved a hand and went silent, the memory burning hard in his chest.

"Too what, Tom?" That was soft, almost comforting.

He stared as his hands, and the kitchen became silent, but for the faint hiss of the stove burners and the sizzle of cheese and buttered bread.

Damaged. Broken. Needy. Unworthy. Useless. Pathetic. All the words Tom had heard over the years. "Too much. Just—too much."

Max didn't reply. He lifted the pan from the stove and slid a grilled cheese onto two plates. Then he ladled soup into bowls, and set those next to the sandwiches.

Max carried both, with a skilled precision that Tom didn't possess, to the table without spilling a drop. "Wine, I think," Max muttered, and stepped out of the kitchen, leaving Tom alone with the meal.

He didn't feel like eating. Or drinking. He also didn't know why. The sex—the lovemaking—had been fantastic. He adored Max. The simple food before him looked gourmet. Max had won his hockey game, and Tom had cheered as loudly as everyone else.

When Max returned with a bottle and two wineglasses, Tom met his gaze. There was such worry there. Guilt. Max set the glasses and the bottle down. "I was selfish tonight," he said. "I'm sorry. I should've been thinking about what you needed and not what I wanted."

The words made no sense. Tom straightened in his chair. "I loved everything that happened tonight."

Max nodded, fished a corkscrew from a drawer under the kitchen counter. "But here we are. I know you prefer the kink over everything else and—ech. I got carried away with nonsense."

There were two different conversations happening simultaneously, one in each of their minds. Tom knew because he didn't grasp what Max was saying. "Wait. Hold on. Can we back up?"

No reply. Max stood at the counter, staring down at the bottle in his hand, and the cascade of emotions that rolled over him was nothing Tom had ever seen before. He rose and crossed to Max, touched his shoulders and turned him so they faced each other fully.

"I think," Tom said when those pained eyes met his, "we're both hungry and tired and not making sense."

Max let out a breath. "Maybe." He put the wine opener down, and Tom wrapped his arms around him.

A moment later, strong arms wrapped around Tom in return. "I want you to be happy, Tom. Only that. Promise me you'll tell me when I fuck up, when I overstep my bounds. I'm not as perfect as you believe me to be."

Max was exactly as perfect as Tom thought he was. "I wish I'd had the courage to talk to you. Or hadn't avoided you so well. That's all. Maybe I wouldn't be so fucked up."

That got him a pained grunt. "You're not fucked up."

"Yeah? Who's making dinner go cold?"

Max chuckled. "Me." He pulled back from Tom. "Probably not the wisest idea, but I'd still like a glass of wine. You?"

Tom nodded.

A few moments later, the wine was poured and they were both back at the table, eating. The "simple" grilled cheese sandwiches were astounding, though Max grumbled that he should have pulled out some bacon, but that would have taken more time.

"Honestly, yours are some of the best dinners I've had in a while. I usually get takeout or microwave something." The glitch in the evening hung in the air like the sword of Damocles. Tom took a sip of his wine and let the sword fall. "I am happy, Max. Happier than I've been in a long time, and that's entirely because of you."

Max glanced up, eyes a little wide.

"That's it. That's all I know how to say. I loved this evening. I don't know why we fell into a mood." Tom went back to eating.

Max grunted, and finished his meal. "Let me clean up things."

"Let me help you."

After an exasperated sigh, Max relented, and together they cleaned the pan and the pot, and put everything else in the dishwasher. Max grabbed the bottle of wine and nodded toward the living room. "Couch?"

When they settled, Max topped off their glasses, then corked the bottle. "I think about that day, too. When we talked. When I asked you what you wanted and you couldn't answer me. All those men you've submitted to and what they've done. I kick myself for not being a better person, not stepping in. I'm terrified I'll let my own desires supersede what you want and need from me." He shook his head. "I don't want to become yet another asshole."

The thought of Max in the same category as all the other Doms skittered across Tom's brain like a rusty nail scraping against sheet metal. He flinched, then sipped his wine.

"See?" Max leaned back against the couch cushions and closed his eyes

Max cared about Tom, maybe too much. "I'm damaged."

Max sat up. "You're not—"

Tom held up a hand. "I *am*. You know it. I know it. My past fucked me up a little. It's nothing I can't handle. I'm not *fragile*, Max."

Max glanced down into his wine. "I know."

"Then stop worrying about being selfish. Tonight, I wanted what you wanted, and I got exactly that. We made *love*. In your bed. It was the best damn—" Tom's voice cracked under a surge of those damn emotions he couldn't keep in check. "Fuck."

Tom set his wineglass down and rubbed his eyes. "I had all these fantasies of what you'd do to me, and you chose the one I never would've expected. You didn't beat me. You didn't use me. You didn't fuck my hole. We fell into bed together and made love."

Max muttered a curse, then drank the last of his wine. "Please tell me that was not the first time you've done that. Please."

Tom hung his head and let out a bitter laugh.

"Oh my god." Max placed his empty glass on the coffee table and pushed it toward the center. "Tom."

"Told you. When we started." Nothing about any of his relationships had been normal.

Max grunted. "Finish your wine, then come here, please."

Following orders was easy. Figuring out what the hell was going on in his head—and dare he say heart? Fucking hell, he didn't know. Tom gulped down the rest of the wine and crawled into Max's arms.

That was simple. Being held, having his hair stroked, and listening to Max's steady heartbeat.

"I adore you," Max whispered. "Absolutely adore you."

That was a good thing. Still scared the hell out of Tom, especially since he was pretty sure he felt the same way. He held Max tighter.

A huff from Max. "I had plans to take you downstairs. Torment you with your clamps and my leather. Stretch you open with one of my dildos, cane your ass, then fuck you in my rack."

A flicker of desire swam through Tom. "I wouldn't have minded."

"Oh, I know." Max patted Tom's ass. "You'd have loved that. I'll save that for later."

Good. "Honestly, I loved this evening. It was so... unexpected." Wonderful and hot. Tender. All the things he'd never gotten before.

Max stroked Tom's hair. "Did you enjoy my order from Wednesday? Being controlled like that?"

"Yeah, I did. You can do that again. Tease me, then make me wait a couple of days."

"Excellent." Max's voice was a rumble in his chest, and he shifted underneath Tom. "I think we should head to bed. It's been quite a night, and I have some other plans for you tomorrow before we head to Le Petit Chateau."

A little spike of heat and anticipation zipped through Tom. "I'm game, for bed and for whatever you have planned." He sat up.

Max wore a tired, but still smoking hot, grin. "Oh, I think you'll enjoy tomorrow." He rose and offered a hand to Tom, who took it. After Max pulled him to standing, they headed upstairs.

The path to bed involved more kissing, touching, and teasing, but nothing that went anywhere but snuggling under the covers.

Tom drifted off to sleep wrapped in Max's warmth, utterly confused at the intensity of the joy flowing through him. Feeling that kind of joy in another's company was foreign, yet here he was.

Everything was absolutely perfect.

———

MAX WOKE in the late morning. Not unsurprising, given the game, their lovemaking, then the emotional rollercoaster afterward. Thank goodness he'd managed to shove enough grading into the nooks and crannies of his other days to clear Saturday entirely.

Tom wasn't roused by Max slipping out of bed, using the bathroom, and pulling clothing on. He was sound asleep, his hair flopped over his brow and his beautiful face mashed against the pillow. Max drank that sight in before heading downstairs.

This was love. Max's heart soared watching Tom, and he itched to tenderly kiss his cheek, to make all the world as perfect as he could for him.

Cynical, tender, wonderfully masochistic Tom.

Problem was, he wanted to entwine his life with Tom's. Too soon? Perhaps. But he couldn't deny what he felt.

Max set the coffeemaker to brewing, and pulled out the pastries he'd prepared earlier in the week from the refrigerator. When he removed the cling wrap, they looked in excellent shape.

He usually didn't overnight this recipe, but with the game Friday, he'd had no choice, since he'd wanted to surprise Tom this morning.

One thing Max needed to rein in was the rage that bubbled to the surface whenever Tom recounted his past experiences. The unfairness ground against Max's righteousness like broken glass cutting and digging in. Except the past was Tom's, not his, and he had no right to the anger.

Max sighed, set the oven to preheating, pulled out the ingredients for icing, and got to work.

When Tom ambled into the kitchen some twenty minutes later, his hair was a mess and eyes wide. "Uh—why does the house smell like cinnamon?"

After finishing the icing, Max had taken a seat at the kitchen table to enjoy his coffee. He grinned, the joy in his chest deep and dark. "Because I'm making you cinnamon rolls."

"Fuck." Tom slumped against the wall. "You *didn't*."

"I most certainly did." Max beckoned Tom to the table, and he came, sweet embarrassment written all over his face.

"I can't decide if you're an asshole or the nicest sadist alive." Tom took a seat. "This is like—being flogged with my own whip."

"I was more thinking you'd be happily surprised, but I'll take flagellated, too." Max's joy dimmed. "I hope you're leaning more toward nice than asshole."

Tom ran a hand through his sleep-messed locks, and smiled.

"If making me eat my own words in the form of baked goods is the worst thing you do to me, you're never getting to asshole."

"I would never make you eat anything you didn't want. If a freshly iced cinnamon roll hot from the oven isn't to your liking..."

Tom crossed his arms. "I damn well better get one of those." The look he gave Max was in no way submissive

Max laughed. "Don't get between you and baked goods, eh?"

"Especially not when you've made them!"

The rolls turned out excellent, despite the overnight in the refrigerator. A perfect blend of sticky, sweet, and fluffy, with that lovely bite of cinnamon Max so enjoyed. He'd made six but they'd only managed to consume three—one each and splitting the other—before the sugar was too much for both of them. Coffee helped, but Max scrambled some eggs for protein.

"You make me wish I cooked," Tom said afterward. "I feel guilty about you cooking and baking for me all the time."

"Don't. It's something I enjoy, and it's nice to have someone to show off for." Max finished drying his pan and put it away in the cabinet. "I appreciate the things you do for me."

Tom scoffed. "What do I do for you?"

"You took me ice skating."

"That...you suggested that date." Tom scratched the back of his neck. "Everything between us has been you doing things for me, Max. I—shit."

That despondent expression wasn't good. Max joined Tom at the table. "It's fine. I'm—" He paused. "How much of those books of Aaron's have you read?"

"I finished one. I'm working on another." He met Max's gaze. "Why?"

"If I said, 'service top,' would you know what that meant?"

From the definitive "oh" that rounded Tom's mouth, the answer was yes.

"I'm a sadist, but I also enjoy taking care of you. And speaking of *that*..." Max nodded toward the basement door. "Would you like to scream for me, Tom?"

He wanted to drink in that dreamy sexy, lust-filled wonder Tom got every time Max shifted gears.

"Yes, sir," Tom said. "Please."

When they reached the basement, Max cupped back of Tom's neck to still him, and mentally worked backward from their dinner reservation. They both got lost in kink, and time had a habit of slipping away. "I'm going to set a timer," he murmured.

Tom moved under his hand, but didn't break the contact. "You have a timer down here?"

"I do. I've used it both in kinky ways and non. In our case, time runs away when we're together, and if we're late for our reservation, Veronique will give me a piece of her mind."

Tom turned, breaking the gentle hold Max had on him. "When you're ready, I'd like to hear the rest of the story of you and Le Petit Chateau."

He owed Tom that. "Perhaps tonight. But for now—" Max strode behind the bar. "Strip, Tom. And come have a seat."

While Max found the timer, Tom took off his T-shirt and sweats, folded both, and placed them on one of the barstools. He took the requested seat on the other.

So many things Max wanted to do to and with Tom. Ways to please him, both with pain and pleasure. Make him scream. Dive into his own dark joy. Now? Something simple to satisfy them both.

He set the timer, placed it on the bar, then drew out what he'd need to make their afternoon pass extremely well.

He cuffed and strung Tom up as he'd planned the night

before, then teased him mercilessly, pinching, biting, and stroking over sensitive flesh until Tom was panting and moaning, his dick hard and balls heavy.

"Please," Tom moaned.

Max kissed his back. "I don't think so."

A delight to see him strung out, similar to when they'd played in Tom's office. Rather than fingers, Max worked a prostate massager into Tom, savoring the gasps and moans that he elicited from Tom, then Tom's extraordinary astonishment when Max switched the vibrations on.

"Oh god. I—can't—oh fuck." The last word was a long moan of carnal frustration. Tom jerked his hips, and the chains holding his ankle cuffs rattled.

"You can." Max kissed Tom's shoulder as he pumped and twisted the massager until Tom arched in abandonment. Didn't take long before Tom was shuddering and jerking through an orgasm, his mouth open wide and tears pricking at the corner of his eyes. Max hadn't had to touch Tom's cock at all.

He didn't remove the massager—kept it in place until Tom was mindless between rapture and agony. The cry Tom voiced was music that Max drank with wicked delight, his heart beating fast with need that had nothing to do with his dick's desires.

Eventually, Max eased the toy from Tom, who hung in the frame, his breath coming in long gasps. "Oh my god," he whispered.

Max wrapped an arm around him, and rained kisses over his back, tasting the salt there. "More? Less?"

"Pain," Tom croaked. "Sharp. Please."

That was exactly what Max had planned, what he needed. "My absolute pleasure."

Max took out his favorite cane. Painful. Whippy. Always left marks. Usually made his subs scream and curse.

Tom did both, tears falling freely as his cries echoed around Max, fueling his blood. Six strokes later, Tom was sobbing in Max's arms, ass welted, body shaking with pain and the torment of earlier pleasure. Everything Tom wanted. Exactly what Max needed to soothe his own soul.

He unclipped Tom's cuffs, gathered him into his arms, and kissed away those tears. "I'm so proud of you. You're so good. Perfect."

Tom clung to Max and didn't speak, but dusted kisses over Max's chin until their lips met. They kissed, again and again, until Max lost track of the world, and all that existed was Tom in his arms.

A soft but annoying beeping brought him back into reality.

Tom sighed. "Well, shit."

Yes, but dinner would be its own pleasure. Because Tom would *feel* this afternoon, all evening long. "I should shut that thing off. And we should shower."

Tom loosened his hold. "What about you?"

Max didn't understand. "What about me?"

"You made me come. And fuck, that was amazing. But you didn't..." Tom trailed off.

No, Max hadn't orgasmed. He wasn't hard now, though he had been. "What I needed, you gave me, never fear. And the night isn't over." He ran a finger over the seam between Tom's lips, opening and slipping it inside his hot mouth. "Do you think you can pleasure me later?"

Tom's eyes fluttered closed, and he moaned around Max's finger, sucking and caressing it with his tongue.

"That's very good." Max withdrew the digit. "Now, up. Shower. I want to see your best suits."

———

AS IT TURNED OUT, Tom's best suits were exceptionally fine, indeed. Nicer than the one Tom had worn earlier that week. As Max drew them out of Tom's closet, he noted the labels, the detailed work, and the custom linings. Hell, Tom's name was embroidered on the inside pocket.

These suits rivaled the one Max wore, which was his absolute best.

When Max had donned his suit, Tom whistled in awe. "Damn, you look amazing. You always do, but that suit—" Tom's gaze had wandered over Max's body, as if he were a work of art.

Max's suit was a heather gray that he'd paired a French-cut shirt with blue accents, and a blue-and-gray silk tie. The clothier in Montreal had claimed those hues brought out the color of Max's eyes. Flirty man, but he made the best suits.

Tom's suits were astounding. "You should wear these more often," Max said.

The answer was a huff. "I'm not wearing my best court suits as daywear."

There was the prideful lawyer, the core of steel in Tom, despite his submissive needs. "We need to go more places where you can wear them, then" Max picked the most colorful of the lot—one made from a deep burgundy wool. Beautiful weave and hand. The lining was a contrast of cream patterned with rabbits in various poses. "Why the rabbits?"

"Uh." Tom's laugh was self-deprecating. "Because I like to fuck like a bunny?"

Max nearly dropped the suit, and then the laughter hit him. He laid the suit out on Tom's bed. "You—wear that *to court?*"

"Yup." Tom had a stunning smile. "Honestly, knowing that's on the inside, and what it means? That keeps me sharp and grounded."

Max pulled out a shirt and tie that matched the suit. "I have this image of courts being dry and stately places."

Tom waved a hand. "They are. But I'm not. Neither is Aaron. God, you should hear us sometimes. We concoct stories about judges and lawyers when we're bored."

Max could only imagine those two minds developing fiction out of boredom. He shook his head, and gestured to the bed. "Any objections to this for tonight?"

"Oh, none. That's practically the exact tie and shirt I wear with that one." Tom dressed while Max watched, and that was mouthwateringly delightful, watching Tom fill out that suit. Another three-piece, stunningly fitted. "I'm not sure whether I need to introduce you to my tailor or vice versa," Max said.

Tom grinned. "We could exchange."

The shoes Tom chose to wear were black and burgundy cloth and drove the look that much higher. "I'm glad it's dry tonight, or it'd be black leather."

Max pulled Tom in for a quick kiss. "You have an issue with black leather?"

"Not at all." Tom kissed him back. "I'd love to see you in full leathers sometime."

Max slapped Tom's ass, earning him a nice flinch. "Let's go have dinner."

The drive was uneventful, filled with Tom recounting some of the more interesting stories he and Aaron had concocted, including the tale of the older judge they'd decided was his sweet wife's submissive, and the whole secret drag king makeup influencer life they'd concocted for one of the DAs.

"Sounds like courtroom fanfic."

"It kind of is, but we would never, in a million years, write that shit down," Tom said.

When they neared Le Petit Chateau, Tom quieted, and Max did, as well, his mind casting back to the last time they'd been here. His bid to save their relationship, to soothe Tom's fears.

Tom cleared his throat. "This is just dinner, right?"

"Yes, and perhaps me showing you off." Max pulled into the lot, parked, and turned off his truck. "Nothing more."

That seemed to waylay whatever fear had built up inside Tom.

This was far too early for talks of long-term commitment or love, no matter what Max felt. Love might not be a topic he'd ever bring up.

They got out of the truck. This time, their attire didn't draw attention from the exiting patrons, though he did catch one person eyeing Tom's shoes.

Inside, the familiar sights and scents greeted Max, as did Gabriel. This time, he spoke in English, though the flourish on Tom's surname was French. "I can take your coats. Your table will be ready momentarily."

Gabriel vanished with their coats. Max had a good idea what would happen next, and he wasn't disappointed when Veronique appeared. She was older than Max by about fifteen years, though he'd never asked—would *not* ask—her age.

"Maxime!" Her voice resonated deeply, and he couldn't help the smile, nor the traditional embrace. "And this is your companion?"

"Tom, may I introduce Veronique Blanc, Le Petit Chateau's owner. Veronique, this is Tom Cedric."

Tom offered his hand, and received Veronique's greeting as if he'd been around Europeans quite often. Then again, he was a lawyer and likely could adapt to most situations with ease.

"Pleasure to meet you. Your restaurant is exquisite," Tom said.

They made small talk as Veronique showed them to their table. Heads turned again, but this time for very different reasons. Max recognized a few university donors, though he doubted they knew his name.

Their table was in a prominent place in the dining room. "Maxime, Tom, do you wish for menus, or do you trust me to create a feast for you?"

Tom gave Max a glance, and Max answered, "You know I trust your judgement, Veronique."

"And I trust Max," Tom said.

Warmth zinged through Max's heart, and Veronique's smile deepened. "Good. Wine?"

"Yes," Max said. "Though a small amount for me. I drove tonight."

Her smile turned sly. "I'll have your rolls and water brought out."

Max chuckled. Veronique gave them both a nod, then headed away.

Tom took in the room, then spoke in a low voice. "I feel on display here."

"That's because we are. Everyone knows who Veronique is."

Tom absorbed that information and turned those sharp eyes onto Max. "There's more to the story of you and this place than dinner rolls."

A lawyer's mind. "A little more. The bakery my parents own is somewhat well-known."

Max started at the sound of Veronique's scoff. She held a basket of rolls, a server trailing behind with water.

Veronique slid the basket onto the table while the server placed the glasses. She tsked, then switched to French. "You're too much, with your deprecation and your humbleness." She mimicked his English. "Somewhat well-known."

Max held up both hands and replied in French. "Barely anyone outside the business has heard of us."

"Oh, *us*, is it now?" She glared at him. "Not *my parents*."

He was going to lose this discussion. "Ech, Veronique. Please. I'll always be my mother's child, and she was adamant about how much fame meant to the bakery." Nothing at all. What mattered was getting up and putting the work in with the best ingredients. Giving their best that day to their customers.

How many times had he and Veronique had this particular discussion?

She softened and switched to English. "Fine. For your mother then."

Tom sat still in his chair, perhaps sensing that it was better not to attract Veronique's attention. The rest of the dining room had become quiet, too. He did meet Veronique's gaze when she turned to him, though.

"The bakery Maxime's parents own is perhaps the best French bakery outside of France, and it rivals several well-known ones inside of France."

Max resisted the urge to roll his eyes. Instead, he focused on the basket of rolls. His rolls, a modified family recipe.

"Oh." There was silence for a moment, then Tom said, his voice low, "I thought you weren't a prince?"

Max jerked his head up to meet Tom's devilish grin. "I'm not!"

That made Veronique laugh exquisitely. "Ah, Maxime! You've found a match at last." That bit was in French. She patted him on the arm and switched back to English. "Enjoy the rolls, gentlemen."

Tom had the look of a cat who'd caught a mouse. "How's your ass?" Max asked.

"Hurts like fuck." Tom's smile didn't diminish. "Son of a baker, huh?"

He'd make sure Tom's ass hurt more once they returned to Max's. Or Tom's. He took a sip of water. "Yes. I'll always be my parents' son." He took up one of the rolls and started breaking it apart. "Would you like to hear the story of the shop?"

Tom grabbed a roll as well. "Of course I would."

So over the course of the meal, which started with salad, included both lamb and escargot, and ended with chocolate soufflé, Max told the tale that had been recounted to him, of his great-grandfather traveling from Paris to Montreal with the family's recipes and a jar of starter, to open a bakery that eventually grew into the one his parents owned today. He included all the apocryphal tales of rivalries in both Paris and Montreal, and the tale of his great-grandfather stealing the recipes from his brother, all the intrigue and subterfuge. The forbidden love that drew his grandparents together, and the more traditional relationship his own parents had. The disappointment of his mother when Max didn't want to go into the business.

Tom asked questions, including the most obvious one. "Why didn't Veronique recognize your name when you first came here?"

"Demers isn't that uncommon a surname in Québec, but also, the bakery is from my mother's side. She kept her surname when she married, but I received my father's."

Tom nodded, then glanced out into the rest of the dining room. "Have you given them other recipes?"

Max smiled. "A few, all with some slight modifications."

"And the starter?"

So the man who claimed not to cook was astute enough to ask *that*. "No. Never." He had some, of course. Kept it fed. But that was a family treasure.

Afterward, Bernard came to chat, and Tom was effusive about the meal, even more so than their past dinner. Veronique saw them to the front, where Gabriel had their coats.

When she pecked Max on each cheek, she murmured in his ear, "Invite me to the wedding."

God, the heat to his face. Thankfully, that had been in French, because that sentence alone would have sent Tom flying for one of the hills outside the restaurant. "Veronique..."

"Ah, ah, Maxime. I know you." She straightened the lapel on his coat. "Give my regards to your parents." That she said in English.

"Of course," he said, still caught on her earlier request. Marriage to Tom. That was—He wanted that. Deep in his soul, to the very marrow of his bones. He was certain it would never happen.

Veronique moved to Tom and pecked him on both cheeks. "Take good care of your prince there. He's a handful."

Tom chuckled. "Not nearly as much as I am, I'm afraid." He met Max's gaze. "But I'll try."

Then they were out into the cold fall night again. The air smelled of smoke and a hint of snow on the breeze. Halloween was next week. The world felt alive with promise, despite the chill and the darkness.

He was in love with Tom Cedric, needed him like fields needed sun and rain to thrive.

He blew out a cloud of breath. "I'm not a prince."

Tom drew his scarf around his neck. "I know. You're a linguistics professor for a liberal arts university in a small town in western PA. But we just ate what was probably a meal that runs three figures in a stellar restaurant, completely on the house. The folks in there adore you—and not just for your family's secret recipes. That makes you damn close to a prince, Max."

He couldn't help peering at Tom. There were moments when Tom had such astounding insight into people, relationships, and the ties that bound one to another. But when Tom faced his own life, he seemed so lost, so unaware of his own worth. "Maybe everyone is royal in their own way."

Tom's smile was beautiful. They made their way to the

truck in silence until Tom said, "I love it here."

"Le Petit Chateau?"

Tom shook his head, then cocked it. "Well, yes, that too. This place is wonderful, magical. But I meant Laurelsburg. And...here. With you."

Oh. A spark of hope leapt in Max's chest. They climbed into the truck and once he'd turned the engine over, Max replied, "I love our time together, and being in Laurelsburg, too." He'd set roots here. Had tenure and a community. He gazed at Tom, and he had an expression somewhere between shocked realization and terror.

There it was; Tom's brain turning over every word said tonight. "Where to?" Max asked. "Your place or mine?"

"Uh." Tom shook his head, as if to clear it. "I owe you an orgasm."

"You don't," Max said. "But if you're offering, I'll gladly take you up on that."

There was another profound look in Tom, then a soft smile. "I'm offering. And your place. You have more interesting toys."

He did, indeed. Max put the truck into drive and headed back into town. "I also have an intense desire to peel that lovely suit off you piece by piece."

Tom took a deep breath. "I believe we can work something out, since I have this intense desire to be stripped, spanked, and fucked, in whatever way you wish."

Max grinned into the darkness of the truck. "Oh, good."

As they drove back to town, Tom revealed he'd been listening to a kinky podcast, and Max had Tom recount what he thought were the best parts. A little unfair to both of them, as keyed up as they were, but he loved Tom's voice. Plus, a hot and bothered submissive was never a bad thing.

When they returned to Max's house, he peeled Tom's suit off, one item at a time, starting with those lovely shoes. When he'd stripped Tom's body, Max tied him up and swallowed his cock until Tom spilled down his throat. Max found those clamps Tom hated, lovingly clipped them onto each nipple, then paddled his already welted ass until tears fell from Tom's eyes. Then he took him down, removed the clamps, and helped him up two flights. In his bedroom, Max laid Tom out in his bed, and made love to him until they both came, breathless and shuddering.

"Max," Tom said, his voice raw and rough. "God, I think I— fuck." He buried his head against Max's shoulder.

A strand of worry wove through Max. "Was everything all right, what we did?" He hadn't asked for consent as much as he had in the past, falling into the flow of their needs and wants.

A choked laugh resounded against his skin. "Oh god, yes. Perfect. Always perfect. You're perfect. I—" Tom shuddered and gripped Max tighter.

Max stroked Tom's hair. "You're perfect too, Tom."

They lay there for a while longer before Max untangled them, discarded the condom, and grabbed supplies from the bathroom to clean them both up. Then he tended to Tom's ass, and crawled back under the sheets. "Tomorrow's a day to do whatever you wish."

Tom grunted against the pillow. "Eat cinnamon rolls and go ice skating."

Max kissed Tom on the cheek. "Sounds ideal." Then he turned out the light.

Marriage might never come, but that didn't matter. Max had learned from his parents that you could only tend to the day at hand. Bake the bread and make the pastries with the ingredients they had. The sun would rise and set regardless of the past or the future. Focus on what you had in front of you.

He would take every day with Tom, and enjoy them to their fullest.

CHAPTER THIRTEEN

EVERY TIME TOM set foot in Bold Brew, the world felt surreal. He'd first seen Max here. Gone to munches. Demos. Bemoaned men over coffee with Aaron. Had some horrible and uncomfortable dates. Then he'd tacked up that ad, which had been a complete failure.

Until Maxime Demers had bought him coffee and he'd finally had the courage to talk to his long-time crush.

Tom shuffled forward in line. It was early on Wednesday morning, just past seven thirty, but a queue had formed at the shop between the students needing caffeine before their morning lectures, and people like him—business folks needing a jolt and a quick breakfast to start the day.

God, Max. They'd done so much in the weeks since that day. Ice skating. Dinners. Coffee dates. They'd had the most incredible kink and sex Tom had ever experienced.

His ass still hurt from their weekend escapade to Le Petit Chateau. His back and legs ached, but that had been from ice skating for a couple of hours before Max "remembered" that he had hockey practice that evening. He'd gotten Tom into hockey gear, and they'd both learned exactly how rusty Tom was.

Extraordinarily rusty. Still, Tom found the back of the net several times, and more often toward the end of practice.

"If you work on that," Charrs had said, "you'd be a good shot."

"Yeah, if I had the wheels, which I don't."

She grinned at him. "You can work on that too, you know."

Tom groaned. "Sounds like *homework*."

Both she and Max had laughed.

While Tom liked shooting the puck around with Max's teammates, he was far happier watching Max play hockey than joining him. He'd done that last night.

The line in Bold Brew shifted forward. A few more people, and he'd be there. Lupé was working, along with the ever bright-haired Blake, who wore devil horns in honor of Halloween. They were moving through patrons fast, all things considered.

Today, Tom had a pretty full day of client meetings, then handing out candy with Aaron for the business district trick-or-treat hour. Tomorrow, he had some big court sessions. Now? Now he needed one huge cup of coffee to get him going or he'd be an actual zombie by the end of the day.

Part of the problem was that Max's game last night had run late, with an overtime, then a shootout. The Shrubs lost, unfortunately. Max was understandably annoyed, so Tom had wrapped him in his arms, despite Max insisting that he smelled like a locker room.

"Shut up and let me comfort you."

Max had sighed, then leaned into the hug. "Merci," he'd whispered.

Even Tom knew the meaning of that word.

They'd parted with several kisses, but Max's eyes had still been sad.

This morning, with the sun shining brightly through the

cloud-dotted sky, the need to make things better for Max was an itch in Tom's bones. He'd never felt like that for anyone.

When he got to the front, Lupé took his order. They looked at Tom, raised an eyebrow, and said, "One extremely large cappuccino with an extra shot and a dusting of cinnamon sugar to go?"

Tom coughed a laugh. "Yeah, that'll work." He handed over his card, and Lupé called out the order and rang him up.

"How's Max?" They had a knowing smile. They'd watched that first day, when everything had gone down.

"Super good. Amazingly good."

"Sounds like someone's in love!" Lupé fanned their face. "Not that I blame you."

Tom tried to stammer a response. Love? No. He... *Shit*.

Lupé handed him his drink. Tom gave a farewell salute with the mug and hightailed it out of the shop.

The coffee was good, hot, and reminded Tom of Max.

Love? Shit. He wasn't going to think about that.

When he got to work, he threw himself into email, then client meetings, then research for his court dates. Work kept him sharp and focused and far away from the word Lupé had uttered.

He managed not to think of that interaction the rest of the week, nor much over the weekend with Max, which was quiet and sedate for them. They were both exhausted from the week and Max had piles of grading to do, so they spent the majority of the time in Max's house, with Tom napping on the couch and surfing the internet while Max worked.

During a break in Max's grading, they ended up talking board games, and they went old school, with Max breaking out an old backgammon set. They were pretty evenly matched, but Tom eked out a win in the end, and a deep part of him was shocked when Max was perfectly fine with that.

"I still get to beat you, nonetheless." His smile was wicked. "But I'm going to make you wait a little for that."

Tom laughed. "Oh, so there *is* punishment for winning, then." He curled up in Max's arms on the couch.

Their conversation drifted from favorite games to hobbies, and Tom confessed he really didn't have any. "I used to sketch, but I was never good enough to make a career out of it, and once I was in law school, I didn't have the time. I keep thinking of asking Will for some tips on getting back into it."

"Why haven't you?"

Tom shrugged. "Inertia, I guess? Also, I'm a little afraid people will ask to see my art if I make some. It's closer to the bone. More personal. Or it was."

Max kissed the side of Tom's neck. "You don't have to show anyone. It could be yours alone."

Tom's heart twisted, but without pain, a very odd feeling. A moment later, he realized that the emotion was gratitude—that Max had both offered support and signaled that he'd respect Tom's privacy.

They were friends. Truly and deeply.

Tom relaxed into Max's arms. "Thanks for saying that. Maybe I'll stop by Kramer's Art Supply next week."

Later that evening, they'd indulged in playful spanking, some domination, and sex that sizzled through Tom's body, the two of them enjoying each other thoroughly.

There were more cinnamon rolls and fresh sourdough bread.

The latter made Tom's heart flip over. "Is this the starter?"

Max had nodded. "Lots of history in this bread."

Tasted sublime, too.

Max fiddled with his plate. "Do you think I should take a loaf to Jeremy's Thanksgiving bash?"

That jogged Tom's memory. The first game he'd gone to,

when he'd met Max's colleagues. God, Thanksgiving was in... three weeks? "Everyone would love it. It's probably the best bread in Laurelsburg."

"Would you like to come with me?" Those gray eyes met Tom's gaze.

A strange, unsettled feeling zipped through Tom. "Yeah, I would.

Max's smile had been brighter than the sun.

Before Tom headed home on Sunday, they'd made plans for the following weekend. "I enjoyed this one, but I'd like to offer you more time downstairs. Take things further than we have before."

He'd said yes to that, too. He'd loved the kink they'd done, but more and further would be welcome too. He'd left excited at the prospects, head full of the delicious, painful, and wicked things Max might do.

Come Monday morning, Tom couldn't shake a mix of trepidation and elation that kept rattling around inside him, like the moment before a rock concert started, or that first glimpse of the ocean over the dunes on a perfect summer day. Both Max's smile and Lupé's comment came back to him at odd times, and even sitting still, Tom felt like he was tripping, catching his foot on some unseen bump in the pavement and pitching forward into something he didn't know or understand.

Not a great start to the week.

He shoved all of it aside, burying himself in work. He demurred when Aaron quizzed him about Max, which Aaron didn't like, but after the third time in two days, he let it go. The looks and the frowns were there, though. The worry. All because of Maxime Demers.

Tom had no idea what to do. Everything was great with Max. The sex, the kink, the friendship. Yet when he thought too long, when he sat in quiet for an extra minute, Max was there in

his head. That gorgeous smile. His laugh. The ripples of
pleasure when Max was moving inside him. How his hair fell
over his forehead when he was cooking. Every time Tom
thought about Max, he got warm and cold and his mind wanted
to do cartwheels.

When he'd crushed on Max, he hadn't been in Tom's mind
like *this*.

This was definitely something other than friend with hefty
side of kink and sex. They were dating. People saw them as a
couple. They were a couple. Every minute Tom spent with Max
was a joy.

He'd said yes to being Max's Thanksgiving dinner date.
Mere weeks ago, that would have been completely out of
character for Tom. His past Doms weren't anyone he wanted to
be around.

By Thursday, Tom had a horrible suspicion about his
emotional state. He checked Aaron's calendar, which was
booked solid for the rest of the day, and sent him an IM.

I don't suppose you'd be free at all this evening?

There wasn't a reply right away, and Tom bit his lip. Damn.
Aaron must be deep in the thick of it. He got back to his own
work.

There were a bunch of snippy letters from the lawyers
representing his clients' exes and several emails from clients
complaining about exes, and one particularly nastygram from
one of the exes that was such a wrong move on the bozo's part.
The court didn't take kindly when you threatened, even
vaguely, the opposition's lawyer. He forwarded that one on to
the opposition and to the judge who had been chosen to hear
the case.

Only then did Tom's IM flash.

I could be. Is this work, or personal?

Personal. About Max.

Shit. Good or bad?

I don't actually know? That's why I want to talk to you.

Aaron owed him this much, especially after the whole Will-and-Kelly fiasco. That had turned into the best thing for Aaron in years.

Okay. How about Sarah B's? Say meet at 6:30? I'll even buy you one of those really expensive beers you like.

Yeah, Tom was probably going to need one of those.

Thanks, man. I owe you.

Nah, this one is on me.

They exchanged a few more messages about work—turned out Aaron had another particularly hard case coming up—then both got back to their jobs for the rest of the day.

―――――

THERE WAS enough time after Tom's last client meeting to run back to his apartment and change into something casual for beers and dinner at Sarah B's. The bar was a bit of a hike from his apartment—away from Main Street and out toward the highway, tucked into the interface between the houses students rented and the older residential part of town. Sarah B's was popular with everyone, due to its good food and large selection of imported beers from everywhere, including Tom's favorite beer haven, Belgium.

The higher prices meant that it wasn't too packed with college kids, but it was crowded enough. Tom got a table in the back and texted Aaron to tell him where he was.

Aaron appeared about five minutes later, holding two glasses. One was a regular pint glass with something that looked like a lager, while the other was a chalice with a lovely golden liquid.

"They had one of those high-test beers I can't pronounce on tap, so I got you one," he said.

Tom took the chalice. "You fucking lifesaver, you."

"Don't say that yet." Aaron wagged a finger at Tom. "You still have to spill your guts and I'm not always known for being benevolent."

Yeah, that was one thing about Aaron, he could cut like a razor. Tom was either going to receive good advice or his ass handed to him.

A server came and took their order for dinner—both burgers —and Aaron leaned back. "So, what's going on with you and your cinnamon roll?"

"He might be too good, too pure for my world?"

Aaron rolled his eyes. "Come on, dude, don't go there."

Tom took a big sip of his beer, which was about twice as alcoholic as Aaron's, so he needed to pace himself. Right now, he needed his brain looser. "Everything's fine between us. He's —my god, I can't describe it. The sex is out of this world. The kink is phenomenal. He's done things to me no one else has and wants to do more unspeakable things to me." He waved a hand. "You know, like Kelly."

Aaron chuckled. "If you're comparing him to Kelly, I don't see an issue here. Sounds like he's ideal for you."

"He *bakes*, Aaron. I told him about the cinnamon roll thing, and the fucker *made* me cinnamon rolls. Best ones I've ever had. Then he took me into his basement and—" Tom stopped. "Let's say it was quite the experience."

"Mmmhmm. I'm still not seeing the issue. He's a keeper."

Maybe? Tom didn't know. "Whenever I think about him, my insides twist into knots, but not in a horrible way. I think I might be in love with him. Other people seem to think I am."

"Of course you're fucking in love with him!" Then Aaron got a strange look. "Tom...have you been in love before?"

"No! I don't even know if I am right now. I've never —*literally*, not figuratively—felt like this about anyone. It's like friendship that someone's overlaid with, well, icing, I guess."

"Huh." Aaron crossed his arms. "Cinnamon roll Dom. Aromantic sub."

"Except if I'm aromantic, I shouldn't be falling in love. I guess I could be demi, but does that really matter?" The beer started Tom's brain buzzing. He sat back. "Maybe I should break up with him." The very thought made his whole body ache.

Aaron sat up. "Thomas Allan Cedric, don't you fucking *dare* break up with him! Not over this!" He waved his hand wildly, which almost caught the edge of plate the server was about to place in front of him. "Oh fuck, I'm really sorry. My friend's being a dipstick, and I have to yell at him."

She gave Aaron a pasted-on smile. "That's okay." Then she placed a burger in front of Tom. "Careful, the plate is hot."

The plates were always hot. Tom thanked her, then turned back to Aaron. "Look, I've never labeled myself other than gay and submissive. You know that."

Aaron nodded.

"But what if this changes me? What if I'm in love, and it makes me a different person? I haven't felt the same since I started seeing him. The whole 'friend with benefits' idea is fucking amazing, and he's a friend and a lover and—"

Tom wanted it to go on forever.

"Oh my god." Arron rubbed his temple. "I should charge you by the hour, counselor." He held up a finger as Tom was about to protest. "No, you've had your time. Let me take mine."

Goddamn fucking lawyers. Tom ate a fry and glared at Aaron.

Aaron took a swig of beer and leaned forward. "We've known each other, what, six years now? And since the day you saw the French professor—"

"French-Canadian."

Aaron balled up a napkin and threw it at Tom's head. It didn't have enough weight and hit his chest instead. "I should have brought your fucking stress ball. You going to let me finish?" Real, honest anger there.

Tom nodded sheepishly.

"You've wanted Max since you saw him. I kept telling you to get his number. To talk to him. To even fucking say hi to him in passing, because he's universes better and kinder and more together than any of the jerks you've dated. I'm not going to have to fucking pretend to be a DEA agent to get him off your back."

Oof. Greg. Tom slid down in his chair at that memory. He'd tried to take a break from men after that, but after a rough court case, he'd been back on Kinkbook.

Aaron nodded, as if reading Tom's mind. "Dude, I've been your shoulder. I've had your back. And I fucking *told* you that you should date Max Demers."

Tom couldn't keep silent anymore. "I *am* dating Max Demers." Even saying it made his heart flop over in his chest and excitement slam through him.

"Yet here you are complaining that the dude is *too good* for you and maybe you should *break up* with him, all because you have no fucking clue what to do now that you've fallen in love."

"I don't even know if I *am* in love!"

"You remember when Will and Kelly came into the office, and you told me Kelly was gooey-eyed over Will and me?"

Oh. Shit. Tom nodded apprehensively.

Aaron got that feral grin he did when he was about to eviscerate the opposing counsel. "You look *exactly* like that whenever you see or mention Max. Exactly. It's love, Tom, and I bet if you don't run away from your damn feelings because he's *nice* to you, you'll figure that out in time." He sat back, took a swig of beer and picked up his burger. "No further questions, your honor."

Ouch. Tom folded his arm, stared at his own burger, and tried not to bite his best friend's head off. Especially since Aaron was right. "Fuck you, Taylor."

"Not part of our contract," he said.

Goddamn it. Tom uncurled, drank another swallow of beer, and tried his burger. Juicy. Tasty. Too bad his stomach was a mess. He put it down.

Aaron eyed him. "Oh, did you want me to tell you to break up with him?"

"No." Tom spat the word out, then groaned and said it again without any anger. "No." He picked up a fry. "I guess I wanted you to talk some sense into me."

"Well, I'm *trying*. You're not listening."

Except he was. "What if it's not love? What if *he's* not in love?"

"Oh my god, dude. He made you cinnamon rolls."

Yeah, okay. "Point, counselor."

Aaron smirked and went back to his burger.

Tom downed a few more fries, then some more of his burger as his stomach unknotted itself. Aaron was right, of course, about the past. He'd been there for all Tom's greatest dating mistakes. He'd also ribbed him continually about his crush on Max.

"I don't know what to do," he said. "Honestly. I don't want what I have with Max to end, but I have no idea what I'm supposed to *do*."

"I have some advice, but I don't think you're going to want to hear it."

Tom lifted an eyebrow and glared across the table.

Aaron's lip twitched up. "Okay, but I warned you."

"Out with it, Taylor."

He grabbed his beer. "Talk to your cinnamon roll. All the shit you told me? Tell him. I bet you the hundred bucks you won from me earlier this year that he'll be grateful and charming, and you'll live happily ever after."

"Oh my god." Tom rolled his eyes. "This isn't a fantasy."

"Nope. It's real life. You've found a good guy. Fucking *talk to him*, rather than running away."

Tom mulled that over while he finished his dinner. Shit, Aaron was right. His advice was sound, so sound that Tom would've said the same to someone else in the same situation. "Fine. But I'm not betting anything."

"That's because you fucking know I'm right."

Bastard. "Whatever." He couldn't keep the smile from his lips, even as annoyed as he was.

Aaron laughed. "Dude, you're impossible sometimes."

Yet Max wanted him. Tom struggled with that thought, struggled with everything swirling in him, then gave up. "I'll talk to him. I won't break up." He paused. "We're getting together this weekend."

"Of course you are. You've gotten together every weekend. And some weeknights."

"You keeping count?"

Aaron waved a hand. "I don't have to. It's easy to spot. Gooey-eyed."

Tom found the balled-up napkin and threw it back. Sadly, it still didn't have good aerodynamics, and bounced off the top of what was left of Aaron's burger, then rolled into his lap.

"Hey!"

"You started it."

"Technically, you started it with that stress ball of yours."

"Ugh." Tom grabbed his beer. "If you weren't so infuriating..."

Aaron mimicked picking up an old phone. "Oh, hi Mr. Kettle. Let me put Mr. Pot on the line for you." He held out an imaginary receiver for Tom.

"Better not be the DEA."

Aaron lost it, and a moment later Tom joined him in laughing. When they quieted down, Tom sighed. "Thank you."

"Hey, that's what friends are for."

Aaron munched on a fry, then spoke again. "You don't need to worry about Max changing you. He already has. You're happy. More so than I've seen since I met you. That's not a problem, Tom."

That was something to digest. The longer what Aaron said rolled around in Tom's head, the more it made sense. He felt *different*, but not in a bad way.

They finished up their meals and Tom footed the bill, despite Aaron saying he'd pay. "Dude, I dragged you out here to yell at me. The least I can do."

Aaron insisted he'd call Will for a ride, and they'd drop Tom off at his place. "You're a little blitzed, dude."

He was. Tired, too. On Saturday, he'd have to fess up to Max about his feelings.

Fucking hell.

Aaron was correct. This was the only course of action. But still, fucking *hell*.

Didn't take long for Will to swing by, and even less time for them to drop Tom off. As he rode the elevator to his floor, apprehension kicked in.

Max cared. Tom was absolutely was sure of that. That was one thing—dealing with Tom's emotions was quite another.

Maybe he should have taken Aaron's bet, because he really wanted to lose that hundred dollars.

CHAPTER FOURTEEN

MAX'S WEEK was a whirlwind of grading, lectures, and panicked students. They were closing in on the end of the semester, with final papers and exams looming on the horizon. He'd had to remind several undergrads that they weren't in a great place, grade-wise.

He hated that, disliked his students not succeeding. He endeavored to give them enough opportunity not to fail his classes, worked hard to make sure they didn't, and yet there were always a few who didn't do any of the work.

That gutted Max. There was only so much he could do before he had to mark assignments as zero. Without any coursework, a failing grade was inevitable.

Monday, one of that group had slinked in during his office hours, and they'd had a frank discussion about what the student would need to do to pass the class.

"But what can I do to get a B? I need at least a B to keep my scholarship."

Max cringed. Fuck, *this* he hated more. The answer to that was, "come to class, turn in the assignments, and take the quizzes" and it was too late. "You're not going to get a B, I'm afraid. The best you'll be able to do is a C, but you'll have to ace the final paper."

Then he'd had to deal with the five stages of the student's grief, cycling through from denial to acceptance. Anger, of course, was the worst, since they always lashed out at Max for being a poor professor.

He wasn't, but the biting comments of his students hurt.

By the time Max was done, all he wanted was to get the fuck off campus and retreat to the safety of his home. Though lately, the space that had been a balm seemed a little...empty.

He wanted to come home to Tom. Didn't know if that would ever happen. Tom was so nervous about commitment.

No, that wasn't correct. Tom was terrified of anyone loving him. Max had been happy enough with their boyfriend arrangement that was closer to friends with benefits, or play partners with a friendship, or however Tom needed their relationship to be framed. That didn't stop Max from longing for Tom's company on a much more regular basis.

Like now, when he was curled up on his couch and wanting to be held. By Tom.

They did send texts back and forth, but lately, Tom's replies had been shorter than normal, so Max had refrained from texting about how awful his day had been.

There were boundaries for a reason, after all. Tom didn't need his issues.

He held on to the memory of the past weekend, of Tom in his arms, their talks, and his voice. The next weekend would come soon enough.

On Tuesday, Max ran into Jeremy in the faculty dining room, and they shared a table. The meal was uninspired and the coffee not strong, but Max was glad for the company. He told Jeremy that Tom would be joining him for the Thanksgiving party.

Jeremy beamed at him. "I knew it! He's got you good."

Max shrugged. "I've dated people before."

"Not like this guy," Jeremy said. "He's interested in *you*, not just your looks or..." He waved a hand.

Was that true? The start of his and Tom's relationship had been entirely based on sexual attraction and kink. That still comprised a large part of how they related, but Tom seemed interested in the skating and the hockey. He didn't resent Max's grading. Enjoyed his cooking and wanted to know about his past. Tom had also shared bits of himself with Max he doubted anyone else knew. His interest in art. Their long-running discussions about podcasts.

"We're friends and we're dating," Max said.

"You're more than friends," Jeremy countered.

Max shook his head. "I hate that phrase. Friendship is divine. Full of deep trust. Maybe it's not sexual most of the time, but it's intense and strong, and can break your heart all the same."

Jeremy sat back, pursed his lips, and nodded. "Yeah, okay. I can see that." He pushed a cube of beef through sauce. "What I mean is that I think you're in love with him."

Max huffed a laugh. "I am, yeah." For better or for worse.

Wednesday morning, Tom texted him.

Hey. Can't do much Friday night. Maybe dinner? A client wants to meet Saturday morning, so it'll have to be an early night.

There was an unhappy face emoji after that. Max looked at the pile of papers on his office desk he still had to grade.

We can meet for dinner, or just get together on Saturday, once you're done. I'm swamped with grading and finals prep. Students are starting to want extra office hours.

Ooof. I'd put all that end of semester stuff out of my head.

Max smiled at that.

Sorry, you're dating an academic. It's burnt into my life.

But you get summers off.

Ech. Mostly. I teach a summer course sometimes. And I get a chance to work on my research.

There was a bit of a pause before the phone showed Tom typing again.

You haven't told me about your research.

Max sat back in his chair. It'd never occurred to him Tom might be interested in that. Jeremy's words from the other day came back, that Tom was interested in Max as a *person.*

Would you like to hear about it? I focus on the intersection of urban and rural areas with regards to the Appalachian dialect.

Sounds cool. Maybe this weekend?

Max nodded to himself.

Sure.

What time on Saturday?

Why don't you come over when you're finished? No worries about time or anything like that.

I can do that.

A student knocked on Max's door. He looked up and caught the anguish in her face. "Rachel. Have a seat."

Have to go. Student meeting. See you Saturday.

Then Max silenced his phone and set it face down off to the side.

Rachel perched on the edge of Max's guest chair, looking distraught. She was one of his better students, or had been until a few weeks ago.

"I'm really sorry, Professor Demers! I just... I can't..." Tears welled in her eyes.

Max pushed his tissue box toward her. "Tell me as much as you want about what's going on, and let's see if we can't come up with a solution, eh? All's not lost."

She took one of the tissues, blotted her eyes, and nodded.

Once he'd worked through Rachel's issues, both with his class and beyond, he shut the door to his office and leaned his forehead against it. He hoped the rest of the week would even out, for everyone, but another night alone loomed for him.

The interest Tom had shown in his research sparked a heat in Max, though. He had no idea how to return the favor.

But by Thursday, he had an idea, and on Friday, he'd decided that this weekend, do he damnedest to make it the best possible time Tom could have.

———

TOM'S SATURDAY client meeting wasn't as bad as he'd feared. Often the harder, more painful divorce cases were the ones he first heard on Saturdays, but his client, a woman about his age, was no-nonsense and didn't come with a huge heartbreak.

"We're not good for each other," she said. "He wants out, too, but Mom always said to get a lawyer rather than go by good will, you know?"

Tom agreed. Sure, there were couples that split in a kind, easy manner, but they were rare, even when both parties wanted divorced. Splitting up often brought out the spite.

He sat down with her, walked her though the steps, and got an idea of what she wanted, then drew up a small plan for the information she needed before they dug into things.

All in all, the meeting took about an hour and a half, then he locked up the office, headed home, and stripped off his suit.

He had no idea what to wear to Max's. He'd never cared with other Doms, because clothing wasn't important, as he'd always been ordered to strip at the door. But with Max—

They talked. Ate. Bantered. Max might order him to strip or undress Tom himself.

Time for new habits. He was going to tell Max how he felt. That deserved some care in clothing, regardless of how he'd be dressed when that happened.

He chose jeans, a simple blue sweater over an old college T-shirt, and his hiking boots. There'd been talk of snow over the weekend, and the last thing he needed was to fall on some slick pavement.

Then he packed an overnight bag with a change of clothes, his own pair of flannel pants, underwear, and his travel kit. He texted Max before he left.

On my way.

A few moments later, the reply came.

When you get here, come in. Door's unlocked. I'm in the kitchen.

Tom's stomach growled in anticipation. He didn't know which he wanted more, whatever Max was cooking up in his kitchen, or whatever torture he'd dreamed up in that basement pub of his.

He walked to Max's, rather than jog or run outright. Patience was a good thing, and the walk helped center him and calm the fear that wove through his heart.

Part of him didn't believe he was seeing Max, that he might be in love with Max. After all those years of pining after the unobtainable, he was going to walk right into Max's house as his friend and lover.

Then he pushed through the gate, bounded up the front stairs, and opened the door. "Hey, I'm here!"

The house smelled heavenly, full of spices overlain with the aroma of butter and sugar. "Kitchen!" Max called.

Tom shut and locked the front door. Last thing he wanted was the unexpected arrival of anyone. He hung up his coat, kicked off his shoes, and dropped his duffel by the stairs. Then he padded to the kitchen.

Max was in his element, with an apron on over his jeans and green Henley, sleeves pushed up to his elbows, hair pulled back into a ponytail. Flour dotted the apron and he held a mixing bowl and had the widest damn grin. He looked like a manic not-so-pixie dream professor.

There was that tumble in Tom's chest again.

"Hello," Max said.

"Hey." Tom didn't know what to do. Kiss Max? Have a seat at the kitchen table? Offer to help? Ever since he'd talked to Aaron, he'd felt off kilter.

Kink was easy. This was not kink.

He stood in the kitchen doorway and wavered. "Um..."

Max rolled his eyes. "Come here and kiss me."

Tom went, and when their lips met, it was all he could do not to take the bowl away so he could take Max into his arms. The kiss lingered, and Max stole another when they came up for air.

"I'm glad to see you," Max said, and Tom believed him. Truly believed him.

"Me too." He peered into the bowl. "What *is* that?" The bowl held a deep brown paste that smelled like chocolate. "Is that fudge?"

"Chocolate filling," Max said. He nodded over at the counter, on which strips of dough were laid out, along with a smaller bowl of something that looked like melted butter and a brush. "I'm making dessert."

Tom had no idea what that was going to become. "It smells good in here."

"Thanks." Max gestured to the table. "Why don't you have a seat? This is going to take me another fifteen minutes to finish. Then it needs to rest. Then I'll put it in the oven while we're eating." He stirred the chocolate more. "Tell me about how the rest of your week went?"

Tom liked—loved this part. The friendship. The bond.

He sat down and chuckled. "Well, my ass is completely unbruised. As is my back."

"Oh, good." That came out darker than the chocolate Max was mixing.

Tom coughed a laugh. "Not much to say about the week, really. Today's meeting went well." He launched into describing his workdays, skipping over his dinner with Aaron. "There's one particular judge who likes to move hearings around. I ended up having to call some clients and explain what was happening."

"They can do that?"

"Pretty much." Tom shrugged. "Sometimes we ask for other dates, and sometimes the opposition does. Sometimes scheduling conflicts happen, other times it's part of the game."

Max grunted. "Sounds frustrating."

Tom waved the words away. "I'm used to it." He cast his mind back over the week for anything interesting. "I stopped by Kramer's and bought some art supplies. Drawing pad. Pencils. That kind of stuff. There's some 'learn how to draw' videos on YouTube, and I thought I'd give it a try."

Max turned around, a spatula in his hand. "That's wonderful!" His smile was so huge, Tom's cheeks heated a little.

"Maybe, if I like something I do, I can show it to you?"

That broad smile shifted to a deeply serious expression. "I'd be honored."

Tom scrubbed the back of his head, ducking Max's gaze. There was that flutter in his heart again. "I also tried the salted caramel mocha latte at Bold Brew on Friday after Vann suggested it. Was good! Nice change of pace."

Max wrinkled his nose. "I'm likely the only person in existence who doesn't like salted caramel."

Tom gasped in mock outrage. "That's it. I guess we're through. I thought you were a man of taste."

That got him a laugh. "I *am* a man of taste. I greatly prefer sweet caramel to salted. Give me those bullseye candies and I'll lavish you with love and affection."

"That's the way to your heart?" He made a mental note to look up which candy Max meant.

"That, sparkling conversation, a good personality, and a

tight, spankable ass." Max paused. "Screaming during sex helps, too."

Tom shifted on the chair and sparks of heat sank into his stomach. "Do I scream?"

Max turned around and pegged Tom with the hottest damn stare. "Yes. Quite loudly when you're coming. It's succulent."

God, how Max could shift the mood with so few words. The urge to start stripping or kneeling hit hard. Except stripping was unhygienic in a working kitchen, and Tom didn't kneel. "Are you going to make me scream tonight?"

That got Tom a very sexy dark smile. "Wait and see."

After Max stuck an entire tray of what looked to be some kind of rolled pastry into the fridge, he dusted his hands on his apron. "I need to clean things here, then myself. Covered with flour isn't exactly a Dom look."

"Flour probably isn't great for the leather, but I'm sure you could make it work." Tom would take Max any way he could get him.

Max lips curled up. He beckoned with a finger. "Come here, then."

Oh, hell yes. Tom stood and crossed the kitchen to Max.

"You'll need to be occupied while I get myself ready, yes?"

Tom swallowed. "Sir?"

"I want to keep your mind on what's to come. We have several *hours* before dinner."

God, he was half hard already. "What do you want me to do?"

Max trailed a finger over Tom's jaw. "Downstairs on the bar, I've placed several items. Go there, strip out of this lovely sweater, and use those toys to play with yourself while I clean up. Two rules: you must be wearing at least two of the items when I join you, and you cannot come. Is that clear?"

Just like that, Tom was dropping into subspace. "The last part, yes, Sir. But the first?"

"You'll figure that out when you go downstairs."

Tom shivered and Max chuckled darkly. He leaned in and took Tom's mouth in a kiss that commanded and stripped Tom bare while fully clothed.

Afterward, Max nipped at Tom's lip, then spoke, a rumble to his voice. "Go, Tom. Do as I say."

"Yes, Sir." He took a few steps back, then headed to the basement stairs.

CHAPTER FIFTEEN

TOM HAD no idea what he'd find when his ventured into the basement. The lights were on but dim, giving the space a quiet glow. The air was warm, which was comforting since he'd be naked soon.

He approached the bar with a trepidation that wasn't relieved when he reached his destination. The items on the bar had him rock hard and full of lust, but what Max asked of him was going to be a feat.

He'd thought one of the objects would be cuffs, given the command to wear two of them, but none were. There were two different gags, a blindfold, a massager, a masturbator, a set of different sized silicone cock rings, clothespins, lube, and a thick dildo laying out on a paper towel. A box of condoms sat nearby. The dildo had been washed, but Tom suspected the condoms were there in case he'd prefer that.

A kinky picnic had been spread out, and all the items were enticing, though he wasn't sure he was ready for gags yet.

Over near the cross and rack, a small futon-style bed had been set up, complete with a sheet and pillows. Somewhere comfortable to play.

The soft sound of running water, and the clanking of dishes echoed from above.

Tom bit his lip and rubbed his pecs. Time to obey. He stripped, folded, and set his clothes on one of the stools, then scooped up all the toys and carried them to the futon. He came back for the lube and hesitated, contemplating the condoms, then decided to skip them. He didn't use them with his own toys, nor had Max used them with toys when they'd played together.

He loved the deviance of using a toy raw, and the one Max had chosen was too scrumptiously thick not to use.

Max *knew* him. That was evident from the items chosen. The dildo and the masturbator were easy—he owned similar. Cock rings were common. The other toys—those were on the edge of Tom's comfort, right where he liked to be. Max had used clamps on him, but Tom had never clamped anything on his own body. There were enough clothespins to be *creative*. He'd seen them clamped to balls and other sensitive flesh.

Tom took one up, used it on his finger, and winced. No. Not tonight.

Those he set aside, along with the cock rings. He preferred willpower to obey Max's order over the cockrings. Besides, he didn't like silicone rings. The blindfold and the gags were items of trust, though Tom would be the one to place them on himself. Still, he'd be unaware when Max entered the room, and that sent heat sparking through Tom.

Yes, then.

That left the two gags. One was a ball type, the other penetrative, with a dildo about as wide as two fingers, but not quite as long as his index. Tom had been gagged with the former type, but not the latter.

He hated being gagged. Doms always seemed to use that as

an excuse to overstep Tom's bounds, and then he couldn't object.

Here, he'd be fucking himself, though. He trusted Max. Maybe loved him.

In the end, he slipped the cock gag in his mouth and buckled it tight, his own dick hardening at the intrusion of his mouth and how he could lick and caress the cock with his tongue. Wasn't Max, but it was Max's toy, and that was nearly as good.

Tom lubed his ass and fingers and stretched himself open, prepped the dildo, and slipped the blindfold on.

Time to enjoy himself.

He was fucking himself hard with the dildo, groaning around the gag when the thick shaft hit him right, when Max sighed from nearby. "Now, isn't this a lovely sight."

Tom nearly lost hold of the toy.

"No," Max murmured. "Keep going. Show me how much you need it."

Hearing that voice and those words drove Tom's orgasm closer. He moaned and did as Max ordered, sliding the thick cock in and out of his hole, so aware of what he must look like with his ass speared and stretched wide. Gagged. Blindfolded. Cock hard and slick with lube. He whimpered and shuddered.

"Ah, no. Don't come. That's a pleasure I control, at least today and tomorrow."

He pressed his forehead against the mattress and tried hard to obey that command.

Max's warmth slid close to Tom's side. Then the sound of a vibrator came to life.

"Don't stop fucking yourself." Max's voice coasted over Tom like a silky caress. "And don't come." Then he pressed the vibrator against Tom's taint.

Tom shouted around the gag and thrust against the toy inside him.

"So sweet," Max murmured. "So wanton. You're lust incarnate, aren't you? Absolutely beautiful."

Tom closed his eyes and whimpered, but kept fucking himself even as Max teased and stroked him with the massager.

He didn't know how long the torment continued, too focused on staving off the orgasm that kept building, only that he was a moaning mess when Max relented and removed the vibrator.

Max stilled Tom's ministrations. "Don't pull that out, but let go."

Body a live wire, Tom groaned in frustration even as his mind soared.

Max coasted hands over Tom's sides, from his ribs to his hips, rocking him back but giving him no friction. "Your obedience is a treat, Tom. As is your body. I'm going to torment you. Make you beg before I let you near that orgasm you so want."

Tom lowered his head and panted around the gag, resigned to his fate. He loved when Max had him like this, riding on the painful edge of pleasure. Almost as good as being flogged.

With any luck, flogging would happen next.

"I'm tempted to leave that cock in you," Max said. "But I have other plans." He eased it out of Tom.

Tom could only groan as the fullness vanished, and even more than before, he ached to jack off and come. Finish what he'd started.

Max placed his hand on the small of Tom's back, his commanding voice all around Tom. "I want you to sit up, and when you're able, stand."

That took effort, and he wasn't graceful about it, not while gagged and blindfolded. Max walked him back toward to bar and sat him on one of the barstools, the leather cool against his lubed ass.

Max traced the outline of the gag. "I didn't think you'd choose this or the blindfold. I am so grateful you did. You look stunning gagged."

Tom shivered and groaned at those words.

"I'm glad you enjoyed that, too, but I need you to see what I'm offering you, and hear your answer, so I'm going to remove both."

Max unsnapped the gag first, and gently pulled it from Tom's mouth.

Tom took a deeper breath and licked his lips, tasting the silicone that had been in his mouth. "I hate gags," he whispered.

"Really?" Surprise there. "Why'd you choose it?"

Truth came easier when he didn't have to look into those gray eyes. "It's *your* gag, and I wanted to please you."

There was a low rumble from Max. "You did, very much so."

"I'd wear it again," Tom said. "For you."

Max's breathing hitched. "Tom. Thank you for that." The words were a caress. "Let me—"

There was a brush of warmth against Tom's hair, and the scent of Max's floral shower gel, then the blindfold slipped down and Tom blinked against brightness of the room.

Then *his* breath caught in his throat.

Max was in leather. Gloved hands, an open vest that exposed Max's glorious chest with its dark hair and darker treasure trail that led down to a leather jock covering his package. Leather boots, too, well blackened.

A picture of a Dom, so different from the sexy academic look, his expensive suits, or the sleek leather pants, shirt and vests he wore to demos or Mansion House.

Max got a devilish smile. "Not expecting this, eh?"

"Not from a nice Canadian boy." That came out before Tom could snatch it back, but Max laughed.

"Oh, I am that, too." Max traced a leather-clad finger over Tom's lips. "But not right now." His voice dipped low, and Tom shuddered.

Those fingers gripped Tom's jaw. "Would you like to wear more of my leather, Tom?"

God, yes. "Please."

The curl of those lips spread joy into Tom's soul, a heat unlike any other.

Max stroked Tom's chin, let go, and strode behind the bar. He pulled out a set of cuffs for Tom's wrists and ankles. "These, I believe, you're familiar with."

His limbs ached for them. He nodded.

Max then pulled out a leather chest harness, and pinpricks of energy showered Tom's whole body. He'd never worn one, but had seen such harnesses at demos and parties, and had longed to be in one.

Before Max spoke, Tom blurted out, "Yes."

"Eager thing, aren't you? Perhaps not so much for the next one." Max placed a simple leather band with snaps on the bar.

It took Tom a moment to realize what he was looking at. "Is that a cock ring?" So different from the silicone rings Max had set out before.

"Yes, and I would love to see it on you."

Max's leather tight around the base of his cock, coupled with his commands. Tom bit his lip. Leather was sensual and tempting.

Max tipped his head. "It's quick to remove if you find it too much."

"I would love to wear it for you." Those words tasted right on Tom's tongue.

"Excellent. I look forward to strapping that on."

Tom shifted on the stool. So did he.

"And lastly..." Max pulled out a collar with several rings on it. "This."

Tom sat straight up, electricity running all through him. Yes. No. *Yes*. He met Max's gaze. Didn't say a word.

"I don't do collaring ceremonies." Max's voice was soft. "But I find collars handy, and I want to see my leather around your throat while we're playing."

A fire raged in Tom's blood, even as a different warmth spread in his chest. Max claiming him. Wrapping leather over his neck. He could almost *feel* the tightness.

Max touched the collar. "I know it carries weight. You can say no. You can always say no."

When Max's gaze locked with him, Tom could barely breathe.

"Do you want me to put my collar around your throat, Tom?"

Tom swallowed and stared at the collar. His to claim or reject.

He lifted his head, held it high, and stared at Max. "Yes, Sir."

Those two words had a profound effect on Max. His lips parted, and Tom saw desire sweep over him. Max dropped a hand inside the leather jock and fondled himself. His voice was deep and full of gravel. "Good."

Tom's breath hitched. Max was jacking off in anticipation of collaring *him*. The urge to kneel hit him again. Would be easy. Slide off the stool to the floor.

Max had made it clear that Tom never had to kneel. Maybe that's what made the idea safe.

When Tom's knees hit the floor, Max gasped. Not loudly, but shock etched itself over Max, and he moved, rounding the bar to stand before Tom.

Tom looked up and met Max's emotion-filled gaze. "Sir."

Max's lips parted, then he cupped his hand under Tom's chin, the leather warm against his skin. "A treasure," he murmured.

"Yours," Tom said. "Make me earn your collar."

Max stroked a thumb over Tom's chin, then pressed it against his lips. Tom closed his eyes, tipped his head back and opened against the pressure, tasting the smooth leather against his tongue.

"Oh, Tom." Soft, soft voice, full of gravity and lust. "You've earned so much more than my collar." He slid his thumb out.

Tom blinked his eyes back open. Max stared down, his smile tender, a contrast from the dark leather he wore. Maybe not, though. All Max, that smile, the leather. The pain and pleasure he could give. His tenderness.

Max lifted the collar from the bar, leaned down, and wrapped it around Tom's throat.

The smell was heady, leather combined with Max's sweat, and arousal, and the trace of his lilac shower gel. Masculine. Gentle. Hard.

Then Max drew the collar tight against Tom's skin, and buckled it on.

He belonged to Max.

Their gazes met, and there was fire in Max's, an inferno that burned Tom to his bones. Max slipped a finger through the front ring, and tugged up, forcing Tom to stand. Then Max devoured his mouth, dragging their bodies together. He gripped Tom's ass, fingers digging in hard, and trapped Tom's cock against the leather that covered Max's.

He groaned into Max, and grasped Max's vest. He wanted Max to fuck and flog and use him until all the world was gone and only they existed.

Tom wanted Max after, too. The laughter and the touches,

the gentleness and light. The food, the caring, and the hockey. That burning desire frightened Tom more than anything. He needed Max like air.

Max broke the kiss. "Time for the rest of my leather on you, Tom."

His very soul ached. "Yes, Sir."

Max had him sit. Good thing, because Tom wasn't sure how much longer his legs would hold him up. The cuffs were next, each lovingly placed with kisses to each pulse point of the wrists. "Beautiful, lovely Tom," he whispered.

Tom wanted to be on his knees, wanted Max's cock in his mouth. Wanted to moan for him.

Max dropped to *his* knees to strap on the ankle cuffs, and that was a sight. Those thick thighs, corded with muscle, and his package prominent, but hidden by leather. His hair cascading over his shoulders and back.

Tom needed Max inside him, wanted to be stretched and filled by him. God, he hoped that happened. Tonight. Tomorrow. Both.

"Spread your legs, Tom. Show yourself to me."

He couldn't help the whimper as he obeyed.

Max purred, then kissed the inside of Tom's thigh, his hair brushing over Tom's dick.

"Oh god." Tom clamped his hands around the edge of the stool, and tried not to come from those silky, teasing strands.

Max laughed, then kissed the other thigh. "Like my hair, do you?" he murmured against Tom's skin.

"I fucking love your hair." That burst out of Tom. "Sir."

A chuckle, then Max buckled each cuff on.

Pulling on the chest harness was less erotic, until Max took each of Tom's nipples and rolled them until Tom was arching off the stool.

"You're too hard for the cock ring now." Amusement in Max's voice.

"You could make me come." Tom looked up at Max.

"I could," Max said. "Or I could order you to sit exactly like that while I set up things in the other room."

Tom blinked. "What other room?"

The answer to that question was a sly look and a smile. Max slid back behind the bar and snatched up several items—Tom couldn't see what—then opened a plain door to the right of the bar. Max vanished behind it, the door clicked closed, and Tom was alone at the bar.

Curiosity flooded into him. He'd assumed that led to storage or utilities. Figured the door on the other side of the basement did too, since none of those things were visible.

Light shone from under the door Max had entered, and he wasn't quick to come out. What *was* behind Door Number Two?

The time Tom had to ponder that felt like *hours*. He kept his legs open wide, and the air—while not cold—was cool enough to quell the excitement in his cock.

The door cracked open, and Max slid back into the room. "That's better." He picked up the last piece of leather on the bar. "On your feet, Tom."

Tom stood, then gasped when Max took his balls and cock in one hand, lifted them and circled the leather strap around the base. Just as quickly, the strap was pulled tight and snapped shut.

Tom panted against the pressure and Max's touch. No pain, but he knew exactly what was there. Like the leather around his throat and across his chest, awareness flooded with each breath and every twitch of muscle.

Max nuzzled Tom's neck and lazily stroked his cock. "How's that?"

"Fuck," Tom murmured. "Oh god." Perfect. Horrible and *perfect*.

The chuckle that rolled off Max vibrated down Tom. "I told you I enjoy cock and ball torture."

"And orgasm denial," Tom said.

Max skimmed lips over Tom's shoulder. "That too." He drew back. "Another choice for you. Crop or cane?"

Tom bit his lip to keep from saying both, because that would be too much. Then he waffled some more, because he couldn't choose. "I—your choice, Sir. I enjoy them both."

"Then the crop. I can work both sides of your lovely body with it."

Oh. Yes. Good.

His reaction must have been written into his body, because Max's smile deepened. "You *are* a pain slut, aren't you?"

He was. Pain, the pleasure of it ripping through his mind, was what grounded him. Kept him on track. The price, though, had been assholes.

Then Max had bought him coffee.

"It's better with you," Tom said. "Everything's better with you."

Max took hold of the ring in the collar again, dragged Tom forward. But this kiss was sweet and belied how much devil rested in Max. A nip at the end drove *that* home.

"Rack," Max said.

When Max pulled the collar, Tom stumbled forward after Max.

He didn't mind. Had any other man led him on a collar, he'd have safeworded and left. This wasn't humiliation, though. Far from it. This was private, for them alone.

When they reached the rack, Max let him go. "Please don't do that in public," Tom said.

Max turned, shock and worry written on his face. "Are you..."

"Here is fine. I like it here. But—"

Max let out a breath. "For us only, then. I promise."

That was enough. Trust. Caring. He could spend the rest of his life with this man.

That ripped through Tom. There it was. "Oh."

Another very concerned look. "Tom, are you okay?" Weight in those words.

He nodded. "Yeah. I—hang me in your rack and beat me until I can't think?"

Max took Tom's face between his hands. "That would be my pleasure."

This kiss crumpled Tom's legs, but Max caught him around the waist, then took another sip of Tom's soul with those lips of his.

"Are you swooning for me?" A murmur, halfway between amused and delighted.

"You kiss too good."

That got him a laugh, then Max pulled him upright. "Arms up, Tom. That'll keep you on your feet."

He did as ordered, and Max hung him from chains on the rack, then chained his ankles too, spreading his legs wide. Vulnerable. All for Max. He met those gray eyes. "Do your worst, Sir."

"Unfortunately for you, I plan to do my very *best*." Max smacked Tom hard on the ass, then headed to the bar.

Oh, this was going to hurt so damn good.

———

MAX'S HEAD and heart whirled. From the kneeling, to Tom's profound look, to the request not to be led by the collar in public, Max didn't know what to make of it all. Tom's plea for pain, however, was true and strong, and he could give Tom that.

Later, they'd need to talk and untangle things. Emotions, expectations. Where this relationship was heading.

Behind the bar, he opened the cabinet that contained his crops and floggers and drew out his favorite, one with a single band of red leather wound with all the black around the handle. It fit perfectly in his hand, and he could flick it with the utmost precision. He intended to do that, all over Tom's body.

When he returned, he studied Tom's splendid back and ass, and chose his target. While the ass was the obvious and most delectable target, Max flicked a blow at his left shoulder blade, then another at his right, then one on both of Tom's thighs.

Tom's reaction was divine. The gasp, the dance, the rattle of the chains, then the low moan of "fuck."

Perfect. Once more Max avoided ass, raining blows on Tom's thighs again, and on his upper back. Same delightful response. He paused to give Tom enough time to breathe and relax before he laid into him on his thighs and finally on his ass.

Tom hissed, yelped, and cursed, and those sounds, especially when Tom started begging Max—to stop, to keep going—sent heat into Max's core and drew out that dark joy. He *loved* this, the flick of the crop, the slap against flesh, the mark left behind, and especially Tom's throaty cries.

Before him, Tom was stretched out, in his leather, chained to his rack, entirely Max's to use until they were done, or Tom said otherwise. He relished the power he'd been handed. The trust. Desire burned through Max as he brought up marks on Tom's body, as Tom danced and shouted and begged.

Max laid out a hard blow to Tom's ass, and Tom rose on his toes, keening in pain.

That was so pretty, Max did it a second time.

Tom arched his back and sobbed. "Oh god, please!"

Stepping in, Max wrapped an arm around Tom, and caught a loop on his collar. "Please, what, Tom?" He pressed his leather-covered dick hard against Tom's ass.

That got him a high moan. "Please...more, Sir. I need...you."

Needed *Max*. He kissed Tom's shoulder. "Shall I delight your front?"

A whimper. "Anything. Just, take me there?"

Tom was such a masochist, maybe more so than he was submissive, and so complementary to Max's needs. He indulged in a hard bite to Tom's shoulder, in one of his favorite spots, and Tom keened under him.

He wanted to make Tom gasp and scream forever. Such pleasure. Such wanton desire.

Max drew back. Deep love for Tom danced at the corner of his mind and tangled with his sadism and his need to give Tom everything he wanted, including pain. He rounded to Tom's front and found those wide dark eyes staring at him. Tom's lips were open in blatant desire, and Max traced his lips before plunging two gloved fingers into that tempting mouth. Even through the leather, he felt the heat of Tom's mouth and the vibration of his moan.

"That mouth of yours was made for fucking, wasn't it?" Max worked his fingers in and out of Tom's lips, while Tom sucked and licked and moaned around them. "Want that pretty gag back, Tom? Need a cock to suck on while I mark you and make you fly?" He withdrew his fingers.

"Yeah." A heady sound there. "Need my holes plugged, Sir."

He caught Tom's chin. "Ass, too?"

Dark eyes met his, full of desperation. "Please. I—need it."

He should have spoken to Tom much sooner. But the past was the past, and the future theirs to made. "You're delectable, Tom. I'll give you what you need."

He let go, hung the crop on a hook he had on the side of the frame, and crossed to the bar to prep one of his larger anal plugs, get lube, and reclaim the gag with the dick. The plug, he placed behind Tom. He wanted Tom's mouth full when he slid the plug home.

The moan would be *exquisite*.

Before he gagged Tom, he took Tom's chin in hand again, and claimed that mouth, demanding entry and plunging his tongue in. Tom surrendered, groaning at the onslaught and shaking the chains that held him up and in place.

When Max drew back, he said, "Yank down three times with your right hand for red."

Tom nodded.

Max eased the gag in, buckled it tightly around Tom's head, then traced those lips again. "Lovely. Not quite as pretty as when you're choking on my cock, but still, lovely." He stepped back, slid his cock free and jerked off a few times.

Tom's moan and the shudder were perfect. Max tucked himself back in. "If you're very good, maybe you'll get a taste of that." Then he stepped to the other side of the frame.

Tom had stretched and lubed his own ass well with that fat dildo. This plug was a little thicker—Tom would certainly feel it in his ass and be unable to escape it pressing against his prostate.

Max slipped off his gloves and got to work lubing the plug. He'd ruined too many good leather gloves by coating them in lube, and he liked this pair.

When it was slick, he ran the tip of the plug up and down Tom's crack, eliciting a wanton moan from Tom. "You want to be fucked so much, don't you? Need that greedy hole stuffed full?"

Tom whimpered and rattled the chains, squirming.

Fuck, Max loved seeing Tom like this. He positioned the plug and pushed it forward.

Tom grunted, then groaned long and loud as the plug stretched him open, bucking his hips. Max worked slowly, dragging out that torment. Tom's groans were music to Max's ears, and watching Tom's ass take the plug an absolute delight that left Tom shaking in his bonds.

When plug was seated, Max cleaned his hands of lube and scooped up his gloves.

With Tom watching him, Max carefully slid his gloves back on. That had the desired effect—Tom was wide-eyed and taut in his bonds, and he gave a short moan. His cock was rampant, the leather cock ring a black band against his ruddy arousal.

"All full and plugged for me, eh?"

Tom whimpered, and Max stepped close. "When we're done here, I'm going to fuck you so hard, that plug will seem a pittance." He stroked Tom's dick slowly. "And you're going to scream like you always do for me."

Tom closed his eyes, his breath heaving in his chest, His cock was rock hard in Max's hand.

"But first, I'm going to make you scream in other ways." Max stepped back and reclaimed his crop.

The front, as he had noted way back during that demo, was more delicate, so he was careful in his cruelty. Shoulders. Pecs. Nipples.

Oh, did Max love tormenting Tom's nipples. So sensitive, and every slap of the crop made Tom jump and squeal behind the gag. The insides of Tom's spread thighs were even better, making him moan and thrash against his bonds.

Max watched for the safeword sign, but that didn't come.

Instead, those moans of agony changed and turned to groans of pleasure and need. Tom thrust his hips forward, and when he locked eyes with Max, those seemed to beg for one thing.

Tom wanted to be fucked. Hard. Now.

Max wasn't done with him yet, though. He worked Tom's

body over, laying down stinging blows on every inch of flesh that could take them.

Then he gently touched the crop to Tom's jutting dick.

Tom jumped in his bonds, eyes wide.

Max stroked the crop up and down the shaft, unable to read whether fear or desire made Tom tremble so much. "I can't tell if you're afraid I'll strike you here, or if you *want* me to do just that."

The short sequence of moans Tom made could've been either sentiment. Or both.

"Three yanks on the chain for red. Two for yellow. One for green. Do you want me to punish your needy dick?" He circled Tom's shaft with the crop.

When Tom met his gaze and yanked once, Max's body flooded with fire and joy. The pain. The *trust*. He let the crop fly, and it struck the head of Tom's dick.

Tom cried out, the sound loud even with that gag filling his mouth. He threw back his head, body shaking and thrust his hips forward.

A wildfire of dark pleasure swept over Max, and he let the crop fly again.

Tom's cries were louder this time, and tears formed at the corner of his eyes. His thrusts didn't stop, though. Neither did the moans. He met Max's gaze and there was desperation there. His whole body shook.

The plug. The pain. "You're close, aren't you?" Max flicked the crop hard at Tom's nipple.

Tears slid down Tom's cheek. He flinched and panted against the gag.

So fucking beautiful. "You want to come from me punishing your cock, from my plug in your ass, don't you?" Max followed that with a strike to Tom's other nipple.

Tom jerked his hips forward, and the moans around the gag changed timbre.

This time, Max gave in to his own darkness and needs, wanting to see that pain Tom so loved, needing to drive him to the edge. He struck hard and repeatedly, leaving rising marks behind on Tom's chest, thighs, and shoulders as Tom rutted his cock forward, chasing an orgasm he couldn't achieve. Those moans of frustration, pain, and need sang through Max's blood.

Finally, Max returned to Tom's dick, laying down three strikes in rapid succession.

Tom shrieked in the rack, screaming behind the gag and rocking himself in every direction.

Tears flowed down his cheeks, and he yanked twice on the chains.

Fuck. Max dropped the crop and caught Tom. "There. I've stopped, Tom." Wasn't the three pulls, but yellow was enough.

Tom trembled and sobbed, and fear shot through Max. "I'm taking the gag off." He didn't know if the words were registering in Tom at all.

But when the gag slipped free, Tom gulped air and pinned Max with a look of pure fire. "Fuck me." Rough, guttural words. "Get me off this thing, throw me on the ground, and fuck me. I need you inside me, and I need to come."

Wasn't a plea. That was an absolute order, and it cut through Max like a hot knife, sizzling against every nerve. "Tom."

Submissive to equal in no time flat.

Tom hissed. "Fuck—just do it!" So much need in his voice and unraveled emotions in his eyes.

Tom wasn't the only one shaking. Max laid a trembling gloved hand on the side of Tom's face. "Tom."

"Please." That was softer. "I'll do anything."

"Wait, and trust," Max reached up and unhooked Tom's

wrist. He had to catch some of Tom's weight, but quickly undid the other wrist.

Tom grabbed him and kissed him. Hard and unrelenting, pushing past all Max's defenses, until he was the one who moaned into Tom.

Fuck, he wanted Tom, but he needed control. Max broke the kiss, bit Tom's lip, and grabbed the ring of his collar. "If you want me to fuck you," he growled, "let me go so I can free your legs."

That got a groan from Tom. "Push me over and take me right here."

"No. We're going to do this my way, Tom, or not at all." Max met Tom's gaze and didn't look away. Didn't let go of his grip on Tom's collar.

Tom trembled and swallowed, his Adam's apple bobbing beneath the leather. "You're too good," he said. "I can't—" A tear slid down his cheek.

Max had pushed Tom hard—harder than he'd intended. Giving in to his own desires. He softened his voice. "You already *have*, Tom. Trust me to finish this, to treat you right and give you heaven."

Tom closed his eyes. "You already did. I—came."

Ah. Dry orgasm. That explained a lot. Max took a kiss from Tom's lips. "Then let me give you paradise, as well." He let go of the collar and knelt long enough to free Tom's legs, then was back standing in front of him.

"We're going to walk to the other room, now."

Tom's tear-stained eyes went wide. "The plug?"

"That's going to stay in you a little longer. As punishment." Max looped a finger through the center ring on Tom's chest harness and yanked.

Tom jerked forward and groaned. "Oh *fuck*! Do you have any idea what this feels like?"

Max pulled Tom toward the door to the back room. "Yes."

That one word was enough to quiet Tom for the rest of the short walk to the door. Max turned the knob, pushed the door open, pulled Tom inside, then let him go.

Tom wobbled forward. "Oh. Fuck," he said. "This is like—is this a porn studio?"

The centerpiece was the bed built specifically for BDSM. A modified four-post style with tie-downs. Around the edge of the room were a few chairs that could be used for a variety of actions other than sitting. There were mirrors everywhere, some movable, some not. From the bed, you could see just about every angle of yourself.

"No cameras. Nothing like that. The only people who've ever been here are me and a few of my partners." Max understood Tom's reaction, though. The room had been built for a voyeur, for Max specifically, so he could watch his partner from many angles, but also so they could watch *him*—flogging or fucking or tying them down.

Max gripped Tom's hips and pulled their bodies together so his package pressed against the base of the plug inside Tom.

"Fuck." Tom's head lolled back against Max.

He kissed the flesh above the collar. "That's next."

"God. What you do to me," Tom murmured. "I've never come dry. Everything aches."

"Did you enjoy that?" Had Max been too rough? Too focused on his own needs?

Tom pushed his ass back against Max. "God, yes. Hated it, too. But that's normal with me."

The worry and tension in Max drained away, and he rutted against Tom's ass.

Tom groaned. "God, Max!"

"That good?" He nipped at Tom's neck.

"Please fuck me. Just—"

Soon. Right now, he wanted Tom on edge. "Jerk yourself off for me. Show me how much you want my cock in you."

Tom's shudder was electrifying, as was his hiss, but he obeyed, wrapping his hand around his ruddy length and working it over hard and fast until he was panting and groaning.

Max held Tom tight against him, feeling those shudders, hearing that keening whine. Sublime. Max kissed Tom's trembling shoulder, right over a welt. "Stop."

That got him a sob. "You're gonna kill me," Tom panted.

Max couldn't help the laugh. "I think not." He nudged Tom forward toward the bed. "Grab that post, high."

When Tom complied, Max ran his hands down Tom's sides, from armpits to hips. "You're strong, Tom. I've not been gentle with you."

Tom sucked in a shaky breath. "I know. I just—don't want to disappoint you."

That chestnut. "You haven't. Trust yourself. Trust me." Max caressed Tom's welted ass. "I'm taking the plug out." Then he did, easing it out of Tom as gently as he could.

"Fuuuuuck." Long slow exhale, then Tom slumped against the post.

Max dropped the toy in a bin he'd left at the foot of the bed for that purpose. "That's what I intend. On the bed, Tom, on your back."

Took Tom a moment to right himself, and he winced as he lay back against the mattress. Then his eyes went wide. "Fuck, you mirrored the ceiling."

Yes, he had. "You're going to see yourself, Tom. Watch when I slide my cock into you. See how you look when you're on the very edge of orgasm."

Tom stared up. "Shit." Then he glanced around and took in all the other angles. "Oh—fuck. I can't not watch."

"I could blindfold you, if you'd prefer." Max crawled up

over Tom, boots and all, and met his gaze. "But I want you to watch me fuck you and pleasure you. I doubt you've ever seen how glorious you are." He leaned down close to those lips. "I want you to see me worship you."

Tom's lips parted. "My god, you are too good for this world."

No, he wasn't. Max kissed Tom, straddled him, and stripped off his vest. "One last choice for tonight," Max said. "Do you want your arms restrained?"

Tom let out a breath. "It'll be easier for me to watch you if I'm free."

Given the angles, yes. Max nodded.

"But tie me down and fuck me here sometime?"

He slipped down the bed to stand again. "Absolutely. There are so many ways to tie you down and use you."

Tom grinned. He was keyed up and hard, but the tension Max had glimpsed a few times today had vanished completely.

Time to give them both what they wanted. Max hooked his fingers around the straps of his leather jock, peeled that off, and tossed it to one side.

The grin on Tom's lips fell away. "I still can't believe we're doing this."

Neither could Max. Tom had been on the edge of his social circle for so long. He'd watched Tom flit from jerk to jerk and worried about him, but there hadn't been a good time to step in. Max put one boot up on the frame of the bed and undid the laces to take it off. Then repeated with the other. All the while, Tom watched, his gaze darting over Max's body.

Then Max was naked but for his gloves. He stood at the foot of the bed and stroked himself.

Tom bit his lip. "I could come watching you do that."

Now that would be interesting to orchestrate. Max filed that away. "Jack yourself again."

Tom groaned. "Please don't make me wait." Then he took hold of his cock and matched his rhythm to Max's.

Max smiled and watched, enjoying Tom splayed out and getting himself off. Max's desire curled deep in his stomach, hardening his cock, and heating his blood. He'd waited and waited, and finally had what he wanted.

Tom's gaze drifted up, and then he gave a little murmur of shock. He stared up seemingly transfixed by the image he saw. "Oh my god."

Max gave himself a final tug before grabbing a condom and lube. "What do you see, Tom?"

"Me." His voice was full of lust and awe. "I look like a fucking porn star. But I don't—" He swallowed. "That can't be me." He slowed down his ministrations and twisted on the sheets. "Oh fuck, it feels so good, though."

"It is you," Max said. He ripped open the condom wrapper, and Tom's attention whipped to him. Max glared back. "No. Look up, Tom."

Tom grunted, then lay back again, fondling himself and breathing hard.

Max had lain in the same spot enough times to know Tom could watch Max roll the condom down and slick himself with lube. He knelt between Tom's legs.

Tom's eyes were wide and staring up when Max positioned himself and pressed in. "Fuck." His hand faltered on his cock. "Oh my god."

"See?" Max's voice was guttural, the heat and tightness of Tom taking away his breath.

That sight, his cock stretching Tom open as it slid inside, glorious and perfect. Max drew out and slammed in deep.

Tom lost hold of his dick, arched his back, and cried out.

"That what you wanted?" Max rammed in again, harder.

"Y-yes!" Tom panted, and stared up. "God, you—you—"

The rest was lost in a series of moans.

Max gave over to his own needs, fucking Tom hard and fast, drinking in the leather around Tom's limbs and neck, across his chest and the strip that encircled Tom's straining cock that pressed his balls down. Tom stared up wantonly, arched and panted as Max took him over and over. That was what Max wanted Tom to see. All those marks he'd laid down.

"Do you see how glorious you are? Like a king?"

Tom's reply was a low groan. "Fuck, you feel so good."

Max tipped his head up and met Tom's gaze in the mirrors, his open-mouthed pants and cries as Max rammed into him. He held Tom's legs open, and Tom's hard cock bobbed against his chest, bound by Max's leather.

Heat and fire overtook Max, and he folded over Tom, kissing his chest, licking the nipples he'd tortured. Tonguing under leather straps of the harness. "So fucking beautiful."

Tom threaded fingers into Max's hair, gripped his shoulders, and met each stroke, stealing Max's breath with a roll of his hips. Max moaned. "Fuck."

Tom laughed breathlessly.

In retribution, Max ground hard and deep into Tom, eliciting a strangled cry, then a whimper. "Please."

Tom had been riding the edge for so long. Max wasn't going to last, the threads of his own control all but ripped apart.

Max reached between their bodies, found the cock ring, and popped the snap free. Then he pumped Tom's cock hard and fast.

Tom nearly levitated off the mattress. His nails bit into Max's shoulders, and he wailed as he came, spilling hot seed over Max's hand.

Tom's ass tightened around Max's cock and sent him flying over the edge, momentarily stealing his vision. He shouted his own release, pounding furiously into Tom until he'd emptied himself.

Afterward, Max could barely hold himself up on his arms, his whole body shaking from the sudden orgasm. Slowly, he met Tom's gaze.

He was glassy-eyed and smiling. "Hey," he said, his voice a beautiful slur of words. "Look up."

Max couldn't from where he was. He levered himself back, still buried in Tom, and gazed up at the mirrors he'd installed.

Both he and Tom stared back.

Tom was smiling, looking so sated and magnificent, Max wanted to paint that expression, though he had no talent there. Max's own reflection looked fey and wild, with long hair everywhere, ruddy chest, face dotted with perspiration, and the black of the leather gloves dark against the light sheet of the bed.

"You're a king too," Tom added, in a low, wondrous tone, "What did I do to deserve you?"

Max tore his gaze away from the heavens and drew it down to Tom, to the man he loved. "You said yes to coffee."

Tom closed his eyes. "Cinnamon coffee from a cinnamon roll."

Max chuckled. "Need to—" He pulled out of Tom, took off the condom, and dropped it into the basin with the plug. He'd clean that up later. Right now? He collapsed onto the bed next to Tom, who rolled onto his side, and threw his arm around Max.

They lay face to face, noses almost touching. "I think I scratched up your back." No regret in Tom's voice.

"I did more than scratch yours."

"Fucking amazing, though Aaron's going to give me shit on Monday when I can't walk straight."

Max stole a kiss. "I'm sure you've done the same."

"Oh, yeah. Hell, Will's had Aaron in a cock cage at work."

Max propped himself up on one elbow and peered at Tom. "Really?"

That look of fear. "Don't you get any ideas..."

Max chuckled darkly. "My dear, I have all *sorts* of ideas. You haven't seen or felt half of them yet."

This time Tom stole a kiss, and lingered. He traced the line of Max's jaw. When he drew back, his smile was sweet and light. "Don't let me go, Max."

He didn't intend to.

Max gathered Tom into his arms, pulled them together, and closed his eyes. "I'll be here as long as you want."

CHAPTER SIXTEEN

TOM DIDN'T KNOW if it was subspace or endorphins, but all he wanted to do was curl around Max and hold him. Be held. Tangle up in Max's life. So different from the past, where he'd been out the door five minutes after he could stand.

When he'd looked up and saw himself being fucked by Max, the emotions that had crashed through him were amazing and terrifying. He wanted those forever.

A king, Max had said, because he was poetic, thoughtful, and emphatic.

Tom had seen what Max saw. Had felt like a king, despite being a mediocre submissive, and Max gave him everything he wanted in kink and sex. Brutal, painful, thoughtful, loving—

Loving.

He studied Max's face. A few of the long locks of his hair trailed over his closed eyes, breath coming slow and easy, as if in sleep. So kind. So cruel. Perfect.

He'd never thought he'd find something like what Aaron had with Will, yet... Thoughts flipped and turned. The future. His past. The way everything with Max could go horribly wrong. All the ways it might not.

"Why aren't you married?" he murmured.

Max cracked one eye open, then the other, and gave a shrug. "I've come close a few times, but ultimately, I wasn't the partner for them. Or they weren't for me. Not for long-term."

"But you've been in love."

Max propped his head up on his hand and pushed his hair out of his face. "A couple times, yes."

"Huh." That was all Tom said, because anything else had too much weight.

Max's lips parted as if to speak, then he smiled and stroked a warm, leather-clad hand down Tom's side. "Do you want to get cleaned up? I don't know the time, but I suspect I should start dinner. In an hour or so, we're both going to be ravenous."

"Could use a shower. And some water. And that ointment of yours." For the welts and bruises that riddled his body.

Max sobered. "I wasn't too rough, was I? The crop on your dick?"

Tom shivered against the memory. That had hurt in ways he hadn't felt before, and had made him come dry. He'd flown so high and wanted so much more of Max. "Not at all," he said. "But I don't think I can take more like that for a while. I loved what you did, but that was a lot to take in."

Max found a mark on Tom's chest and traced a finger over it. "For me too."

"When you push me, do you also push yourself?" Even Doms had limits.

"In this case, yes. I don't let myself go like I did with you. It's not always safe to give into my needs."

"Dangerous to fall into topspace?"

"You've been reading again." Max stroked Tom's arm. "Not exactly. Dangerous to give into my raw desires, maybe." He levered himself up. "Come on, let's head upstairs."

Tom's body protested as he moved. Still, Max was right,

they needed to clean up. "What about these?" He held out his wrists. "And the mess we made."

"Ech, I'll clean up later. As for my leather—shall I take those off?"

Tom considered, aching for the connection the leather gave him to Max. That reminder. "I don't think you want me showering with all this on. Maybe—" He paused, a vague idea forming in his mind, but he pushed it away. "Never mind. You should take them off." He held out his wrists.

Max watched Tom for a moment, his expression unreadable, then he unbuckled the cuffs from Tom's wrists. He laid both on the bed. "Legs, please?"

Tom obliged, and Max removed both. The harness came next. Then Max framed Tom's face with his hands. "I'm not going to ask you what you were going to say, but know you can request anything of me." Then he loosened the collar around Tom's neck and removed it.

The loss of that band send a wave of emotions tumbling hard and painful through Tom. His voice shook. "I'll keep that in mind."

Max stood and offered Tom a hand. "Come with me?"

He let Max pull him up. "That shower of yours is divine." He shoved the rest of what he wanted to say away. Boxed it up and stuck it on a shelf in the back of his mind. Later. He'd ask later. Or never. He didn't know.

On the way upstairs, Tom grabbed his overnight bag. His body did ache in ways he wasn't used to despite the years of kink, and his mind still whirled and twisted.

In the middle of enjoying that huge shower with Max, haze and exhaustion overcame Tom. He leaned back against the slate wall and closed his eyes. "Wow, I'm a little out of it."

Max trailed fingers down his arm. "I don't doubt it. Let's

finish up and dress. I'll get you some water, and you can relax on the couch while I work on dinner."

That sounded ideal, and Max made all of it happen.

Max really should be married. He didn't strike Tom as the type to divorce over dish patterns or because a partner went out with friends, or when finances got tight, or any other of the other reconcilable differences he'd seen over the years.

Why the hell was he dating Tom? There were tons of better partners out there.

He must have had a faraway look, because Max rubbed both of Tom's arms, as they stood in the bedroom. "Hey, you there?" A little smile cracked through the worry. "Do I have to carry you downstairs?"

Tom shook his head. "Just—thinking." He took one of Max's hands in his own, then twined his fingers in Max's.

Felt good. Right. Aaron said Tom loved Max. Tom thought he might, too.

Max pushed a few stray strands of wet hair from Tom's forehead. "Thinking about what?"

"You. Us. I don't know. It's all—" He waved a hand. "Out there."

"Well, if you want to talk about it, I'm here."

Tom nodded. Max was, and that was so unexpected. "Couch, I guess? You don't have to carry me."

"All right."

Max led him downstairs. The couch ate Tom as soon as he settled into that soft surface. His ass and back stung, but that was nothing compared to the relief he felt curling up and sinking in.

Max chuckled. "I'll get you some water and a blanket."

The water was cool and crisp as it spread out inside Tom. "God. I needed that."

Max sank down on the edge of the couch with a glass of his

own. "We spent a lot of time in that scene. It's going to take time for you to come out."

"You're out."

"Not really. Cooking will help. It's meditative and orderly."

Hence why he wasn't joining Tom on the couch. "You can be in control there?"

"Cooking has a way of humbling anyone with rigid plans." Max patted Tom's thigh, set his glass down on a coaster, then rose. "Finish your water. I'll get you a blanket."

That was an order. Tom smirked and muttered, "Yes, Sir," before taking another drink.

"Heard that." Max pulled out a rainbow blanket lined in fleece from a wicker trunk in the corner. "I'm still going to give you my most comfortable throw, though." He draped it over Tom's shoulders.

"Do you do all this for your subs?"

Max reclaimed his glass, and swirled the water. "No." He met Tom's gaze with a look that was shockingly vulnerable. "Precious few. There've been two others, and none recently."

Tom stared up at Max.

Max gave a huff that might have been exasperation or amusement. "I love you, Tom Cedric." Then he turned and headed into the kitchen.

Tom stared into the glass of water in his hand, his whole body vibrating and going numb at the same time. Max *loved* him. Holy fuck.

He—liked Max. More than a little. More than normal. More like love. He was going to fucking lose that bet he hadn't made with Aaron. Thank *god*. Everything felt light and heavy and *perfect*.

He still didn't believe this was happening, but it was. He drank the last bit of water in the glass, set that down on the coffee table, then wrapped Max's blanket around him.

Exhaustion from the scene merged with the absolute joy at Max's words, so when Tom curled up, he was out like a light, falling into a dreamless sleep.

————

MAX STOOD at the sink and tried to compose himself, not sure if he wanted to laugh or cry. Tom was sexy. Breathtaking. So frustratingly unaware of himself.

He was in love with Tom. Maddeningly so. Wanted to sweep him off his feet. Woo him with everything he could. Be the best Dominant Tom had ever had.

The last bit was easy, since Tom hadn't had a Dom worth any weight of salt. He still wanted to track them down and kick them in the balls. Some were still in the area.

Ech, leave it, Maxime.

At the best of times, he was a touch protective of the people he cared for. This was not the best of times.

He rubbed his hands together and grabbed an apron off the hook on the wall. Cooking, as he'd told Tom, would help. He mentally ticked off ingredients and timing in his head, then started pulling out what he needed.

As for wooing, Max could be impossibly romantic under the right circumstances. These were not those, either. Tom said he wasn't romantic at all, and whether that was due to circumstance, nature, or both didn't matter. Not the best relationship combination.

But after that scene, Tom had been sweet. Responsive. And even *romantic*. Despite, or maybe because of, the torment and pleasure Max had put Tom through.

He drew chicken cutlets out of the refrigerator, along with several other items, and set them on the counter next to his cutting board. The red wine he used for cooking was already out. He popped the cork off, pulled out a glass, and splashed a little into the bottom.

He should drink more water, but the sharp bite of the tannins of the wine and the alcohol helped.

The crop wasn't his most painful toy, but he could inflict such exquisite torture with it, and striking Tom on his dick? The pleasure of seeing and hearing Tom's cry, his pain and ecstasy, pulsed through Max. That hadn't been *kind*, even by his own standards, and it had driven Tom to an orgasm.

Max leaned against the counter. As a sadist, he'd only dreamed of a sub who wanted pain like that. Now that he'd found one, he was terrified he'd push Tom too far, or not enough to meet Tom's needs, and he'd move on, looking for someone else to *scratch that itch*.

And yet, Tom didn't always need those heights. He'd been equally as touched by ice skating, simple lovemaking, and a coffee shop date. Not the sign of someone who'd lose interest from not enough kink.

Max found his water glass, took a long drink, and got back to cooking. There were mushrooms to slice, chicken to sauté, and a red wine cream sauce to make.

There'd also be conversations over dinner, especially after Max had blurted out his love for Tom.

Max set the oven to preheating. If nothing else, there'd be chocolate croissants to ease away whatever came out of that discussion.

An hour later, the table in the breakfast nook was set with linen, plates, stemware, a few rolls from dough he'd thawed out the day before, and a candle. Dinner only required plating, and the croissants were cooling. The whole setup looked intimate. Loving.

Romantic.

Max shook blew out a breath, then headed to the living

room to wake Tom. He'd stuck his head in a few times while cooking, but Tom had been gone to the world. He was still out cold.

Max sat down on the edge of the couch, near Tom's curled-up legs, and that movement was enough to cause Tom's eyelids to flicker.

"Hey, Tom."

Tom's eyes flickered open. "Uh. God. Hi." Tom stretched out an arm, then rolled onto his back. Then he flinched. "Ow. Fucking hell."

"We had a harsh scene earlier."

"I remember." Sleep in his voice. "Wasn't harsh. Was perfect."

Max's heart lifted; the sadist in him was so pleased. "Glad to hear. But I did a number on your body, so be gentle with yourself."

Tom took a deeper breath and looked more clear-headed than when he'd curled up on the couch. "Man, what did you make? Smells fantastic!"

"You'll see in a bit." Max patted Tom's blanket-covered legs. "Feel better?"

A nod. "Yeah. I needed the nap. How long was I out?"

"About an hour."

"Huh." Tom swung his legs off the couch. "How are you?"

"Better. More down to earth."

"Is that a good thing or a bad thing?" Tom pushed the blanket off and rolled out his neck.

Interesting question. Max cocked his head to one side and studied Tom. "Neither. Why?"

"It occurs to me that we always have serious conversations over food. What you've made smells divine, so I'm guessing this won't be an easy discussion." Tom met his gaze. "Also, you have your sadder smile, which isn't a good sign."

Max opened his mouth, then paused, because the thoughts ramming through his brain were a tangle of two languages. He found the correct words. "You're startlingly perceptive."

"I'm a lawyer," Tom said. "Plus kink clears my head, when it's good." His lips twitched up. "And that was so much better than good, Max."

Embarrassment coursed through Max's body. "I'm—thank you," he said. "Please tell me you're hungry, though, because dinner will only keep for a little longer."

Tom laughed, and that lit up his entire being. "Yeah, starving. Let's eat."

The shift in mood caught Max off guard, so it was Tom who strode into the kitchen first, with Max following, bewildered in his wake.

Tom stopped when he saw the table. "Shit. This is fancy."

"Is it too much?" Some of the worry Max tried to hide slipped out.

"No, it's lovely. This is..." That brilliant smile returned. "Serious."

Joy suffused Max, relaxing his muscles and soothing his heart. "Have a seat." He plated both dinner dishes, and poured the wine. Then he stripped off his apron and took the other chair.

Tom watched him, amusement evident. "Did you just serve me?"

Max rolled his eyes. "Yes. This is dinner, not a scene."

Tom shrugged. "Sometimes you switch to Dom so fast, it's hard to tell."

Max sat back and considered. "I don't mean to. But you inspire me."

"We both have our blinders, I guess." Tom took a bite of the chicken, then closed his eyes. "Oh my god."

"You say that a lot." The dish was cooked well—chicken and

mushrooms in a red wine cream sauce over wide noodles. Max had steamed asparagus, and drizzled that with lemon juice and almond slivers. A pretty simple meal, all told.

"That's because everything you do is really fucking good." Tom took one of the rolls. "Did you make bread while I was asleep?"

Max laughed. "No, no. Every so often, when I'm in a mood, I wreck my kitchen making dough. Then I divide it up and freeze most of it. I just need to thaw, let it rise, and then bake."

"Just." Tom shook his head.

"Tom..."

He waved that away. "I know. It's not much for you, because you're a fucking bread prince. But look, you've seen me. I'm a mess. I'm so out of my depth with you. I'm—"

"Tom." That came out more forceful.

He quieted, but glared at Max.

The only thing Max could do was laugh. Then he picked up his glass of wine. "A toast?"

The glare remained, but softened. Tom picked up his glass. "To what?"

"Us," Max said. "You, and your worries that you're not good enough for me, and me and my worries that I won't be good enough for you."

Ah, that stupefied look. So endearing. Max clinked his glass against Tom's. "Santé."

"What do you mean you won't be good enough for me?" Tom looked at his wine, then at Max.

Max sipped. The wine was from a good bottle. Not the best of his collection, but one befitting a dinner for two with a man he'd love to have in his life a long time. "I worry that you'll tire of this." He gestured to the table. "When the novelty wears off. But all this—cooking, baking, treating you like the amazing person you are—isn't something I can turn off. It comes with the kink and with the sex."

Tom watched him. "Let me think about what you said." He set down his glass and picked up his utensils. "Also, I don't think you want this to go cold, or go to waste."

Max huffed a laugh, and also set about eating his meal. The silence that fell between them wasn't uncomfortable, and Tom seemed relaxed and comfortable in his skin.

When Tom cleared a good portion of his plate, he claimed his glass again and sat back. "I think I do push your limits, too."

That zipped through Max like the sound of a bell being stuck. It reverberated true. "You do." He took up a roll. "I had no idea I'd feel so strongly about you when I ordered that coffee."

Tom sipped his wine. "I've always thought you'd be a remarkable person to know, but with everything else?" He shook his head. "You're the best Dom, the best sadist, I've ever had. And the sex—my god." He shivered.

"Same, actually, except the other way around." Max tipped his wineglass to Tom.

Tom set down his glass. "See, now *that* I don't understand. How am *I* any good?"

Max closed his eyes, because the absolute rage that dwelled in him whenever this subject came up bubbled to the surface. He muttered a few choice words in French, then opened his eyes. "Forgive me. I'm not angry with you. But if I ever see any of your former Doms, I may kill them." He took a sip of wine before setting his glass on the table. His hand trembled.

Tom stared at Max's hand.

"Tom, beyond your intelligence—you're a lawyer, for goodness sake—your stunning looks, and the way you fucking light the world up when you smile, you're also deeply and passionately masochistic. You don't flirt with pain, you crave it, seek it out, and demand it. You're submissive, but only to a certain point. That's a heady combination for someone like me. What we did today—" Max paused and shook his head. "I could lose myself in your desires. Set myself free. I've never—" He stopped, because voicing his own dark need was hard.

"You're—frightened of *me*?"

Max turned the words over in his head. "In a way, yes." He rotated his wineglass but didn't pick it up. "I *want* to push you, not only because you want that, but because I can explore my own desires. That's horribly selfish, maybe to the point of being one of your jerks." He met Tom's gaze. "I'm afraid I'm going to *hurt* you. Physically, mentally, or emotionally, like those other men."

There. That was out. He sat back in his chair and closed his eyes. "I'm also so in love with you. I want to offer you every wonderful thing that's in my power to give." He opened his eyes. "Every moment with you is extraordinary, regardless of what the moment is."

"Even these ones?" Tom choked the words out.

Max croaked on a laugh. "Especially these ones. They're the most important."

Tom looked away, stared outside, where twilight darkened the sky. "I spend a lot of time splitting people apart. Maybe it's made me cynical about relationships. I understand the enduring nature of friendships, though. There are times I've gotten so fucking mad at Aaron, and him at me, but I wouldn't want to practice law with anyone else, ever." He fell silent.

"You don't have sex with Aaron. Nor indulge in kink."

Tom looked back at Max. "One, he's married. Two, he's a sub."

"I'll grant you two, but he and Will aren't monogamous."

"But I am. I did the multiple partners thing when I was younger, and it wasn't what it's cracked up to be, at least for me." He gave Max a rueful look. "You can see how great I am dealing with *one* relationship."

"You're not doing badly." Max spoke those words quietly.

Tom sighed. "I know. This is—" He gestured at the table, then more encompassingly. "Absolutely wonderful. But it's fucking with my head *because* it's wonderful. I don't know what to make of my feelings."

"Do you need to know right now?"

"Maybe? I don't want to lose the best thing that's happened to me because I can't sort out how I *feel*." There was derision there. Disparagement.

"Tom." Max couldn't keep the sharpness from his voice

Fire in Tom's gaze. "You hate when I put myself down."

"I do."

"I like that about you, how damn much you care. Even your fears are wrapped in care. You're afraid of letting yourself go during kink because you believe your desires are worth less than mine. Your entire focus is on me."

That was embarrassingly close to the truth. "I—not my *entire* focus."

Tom raised an eyebrow. "Most of it."

Max couldn't counter that.

"I'm so used to the opposite. My will, desires, and needs are an afterthought, if any sort of thought at all."

Max rubbed his temple, his ire rising again.

"I know," Tom murmured. "Those fights with Aaron? Inevitably over my taste in men."

"But why?" The question burst painfully out of Max. "Why did you put yourself through that?"

Tom looked out the window again, arms crossed over his chest, a furrow between his brows. He was silent for a long time.

"That was unfair of me to ask. I'm sorry" Max was fucking this up. "I should clean." He made to rise.

Tom swung is gaze back and pinned Max with a look so strong, it froze his movements. "Max, no." He spoke softly. Calmly.

Max sank back into his chair.

"It's not an unfair question. Aaron's asked. Candace, too." Tom gave a shrug. "I don't have a good answer, except the kind of pain I like—the type that makes you afraid to lose control—is easier to find with men who don't give a fuck about me. But they have no qualms about hurting me or tromping all over my boundaries or using me in ways I don't want. None at all."

Max's insides twisted and ripped so hard tears sprang to his eyes. For Tom to live like that, subject himself to that.

"Ah, shit," Tom said. "See, you really fucking care."

"Is that a problem?" Max managed to get the words out.

Tom shook his head. "No." He uncrossed his arms. "It's the exact opposite. But I conditioned myself badly for what you're offering. I enjoy dating you, but I don't trust my head, and I've no fucking clue what to do with my heart." He blinked a few times. "I still can't fathom that I'm here, in your house, with you telling me you love me."

This conversation had spun so far out of Max's control, all he could do was keep his ass in his seat, and let Tom—beautiful, intelligent Tom—take the lead. "You *are* here."

Tom's smile was a miracle. There was an undeniable brightness to it. "Yeah, and you want me to be here, so everything's going to be okay."

Max felt the tension leave his body. "Just okay?"

Tom arched both eyebrows, pushed back his chair, and stood.

Though everything in Max protested that he should rise, he remained seated and watched as Tom stalked around the table. He pulled Max's chair from the table and rotated it, his gaze sharp, eyes bright. Then he sat in Max's lap and kissed him.

Max's heart soared and he wrapped his arms around Tom, took over the kiss, deepened it, and drank Tom down.

They both moaned. Tom squirmed and cursed. "I forgot how bruised my ass is, and your thighs are harder than that chair." He combed fingers through Max's hair. "Better than okay. You're the best thing that's ever happened to me." He kissed Max again.

Max didn't know how long they remained wrapped in each other's arms, kissing and nuzzling. He didn't try to gain the upper hand this time. Wasn't needed. This was perfect.

Tom pressed his forehead to Max's. "Do you know why I've never safeworded, even though you pretty much told me I should test you?"

"No," Max whispered.

"I don't need to test you. I've always felt safe. You've never pushed me beyond what I can take. You don't need to worry about losing control. I promise I'll tell you if you need to stop." Tom kissed his forehead. "You have to trust me, too. I may be broken in some places, but that's not one of them.

"You're not broken at all."

A smile touched Tom's lips. "I've never been in love."

"Not everyone falls in love."

Tom rolled his eyes. "I know that. I don't know if I'm aromantic. My kink and sexual relationships have been shit, so the data isn't there. My friendships have been stellar, but the way I feel about you doesn't fall in line with, say, my friendship with Aaron."

"God forbid you feel about me like those men you dated." Max couldn't help it.

"Oh god. The stories I could tell."

"Not if you want my blood pressure to remain normal."

Tom pecked his nose. "What I feel for you is nothing like those guys. Aaron says I get gooey-eyed when I talk about you."

Max ran a thumb over Tom's cheek. "Do you?"

From so close, Max saw the sweep of Tom's lashes as he looked down. "I'm unbelievably happy. Joyful. Like my heart might burst. Like I'm standing in sunlight."

Oh. Max knew those feelings well. But he wouldn't label Tom's emotions for him.

When those eyes met his, Max's heart tumbled and tumbled. He cupped Tom's face. "Those are good feelings. I'm honored."

Tom searched his face and took a deep breath. "I haven't felt like this before. I think I might be in love with you, too."

Max smoothed his thumbs over Tom's cheeks again. "Maybe we should keep doing what we're doing, and you can see if you are?"

Tom laughed. "That sounds better than my other plan."

Curiosity got the best of Max. "What was your other plan?"

"I asked Aaron if I should break up with you." Tom whispered the words.

"Oh, Tom." It came out like a sigh. He leaned his forehead against Tom's.

"He told me I was being an absolute fool. It was obvious to *him* I was in love, and running away wasn't going to change that, only make everyone's lives worse."

"He has a point, your partner." Aaron had always seemed to have a good head on his shoulders. Max had always liked Will, and was growing fond of Kelly.

"Yeah. So here I am, trying to tell you how I feel."

That reminded Max, and this seemed as good a time as any to bring it back up. He opened up a little space between them. "There was something you wanted, downstairs, when I took my cuffs off you."

Tom looked down and bit his lip, which was the sexiest

fucking thing Max had seen this close up. He placed a finger under Tom's chin. "Anything within my power, Tom. Just ask."

"It's silly. But is there something you could give me to remind me we're together? I was thinking the cuff, but that wouldn't do well in work settings."

"Oh!" Max's heart soared and mind whirled. Then his desires caught, and he smiled at Tom.

Tom smacked him on the chest. "Not a cock cage." He shivered. "Okay, maybe a cock cage sometimes, but not for this."

Max laughed. "I think you'd thoroughly enjoy walking into work on Monday all caged up, but I understand what you're after. Let me think about something discreet enough that you can leave on."

Tom bit his lip again. "Can we talk about Monday, too? Can I try a cage on? See how I feel about it?"

"Always. Any toy."

That smile he loved broke out on Tom's face. "You're amazing. Thank you."

Max clasped the back of Tom's neck and pulled him in for a long slow kiss. When he finished, and Tom was breathless, he whispered into Tom's ear, "I made chocolate croissants for dessert."

"Fuck. French baker prince."

Max kissed his neck. "French-Canadian." Then he bounced his thigh gently. "If you want one, you're going to have to let me up."

Tom mock-pouted, the slid off Max's legs and winced. "You wield that crop so well."

Max rose. "I used to play with it while studying in grad school. Practicing blows, flicking it through the air. It's a comfort sometimes." He crossed to the counter, and plated a half-dozen croissants.

"Beating people soothes you?" Teasing in Tom's voice, which heartened Max.

"Kink...frees me. Playing with the crop kept me focused by letting my hands work while my mind churned through everything else." He took the plate and presented the croissants to Tom.

Tom stared at them. "Those look amazing. We're never going to eat that many, though."

"Ah, have faith in yourself, Tom. These are *my* croissants." Max reclaimed his seat and patted his lap.

Tom's laughter was magical as he sat on Max.

They only managed to eat four of the six, feeding each other bites and kisses, then licking the chocolate from lips and fingers until they were both wrapped in each other, breaths coming heavy and cocks hard again.

"God," Tom murmured against Max's lips. "I'm not sure I can take being fucked again tonight."

Max pulled Tom's T-shirt to one side and nipped his shoulder. "I'll take that as a compliment for earlier."

"It is." Tom rolled his head back. "You're so damn good."

"There's plenty of ways for us to get off that don't require my cock in your ass, you know."

Tom groaned. "Maybe we should take this elsewhere and you can show me?"

Max bit the junction of Tom's neck, below where a collared shirt would show the bruise, then gripped Tom, one arm under his legs and one braced against his back.

"Oh shit, you're not going to—"

Max stood, hauling Tom into his arms.

Tom yelped and wrapped his arms around Max's neck.

"I've wanted to do this," Max said. "Sweep you off your feet." For several years, if he thought about it.

Tom laughed. "Well, you have, in a couple of ways."

Good. "Bedroom, or basement?"

Tom considered. "Basement? We have to clean up there, and no wet spot on your bed." He paused. "Are you going to carry me downstairs?"

He'd done that with other partners, though Tom was closer to his height than any of them. Still, he fit comfortably in Max's arms. "Let's find out."

They made it to the basement fine. Max headed for the room in the back and the large bed they'd used before. "I'd like to suck you off again."

Tom hissed when his ass hit the bed—probably from the beating he'd taken. "I was thinking I'd rather like your dick in my mouth."

That solved that problem. Clothes came off, and they took time kissing and tasting each other. Touching and stroking until they were both achingly hard. This wasn't a scene. Max had no intention of dominating.

Tom nibbled his way down Max's ribs. That made Max gasp and thread his hands into Tom's hair. "Shit, no, ticklish!"

Tom grinned up. "Is that a safe word?"

Max groaned and hauled Tom around until they were in a sixty-nine position. "More like an I-need-your-cock-in-my-throat word."

Tom laughed, then gasped as Max wrapped his lips around Tom's dick. "Oh fuck."

Max went to town, sucking and licking and listening to Tom's moans, until Tom sucked down Max's cock with such gusto that Max had to gasp for air.

Tom's chuckle around Max's shaft was full of mischief.

Well, that wouldn't do. He returned to his ministrations with greater fervor. Tom cursed, thrust, then tried to outdo Max's blowjob.

Given Tom's gusto, he might manage that. Max wasn't going

to last. Between the relief from their conversation, Tom's clever mouth, and the absolute joy of sucking cock, Max was on the edge of orgasm, his control rapidly fraying, and nerves on fire. Each pull of Tom's mouth over his shaft threatened to undo him completely.

The only response he had was to work Tom's dick harder.

In the end, Max won, but barely. Tom thrust his cock between Max's lips, seeking his pleasure and groaning around Max's shaft, until he was spilling his seed down Max's throat and shouting around his dick.

That was all it took. Tasting, hearing, and feeling Tom come had Max to flying up into his own orgasm, groaning out a string of curses, until he lost himself in the sweet heaven of Tom's mouth.

Afterward, they lay panting on the bed, and Max stared up at the ceiling, into mirrors that displayed what a fine and debauched couple they were.

In their reflection, Tom caught Max's gaze and chuckled. "Well, that was a nice way to end dinner."

Max closed his eyes and smiled. "Agreed."

"Hey, Max?" Tom's call was soft and full of weight.

Max blinked both eyes open. "Hmm?"

"Pretty sure I'm in love with you, but I'm going to have to stick around a while longer to make sure."

Joy swept through Max, stronger and harder than his orgasm, and it took him time to breathe, and then another minute to speak. "You can stay as long as you'd like. However long you need, to be absolutely certain."

Tom sat up, then flopped down face to face with Max. "Too good, too pure—"

Max put a stop to *that* with his lips. When he broke the kiss, he rested a finger against Tom's lips. "Not too good or too pure for your world, Tom Cedric."

"No." Tom spoke around Max's finger. "And with the right amount of bite."

Max laughed, then replaced his finger with his mouth. Tom was correct. Everything was going to be okay.

Better than okay. They were going to be perfectly fine.

EPILOGUE

MAX PRESSED his cheek against Tom's back and closed his eyes. He'd heard this particular story of Jeremy's about a dozen times. Didn't begrudge the telling, but he was happy this time to have Tom in his lap and a nice warm sweater to lean against.

Perfect place to be when attending the annual Thanksgiving party at Jeremy's house.

"—and then I stepped in a hole that I didn't see and fell face first into a muddy puddle where they'd been cleaning dirt off our tools." Jeremy shook his head. "When I got up, there were bone fragments stuck to my skin. Turned out they were mice, but after that, everyone called me Bones. That's how I got the nickname."

"Also, he's a fucking archaeologist," Max said. "Digs up bones."

"I dig up pottery fragments, Demmy." Jeremy sounded absolutely indignant.

Amusement vibrated through Tom. He patted Max's thigh. "Be nice, or I'll tell them *your* nickname."

There was a general round of laughter in the room. "Which

one?" That was Will Taylor's voice. He and Aaron were both at the party.

Max shifted Tom on his lap so he could peer around and glare at Will. "Don't you start."

Will held up his hands. "I'm just saying that I've heard a lot of nicknames for you, Max."

"Professor Hot Pants," Madeleine said. "Doctor Hot Lips. Sexy French Professor."

Max groaned. "Oh my god, please."

There were more. Lots more, and they were all recounted by the various faculty members in the room. Eventually they moved on to the nicknames of other faculty members, and that led to another round of stories.

Tom leaned back in Max's lap. "What's wrong with Cinnamon Roll?" he murmured.

Max ran his fingers along Tom's neck, catching the gold chain there. *His* chain, which held a gold fleur de lis charm against Tom's chest. "Nothing at all, except it's ours, and I'd rather keep it that way."

"Aaron and Will know. Probably Kelly, too."

"But they know that's personal." Max fiddled with the chain, then kissed Tom's neck.

Having Tom here was amazing. Since that Saturday when Tom confessed that he probably loved Max, their affection for one another had grown. Every so often, Max would catch Tom touching the chain or the charm and see a look of wonder spread over his beautiful face.

That probability of love became more solid every day. Max never pushed, but Tom said—or texted—those three words more often than not. Max replied in kind, wholeheartedly.

"Hey, do you two need a room?" Jeremy again.

Max pecked Tom's neck again, then grinned at his friend. "This one is quite lovely, thank you." Warm, with a fireplace, painted wainscoting, and a lovely, colorful rug. A table had been pushed off to the side and held several different dishes that comprised their potluck feast.

"Eh," Tom said. "It's not quite my style."

Warmth zipped through Max. That was something else they'd discussed—the third floor. Max had offered Tom that space for his own and they'd already had discussions about him moving in with Max. Tom had spent some time up there and had commented that it would make a lovely artist's loft.

There was no hurry to decide—Tom's lease wasn't up until late summer. Even then, they need not work on the third floor immediately, though Tom had mentioned he'd been watching videos on how to remove wallpaper.

That was a good sign. So was the fact that several of Tom's suits now hung in the closet of the main bedroom. Max had made it clear he was welcome in the house at any hour and on any day, and Max's key hung on Tom's keychain.

Max had no idea what Tom's style was, but like their relationship and their love, that would unveil itself in time.

Madeleine crossed the room to where they sat. She wore a long red sleeveless dress that showed off her arms and a colorful tattoo of a vine with tropical flowers in yellows, reds, and purples. She towered over them both, her heels adding to her already impressive height. She peered down, meeting Max's gaze. "What I'd like to know, Dr. Demers, is when the wedding is going to be?"

Unexpectedly, Tom laughed, a joyous sound. Two months ago, he would've leapt off Max's lap and headed for the door.

Max's brain skipped like an old, bumped CD player, and he stammered, "I—we've not discussed that. I don't even know if Tom wants to be married in general, not just to me."

"I am a divorce lawyer, after all." Tom's smile was wide and wonderful.

"Not just divorce," Aaron said. "Your card reads 'and other family law.'"

"Duly noted, counselor," Tom said, dryly.

"Well?" Madeleine sipped her wine, then turned her gaze on Tom. "Marriage?"

"Maddy, really?" Annabell, her wife, joined her and wrapped an arm around Madeleine's waist. "Leave the boys alone."

Tom chuckled. "Marriage is a fine institution, especially when it works. It can be a trap when it doesn't. Love doesn't require marriage, nor marriage love."

Madeleine considered that while she draped an arm over her wife's shoulder. "It does provide legal protections."

"Oh, don't I know *that*," Tom said.

Max and the rest of the room chuckled.

"But to answer your question..." He patted Max's thigh. "And yours too, I've no objection to marriage. I didn't think I'd be in a position to contemplate it."

That seemed to satisfy Madeleine, at least enough that she moved on to needling one of her fellow physics professors.

That gave Max the privacy to whisper against Tom's neck. "Do you like your position?" He was bit tipsy from the very good wine Will had brought to the party.

Tom patted his thigh again, then turned so he could whisper into Max's ear. "I adore *all* the positions you put me in."

That warmed Max more than the wine. He tightened his grip on Tom and returned the whisper. "Oh, good, because I have some thoughts about tomorrow."

"Tell me later," Tom murmured. "Or surprise me."

"Ugh," Aaron called from across the room. "You guys are too stinking cute. Stop it."

This time it was Max who laughed. Tom merely gave his law partner the finger. They settled down after that, and the party flowed on to other topics. There was food, wine, dessert, and end-of-Thanksgiving cheer. Everyone had loved Max's bread, along with his chocolate croissants.

At the end of the night, Max was glad they'd walked to Jeremy's place, because he wasn't in any condition to drive. Besides, the night was clear and crisp, with hints of wood smoke and pine on the air. He stared up at the sky. "It's beautiful out."

Tom huffed a laugh. "Yeah. It is."

But when Max looked over, Tom was entirely focused on him.

"Ech, *stop*."

That only made Tom grin wider. "You really are good and pure, Maxime Demers. And you bite very, very hard. Let's go home so you can do unspeakable things to me."

"Tomorrow," Max said. "Can't Dom when buzzed."

"Then let's make love." Tom slipped his arm around Max's waist, and they set off toward their home.

THANKS FOR READING!

Dear Reader,

Thank you for reading *Cinnamon Roll*! I hope you enjoyed Max and Tom's story as much I enjoyed writing it!

Next up in the Bold Brew series is *Double Shot* by Gwen Martin, featuring Tom's landlord, the photographer Rhys Campbell.

If you're curious about Aaron, Will, and Kelly's story, you can find that in *Extra Whip* by LA Witt.

If you enjoyed *Cinnamon Roll*, and would like to read more steaming hot stories with BDSM from me, I'd suggest either the *Takeover* series of office romances, or the *Twisted Wishes* series, featuring a found family of rock stars, though most of my catalogue features loving, consensual kink of some kind.

To find out more about my books and new releases, you can follow me on BookBub, join my facebook group or sign up for my newsletter.

Thank you so much!
-Anna

BOOKS IN THE BOLD BREW SERIES

ACKNOWLEDGMENTS

First and foremost, I have to thank Annabeth Albert for creating and inviting me to be a part of this project. I'd been in the depths of a particularly bad case of writer's block since my last novel. Coupled with the awfulness that was 2020, both with COVID-19 and also with some personal loss, I was starting to believe I might never write again. But once we all got started on building the town of Laurelsburg, I found the words that had so eluded me, and I can't be more grateful for that.

I decided for *this* novel, I was going to write what I enjoyed and throw all my loves into it (hence all the sex, kink, food, baked goods, and hockey), and just hope that readers would be willing to come along for the ride. If you've read this far, *thank you* for indulging me. I owe so much to my readers.

The lovely cover, featuring Tom, was by Cate Ashwood.

I couldn't have written this book with out all the writing sprints with Annabeth, Cate, Crystal Lacy, Gwen Martin, Wendy Qualls, and Layla Reyne.

Special thanks to LA Witt for the use of Aaron, Will, and Kelly in this book. We tossed scenes back and forth to perfect the snark, and worked out the history of Tom and Aaron's firm together.

Thank you to Lynda Ryba for copy edits and catching all the little things.

Finally, so so SO much thanks to Mackenzie Walton for editing what was a messy messy draft. I'm so glad I could work with you again. I owe you many croissants.

ALSO BY ANNA ZABO

Close Quarter

Close Quarter

Slow Waltz (a Close Quarter short story)

Takeover

Takeover

Just Business

Due Diligence

Daily Grind

Twisted Wishes

Syncopation

Counterpoint

Reverb

Standalone Works

CTRL Me

Outside the Lines

Weave the Dark, Weave the Light

Cinnamon Roll

ABOUT THE AUTHOR

Anna Zabo writes contemporary and paranormal romance for all colors of the rainbow. They live and work in Pittsburgh, Pennsylvania, which isn't nearly as boring as most people think.

They can be easily plied with coffee or a chance to see the Pittsburgh Penguins.

Anna has an MFA in Writing Popular Fiction from Seton Hill University, where they fell in with a roving band of romance writers and never looked back. They also have a BA in Creative Writing from Carnegie Mellon University.

Anna uses they/them pronouns and prefers Mx. Zabo as an honorific. They can be found online at annazabo.com.

twitter.com/amergina

instagram.com/amergina

bookbub.com/authors/anna-zabo

amazon.com/Anna-Zabo/e/B00A7LA6OC